THE CURLEW'S CALL

JAYNE DAVIS

Copyediting & proofreading: Sue Davison

Cover design: Penny Johnson

ACKNOWLEDGEMENTS

Thanks to my critique partners on Scribophile for comments and suggestions, particularly Ysobel, Rachel, Monique and Jim.

Thanks also to Alpha readers Tina and Dave, and Beta readers Barbara, Carole, Cilla, Claire, Corinne, Dawn, Doris, Frances, Geogianna, Helen, Jeanne, Julie, Karen, Leigh, Lucy, Lynden, Mary G, Mary R, Melanie, Melissa, Nicky, Patricia, Sarah H, Sarah M, Sue, and Teddie.

MAP

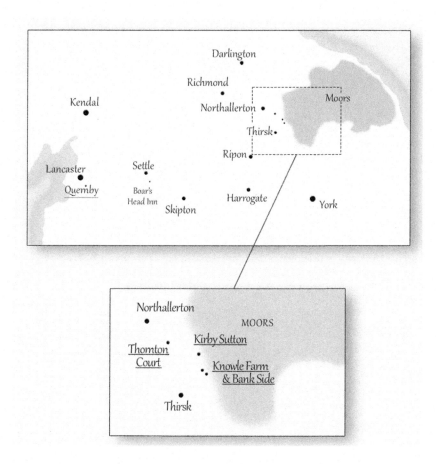

Some of the places mentioned in the story.

Fictional places are underlined.

CHAPTER 1

Quernby, Lancashire—March 1812

Eleanor Wilson shifted on the hard pew, trying to get comfortable as her father—the Reverend Dennison—conducted the funeral service for his sister, Ellie's Aunt Harriet.

"As all good Christians should, Harriet Dennison always knew her duty to God and Man," Father declared, looking directly at Ellie. "The duty of a woman to the head of her family, and the duty of a daughter to her father."

"But not the duty of a wife to a husband," Aunt Elizabeth muttered beside her, her voice so quiet that Ellie hardly heard it. Ellie kept her eyes on the pulpit but pressed her lips together. It was wrong to speak ill of the dead, particularly at that person's funeral, but she had to admit that Aunt Harriet's exacting standards, and her incessant demands that everyone live up to them, had not endeared her to many people. Not to any possible husbands, certainly.

As her father droned on about duty, Ellie's attention wandered back to her brother's plaque on the church wall. Ben's memorial service in 1810 was the only other time she'd returned to Quernby since her marriage five years ago, and the plaque hadn't been completed then.

She had stood beneath the plaque for a few moments before taking her seat. The two crossed flags at the top of the plaque depicted the regimental colour of the 52nd Foot and the king's colour—Ben would have been pleased at that. Less so, perhaps, with the text beneath, praising Ben's sacrifice in giving his life for king and country. Ellie could imagine Ben sitting beside her, rolling his eyes and muttering that the last thing on his mind had been the mad king or his fat son. Ellie swallowed a lump in her throat—she still missed him.

Perhaps she would miss Ben less if her relationship with Martin was as close as her sister's was with her husband. Martin had been a friend when they married, and although she'd hoped their friendship would develop into something closer, it had not. She'd shared more of her thoughts and feelings with Ben than she ever had with Martin, and surely a husband should feel close in more intimate ways as well? She might not have minded the lack of love if they had been blessed with children, but there was no possibility of that now Martin had stopped coming to her bed.

Ellie dragged her mind back to the service, sighing in resignation as Father began talking about Aunt Harriet's activities in the parish, which demonstrated the kind of piety he thought others should emulate. And she tried to ignore Aunt Elizabeth's little hmpfs of disbelief at descriptions of Harriet's kindness. Aunt Elizabeth was Mama's sister, and very different from Aunt Harriet. Aunt Elizabeth had come to stay often during Mama's long illness. As well as being a friendly face, her visits had been a great practical help; when her mother could no longer manage things, Ellie had been the one to run the household and look after Mary and Ben.

Aunt Harriet had moved into the vicarage when it became clear that Mama was unlikely to ever recover completely, but she had done little other than issue orders and find fault, making Ellie's life more difficult. Too often, she felt as unloved as Aunt Harriet had been—although Aunt Harriet had the benefit of either not realising it or not caring, Ellie didn't know which.

When the interminable service finally ended, the congregation followed the coffin out into the churchyard. There were a remarkable number of parishioners present; more than Ellie would have expected. Perhaps they wanted to be sure that Aunt Harriet had really gone.

Only the squire and the doctor went to stand by the newly dug grave to hear the final words of committal. The earlier heavy rain had left the long grass in the churchyard sodden and the lane beyond the lych gate even deeper in mud than usual. Patches of blue were appearing in the sky to the west, but the chill breeze that set the daffodils dancing would probably blow in more rain clouds later.

"I'm sorry I couldn't get here earlier," Aunt Elizabeth said, as the first handfuls of earth struck the coffin and the parishioners began to leave. "I haven't seen you for too long. And I must set off home tomorrow. Will you walk with me, or come to the inn for a while, so we may talk in private?"

"Father expects me to preside over the refreshments," Ellie said, with regret. He was always ready with orders and instructions, but never with thanks or praise.

"He cannot need you all afternoon. Has he invited many from the village?"

"The doctor and the squire and their wives, and a few more, I think. But Father has a list of things for me to do before I return to Yorkshire, and I must meet the coach at Caton tomorrow."

"Oh, well—I shall enjoy a good coze with the wives. They were friendly with your mama, as I recall. I don't expect their husbands will wish to linger for long, either."

"No." It was a sad fact that Father did not endear himself to those around him any more than his sister had.

"Dennison is far too fond of enumerating the sins of others," Aunt Elizabeth went on, more outspoken with her opinions than Ellie. "If you cannot find the time to talk today, I will take you to Caton in my carriage in the morning. What time do you need to be there?"

"Eleven o'clock." Ellie was grateful for the offer. It would save complaints from her father about depriving him of the gig and their outdoor man for the morning.

At the graveside, the verger's men began to shovel earth. Ellie set off to warn Cook that their guests were about to arrive. Aunt Elizabeth followed with Mrs Knox, the squire's wife.

In the dining room, the mirror above the fireplace was draped in black crepe, but the only other signs of mourning were the black gowns and black armbands on the guests. Cook had laid out a cold collation, with raised pies, glazed ham, jellies, fruit tarts, and sweet pastries. Ellie smiled and began to fill a plate. Aunt Harriet would never have approved of such rich food; Cook had clearly taken the opportunity to show what she could do when given a free hand.

"Ah, splendid!" The squire rubbed his hands at the sight of the laden table and proceeded to heap food onto a plate. Not for the first time, Ellie wondered how Mr Knox managed to stay rail-thin while eating so much.

His wife did show the signs of too much culinary indulgence, but plumpness suited her. "It seems your father's cook can manage very well without Harriet's supervision," she said to Ellie, running an appreciative eye over the food. "Whether your father will approve is a different matter. How is life in Yorkshire treating you?"

Ellie put her plate down with a smile. "Very well, thank you."

"It's a pity Mary was not able to come—I have not seen your sister since she came to your wedding."

"She is happy with her husband and children and expecting another. She is a few months from her time, but too big to travel this far."

"Oh, that is good news." Mrs Knox nodded and smiled, then a look of concern spread across her face. "But is there still no sign of a happy event with you?"

"I'm afraid not." She should be used to her childless state by now, but being questioned always brought some of the sadness back.

"Oh, well, there's time enough yet." Mrs Knox patted Ellie's arm. "Is your husband well? Such a pity he could not accompany you."

"I don't mind," Ellie said, which was true about Martin's absence, at least. She'd met him while staying with Mary in Harrogate, so he didn't know these people, and they didn't know him. Father had taken a dislike to him, for no reason that Ellie could discern, so his presence would have made her stay here even more uncomfortable.

"You look very well, Ellie."

Ellie glanced down at her gown, one of the black ones she'd bought when mourning Mama's death. She hadn't seen the point in buying a new dress that she would only wear for Aunt Harriet's funeral. Papa might disapprove, but she would not be wearing blacks when she returned home.

Mrs Knox was smiling, but Ellie shook her head. The dark gown made her grey eyes and pale hair look insipid. "I know black does not suit me, ma'am, but one must show respect." Even if she didn't feel it.

"Hmm." Mrs Knox patted her arm again. "It's a pity I could not call you daughter. Albert's wife is a pretty little thing, but with not a sensible bone in her body, bless her, so the house is always in chaos. You would have been a much more suitable wife for him."

A much better housekeeper, Ellie thought, suppressing a sigh. It would be nice to be more than merely useful. To have someone who wanted *her*, not just a household manager.

"I wish you well, Ellie. Now, I must dissuade my husband from eating another plateful." She nodded and hurried over to where the squire was eyeing the remaining slices of game pie.

Would life have been different—better—if she'd encouraged Albert Knox? But he'd started to court her only a few months after Mama died. Father had said her duty then was to her family, and to the parish, and Ellie herself hadn't been ready to take such a big step at that time. Albert had accepted her excuses with depressingly little protest, and married a girl from the next village only a few months later.

Wondering about might-have-beens was futile, and Ellie forced a smile as the doctor's wife came to talk to her. That conversation went much the same way, but without a reference to courtship. Then people were taking their leave, and Ellie found her father beside her.

"I noticed your attention wandering during the service, Eleanor." Father's expression was his customary, irritating combination of reprimand and sorrow.

"I was thinking about Ben." Snatches of talk drifted in from the hall—the fuss of greatcoats and pelisses being found and bonnets donned, then the front door closed and the maid's footsteps receded to the kitchen.

"Ah, yes. A great pity I permitted him to join the army. It was not well done of your Aunt Elizabeth to give him the money for his commission."

"He would have gone as a volunteer if he had not been able to buy his commission."

Father's brows drew together. This was not the first time he had made that complaint about Aunt Elizabeth, but it was the first time Ellie had voiced her opinion.

"Yes, well. Now that Harriet has gone to her eternal rest, I am left without someone to run the house." He pointed to the table, still with plenty of food left. "You can see from this extravagance that Cook needs better supervision. It was not well done of you to marry, Eleanor. I disapproved at the time, and I was right."

That had been an unpleasant time, but Father's attempts to persuade her against her marriage had only made her more determined to escape. "Marriage is an estate ordained by God, Father."

"It is ordained for the procreation of children—and you have failed at that. What use is a barren wife? You would have served God better by remaining here to help in the Parish."

Ellie took a deep breath, suppressing a mixture of anger and hurt. She had long thought that Father saw people only in terms of how they could be of use to him, but he had never been so brutally clear about it. She clenched her fists to stop her hands shaking and made an effort to steady her voice. "Marriage is also ordained for mutual society, help, and comfort." Thanks to her upbringing, she could quote the prayer book nearly as readily as he.

Father went on as if she hadn't spoken. "It is clear that this house needs a competent housekeeper. Before you return to Yorkshire, you should find one for me and ensure she is trained in my requirements."

"Martin is expecting me back." In truth, he had probably gone up to the other farm, and wouldn't mind if she was a week late. "Excuse me, Father, but you did say there were a number of things I need to deal with before I leave in the morning."

"Very well—but we will speak on this again later."

It would make no difference. He had no power to make her stay.

One of the tasks Father had set Ellie was to sort through Aunt Harriet's things, deciding which items should be given to the poor—the *deserving* poor, naturally—and which should be kept in the family. There was little of the latter, Aunt Harriet being of the mind that jewels and adornments were mere vanity, and her only books being of an improving nature. Of a particularly repetitive and sanctimonious nature, Ellie thought, flicking through a volume of sermons. Perhaps she should keep one to help when she couldn't sleep?

Father would protest, she was sure, if she decided that neither of his daughters wanted a keepsake from their aunt, so she picked out a book for herself and one for Mary. Slim volumes, so as not to take up too much space while remaining unread on a shelf.

She put the books down on the table, resting one hand on them as she looked around Aunt Harriet's room. It was a sad end to a life, with only Father regretting her death.

Would she end up the same way? If only she'd been able to make a love match like Mary's. Mary had met Henry by chance, not through any attempt by Father to find her a suitable husband. Nine years ago, with their mother ill and not long after Aunt Harriet inflicted her presence on the vicarage to 'help', the eighteen-year-old Mary had accompanied Mama to Harrogate for a month, to see if the sulphurous spa waters could improve her health. Both Father and Aunt Harriet had insisted that Ellie was needed at home and so she had stayed behind, as an obedient daughter should.

The waters hadn't helped Mama, but the trip had given her the satisfaction of seeing Mary fall in love with Doctor Henry Cowper. Henry had ridden over the Pennines a few weeks after Mama and Mary returned to Quernby, and formally asked their father for Mary's hand. Mother had insisted he agree, and they married soon after.

The following months had been hard for Ellie, with Mama declining fast and Mary gone, but Ellie did not resent her sister's escape. Mary and Henry had returned for Mama's funeral on a cold April morning, and that was the last Ellie had seen of her for a few years, although they had corresponded regularly.

Ellie had become closer to Ben after Mama's death. He was four years younger than her but, at sixteen, he was old enough to understand her feelings and to sympathise. They would escape up to the moors as often as they could, alone or together. Ben had gazed west, to where the Irish Sea glittered on sunny days, dreaming of seeing far-off lands. Ellie had mainly enjoyed the peace of being alone where there was no-one to make demands on her, where she could hear nothing but the wind in the heather and skylarks singing, or curlews' whistling calls. Even when he'd joined the army, she'd found comfort in reading his letters, and in knowing that he was somewhere in the world and thinking of her now and then.

But she should not regret her marriage, loveless and childless though it was. Not when the alternative had been remaining here at the beck and call of her father and Aunt Harriet.

CHAPTER 2

*Y*ork

Captain Thomas Allerby knocked on the door of his older brother's house in Micklegate. Frank had come up in the world, judging by the looks of his new home. Three years ago, the last time Tom had been on leave, his brother had been enjoying his bachelor life in rooms above a shop on the outskirts of the city. Frank had said in his letters that his new partnership with an established York attorney was going well, although it did take him out of town often. Now he was living with his new wife in this fine house in one of York's oldest streets.

Tom had given Frank no notice of his arrival, having intended to see their mother first. But the offer from a fellow officer to take him as far as Lincoln in his hired—and very comfortable—post-chaise had been too good to refuse, so he'd decided to visit Frank first. If Frank was away on business, he'd hire a horse and set off for Kendal this afternoon. He had time to return to York before he was due to rejoin his regiment.

Micklegate was busy with pedestrians, carriages, and carts, the air full of noise and coal smoke. Tom stood with his back to the door while he waited, wary of being walked into. His leg was mending well from a bayonet slash and possibly cracked bone, but a knock could set it aching again.

Finally, the door was opened by a young maidservant, who bobbed a curtsey. "Can I help you, sir?"

"Is Mr Allerby at home?"

"No, sir."

That wasn't too surprising. It was the middle of the afternoon on a business day—he should have gone to Frank's office.

"Who is it, Morris?" A petite woman appeared behind the maid, attractively clad in a moss-coloured gown that brought out green highlights in her eyes. Her glossy black hair was fastened up behind, with ringlets framing her face beneath a delicate lacy cap that matched the lavish trimmings on her gown. Frank had described his wife as beautiful, and Tom had assumed the bias of affection—but she was indeed very pretty. And young—very young. She must be at least a dozen years younger than Frank's thirty-four. More, probably.

Tom bowed. "Captain Allerby, at your service, ma'am."

Her eyes narrowed a little as she inspected Tom, then she smiled, showing even, white teeth between rosy lips. "You have a look of Frank."

When they were young, no-one had failed to notice their resemblance to each other—the shape of their features as well as the same brown hair and eyes. Since then, Tom's fourteen years in an infantry regiment had made him broader in body compared to Frank's slim build, and with a more weathered complexion.

"Do come in, Captain. Frank has told me much about your exploits in the Peninsula. If you have come all the way from Spain, the least I can do is to give you tea. I'm afraid Frank is away on business."

He'd only come from Pontefract today, after a leisurely and excellent breakfast, but he was curious to see what this new house was like. "Thank you, ma'am."

Mrs Allerby led the way into a parlour on the first floor, furnished with spindly chairs that looked as if they would not stand his weight. She sat at one end of a sofa and Tom took a nearby chair, lowering himself gingerly onto the pale silk upholstery. The fine furnishings made him feel shabbier than ever, in his civilian clothing kept too long in the bottom of his trunk.

The only sign of his brother in the room was a framed print above the fireplace showing racehorses in mid-gallop, similar to the painting that still hung above their mother's fireplace in Kendal. All else was pretty frippery, flowered fabrics, and ornate figurines and vases. Tom spared a sympathetic thought for the poor maid who had to dust them all.

"Such a bore that Frank isn't here," Mrs Allerby said. "But needs must, I suppose."

"At what time do you expect him to return, ma'am?"

She shrugged, a delicate movement of her shoulders. "Sometime this week."

"When did he leave?"

"Not long ago. Did you have a good voyage, Captain?"

Tom bit back his impatience—from her answers, Frank could be back tomorrow or in several days' time. "Tolerable, thank you." That was as good as one could expect, crossing the Bay of Biscay at this time of year. "The journey from Portsmouth was comfortable enough." He spun out an account of his journey until the tea tray arrived. Mrs Allerby poured the pale liquid into fine china cups and handed him one. The thing was lost in his large hand, and he sipped at the insipid brew. "This looks a lovely house." It wasn't to his taste, but Frank must like it.

"It is now. Frank took out the lease when we married, but it has taken me nearly two years to have it decorated properly."

"I gather Frank's business is doing well?"

She nodded, her ringlets bobbing. "He says so, yes. He certainly spends a lot of time at work, or travelling." A frown briefly formed on her brow. "It is most inconvenient, being left to fend for myself so often. Do you have a long leave, Captain?"

"A few weeks only."

"Well, you must stay in York until Frank returns. You may escort me to the next assembly, or I believe there is a concert tomorrow."

"I... Thank you, ma'am, but I don't have suitable clothing for such events." He'd left his dress uniform stored in Lisbon, together with most of the rest of his meagre possessions. That was a more diplomatic excuse than pleading a dislike for sitting on hard chairs for long periods. And what use was a man with an injured leg at an assembly?

"Oh, do say you'll stay, Captain. My days are so tedious while Frank is away." There was a note of pleading in her voice.

Tom drained the remaining tea in his cup and set it on a nearby table. "I'm afraid I am otherwise engaged, Mrs Allerby. I am setting off to see my mother this afternoon. If you can tell me on which day you expect Frank to return, I will try to make time to see him then."

Her bottom lip stuck out in a brief moue of disappointment, but she rose gracefully and walked over to an escritoire in a corner of the room. She flipped through some pages in a notebook. "At the end of the week. Friday or Saturday."

Tom stood. "Thank you. Do give him my best wishes."

"I look forward to your return, Captain. The maid will show you out." She rang the bell, her smile a little wistful.

He supposed it could be hard on her if Frank was away often, but from what his brother had said, Frank was much younger than the senior partner and would usually be the one to travel for business matters. He found his pocketbook and looked up the address of Frank's office. He would ask the clerk about Frank's movements for the next few weeks and leave a note for his brother, then set off for Kendal. There was enough daylight left for him to get twenty or more miles on his way. That would mean two nights on the road instead of one, but he had nothing else to do in York.

Aunt Elizabeth's coachman knocked on the vicarage door at nine, just as Ellie and her father were finishing a silent breakfast. Ellie, suspecting that her aunt would make an early departure, had her valise packed and ready to go. She bid a hasty goodbye to Father before he could say—again—that he was disappointed in her refusal to accede to his demands.

The overnight rain had stopped, but clouds still filled the sky. The coachman put her bag on the rack, and Aunt Elizabeth greeted her with a smile as she took her seat in the chaise. They set off through the village and over the narrow bridge, the stream below running high in its banks, tumbling down the slope and swirling around tree trunks. It hadn't been a particularly wet spring so far in Yorkshire; it must have rained more on this side of the Pennines for the water to be so high.

"I hope you have a safe journey on the stage coach," Aunt Elizabeth said, following her gaze.

"I'm sure the coachmen know the route well." She'd rather suffer an uncomfortable journey than remain to be berated by Father. Her aunt's route north to Carlisle would not be any easier.

"Your father did not wave you off." Aunt Elizabeth's words were half statement, half question.

"He didn't want me to return home. He wanted me to stay until I've found him a new housekeeper and explained his ways to the poor woman."

"That is *his* job, not yours." Aunt Elizabeth pressed her lips together. The expression looked quite odd on her normally kind face. "You did right not to do as he demanded. I know he's your father, my dear, and that your mama held him in affection, but I'm afraid I do not like the way he treats you. Or anyone else, come to that. I suppose he means well—by his standards, and by his interpretation of God's will, but I cannot like him. I am pleased your mother stood up to him and insisted that Mary would marry her doctor. She is happy, I think?"

"Very much so." Harrogate was only half a day's drive from Ellie's home, and she visited her sister often. "You have been very good to all of us."

Aunt Elizabeth's lips drooped. "I try, but I do often regret buying Ben his commission. He might still be with us if I had not."

"Don't think that, Aunt. It was what he wanted. He said he enjoyed the life, although I find it difficult to understand how he could."

She recalled the time he'd come to visit her in Yorkshire, nearly four years ago now. It had been a hot day, and they'd walked up onto the moors.

"It's a good life, mostly," Ben had said as they sat in the heather, eating bread and cheese, and drinking ginger beer still cool in its stone bottle. "If I don't come back..." He ignored her protest. "Be realistic, Ellie, not every soldier returns unscathed. I chose the life, and don't regret doing so." He waved his hand at the blue skies and white puffy clouds above them, pausing as a curlew called somewhere in the distance. Her memories of Ben seemed inextricably linked with birdsong and, like the curlew's call, were sometimes cheerful and sometimes melancholy.

"If I don't come back, Ellie, don't wear the willow for me, but remember days like this together. What would be the use of becoming Father's curate, as Mama wanted, and living a tedious life?"

"A long life?" Ellie suggested.

"Tedious," he repeated. "*Carpe diem*, Ellie. Seize the day." It was a phrase he used often. "Live the life you've got." He lay back, gazing up into the blue infinity. "There's nothing worse than regretting what might have been. Things you might have done but didn't dare. Or things you avoided because you worried what other people might say."

"You don't have such regrets, do you Ben?"

He laughed. "Only minor things—schoolboy things." He rolled over, raising himself on one elbow to look into her eyes. "I would have regretted not buying my commission."

At that moment, she had believed him. It was only later that her doubts returned, as she recalled the hardships of being on campaign, and the ever-present risk of death or crippling injury. Things she had only read about or inferred, for Ben had been reluctant to talk about his experiences, and his letters had merely mentioned that he was well, or related trivial incidents of army life. She had to take Ben's word that he'd enjoyed being in the army, but she didn't understand what satisfaction there could be that would outweigh the dangers and discomforts.

"Ellie?" Aunt Elizabeth was staring at her in concern.

"I was remembering, Aunt. Ben told me that he had no regrets about joining the army, and not to mourn him too long if he died. He said it was far better than a boring life as Father's curate."

"Thank you, my dear." Aunt Elizabeth did look happier for hearing it. "And what about you—how are you going on? Still no sign of children?"

The words could have been as censorious as Father's had been, but Aunt Elizabeth's expression held only kindness.

Ellie shook her head, swallowing a lump in her throat.

"You are young, still—there is plenty of time."

"I don't think so. Martin… He doesn't…" Her cheeks burned, and she turned her gaze to the moorland rising to their right. "He doesn't come to me any longer." Not for the last six months or so.

"Oh, my dear."

She shrugged. "I don't miss the… the act." Martin had come to her bed regularly for four years, each visit an embarrassing and uncomfortable fumbling in the dark. At least it didn't last long. "But I would have liked children of my own." Her throat tightened—somehow saying it out loud made the disappointment feel worse.

"Ellie—the…" Now it was Aunt Elizabeth's face that turned red. "The act between a husband and wife is something to be enjoyed, something that should bring the two of you together. It is not only the means to have a child."

Perhaps it was, if you married for love, as Mary had. But Ellie had married a man with whom she got along well, not one she loved. She had married for a home, and a family, of her own. To not be at Father's—and Aunt Harriet's—beck and call at all times, with everything she did subject to their critical eyes. Mary had said that affection, or even love, would come. But she and Martin were still only friends, sharing the running of the farms amicably, but nothing more.

She thought again of the squire's son—would marriage to him have been different? If he had really desired her, would he not have persisted?

Was she only wanted when she was useful? Perhaps no man would ever desire her.

~

Tom reached Skipton by early afternoon the next day, in spite of the muddy roads and continuous drizzle. He stopped there to give the horse a rest, and to warm himself by the fire in the taproom of the Castle Inn. It was just as well he hadn't chosen the northern route through Leyburn and Wensleydale. That was a lovely ride in the summer, but more likely to be affected by flooding than the turnpikes he was following.

He warmed his insides with a chicken stew followed by bread and butter pudding. As he watched the raindrops spattering on the windows, he enjoyed the luxury of knowing that no-one was about to order him to march on, and he could spend the rest of the day here if he wished. But he'd planned on getting as far as Settle today, and that was another fifteen miles, so he forced himself to move. He'd ridden longer distances in far worse weather in the Peninsula, although without a damaged leg. But tomorrow there would be a warm welcome from his mother, not a devastated village with murdered inhabitants.

The drizzle had turned to rain while he'd been eating. It leached the colour from the buildings and turned the castle into a threatening hulk behind him. Once he was beyond the town, the fields and moors to either side blurred into a grey distance. Still-bare trees stuck up like black skeletons, their branches bending in the rising wind, and the streams that ran beside the road foamed white. Tom turned his collar up and urged the horse on, trying to ignore the rain lashing his face and getting inside his jacket.

As he rode over a stone bridge, he paused to watch the river swirling beneath. It looked to be running higher than usual, with grasses on the banks partially submerged, but was far from filling the arches. Unless the weather got much worse, he should get through to Kendal tomorrow without having to divert around flooded roads or washed-away bridges.

Trees might be a different matter, he thought a little later, passing through a small belt of woodland. Numerous twigs and a few small branches lay scattered across the muddy road. A milestone in the verge informed him that Settle was still six miles away—the going was slow with a tired horse.

As he rode on into the open again, a coach came into view around a bend ahead. He pulled the horse to one side, its hooves sinking into the sodden verge, and the coach trundled past, jolting over stones buried in the mud. The men on the box appeared well-protected in many-caped greatcoats with oilcloth covering their legs, but the sole outside passenger looked thoroughly miserable, hunched into his greatcoat with his head down.

Tom had almost reached the bend in the road when the high-pitched scream of a horse in distress made him stop and look back.

CHAPTER 3

*E*llie leaned her head against the side of the coach, appreciating the extra space beside her after one of the passengers left them at Settle.

"I was within my rights," Mrs Crabbe said again, the lines beside her downturned mouth deepening as she peered around her rotund husband to scowl at the other female passenger, a thin woman in the far corner with a child on her lap. She had hardly stopped complaining since Ellie boarded the coach and everyone introduced themselves. Mrs Hart sniffed into a handkerchief while the little girl sucked her thumb. They both looked delicate as well as unhappy. "Your husband only paid for an outside seat," Mrs Crabbe went on, "so he should not have been taking up space in here and spreading damp."

Ellie would not wish anyone a ride on the roof in this weather when there was space inside. But when the coachman had suggested at Settle that Mr Hart move inside and pay the difference, Mrs Crabbe had threatened to write to the coaching company, accusing the coachman of wanting to pocket the extra fare. The coachman had shrugged and given up.

Did Mrs Crabbe feel guilty? She continued to try to justify her action even though no-one bothered to respond. The remaining inside passenger—who had briefly introduced himself as "Easton, apothecary"—continued to hide behind his newspaper as he had done for most of the journey.

Ellie kept her gaze on the passing landscape, not wanting to meet Mrs Crabbe's eyes and possibly get drawn into discussion on the matter. But there were few houses along this stretch of road, and not many villages. Nothing to distract her from the thoughts that had been plaguing her since she boarded the coach in Caton—her father's remarks about barren wives, and his unreasonable expectation that she abandon her own life and responsibilities for some weeks to satisfy his whims.

She tried to turn her thoughts to more cheerful subjects. Spring was on the way, with daffodils and primroses in bloom, and longer days. Looking forward to summer was better than repining about things that could not be changed. She had a home of her own and plenty to keep her busy. If she felt in low spirits, she would pay Mary a visit—there was no-one like her sister for taking a sunny view of life.

A gust blew a spatter of rain against the window, and the view darkened as they passed into a band of trees. There was a loud crack and the coach shot forward, setting Ellie's heart racing. The forward jerk became a sickening sideways lurch and she slid down the seat into the apothecary as the coach came to a grinding stop. On the opposite seat Mr and Mrs Crabbe had fallen on top of Mrs Hart and her daughter. Mrs Crabbe began to screech, and the little girl wailed in distress.

The coach was tilted, but had not fallen completely on its side. The glass in what was now the lower window was shattered, the broken end of a tree branch poking through it, but nobody appeared to have been harmed. The tree, and the stone wall below it, had prevented the coach overturning.

"Mmpf." The apothecary pushed Ellie, and she slid around him until she was resting against the side of the coach. Her position didn't feel very safe—she was partly resting on the door, which might not withstand her weight if it had been damaged by hitting the wall. She reached out to take the little girl.

"Sir," she addressed Mr Crabbe. "If you support yourself and your wife for a moment, Mrs Hart could move out of the way. You are crushing her."

"Pass the child to me," the apothecary said. Ellie did so, and then managed to ease Mrs Hart away. She appeared to be on the verge of swooning, but had made no cries of pain as she moved, so Ellie hoped she was unharmed. Voices came from outside, then the top door swung open and crashed onto the coach body. The head and shoulders of a man appeared, silhouetted against the daylight.

"Is anyone hurt?"

As he approached, Tom saw that the coach was tilted to one side, its body resting on the stone wall that separated the trees from the road. There was no sign of the passenger who had been riding on the roof, and only one of the coachmen was attempting to calm the lead horses. He was glad he'd turned back—these people needed him.

He dismounted by the coach, looping the reins of his mount over a tree branch on the opposite side of the road. Crossing the mud carefully, he winced as his foot slipped over a hidden stone and sent pain shooting up his injured leg. Cursing himself for thinking he could manage without the cane he'd been using for the last few weeks, he grabbed the bridle of one of the wheelers and talked to it and its pair, gradually bringing calm.

"Thank you, sir." The coachman was young, white faced. "Falling tree-branch frightened the horses. Josh tried to slow them, but there's a bit of a ditch by the wall and the wheels went in. One hit a stone, I think."

"Josh?"

"Driver, sir. He fell off the box."

"And you are?"

"Dodds." He swallowed hard. "I'm new to this business—only my second run."

"What happened to your outside passenger?"

Even as the lad spoke, they heard a string of fluent cursing from beyond the wall. Tom's lips twitched—one of the missing men was conscious.

"That sounds like the passenger, sir. I didn't see him—I was trying to stop the horses running on."

"Good man." Dodds seemed to need reassurance—and he had done the right thing. If the animals had managed to pull the damaged coach further, more harm could have been done. The pole and harnesses appeared to be undamaged, but that was no use unless the wheels were intact.

"There's five inside, sir, and a little girl."

"You keep an eye on the horses." They were still nervous, and it wouldn't take much to set them panicking again. Tom walked back to the coach and reached up to turn the handle and lift the door open. He found himself looking down the floor to a pile of bodies at the far side. Moving and complaining bodies, thank goodness, although he couldn't see clearly in the dim interior.

"Is anyone hurt?"

"Get me out of here! I will be demanding a refund, you—"

"Is anyone hurt?" Tom repeated the question in his best reprimanding-recruits voice, and the woman fell silent.

A different female voice responded—calmer and more measured. "Bruises, perhaps, sir, but I don't think there is anything more serious."

"Thank you, ma'am. I need to see how the outside passenger and the coachman fared."

"You can't just leave us here!" the shrill one complained. "I demand—"

"Go, sir. Do what you need to." The interruption came from one of the male passengers. Thank heavens there were a couple of sensible folk inside.

"Thank you. Try to get yourselves out." That had come out more like an order than a suggestion, but this was no time for pleasantries. He went to investigate the fate of the remaining men.

Twenty minutes later, Tom had everyone gathered behind the coach, sheltered only a little from the wind and not at all from the rain. He'd sent Dodds for help, riding awkwardly without a saddle on one of the coach horses; the lad was confident that it was only about two miles back to Long Preston the way they'd come, and seemed glad to be free of responsibility for the passengers.

The outside passenger—a young man who looked to be in his twenties—had jumped from the roof as the coach tilted, landing beyond the wall without impaling himself on fallen branches, but he had either broken his ankle or badly sprained it. He stood now, leaning against the wall with one arm around a thin woman; the child huddled close to them. The driver, busy trying to control the horses, hadn't been able to save himself as the accident happened and had taken a nasty knock on the head as he was thrown over the wall. He was conscious, but pale and shivering, and in no state to make decisions.

The expressions facing him varied from belligerence—the sharp-featured woman in the blue pelisse—to tears from the woman with the child, and resignation from the others. All looking to him.

"There is an inn in the last village you passed through," he began. "Although that is only a few miles away, it is likely to be an hour or so before anyone the assistant driver can find will arrive." He'd requested a cart, at the least, to take people and baggage to shelter, and men to extract the coach from its position blocking the road. One wheel was damaged, but a wheelwright, at this time of day and in this weather, was too much to hope for.

The belligerent one opened her mouth, but Tom raised his voice and continued. "I know you are heading east, but there is no habitation that way for many miles."

"Sir, if it is only a couple of miles, should some of us walk? We will get very cold waiting, even if we shelter inside the coach, and it cannot hold all of us at that angle." It was the same person who had calmly answered his earlier query about injuries. The speaker was tall for a woman, with steady grey eyes. She was swathed in a long pelisse that hid her shape.

It was a valid suggestion, but most of the passengers would not be able, or willing, to attempt it. He was about to say so, but the outside passenger spoke up first.

"I don't think that would be wise, sir. The road is deep in mud most of the way—not enough to have slowed the coach much, but on foot?" He shook his head.

"Walk? In this weather? I've paid for my ticket and…"

Tom lost patience with Mrs Blue Pelisse and stepped away before he gave her a piece of his mind. One of the men and the sensible lady followed him.

"Sir… Major, is it, perhaps?" Her brows rose, and the corners of her lips turned up a little.

"Only a captain, ma'am. Captain Allerby. Is my profession so obvious?"

"To me, sir, yes. It is a happy chance for us that you stopped." She glanced behind, then indicated the man beside her. "Mr Easton and I questioned the others. He is an apothecary. The crying woman is Mrs Hart, and her husband has the damaged ankle. My name is Wilson. The lady in the blue pelisse is Mrs Crabbe, travelling with her husband."

That would be the corpulent man who rolled his eyes at his wife's complaints.

"Mrs Hart is not well," Easton added. "Not long recovered from the influenza, her husband says. And Jennie—the child—is certainly too young to walk so far in this weather."

"I thought perhaps we might use your horse to get Mrs Hart out of the rain more quickly," the woman said. "It is the only one with a saddle."

"Mrs Wilson's suggestion is a good one," the apothecary said. "The other person most in need is the coachman, but I do not think he should attempt to ride—with or without a saddle. If he fell again, it could have serious consequences."

"I doubt Mrs Hart is well enough to ride on her own," Mrs Wilson said, "but I think your horse might manage two and the child for a short distance. You could take her up in front of you."

Alone with a weeping woman and a wailing child?

"Or someone else could ride with her." Mrs Wilson was amused—with him. He must have let his thoughts show on his face.

Who, though? The apothecary would be looking after the coachman, and Mr Hart's ankle ruled him out. Mr Crabbe?

"I'm afraid I'd need the saddle, though," she went on. "I cannot be sure to keep myself from falling off without that, let alone keep someone else on, so I cannot take one of the carriage horses."

He looked at Mrs Wilson with more interest. Why had he not considered her? "Good of you to volunteer, ma'am."

"Oh, not at all. I leave you to the complaints of Mrs Crabbe!"

He winced, and her lips twitched.

"But to be practical, sir, I think you are the best person to find some way of using what there is to shelter those who remain. The tarpaulin over the luggage in the boot, for example, and the coachmen's oilcloth. It cannot be unlike making do on campaign?"

Tom sighed—the idea of riding on, even with a crying woman, was beginning to seem rather more attractive, but she was right. "Very well—as long as you can persuade Mrs Hart and her husband."

She nodded. "I think talking of little Jennie's welfare should convince them, if necessary."

Tom brought his horse over as Mrs Wilson went to talk to the Harts. He checked the girth and lifted off his saddle bags. The top of Mrs Wilson's head had come up almost to his nose, so he shortened the stirrups by several inches. By then Mrs Wilson had returned with the child in her arms and Mrs Hart was helping her husband to hobble over.

Tom cupped his hands to provide a step. Mrs Wilson made no fuss, but settled herself in the saddle, wriggling to pull her skirts down as far as they would go.

"Try the stirrups, ma'am," Tom said, attempting to ignore the shapely ankle and calf that her skirts wouldn't cover. Her legs were well muscled for a woman, and she wore practical half-boots. *Mrs Wilson*, he reminded himself.

"Just right, Captain, thank you."

"When you arrive, can you make sure Dodds has made clear the urgency? He was the best person to send, being an employee, but he's new."

"I will do my best, sir."

There was some hesitation when Mrs Hart realised she would have to ride astride, too, but the argument that it would be the safest way for her to hold Jennie convinced her. Mr Hart handed up his own greatcoat and draped it around his wife and daughter, managing to provide a reasonable covering for the two of them.

"Are you sure?" Tom asked Mrs Wilson, still wondering about the wisdom of sending two women and a girl off alone. The rain had not let up, and the wind continued to gust.

"I used to ride on the moors often with my brother, Captain. We got caught out in worse weather than this. At least here, I cannot get lost if I follow the road."

They had little choice, but she sounded confident, and Tom had to trust her judgement. He stepped back and gave the horse a slap on the rump as Mrs Wilson urged it into motion. He watched until she went out of sight around the bend in the road, feeling a twinge of regret. Her calm good sense would have been useful in dealing with the other passengers. He squared his shoulders and turned to the business of trying to keep the remaining people warm enough until help arrived.

Ellie squinted into the rain, wishing that she had her oilcloth-covered bonnet instead of her smarter straw one that was fast turning into a sodden mess. It was doing little to keep her head dry, and even less to stop the rain running into her eyes.

The horse plodded on. The poor animal must have already been tired when Captain Allerby stopped to help, and had then stood in the rain for half an hour or more. Mrs Hart's head drooped, but when Ellie leaned forward to check whether she was still awake she was reassuring her daughter, telling her they would be in the warm soon.

Her thoughts turned to Ben. It was eighteen months since the news of his death; she had grieved for a while and then got on with her life, as he wished, remembering their shared times together. But reassuring her aunt about buying his commission, and then encountering Captain Allerby, had brought him to the forefront of her mind again.

She smiled, despite the cold water trickling down the back of her neck. Ben would have taken charge just as the captain had, impatient of complaints. Not that the two were alike, really. Ben, like all the Dennison family, had been tall and slim. The captain was a little shorter, but broader in face and body with dark brown hair and eyes, and some years older than Ben would have been now. She could imagine Ben rolling his eyes at Mrs Crabbe, or even imitating her nose-in-the-air manner behind her back. Captain Allerby had been more direct and to the point, but perhaps he would have a sense of humour, too, in easier circumstances. There had been a brief twitch of his lips when she mentioned leaving him with Mrs Crabbe.

Both were soldiers, though, used to marching in all weathers—searing heat and freezing cold, often with little prospect of shelter at the end of the day. Well, a tent, she supposed, but how could that compare with the comfort of a solid roof and a roaring fire? Ben had had a sense of adventure that she did not, and would have thought nothing of this ride, even with the unrelenting rain and the thick clouds bringing darkness early. Ellie still found it hard to accept that he could truly have enjoyed such a life. Did Captain Allerby enjoy being a soldier?

Damp was soaking into the shoulders of Ellie's gown. Her pelisse was not proof against this weather, and chill was creeping into her bones. She kept reminding herself that she only had to follow the road. There *was* habitation somewhere ahead, and it was only the weather that made yards feel like miles.

CHAPTER 4

*E*llie could just make out the glimmer of lighted windows in the distance when a wagon appeared with two men on the driving bench. Reining in, she waited for it to reach her—if it was not the expected help, she could ask where to go.

But it was. She hadn't taken much note of the coachman and his assistant when she boarded the coach in the rain, but the assistant recognised her.

"Has something else happened, missus?"

"This lady needs shelter urgently," she explained. "Is the inn nearby?"

"My place. The Boar's Head, on your left," the other man answered, jerking a thumb over his shoulder.

Ellie nodded her thanks as the wagon trundled off. "We're nearly there," she said to Mrs Hart, who nodded and bent her head to tell her daughter.

The Boar's Head was not a large establishment but looked big enough to put up the coach party. Not that it mattered; by now Ellie would have happily spent the night in a stable, if that was all there was.

Someone must have been watching, for the door opened as she

approached, and a couple of men came out into the rain to help Mrs Hart and her little girl down. Ellie, stiff with cold, swung one leg awkwardly across the saddle and kicked her other foot out of the stirrup.

"Here, steady, miss." Someone caught her under her arms as her cold legs almost refused to support her, then she was hustled indoors and into a warm parlour. Mrs Hart drooped on a settle, clutching her daughter, both looking alarmingly pale.

The landlady—a plump woman with greying hair—tutted. "That boy said nothing about poorly ladies and children. Just said a coach was stuck and he needed a wagon for the passengers." She turned to examine Ellie. "I'm Mrs Sellars. You don't look to be in such a bad way as her."

"I'm not," Ellie confirmed, although a hot bath would be lovely. "Mrs Hart has been ailing recently. An apothecary travelling with us said she needs to be made warm."

"Well, I can see that. Jane!" Ellie winced as Mrs Sellars shouted.

A girl came running.

"Light the fire in bedroom two. And fetch towels—she needs to be dry." Mrs Sellars' orders sent Jane hurrying off again.

"Her husband is still with the coach—he has a broken ankle."

Mrs Sellars bustled to the doorway and shouted up the stairs to tell Jane to prepare one of the large back bedrooms instead. "Now, my husband took lamps and some tarpaulin with him, for shelter. Mrs Hart needs dry clothes and a warm bed. And something hot to eat—soup perhaps?"

Ellie nodded.

"The same for the little girl, although she is not as wet. How many other rooms will be needed?"

Mrs Sellars nodded as Ellie listed the other passengers. "As much hot water as we can manage, then. It'll take me a while to get all them rooms made up." She eyed Ellie's wet gown doubtfully.

"I will do well enough by the fire for now. And I have nothing to change into until my bag arrives."

Mrs Sellars smiled. "I do like a woman with sense."

Ellie grimaced. "You won't like Mrs Crabbe, then."

"Ah, well, that's trouble that can wait. I'll deal with these two, then I'll get a room ready for you." Mrs Sellars took Mrs Hart and Jennie away. Ellie removed her pelisse with fingers still chilled and numb, and settled down to wait by the fire.

"Taproom, parlour. Both be warm by now." The innkeeper jerked his head towards doors either side of the entrance passage as he spoke. As Tom had discovered on the road, he was a man of very few words. Two grooms helped Mr Hart and the coachman indoors, and a woman who Tom took to be Sellars' wife escorted Mr and Mrs Crabbe into the parlour.

Tom headed for the taproom. The apothecary must have accompanied the two injured men to wherever Mrs Sellars had put them, and he had the room to himself for the moment. Unsurprisingly on such a night, there were no local customers. He draped his sodden greatcoat and his damp coat on the backs of a couple of chairs near the fire. A jug of ale stood on the hearth, next to a clean poker and several jars, which, on closer inspection, turned out to contain lumps of sugar, cinnamon sticks, and cloves. All he needed for mulled ale. Giving silent thanks to whoever had thought of it, Tom pushed the poker into the fire to heat it up and brought over a mug from the bar. Then he sank into a chair by the fire; his leg hurt, and he was glad to take the weight off it. Glad, too, of the warmth now raising steam from his wet breeches.

He stood as Mrs Wilson entered the room. She'd shed her pelisse and bonnet, revealing pale hair neatly arranged in a knot behind her head. Her black gown was sensible rather than fashionable. But the high neck did not hide her curves, and she had a frankness in her gaze and colour in her complexion that appealed to him. He wondered if she spent a lot of time out of doors.

"Are you well, ma'am? It was courageous of you to set off in those conditions."

She smiled, with a quirk to her lips that showed amusement. "On the contrary, sir, I reached warmth and food before everyone else."

"I cannot believe that was your motive."

She shook her head. "There was little courage required, Captain. I have been taken unawares by sudden storms before, and today I knew the road would lead us to safety. As to the others, Mrs Hart is warm, dry, and in bed with soup inside her. Jennie is with her, also full of soup and, in her case, a considerable quantity of cake as well."

The talk of food... The chicken stew in Skipton seemed an age ago now. Tom's stomach rumbled at the thought.

Mrs Wilson pretended not to hear, but her lips twitched. "Mr Easton is with the injured men, and Mrs Sellars tells me that dinner will be served shortly. We are all to eat together in the parlour—the passengers, that is. What of the coach—is it still blocking the road?"

"No. Sellars brought rope, and we righted it. A wheel is damaged, but Dodds managed to get it to a wider part of the road before coming on with the horses. Not that anyone in their senses would be travelling this night—the rain is as heavy as ever."

"We will be delayed for a day, I imagine."

It was a statement, not a question, but he answered anyway. "I think so. Even if the wheel can be mended or replaced in the morning, the roads will be difficult. And they'll need to provide another coachman—I doubt that Dodds can manage alone."

"No matter. I have enough coin for an extra night." She chuckled, her eyes lighting up with amusement. "Mrs Crabbe will not be pleased."

He couldn't help a grimace. "She wasn't. She asked... No, she demanded to know when she would reach York. Luckily the back of a farm cart in a storm is not the best place to deliver a..." How to describe Mrs Crabbe's diatribe?

"Scold? Tongue-lashing?"

Tom returned her smile, his irritation with Mrs Crabbe ebbing. "Indeed. Is that why you're here instead of the parlour?"

"A strategic retreat, Captain. Apparently the rain is your fault, too, not to mention the potholes in the road, the lack of shelter in Mr Sellars' cart..." She rolled her eyes in an exaggerated expression that made him laugh. "I also came to find how you are. We would have been in the suds indeed had you not stopped to assist us. I suspect Mr Easton is too diffident to have taken command as you did."

The apothecary's good sense had been helpful, though. As had her own suggestions. "Do not underestimate yourself, Mrs Wilson. You are a useful person to have around in a crisis."

The smile left her face, and he wondered if he had offended her in some way. But she turned her gaze to the hearth, and the sad expression vanished. "Is that mulled ale?"

He picked up the poker and knocked the ash from its end. "It soon will be." He plunged the glowing poker into the ale, and the smell of hot spices filled the air.

Useful.

Ellie had heard how useful she was too often in the last few days. But the captain hadn't meant it in the disparaging way her father had, as if it was her only good quality, and she did her best to dismiss the feeling of inadequacy. She accepted the mug of warmed ale he offered and inhaled the scents. "Just the way to warm me from the inside. Thank you."

He settled into a chair with his own mug, legs out towards the blaze.

"Have you come far, Captain?"

"I left York yesterday afternoon. The roads are not quite as sodden on that side of the Pennines. Talking about the weather, eh, as one does? But pertinent at the moment."

"It could be worse," she said. "It could be snowing."

"I doubt that thought would have pacified Mrs Crabbe."

She bit her lip against a laugh.

"I'm bound for Kendal," he went on. "To visit my mother. It is where I grew up."

"I've heard it is a pretty town, although I have never been there." Father took little interest in places beyond his parish.

"It is. There are pleasant walks beside the river, and high ground close by." He glanced up at her, as if debating what to say. "When I was a youth, I often escaped from my lessons and went up there. Looking at the fells to the north and the sea in the distance made me want to explore further. We—my brother and I—did travel a little with our father, but only to places such as York or Doncaster. My youthful self wanted to find out what was beyond the sea."

Foreign travel had been part of Ben's reason for wanting a commission, too.

"I used to do that as well. But in my case, I merely admired the view rather than wanting to see distant lands." She broke off as the door opened and Mrs Sellars entered.

"Your room's ready, Captain. Room five."

He drained his mug and stood. "Thank you, Mrs Sellars."

She gave a brisk nod and left.

The smile the Captain turned on Ellie was warm. "I will see you at dinner, Mrs Wilson. I enjoyed our conversation."

Ellie was sorry to see him go; he'd been easy to converse with. And to laugh with, as she often had with Ben.

When dinner was served, Ellie took a place at the opposite end of the table to Mrs Crabbe. Captain Allerby had an amused twinkle in his eye that said he knew her reason for choosing that seat. The landlady placed a roast leg of mutton before the captain and the maid set out dishes of roast and boiled potatoes, turnips and leeks, and a jug of gravy.

Mrs Crabbe glowered at the food. "Is this the only choice we get? For the price you are—"

"This looks lovely, Mrs Sellars." Ellie spoke a little louder than necessary. "How good of you to provide such a splendid meal at short notice."

"Plum pudding and custard after, if it's wanted," Mrs Sellars said, not even glancing towards Mrs Crabbe. "There's some wine to be had, or ale. Sellars brews his—"

"Wine," Mr Crabbe stated. The other men all opted for ale, although in a more polite manner. Ellie asked for wine, and Mrs Sellars went to get the drinks. Captain Allerby carved, and Mr Easton and Mr Hart passed the plates and dishes of vegetables.

"How is the coachman, Mr Easton?" Ellie hadn't seen him since he'd arrived.

"In need of rest," the apothecary said. "A doctor should see him, but in any case he'll be in no state to drive for several days."

"Days?" Mrs Crabbe exclaimed. "I thought the captain must have been mistaken. I must be on my way tomorrow. I have an important meeting of the Society for Moral Improvement."

A muffled snort came from Captain Allerby, and Ellie had to press her lips together. Pity the poor subjects of Mrs Crabbe's attentions.

"It is inconvenient for all of us," Mr Easton responded calmly.

"But—"

"It is of no use complaining to me, madam, or any of us here," Mr Easton interrupted. "*We* are not responsible for the weather, the coachman's injury, or the damaged wheel."

"I expect Dodds will ride back to Settle tomorrow and arrange for another coachman, and a coach, if the wheel cannot be mended." the captain said, while Mrs Crabbe's mouth was still open in surprise at the reprimand.

"Where are you bound?" Ellie asked Mr Easton, in an attempt to ward off further complaints.

"Only to Skipton, ma'am. I will attempt to hire a horse in the morning to complete my journey."

"I will have to wait for the coach company to make arrangements," Mr Hart said, speaking for the first time since he had hobbled down the stairs with the aid of a stout stick. "It will do my wife good to rest here for part of the day tomorrow. I must thank you, Mrs Wilson, for getting her to warmth. Mr Easton thinks she will be well once she is rested."

"I am glad, sir." Ellie glanced in Mrs Crabbe's direction, wondering what the woman would find to complain about next, but her attention was now on Captain Allerby.

. . .

"Are you on furlough, Captain?" Mrs Crabbe asked Tom.

"Yes, ma'am."

She leaned forward, her face full of avid curiosity. "You must have been in many battles. What is it like on a battlefield? Is it very dreadful?"

It wasn't battlefields that he sometimes saw in the dead of night when he couldn't sleep, but that Spanish village. "That is not a subject for mixed company, madam."

"Pass the wine, Augusta," Crabbe muttered. He'd emptied the bottle in front of him already. Mrs Crabbe did so, then turned her attention to Mrs Wilson.

"Are you going far?"

"To York on this coach."

"So you live somewhere near there?" Mrs Crabbe waited in silence for several seconds before it became obvious that Mrs Wilson was not going to provide any more details. "Will your husband not be worried when you are late returning?" Her eyes dropped to Mrs Wilson's black gown. "Or have you no husband? It must be a lonely life, being a widow. And so young! I must say, you have kept your gown very neat for such an old garment. Skirts are much less full now, you know."

Mrs Wilson put her knife and fork down, a sadness in her eyes. "My personal life is no concern of yours, Mrs Crabbe. Now, I wish to finish my dinner in peace, if you please."

For a moment, the only sound in the room was the crackle of the fire, then a "Well!" from Mrs Crabbe.

She's a widow?

"I'm for Kendal, myself," Tom said. Better that Mrs Crabbe's attention was on him rather than Mrs Wilson. "That is on the edge of the Lake District, you know. The mountains there are tame compared to some of those in Portugal, but greener."

"All the rain, I expect," Easton put in. "Keeps the lakes full, too."

"It is quite the fashionable thing, I understand, to tour the Lake

Country," Tom added hurriedly, as Mrs Crabbe opened her mouth to speak.

"Indeed." Easton looked as if he was trying not to smile. "The Lake poets—Wordsworth, you know, and Coleridge—are all the rage in some circles."

Mrs Wilson had resumed her meal, her face no longer sad.

"Ah, yes. Who can forget the daffodils?" One of Tom's lieutenants had a book of poetry that he recited from on long winter evenings. "I wandered lonely as a cloud, that floats on high o'er vales and—"

Mrs Crabbe pushed her chair back, the legs scraping on the floor. "I have had a trying day. I will retire."

"Order another bottle on your way out," was all her husband said as she stalked out of the room, slamming the door behind her.

Mrs Wilson had her lips pressed together, her eyes crinkled in amusement. Easton shook his head, a wry smile on his face. "Do you recall the whole poem, Captain?"

"You will, I'm sure, be pleased to know that I do not."

His answer earned a chuckle from Mrs Wilson, and outright laughs from Easton and Hart.

Ellie found the conversation after Mrs Crabbe's departure far more pleasant. She listened with interest while the men discussed the progress of the war—not in the rather graphic way that Mrs Crabbe had seemed to want, but in terms of plans and problems, strategies and tactics. Both Mr Hart and the apothecary were well informed about events in the Peninsula. Ellie read the main news, but had lost interest in the details after Ben's death. Mr Crabbe said little, merely drinking his way through more wine. The little gathering broke up less than an hour later.

The upstairs landing was dark, lit only by a lamp at the top of the stairs and the flickering candle in Ellie's hand. She had just taken the key from her reticule when a door banged below stairs and a sudden draft blew the candle flame out. She muttered a curse, but the fire in her room would still be glowing and she could relight it easily enough.

If she could get the key into the lock, that was. Finding a small hole in a dark door when the only, feeble, light came from directly behind her was proving difficult.

Footsteps sounded on the stairs; Captain Allerby appeared on the landing, lit candle in one hand and a bottle and glass in the other. "Can I be of assistance, Mrs Wilson? A light, perhaps?"

"Thank you. It seems you are always coming to the rescue."

He chuckled in the darkness. "Some rescues are easier than others."

She touched her candle to his, then fitted the key in the lock and turned it. But she hesitated with her hand on the latch. The questions she'd asked herself as she rode here—would the captain answer them? Ben had always given light-hearted, even flippant, answers when she'd asked about his chosen career. She'd believed he enjoyed it—mostly— at the time, but now she wanted to know more about that life. The captain was easy to talk to, and she was unlikely to meet anyone else who could answer her questions.

"Can you manage now, Mrs Wilson?

"Yes…"

He would be on his way first thing in the morning. It was now or never. And if she didn't ask him, she would regret it later.

Carpe diem.

She took a deep breath and stepped into the room before turning to face him. "I would like to ask you something, Captain, but not here on the landing. It may not be a quick answer. Would you come inside for a few minutes?"

CHAPTER 5

Captain Allerby had started to turn away, but now he froze. Ellie's face heated as she thought how her invitation could be interpreted. But she felt he would not take advantage, as other men might. Although why she felt that, she could not say.

Finally he nodded and followed her in, latching the door behind him. Mrs Sellars had given her a handsome room, large enough for two chairs by the fire as well as the bed and a small clothes press. It was warm, the fire needing only a little poking to make a friendly blaze; its crackling almost masked the sound of rain against the window.

"How may I help you, Mrs Wilson?"

"Won't you sit?" She gestured to one of the chairs and seated herself in the other. "I wanted to ask you about... about being a soldier."

He frowned as he sat, and she recalled his expression when he had evaded Mrs Crabbe's questions. "Not details of battles and injuries—I can imagine enough of that." She sat back in the armchair, trying to relax. "Ben was a lieutenant. The last time I saw him, he told me not to grieve if he did not come back, as he'd chosen the life and had no regrets. He told me he enjoyed it."

The captain nodded. Waiting for her to get to the point, no doubt.

"But what I read in the papers describes horrific losses in battle, long marches with not enough food, men dying of fever. It is some time since his death, but I still wonder what could outweigh that sufficiently for someone to enjoy the life."

His brows rose, then one side of his mouth turned up. "That is not a question I was expecting."

"I'm sorry. I… Is that too personal?"

"Not at all. But the answer would vary from man to man, and on their particular experiences. I can only answer for myself, if that is of any use?"

She nodded. It didn't really matter if his answer was the same as Ben would have given. She just needed to know that it *was* possible to enjoy such a life. "You said earlier that you chose the army to see the world," she prompted, when he seemed to be hesitating.

"That was one reason, yes. I had no fancy for anything that involved being in an office all day. And I was very young. The army offered excitement, the chance for glory." His lips twisted as he spoke.

"I take it you no longer agree with your younger self?"

"Not entirely—not the glory part, at least. I have been to parts of Europe I would never otherwise have seen, and there has been plenty of excitement. But much of the time is spent in training the men or marching from place to place, both of which are as uninteresting as they sound. Although certainly more interesting to me than being cooped up indoors, poring over account books or legal documents. However, there is also time spent in the company of comrades, particularly in winter quarters. I think friendships made in the army are unlike those made in other professions, a camaraderie that comes from working together. There is also a degree of satisfaction in a job well done."

"Battles won?"

"Not necessarily. And not all battles won are a matter for satisfaction, either."

"How is that?"

He frowned and did not reply. Had she touched on something he would rather not talk about?

She did not want this conversation to end, not just yet. The bottle and glass he'd brought were on the floor by his feet. She was already risking gossip if his presence in her room became known. Drinking together was a step further, but no-one would know.

"Could I share your drink, Captain? There is another glass on the clothes press."

"Of course." He'd been considering how much he should say, and wishing he'd thought more carefully before speaking. He poured two glasses; their fingers touched briefly as he handed one to her. Her first sip brought a nod of approval, and he settled back into his chair. The brandy was surprisingly good for such a modest inn, and the present company far more enjoyable than he'd expected to find. A pity that he'd led the conversation into the darker parts of army life.

"You said that battles won weren't always a matter for satisfaction," she prompted. "Too many losses?"

"That, yes." She was waiting for him to continue, but there was no need to describe the details. "Sometimes the aftermath is shameful. At Ciudad Rodrigo..." Did she know of that?

"The recent capture of the city?"

"Yes. Assaulting a fortress is always a bloody affair, but this time the men behaved disgracefully once we took the city. Looting, rioting. The enemy were the French garrison, not the Spanish inhabitants, but it was the latter who suffered from our troops. We took the fortress, but overall I cannot celebrate our victory."

And the memories of that night, with the men out of control, reminded him of the Spanish village that still sometimes came to him in his dreams. His fellow officers knew what had happened and had not criticised his actions, but he still couldn't help wondering if he'd made the correct decision. He could possibly talk it over with Frank when he saw him, but what would he do if Frank *did* believe he should have acted differently? He didn't want his brother to think badly of him.

"Captain?" Mrs Wilson's voice was soft, concerned. "I'm sorry—I did not mean to resurrect painful memories."

He shook his head. "I did that myself—and you asked me why I found satisfaction in army life, not for tales of death and destruction." He looked up, to find her gaze fixed on his face.

"I find that telling another person my worries can sometimes help. If you want to tell me about something, please do so. Women are more resilient than men generally give us credit for."

He didn't want Mrs Wilson to think badly of him, either. But he would not be seeing her again after tonight—unfortunately—so it should not matter if she did.

Leaning forward, he looked at the fire rather than her. "We were a foraging party, ten of us, looking for food in a Spanish village. The French had been there before us. They take provisions, they do not buy them. And some—most—do not treat the villagers well." Houses burning, bodies in the street. He took a mouthful of brandy.

"I have heard that."

"The survivor we spoke to thought their attackers had been French deserters, although none of them understood much of what the Frenchmen had been saying. They had not been gone long, and my men wanted to go after them. As did I. I left a few men behind to see if they could help, and the rest of us caught up with the French very easily. Half of them were almost too drunk to walk, and they all surrendered as soon as they saw us, even though there were fifteen of them. We set off back towards the village." He looked up. "That's when we found out why they'd left when they did, before they'd looted everything, and why they'd surrendered to us so readily. They'd learned that a band of guerrillas were about to arrive and felt safer in our custody. We were surrounded by the guerrillas just before we got to the village."

"The guerrillas fight the French, do they not?" Mrs Wilson asked. "They would be on your side."

"They do, but they held us at gunpoint because they wanted our prisoners. To kill them."

Ellie didn't understand the problem. "Those men would hang if brought to trial, wouldn't they?"

"Most likely, yes." The captain finished the brandy in his glass and poured more. "It is one thing to turn men over to army justice, but with the guerrillas it would not have been a matter of a trial and hanging. The Spanish treat French captives the same way as the French army treats them, and even though one might consider it an eye for an eye, my duty as an officer was to take those prisoners back for trial. But I *did* hand over one of them."

She could tell from his expression that he would not have voluntarily given up even one prisoner. "What would have happened had you not done so?"

He shrugged. "There were thirty guerrillas, well armed, and only ten of us. And, to the guerrillas, by sheltering the prisoners we would be taking the side of the French."

Ellie understood why he might believe he'd failed in his duty. But it must be preying on his mind for him to confess like this. He was watching her, now, not the fire, with an intent look on his face. Awaiting a verdict?

"So, if I understand this correctly, you had to decide between handing over the prisoners or fighting the guerrillas."

"Yes."

"You could not know how the guerrillas would have treated you if you fought and lost. The deaths of your men—and yours, too—could have been as... as painful as the ones intended for the French. Could you have asked them to risk that?"

"I... No. Not even if they'd been willing. There was an officer with the French, a subaltern. It was possible that he'd tried to stop them and been ignored, but it didn't look that way. The others were still taking their lead from him. I persuaded the guerrillas to take him and let the rest of us leave."

One prisoner handed over instead of fifteen. It seemed to Ellie that he'd made the best of a difficult situation.

"You should not blame yourself, Captain. Far from failing your duty, it sounds as if you made the best choice you could in very difficult circumstances."

He was staring at her face, although his gaze appeared unfocused. Then the frown went and he shook his head. "I suppose so. I will remember what you said next time the guilt creeps up on me."

Ellie wondered if Ben had ever had to make such decisions, if he'd worried about what he'd done. If he had, it had not been apparent when he'd come home on leave. And the captain had made her see how Ben really could have been happy with his choice of career, in spite of the hardships.

But although his frown had gone, he still appeared troubled—a trouble she wanted to ease, to see his smile return. She took a sip of her brandy, the liquid burning fire down her throat. "There is often more than one way of looking at something, Captain. My father is a vicar. He is always certain that his interpretation of the scriptures is the only correct one. When I was old enough to help in the Parish, I soon learned that his flock had other ways of interpreting God's word. Not *all* of them proper excuses for their behaviour."

"An eye for an eye excusing a fight?"

"Sometimes," she said. "The more usual one was that turning water into wine means drunkenness is not a sin."

He laughed, a rich sound that stirred something within her. A warmth that had nothing to do with the fire or the brandy. "I've heard that one many a time—usually with feigned penitence and a sore head!"

When had she last had a conversation like this, with such a sharing of inner thoughts and feelings? She talked with Martin often enough, but that was usually about events or tasks on the farm. The captain seemed to be enjoying her company, not merely discussing daily practicalities, and she had not felt so close to someone since Ben died. Although this closeness was quite different—there was a breathlessness inside her. Almost as if she was nervous.

What had he said earlier? "You said satisfaction could come from things other than battles won. What did you mean?"

Somewhere a clock struck the hour, the sound faint amid the soughing of the wind in the eaves. Subconsciously Tom counted the chimes—eleven or twelve. It was late; he should leave, but he didn't want to.

"Things like seeing a company of raw recruits develop into a unit that can withstand a French cavalry charge. Or successful skirmishes, such as the time we were covering a retreat. My company was providing covering fire for a unit of engineers setting charges to destroy a bridge. We held the French off long enough, and we all escaped with no more than minor injuries."

She nodded. "Working together for a common purpose?"

"Exactly."

He really should go. It was some time since he'd spent such an enjoyable evening with a woman. She was not only intelligent but attractive, too. Too attractive for his comfort.

He stood and crossed to the window. "The rain has stopped."

She sighed. "You will wish for an early start, I suppose. Thank you for setting my mind at rest."

He turned back to face her. "No, thank *you*. I had kept my doubts about my actions in that Spanish village to myself for too long. What you said has been very useful—it helped me to see things more clearly."

There was that sudden unhappiness in her face again, as in the parlour earlier when he had said she was a useful person to have in a crisis. "What is wrong?

She shrugged, smoothing her face, but did not answer.

"I'm sorry. It is none of my business."

She shook her head. "It's not that. I am just tired of being valued merely because I am useful or helpful."

"Merely useful? Do not think that." Was that really her life? How she saw herself? "You are compassionate, easy to talk to…" Calm in an emergency, but that was perhaps too close to 'useful'. "It has been my pleasure to have your company this evening."

She gazed at him, a small crease forming between her brows. He took a step towards her. "I mean that."

Her brows rose a little, then she smiled. "Thank you, Captain."

The next words came out without thinking. "Tom. My name is Tom."

Surprised, Ellie looked into his eyes and her heart beat faster. No-one had looked at her in such a way before. As if he was hungry. For *her*.

"I'm sorry," he added. "That is too familiar."

It didn't feel that way. Not after all they had talked about. Not the way she was feeling now. Because of his nearness, and because she wanted to believe what he said.

"Not at all. My… That is, please call me Ellie." She rose as he came back to the fire and stopped in front of her.

"A pretty name," he said, looking into her eyes. "For a beautiful woman."

She felt warmth in her chest and her belly. An urge to move closer to him.

"Thank *you*, Ellie," he went on. "I have not enjoyed an evening so much for a long time." He put a hand up towards her face, but checked it.

She wanted him to touch her—the first time she had felt that with any man. Her head moved towards his hand, just a little, and his fingers cupped her cheek. Was it her imagination, or was his breath coming as raggedly as her own?

"I should leave." But he made no move to do so, and his eyes dropped to her mouth. Tom *wanted* her. Wanted *her*. As no other man had.

If she could not have passion in her marriage, could she not experience it just once, with this man?

"Stay with me?"

CHAPTER 6

*S*tay with me.

The words echoed in Ellie's mind. She had met this man
—Tom—only hours ago. He must think her a wanton.

It was wrong, she knew that, but could she ignore this chance?
No-one would know what she had done, but *she* would know what it
was to be desired.

He stood still before her, the hand that had caressed her face now
tense by his side.

"What…" He swallowed and began again. "What are you asking?"

There's nothing worse than regretting what might have been. Things you
might have done but didn't dare.

Her eyes focused on his mouth briefly. "A kiss?" Stepping closer,
she put one hand on his shoulder, then up to his face. Then closer still,
until their bodies were almost touching, and her face tilted up.

She had a moment of doubt when he didn't move, then he let out a
long breath and bent his head to hers. One hand went to the small of
her back, pulling her so close she could feel that yes, he really did
want her. His other rested on her shoulder. The touch of his lips on
hers was light at first, a mere feather-stroke, but enough to warm her
from the inside. But that was as nothing to the liquid fire that shot

through her when she opened her mouth and he deepened the kiss, tongues meeting and his hand moving to cup one breast.

This is what it should be like.

It could not last forever, and he lifted his head from hers, leaving her breathless but wanting more. The lamplight flickered off the planes of his face, his breath fanning her cheek. "Ellie, I should go."

"No." Uncertainty struck again. "I mean, please stay. If you want to."

"Oh, I want to," he said, his voice rough. He pulled her close again. "But are you sure?"

She would never get another chance like this.

Carpe diem, Ellie.

Nodding, she began to unfasten his waistcoat, fingers clumsy on the smooth metal of the buttons. His hands fumbled at the back of her gown, finding and pulling the ties, and her need grew stronger as he slid it off her shoulders.

Tom lay in the bed staring at the ceiling, now illuminated only by the feeble glow from the fire. Ellie's steady breathing as she lay curled up beside him, and the warmth of her back against his side, only added to his feeling of contentment, his mind more at peace than it had been in some time, and his body more relaxed. And that was due to the woman beside him—lovely in body and character.

Sleep didn't come, although this time it wasn't due to guilt. He turned his head to one side, a strand of her hair tickling his nose. The delicate scent of lavender, the rounded shape of her hips beneath the bedcovers, the way her hands had felt on his skin—all made him want to wake her and start again, but he would not. He should leave her soon—before anyone was about, and with enough time to make his own bedroom look used. He would be gone at dawn, but Ellie would most likely have to spend half the day here, or longer. Any suggestion that they'd spent the night together, even if nothing more than his own room looking unused, could be amplified and spread by that venomous Mrs Crabbe.

His usual couplings with camp followers were enjoyable for both parties—he hoped the pleasure was mutual—but they were purely physical acts. With Ellie it had felt much more than that, as if there was some connection between them. He'd shown a part of himself to her, a part he'd been ashamed of, and she hadn't censured him. She'd helped him to accept that he'd done the best that was possible under the circumstances. Those feelings of guilt would return, no doubt, but Ellie's words would counter them.

What had he done for her? Reassurance that her husband might have enjoyed his life in the army? He hadn't been a very attentive husband, from the way Ellie had responded to his touch, to his kisses. Some of her reactions had been surprise—he'd swear to it. When he'd asked again, before their final consummation, the sadness in her eyes when she said she could not have children had almost undone him. But he'd withdrawn anyway, spilling most of his seed on her belly.

The church clock struck three, its chimes giving him notice that he should be gone. He pushed the covers back, trying not to disturb her, and felt for his clothes still strewn across the floor.

"Light a candle." Her voice was sleepy, but the sheets rustled as she sat up. "There's one on the mantelpiece."

He lit it from the remains of the fire and sorted the clothing, laying Ellie's gown and shift over the back of a chair, conscious all the while of her eyes on him. Breeches and shirt pulled on, waistcoat and coat donned but left unbuttoned, stockings, neckcloth stuffed in a pocket... only his boots were left.

"I was going to wake you before I left." He sat on the edge of the bed. "If... If you need anything..."

If he hadn't withdrawn in time. If any scandal befell her...

"Ellie, I will not be in one place for long, and I've to be back in Spain next month, but a letter to my mother will be forwarded. She will know where I am. King's Road, in Kendal."

"I..." She shook her head, as if to wake herself, and rubbed her eyes. "Thank you. Keep yourself safe, Tom." A corner of her mouth turned up, although the smile was bittersweet. "Not the best instruction to a soldier."

"I do my best." He leaned across and kissed her—a lingering taste of what they'd shared earlier, making him regret even more that he had to leave. Then he stood, seeing a similar regret as their eyes met.

Then, with boots tucked under one arm, the brandy bottle and glass in that hand, he turned the key as quietly as he could. The latch made only a faint click as he closed the door behind him. A quiet end to an interlude he would remember for a long time.

King's Road. As Ellie drifted into wakefulness, the address ran through her mind. Grey light shone through a gap in the curtains; a faint smell of frying bacon indicated that breakfast might be ready soon. Normally awake with the dawn at this time of year, she had slept longer than usual. Her mouth felt dry, her head as if it was stuffed with wool.

Brandy. She'd been drinking brandy.

King's Road? Why was that in her head...?

Good heavens! She stiffened as the remaining fog of sleep cleared from her mind. Had she really been intimate with a man who was not her husband?

It was no dream—she could not possibly have imagined the way his touch had warmed her, made her breath come faster. The feel of his hands stroking her *everywhere*. The way the whole world had become only delicious sensation.

She blushed at the memory—but equally sweet was the knowledge that he had wanted her to touch him, too. She had given pleasure, as well as receiving it.

He must be miles on his way by now. They would not meet again, but she dearly hoped he came to no harm in Spain. She had enjoyed his company, as well as his lovemaking. Although *enjoyed* seemed too pale a word. An experience to remember, but not to repeat. She hoped he had not thought her a lightskirt.

But no matter what Tom's opinion was, the people in the inn would think ill of her if they knew what she had done.

Ellie flung the covers back and reached for her shift. This was not the time to contemplate her sins. She would deal with those thoughts later. Now, she had to ensure there was no hint that a second person had slept here.

She dressed quickly, then brushed and pinned her hair, looking around the room for anything not hers. Nothing beneath the bed, no sign on the chairs. She piled the pillows one on top of the other in the centre of the bed and smoothed the sheets a little—not too much. There—it looked as if she'd been sitting up in bed reading.

Satisfied, she went down to the dining room, where Mr Hart was tucking into a substantial breakfast. Mr Easton arrived behind her; they sat down and Mrs Sellars came to take their orders.

"Dodds rode off to Settle before first light," the landlady informed them when she returned with tea and rolls for Ellie, ham and eggs for Mr Easton. "He's just returned, says the coach might be ready early this afternoon."

Ellie buttered a roll. "How is your wife, Mr Hart?"

"Feeling much better, thank you, ma'am, but taking breakfast in our room. I cannot say I am sorry, though, that we have to wait a few more hours."

"Where's Captain Allerby?" Mr Easton asked.

Ellie felt her face heating at the mention of his name, and hastily gulped her too-hot tea.

"Left before dawn, according to Mrs Sellars," Mr Hart said. He grinned. "You will be pleased to know that Mrs Crabbe has requested breakfast in her room."

Good—Ellie would get to eat in peace. But it would be a long trip to York, cooped up in a coach with that woman.

"Mrs Wilson?" It was the apothecary this time. "I am about to enquire for a horse to take me on to Skipton. If you wish, I can see if they also have one with a side saddle. If your luggage is small enough to be strapped on, that is. You might find another coach there, if you don't mind paying the fare again. The weather is not clement, but it might be preferable to travelling with... with that—"

"Virago?" Mr Hart muttered.

"Thank you, sir. I would be very grateful." Her skirts might just be full enough to preserve her modesty on a side saddle—it was all very well riding into this village astride when necessity demanded; it would be quite improper to ride into Skipton in such a manner. Although far less improper than what she'd done last night. She took another mouthful of hot tea.

They set off an hour later. Mrs Sellars had found a length of oilcloth for Ellie to drape over her legs, both for warmth and for modesty. She was in no mood for talking, and Mr Easton seemed to sense her feelings, only casting the odd glance behind to make sure she was keeping up as the two horses trudged along the muddy road. She was finally alone with her thoughts.

Did she feel guilty?

Yes. She had broken her marriage vows.

Did she regret doing it? That was a harder question to answer honestly. She was ashamed to admit to herself that the guilt of breaking her vows was outweighed by understanding what she was missing in the marriage bed.

She would not have that pleasure again—so would she have been better not knowing?

No, she would not. Now she knew it was not *her* who was lacking, who was not attractive enough to please, who could not respond to a man in that way.

Why wasn't it like that with Martin? She supposed that men had to learn what pleased a woman—perhaps Martin just had no experience. Although it hadn't just been that—Tom had *wanted* her, looked at her in a way Martin never had.

But Martin was her husband and, even if she encountered Tom in the future, there must be no repeat of her infidelity. Her conscience would not let her.

There was no point dwelling on it. Life would go on much as it had since she married, and apart from regret at her lack of love and children, she had been reasonably content. But her father's pointed comments about her being useful had reminded her of those regrets and she had taken the opportunity to experience something more—some passion, even if she could not have children.

She had her own home, where she helped to manage the farm and discussed the lambs or the price of cheese with Martin in the evenings. And she was away from her father and his incessant demands. She *should* be content with all that—but could she be, now that she knew what was possible in a marriage?

Tom rode into Kendal late in the afternoon, as dusk was falling. Although the roads were as muddy as the day before, and the weather still gloomy, the day seemed to have passed quickly. His time with Ellie continued to fill his mind, and he wished he'd said more in those few brief minutes before he left her in the early hours. Asked where she lived, if he could write to her. If he could see her again.

But that was foolish—he would be returning to the Peninsula within a few weeks. She had the means to contact him if she wished to. He hoped she would, and because she wanted to, not because she needed to.

After leaving the horse at the livery stable, he slung his saddle bags over his shoulder for the walk up the hill to his mother's house. The limp he'd had when he first started to walk on his injured leg had come back—hardly surprising after riding for three days and helping to right the tipped coach. At the house, the fanlight above the door had a welcoming glow. He knocked, and a young maidservant opened the door, new since the last time he'd been home. "Captain Allerby," he announced, to her look of enquiry.

"Tom!" Mama came hurrying from the parlour, her hands held out in greeting. "I got your letter, but I wasn't sure when to expect you. How are you? Is your leg mended? But you're wet! Maisie, take the captain's coat and put the kettle on."

Tom let himself be ordered about—leaving his boots in the

scullery for the boy to clean, putting his gear in his room, then sitting by the fire to warm himself. He knew from experience that Mama's first rush of words would abate once she'd assured herself that he was well.

Maisie was a sensible lass and brought a large slab of fruit cake along with the tea. Tom tucked in with a will, then settled back to be interrogated about his doings since his last leave, three years ago. Mama always complained that he never gave enough details in his letters.

"I came via York," he said, once his highly edited recital was done. "Frank was away on business, but I met his wife."

"Hmm." Mama pursed her lips.

"A pretty woman."

"Pretty is as pretty does. She seems a little… flighty to me." Mama sighed. "He appears to be happy with her, so it's not for me to judge. I'm just pleased he's doing well enough to afford such a house."

And to completely redecorate it. He looked around the parlour—this was more to his taste than Frank's new house, although perhaps only because he'd grown up here. The familiar clock ticked the time away above the fire, a single porcelain shepherdess stood on a side table, and the painting of Daedalus winning the Derby in 1794 hung above the fire. A lucky bet on the animal at good odds hadn't exactly made their fortunes—Father's legal business had been doing well enough—but it had allowed the Allerby family to move into this bigger house. Later, the remainder of the winnings had paid for Frank to gain wider experience by finishing his period as an articled clerk with a prestigious firm in York, and purchased Tom's commission without straining the family finances too much. Their late father's love of horse-racing had passed down to Frank; Tom enjoyed a day out and placing small bets, but he wasn't as enthusiastic as his brother.

"How long can you stay, Tom?"

"A week, perhaps a little longer. I'll go back via York, see if I can catch Frank this time."

"Mrs Simpson was asking after you…" Mama talked about the local news, about the families he'd known when he was growing up, which of the sons of his age were still in Kendal, who had married... He paid enough attention to make sensible remarks when she paused, but he'd lost touch with many of the people she mentioned. He was happy, though, to know that she was still as sociable as ever. And there were enough of his old friends around to make for several convivial evenings in the town.

On his final day, Mama came into his room as he was packing his saddle bags ready for an early start the next morning.

"Maisie put this in my drawer, Tom, but it isn't mine. Nor hers."

This was a white handkerchief with a flower embroidered in one corner. A small, woman-sized handkerchief.

"It's not mine, Mama."

"I know that! But Maisie washed all your things and wondered why it was with your shirts and stockings."

Was it Ellie's? In that hurried gathering of clothing in the dark, he could easily have picked it up with his other garments and not noticed. He reached for it, but Mama moved her hand away.

"Is there something you're not telling me, Tom?" She had a hopeful smile on her face.

"No, Mama."

Her face fell.

"A chance encounter, no more." Unfortunately. But he had to say what he'd been putting off all week. "Mama... If a... a friend writes to me here, you will send the letter on, won't you? You're the best person to know where I'm to be found."

"Of course I will—you didn't need to ask." She looked at the handkerchief. "You won't be wanting this, then. What a pity."

That was all she said on the matter, although he did have to put up with some knowing smiles over their final dinner together.

But that evening he had a quiet word with Maisie, and the handkerchief went into his pocket the following morning.

CHAPTER 7

*E*llie thanked the farmer for giving her a ride and set off along the muddy lane. She'd reached York last night, a day later than planned, and had been lucky to get an inside seat on this morning's coach to Thirsk. The lad from home, understandably, had not been in the Market Place to meet her, so she'd been luckier still to find someone who was willing to take her to within a mile of home.

She kept up a brisk pace, as the wind was chill in spite of the sunshine. From the sodden grass in the fields and the puddles in the lane, they'd had heavy rain here, too. When the red roof and warm sandstone walls of Knowle Farm came into sight, she hesitated before turning into the track that led to the farm—would Martin be at home?

On the coach to York, and then again this morning, she'd debated whether or not she should confess her sin. Would Martin forgive her? She did not think he would make her destitute, but she could not be sure. If he did disown her, returning to her father would not be an option and what would she do then? Might Aunt Elizabeth take her in? Carlisle was far enough away to avoid gossip reaching it.

The thought crossed her mind that it would be unfair for Martin to resent someone else having what he did not seem to want, but that was no excuse for her actions. In any case, it could not be undone, and would not happen again. Even if Martin forgave her, telling him would cause hurt and upset.

It's just as well I'm barren. A babe could not be hidden.

No, she would not tell him. She could change her mind later, whereas once told, the confession could not be taken back. She must try to greet him normally, so he would not guess from her manner that something had happened and ask her about it.

The decision made—for now—she moved on, past the lavender bushes lining the path to the front door. Then she looked at the mud caking her boots and walked around the house to the farmyard, heading for the scullery.

Jake, their odd job boy, was leaning on the wall. Weariness showed in every line of his thin body, but he limped over as fast as he could when he saw her. "Master's still away at Bank Side, missus. I took the gig into Thirsk yesterday, like you said, but you weren't on the coach."

"There was an accident on the journey. I'm well, Jake," she added, as he frowned.

"I'd have come for you if I'd known you'd be back today, but Bates wanted me to help with the lambing."

"Don't worry—you had no way of knowing when I'd return. But if you have time this afternoon, would you ride into Thirsk and collect my bag from The Three Tuns?"

"Aye, I will. Most of the lambs have arrived now." He glanced towards the back of the house, trouble still on his face. "The hens…" He shrugged. "Agnes'll tell you." He shuffled off back to the barn without waiting for a reply.

Hens?

Ellie was unlacing her boots by the back door when their cook appeared, the worry lines on her face deeper than usual.

"Oh, I'm glad you're back, missus."

Ellie waited for the tale of disaster, but Agnes just stood there, hands clasped in front of her. "What's wrong, Agnes?"

"Three hens killed. Fox got in, took one, left the other two. They're in the pantry now. No-one heard owt, missus, or we would have tried to stop—"

"I know, Agnes. I know." The cook's agitation seemed too much for what was, after all, only a small loss. "Make us a pot of tea and you can tell me all about it. I need to change my gown."

"It's my fault," Agnes said, when they were sitting at the kitchen table with a pot of tea brewing in front of them. "The master'll be angry when he finds out."

Ellie shook her head. Martin might grumble, but she'd never seen him angry about anything other than outright carelessness. "How can a hole in a henhouse be your fault?"

The knuckles on Agnes' clenched hands showed white. "Master won't turn me off, will—?"

"No. Why should he?"

"We were told not to let Mr Palmer onto the farm. But he wouldn't go when we said."

Luke Palmer had been here? For herself, she was glad she'd been away. Martin's cousin missed no opportunity to remind her of her childless state—and gloat about it. Why, she didn't know.

"When did he come, Agnes? And what did he want?"

"Yesterday. Said he'd come to see the master. When he found out you weren't here, either, he said he'd look around to make sure everything was reet."

"And the men were busy with the lambs, I suppose." Martin never let Palmer wander around unescorted, but she could see how that might have been difficult with neither her nor Martin here.

"Yes. Fanny was doing the butter, and Kate had just burned her hand and I had to see to it."

Agnes' daughter was always having accidents—Kate's clumsiness and simple mind were the main cause of Agnes' perpetual state of worry. She could never truly believe that Martin would not turn the pair of them off for minor mishaps that her fears turned into major disasters.

"We didn't know the hens were gone until Kate went to get the eggs this morning."

"You'd better show me."

The path to the henhouse was usually kept swept, but Ellie put her pattens on anyway. Agnes removed a piece of wood resting against the far side of the henhouse, held in place with a large stone. "There, missus." She pointed to a gap easily large enough for a fox to get in.

Ellie bent down, one hand holding her skirts away from the wet grass. The whole end of one plank was missing, leaving a splintered edge where it had broken. Palmer must have levered the end loose, and then managed to bend it far enough for it to break.

Why would he do that?

"We left it so you could see, missus."

"Quite right, Agnes. I'll see if Jake can fix it." Jake would have to replace the whole plank, but she'd tell him to keep the damaged one to show Martin when he returned.

Martin rode into the yard as Jake was fetching the hammer and nails. He slid off the horse, a smile on his face and his loose-fitting breeches and jacket showing signs of having spent most of the last week in the stables.

"Sorry I'm late, Ellie. One of the mares began foaling early, and there were complications. I stayed until she'd finished."

"I've only just returned. Did the foal survive?"

Martin's smile turned wry. "So far, yes. It's a bit too soon to tell how well he'll do." He looked at the tools in Jake's hands. "Repairs?"

"Henhouse."

Martin reached for the hammer. "I'll do it."

Jake surrendered the tools and led Martin's horse away.

"Come, I'll show you." Ellie repeated what Agnes had told her as they walked to the henhouse together. "Do tell Agnes it's not her fault, will you?"

"Her fault?" Martin removed his hat and ran his hand through his sandy hair. "Silly woman, of course it's not her fault. Luke's never done anything like this before." He scowled. "It would be pointless to confront him about it. There's no proof he did the damage."

"No-one else would do it."

"Oh, I know. I wasn't doubting Agnes. But for the price of three hens, it's not worth me accusing him of it."

"Only one, really. I expect there'll be chicken pie for dinner."

He laughed, and stood back, head tilted a little as he assessed the repair needed. "I'm not sure we've got a plank the right size, but I'll find something to patch it up until I go into Thirsk." He straightened. "How was Lancashire?"

"Wet."

He grinned. "As ever. Did you say you'd just returned?"

"There was an accident with the coach." It was only as she told him the bare bones of the story that she recalled her worry that he might know from her manner that something had changed her. That moment had passed, now, thanks to some dead hens. He went off to find some wood while Ellie went on to the vegetable patch to see how many weeds had thrived while Jake had been busy helping with the lambing.

There was indeed chicken pie for dinner, along with heaped dishes of boiled potatoes and roasted carrots and parsnips, and they all ate, as usual, around the large kitchen table. Although the clear skies of the day had turned to a cold dusk, heat from the range made the kitchen almost too warm.

Also as usual, Bates and the other outdoor men said almost nothing during the meal. They'd have a mug or two of ale in the barns later, if they weren't busy with the animals, and Bates would make a last check on the ewes still in the fields—the ones not yet close to their time. Kate ate in silence, happy with whatever was put in front of her.

Martin asked Fanny about the milking and butter making while he'd been away, and when the next batch of cheese would be ready for market. Ellie would go over it all again tomorrow, entering the amounts in the ledgers, but mealtimes were a good opportunity to discuss the farm with all involved. Then he moved onto how many lambs were yet to be born.

Even with Agnes still worried, and Fanny frowning over something, there was a more convivial atmosphere than the last morning's breakfast at the vicarage in Quernby. Although the farmhouse was smaller than the vicarage, this was her home, and had been for nearly five years. All here had warm beds and plenty of food, and there was enough put by to last even a couple of bad years without having to worry too much. She should count her blessings rather than wish for someone to share her bed who *wanted* her.

She poked at the rather solid pudding beneath its coating of lumpy sauce. Agnes' cooking wasn't one of those blessings, to be sure, although she did manage a reasonable pastry. Ellie hadn't really noticed before—the meals here were more substantial and varied than the bland diet Aunt Harriet had insisted on when Ellie lived with her father. But the cook at the vicarage had produced a much more appetising and varied selection of dishes in the few days Ellie had been there.

Perhaps she would buy a book of recipes next time she was in Thirsk, and they could try out some new dishes together. This was her life, and it was a good life even without passion and children. She should be content with it.

Fanny asked her to step into the dairy while Agnes and Kate were clearing the dishes.

"Is something wrong?"

"I dunno, missus. It was something that Palmer said while he was here."

"He didn't bother you, did he?"

Fanny shook her head, a few dark curls falling out of her cap. "Not in that way. I'd have put my knee where it hurts if he'd tried."

Ellie didn't doubt it—Fanny was as tall as she was, and had developed a fair set of muscles from her years of regularly turning a butter churn.

"I told him to be about his business when he came into the dairy, and he said it *was* his business, or it would be when justice was done. What did he mean, missus? I wouldn't want to work for the likes of him."

"No, indeed."

"He was muttering about Jake being useless, too. Just because he has a limp!"

"I'll ask Mr Wilson about it, don't worry. And thank you for telling me."

Fanny nodded and went to help Kate dry the dishes, saying she would have a pitchfork handy next time. Ellie believed her. Fanny had been running the dairy since before Ellie came. She'd been with child and without a husband when Martin took her on. The babe had died, and Fanny never again took any nonsense from a man. Or woman, come to that.

Martin was in the parlour with his decanter, and she took her place in the chair on the opposite side of the fire. Martin poured her the usual glass of port.

"How are the horses?" she asked. Alone with Martin for the first time since she returned, she had to make an effort to behave normally, to say the kind of things she usually would.

"All doing well—except the early foal I told you about. There are a few ready for the army—I'll get them sent off next month. You should go over each week, Ellie. There are two mares a bit small for army work; you could get them used to a side saddle. Be a nice day out for you up on the moors, if you fancy it." He grinned. "The stable lads will ride side saddle in the paddock for training, but won't be persuaded to go beyond the farm where someone might see!"

"I'd like that, thank you." She hadn't been to the horse farm often, as there had always been plenty here to keep her busy, first learning about farming life and increasing the profits from the dairy, then overseeing changes to the kitchen that made life more comfortable. Bank Side was tucked closer to the edge of the wooded slope leading up to the moors. "Will the mares bring as much as the cavalry horses?"

"Possibly more—they're good-looking animals, and if their dispositions are sweet, too, they'd do nicely for a fine lady."

"What about Fleet?" Martin's interest wasn't just in breeding cavalry horses. He'd picked the bay stallion as an animal worth trying out on the racecourse—although so far none of his previous horses had fulfilled his dream of winning and then earning a fortune in stud fees. Martin talked about the young stallion's progress, and his ideas about when to take him to his first local race meeting. Watching his enthusiasm as he talked, Ellie felt ashamed for her dissatisfaction. She should be able to find more interest in running the farm and working with the horses. She had a good life here, even if it wasn't quite everything she wanted.

When Martin had finished singing the stallion's praises, Ellie told him what Fanny had said. He scowled as she talked. "Martin, what did he mean, 'when justice was done'? He's said spiteful things often enough, but he's never said that."

"He didn't mean anything," Martin said, tight-lipped.

"I know he's your cousin, but it does seem odd that he keeps calling when he gets no welcome." Ellie waited, but Martin only shook his head. "Martin, it *is* my business if he's going to force his way in when we're not here, and damage things."

He sighed. "I suppose so." He poured himself another glass of port. "You know I was born at Bank Side, but did most of my growing here after my parents died?"

"With your mother's father, yes."

"Grandpa Palmer had only two children—my mother and Luke's father. He'd already given my mother Bank Side as a dowry of sorts, and she left it to me. Luke's father died before Grandpa, so when Grandpa died what he had was shared between Luke and me."

"And you got this farm as well as Bank Side." It seemed a little unfair towards Luke.

"He discussed it with us beforehand. He'd made some canny investments in mines and so on, and it was clear Luke didn't have the aptitude for farming."

"Farming can be learned, can it not?"

Martin grimaced. "Well, Luke never did like hard work, and Grandpa knew it. He'd worked hard himself on this land. At the time this was all discussed the mine shares were roughly the same value as the farm."

"That seems fair, then."

"Indeed it was. Luke even gloated that he'd got more than me out of it—after all, I'd have to work to get an income. But he always lived more expensively than he could afford, and he's had to sell most of his shares by now. He even persuaded me to buy some to help him out. I gave him some money, too, but he only asked for more."

"And he's run out of money and shares?" Ellie guessed.

"Not quite. But the shares increased considerably in value a few years after I bought them from him—they found a new coal seam. That was not long after we married. Luke wanted to buy them back at the price I'd paid."

"But you wouldn't sell." Why should he?

"No. I could have sold him some of them, I suppose, but he would only have come back for more. He'd bleed us dry if I let him. But since then he's taken every chance he could to do me a bad turn. Luckily the folks around here know me, and they know him. They won't believe any calumny coming from him."

Calumny? "What is he saying?" Ellie had never heard anything to Martin's detriment.

Martin shrugged. "Oh, who knows with him? He'll make something up. Do you want to come to Bank Side with me tomorrow to try out the grey mare?"

"Yes, I'd like that." Helping to train some of the horses might be a distraction from her new discontent.

CHAPTER 8

a thin mist clung to the ground the next morning, and the sky was only a milky blue, but it felt like the kind of morning that would turn into a sunny day. When Ellie emerged from the house Martin was already sitting in the gig with Lass harnessed to it. The mare was an old lady now, but still up to pulling the gig or wagon as long as she wasn't asked to go fast.

"What's in there?" Ellie asked, spotting a saddle bag at his feet as she settled onto the seat beside him. The air was fresh, smelling of damp earth, but the sky already had more blue in it than earlier.

Martin flicked the reins and Lass lumbered into movement. "I thought we might eat up on the moors if the weather holds. But even if not, it's safer than eating what Bill cooks up."

Ellie smiled. Bill was one of the stable hands at Bank Side; he came to collect bread, meat, and vegetables from Agnes two or three times a week. "Were you living on mutton stew for a week while I was away?"

"I did come home to be fed by Agnes on some days," he admitted.

Bank Side was only a couple of miles from Knowle Farm by the path across the fields, but more than twice the distance by road. The last part of their journey was uphill, as the land rose towards the tree-covered slopes that bordered the high moorland beyond.

The buildings at Bank Side were smaller than at Knowle Farm, but it had a sizeable barn for hay and turnips, and stabling enough for the stallions and the mares about to foal. Bill came out of the house to take Lass.

"Let her into the paddock," Martin said. "I'm taking the bay with the blaze onto the moors, and Mrs Wilson's going to ride the grey lady's mount. Can you get them saddled up?"

Bill nodded and led the horse away, and Ellie followed Martin into the house. It always felt a very male establishment—clean and tidy, but with little to brighten the rather dim kitchen and a background smell of tobacco smoke, not strong enough to be unpleasant. There were only enough cooking pots to boil vegetables and stew meat, and few serving bowls or platters. They probably dished up their dinner straight from the pot. Ellie wondered if she should have Agnes make some cakes and pies to be sent up each week. Just because they didn't seem to have the inclination—or the skills and equipment—to cook more elaborate dishes didn't mean they wouldn't enjoy them. That was probably something she should have thought about long ago.

"Mrs Wilson." Sam Barnaby had come into the kitchen, his weather-beaten face smiling a welcome. His short, slight form had made him suited to be a jockey; that, and his love and knowledge of horses, had led him to his current position running the horse farm for Martin. "Mick's been training the grey, says he's done all he can with her in the paddocks."

"What's her name?" Ellie asked.

"White Socks, in the record books," Martin said. "She has white on her front legs."

"That's a very... practical name."

"It doesn't do to get attached to them, Ellie," Martin said. "And the new owners will give them their own names."

Sam shrugged. "We do get to like some of them." He looked out of the window, to where Mick was leading a chestnut horse across the yard. "Mick calls that one 'Mischief'. Likes to squash you against the side of his stall if you let him. Nothing that would bother an army groom."

Ellie hid a smile. Mick probably called the animal far worse things than Mischief when it misbehaved.

"The grey mare has better manners," Martin said, walking out into the yard again. "Ellie, come and meet your mount."

Bill had led out a dainty mare and handed Ellie half a carrot.

"I'll call her Mist," Ellie declared, stroking the mare's nose then offering the carrot. She glanced at Martin. "Yes, I know she's not mine, but you did say I could use her as a hack for a while."

Martin rolled his eyes, but nodded. "We might need another hand at the farm, if she's to be stabled there. Jake has enough to do with the vegetable garden and helping with the cows." Ellie led Mist to the mounting block and settled into the saddle, leaning forward to pat the mare's neck and talk softly to her, wondering if the skirts brushing the animal's flanks felt strange to her.

Martin mounted his own horse and led the way further along the lane, to where it turned into a narrower track winding upwards. It was almost cold beneath the trees, the faint warmth of the spring sunshine not penetrating the bare branches. Then they were out on the open moor, drab at this time of year. But this place had beauties beyond the purple heather in late summer—the open skies, the hazy bulk of the Pennines beyond the vale to the west, and peace.

It had been different that last day with Ben—the sun warmer, the heather in bloom, curlews and skylarks calling. After the news of his death she hadn't wanted to come up here. She'd told herself she didn't have the time—it was a longer walk from Knowle Farm to the moors than the ride up from Bank Side. Now, she wondered if avoiding the moors had been part of mourning Ben's loss. Today she felt the same lift of her spirits she remembered from that day, and the memory was less coloured by grief.

Ben had told her to only remember the happy days with him, and thanks to that talk with Tom, she might be able to do as he'd wished.

Martin had drawn ahead while she'd been lost in thought. She loved this place, and the uncomfortable mixture of guilt and discontent that had been with her since she returned gave way to anxiety. If Martin found out and sent her away, she would lose all this.

Ellie shook her head and urged the mare onwards; there was no reason Martin would find out. And Tom was part of her past, not her future—she must remember that. "Come on Mist. We'll catch up with Martin and try you at a canter."

Ellie rode Mist up onto the moors near Knowle Farm several times in the following weeks, but didn't linger—the winds were from the north, and cold enough to bring tears to her eyes. But the Monday that Jake was due to drive into Thirsk with the ripened cheeses dawned calm and sunny at last. Agnes would go with him to do the marketing, and Martin suggested it was time Mist was introduced to the noise and bustle of a town.

"Are you sure?" Ellie had ridden many different horses over the years, but all had been more mature. "On market day?"

"Leave Jake to deal with the cheese and ride her through quieter streets to start with." He squeezed her shoulder where she sat at the breakfast table. "You're a good rider, Ellie, and you get on with Mist. If you do have any problems with her, you can bring her back tied to the wagon, and Agnes can ride in the back with the flour."

"All right, then." She would look for a book of recipes at the same time, and buy some herbs and spices and more sugar. And it would be time away from Martin, whose presence reminded her too often of what she was missing.

All went well; Mist gave her no problems as they approached the town and crossed the bridge over the beck, walking quietly behind a cart with small cages of clucking hens. The road here was flanked by houses, and led to one corner of the Market Place. When they came out into the open square Ellie turned left, intending to do as Martin had recommended and allow Mist to get used to the people and buildings around her before braving the crowds that would soon be gathering around the stalls in the square.

It had been good advice, Ellie thought half an hour later. Mist had done no more than flick her ears at shouts or passing carts. But the streets ahead were crowded, and Mist tossed her head as a dog approached with a leg of mutton in its mouth, chased by three more dogs and an irate stall keeper.

"I'll dismount and lead you now, Mist," Ellie said, patting the mare's neck before taking her foot from the stirrup. She was about to slide off when the stall keeper ran into a man coming out of a nearby alehouse with two full tankards in his hands. They sprawled in the road at Mist's feet, splashing ale over her and a nearby woman, who began to screech her protest.

Mist skittered sideways a few steps and Ellie fell, losing her balance when she landed. As she sprawled onto the cobbles, Mist tossed her head again, pulling the reins from her hand. Heart racing, Ellie scrambled to her feet, fearing what would happen if the mare tried to escape along this crowded street. But as she stood a man grabbed Mist's reins near the bit with one gloved hand. Mist pulled against his hold, but he put his other hand up and stroked her neck, talking to her, and she gradually calmed.

Ellie brushed dirt from her skirts. All she could see of the man was the back of a shapeless hat, and a jacket and trousers that had seen better days.

"Thank you for stopping her." She should give him something for his help.

The man half-turned his head towards her, showing little more than a tanned cheek. "You all right, missus?"

Ellie rubbed her elbow; her knee hurt, too, but not badly enough to prevent her walking or riding. "Well enough."

The man nodded, spoke to Mist again in a low voice, then held the reins out for Ellie to take. She sucked in a breath as she saw him clearly for the first time. The left side of his face was a mass of scar tissue, red, with twisted, rope-like scars running down his cheeks. Burns?

His mouth turned down, then he touched his hat and spun away, striding off.

"Wait! Please!" Ellie called, trying to make herself heard above the surrounding hubbub. She had offended him, and hadn't meant to. He didn't return, but he did stop.

One hand on Mist's reins, the other holding her skirt above the muddy cobbles, she caught up with him. "I wanted to thank you properly. Mist is young, and not used to so many things going on around her."

He turned to face her, chin lifted in what looked like defiance. Ellie met his eyes, keeping her gaze from wandering to his scars. After a few seconds his chin came down, and he nodded at her before returning his attention to Mist. "She'll get used to it. Best lead her about the town a bit, so she learns that noises don't mean no harm."

He sounded as if he knew from experience. "Do you work with horses?"

"When I can get the work." His shoulders slumped.

"Are you employed at the moment?"

"I were working at the Three Tuns, but they sent me off yesterday. A lady took exception to my face while I were helping to change the horses on a private carriage."

"How unfair!"

"It happens, missus." He stroked the mare's nose. "She'll be all right now."

Ellie remembered the book she was going to look for. The wagon wasn't waiting at the place she was to meet Jake and Agnes, so she still had time. "I wonder—I have some business in town; would you walk Mist around for me? I will pay you, naturally."

The man gaped for a moment. "You trust me, missus?"

"Not entirely, Mr…?"

"Cole. Dan Cole." He stood up straighter. "Late of the 48th Foot. Until this." He gestured at his face and held up his hands. They were still gloved, but while the fingers on his right hand were straight, those of his left remained bent. More than his face had been injured.

"Mrs Wilson. To be frank, Mr Cole, if you do make off with Mist, you are easy to describe." Ellie wondered if she'd offended him again, but the good side of his mouth lifted. "I should not be above half an hour, and if you stay close to the Market Place, I will send someone to find you when I am ready."

"Yes, missus." He touched a finger to his hat, and Ellie watched as he led Mist off around the outside of the square. She hoped she hadn't just made an expensive mistake.

It took Ellie more than half an hour, for once she'd found a suitable book of recipes, she spent rather too long looking through it, and then searching for ingredients that Agnes didn't have in the house, such as cinnamon, cloves, and lemons.

Dan Cole must have been keeping an eye on her, for he was waiting with Mist when she emerged from the grocer's. His walk with the mare had done her good, for although the crash of a falling crate made her ears twitch, she merely tossed her head once and calmed down without Cole's intervention. A man like him would be useful at Bank Side. Ellie didn't know if Martin needed more men there, but he had mentioned needing someone at Knowle Farm. She could, at least, offer Cole a few days' work at Knowle so Martin could meet him. She'd been considering extending the vegetable patch.

She walked beside him as they made their way to the east side of the square, two boys from the shop following with her purchases. "If you don't mind labouring work, Mr Cole, I can offer you employment for a week."

He halted momentarily, surprise on his face, then nodded. "Thank you, missus. I'm glad of anything."

"You can return with us in the wagon, if you wish, or find your own way." She pointed to where Agnes and Jake were now waiting.

"I'll come with you, if I can have a few minutes to get my bag?"

Ellie nodded, and took Mist's reins while Cole hurried off towards the Three Tuns. He returned not long after Ellie had supervised the stowing of her groceries amongst Agnes' purchases and given the two lads a penny each for their trouble. As she was explaining to Agnes and Jake, Cole arrived. He helped her to mount, then climbed into the back of the wagon.

As Ellie followed the wagon out of town, Agnes turned to speak to Cole, and he appeared to be answering. She would ask Agnes later what Cole was saying, but it was a good sign that they were talking to each other. She touched her heel to Mist's flank and trotted past the wagon. It would be well to warn Kate, in particular, not to be frightened at Cole's appearance. And to tell Martin he had another employee, even if only a temporary one.

"You didn't mind me offering him work?" Ellie asked, when she and Martin were sitting in the parlour after dinner that evening. Martin had been out when the wagon reached the farm, and by the time he returned Cole had already begun taking up the rough grass in the unused patch of land next to the chicken run. Martin had gone out to talk to him and come back looking satisfied.

"No, but don't do it too often, Ellie. There's a limit to how many misfits we can use."

"Misfits?" That wasn't very kind.

"Martin's Misfits. It's what Henry said last time he came." Martin laughed. "I think Fanny had just banned him from her dairy."

Ellie liked Mary's husband, and he'd probably said it in jest. Some of them were misfits, in the eyes of many. But it wasn't Agnes' fault her daughter was simple or that her husband had died, or Jake's that an injury meant he could not walk far or fast. Fanny perhaps could have thought harder before believing the promises of the wastrel who had fathered her child, but she was far from the only woman who'd been persuaded by a plausible rogue.

"What were you talking to Dan about?"

"His background." Martin refilled his glass. "Grew up in a coaching inn, he said. Joined the army because he encountered a recruiting party when he was drunk."

Ellie grimaced—that didn't sound too promising.

Martin chuckled. "He says he learned his lesson from that. It'll be clear soon enough if he was telling the truth. I asked why he didn't try for a transfer to a cavalry regiment, but he said he liked horses too much."

"Odd."

"Not really. Said it was bad enough seeing dead and injured horses on a battlefield, without them being his mount, or one he'd looked after."

"He was very good with Mist this morning." Ellie described what had happened.

"I'm sorry, Ellie, I didn't think Mist would give trouble. I won't ask you to—"

"I want to. It makes me feel properly involved with the business." The more things she had to concentrate on, the less time she would have to dwell on what was missing from her life. "I'll take better care if I do it again." She held Martin's gaze until he nodded.

"Perhaps not market day, next time. There's still the other mare to do the same with." He swirled the port in his glass. "I'll try Cole out at Bank Side once he's dug the vegetable patch. That is, if Fanny doesn't see him off first."

Ellie smiled, and told him about the recipe book, pleased at his enthusiasm for a bit of change in Agnes' cooking.

CHAPTER 9

*L*ying alone in her bed that night, the misfits phrase came back into Ellie's head. Was *she* one of Martin's Misfits too, courtesy of Mary and her husband? Not that a vicar's daughter was a misfit in the same way as a wounded veteran or an unmarried mother, but she had felt trapped with Father in Quernby. Perhaps Mary had set out to rescue her?

When Ben left for the army, their increasing closeness over the preceding two years had made his absence hard for her. She'd tried not to let her loneliness show in her letters to her sister, but Mary had always been perceptive. That must have been why, a year after Ben's departure, Mary had written asking—pleading, almost—for Ellie to come and help look after her two children now that she was growing too big with her third to move around easily. The letter had been couched in such terms that Father and Aunt Harriet could not deny Ellie's wish to go.

Ellie smiled in the darkness, remembering her surprise when she arrived on a fine summer's afternoon to find the nursemaid coping easily with little John and Margaret, and Mary nearly six months from her expected confinement. The only indication of her pregnancy was a tendency to feel nauseous.

"You lied to Father!" Ellie accused, once she'd washed away the dust of travel and they were drinking tea in the small parlour behind Henry's consulting room.

"I exaggerated a little," Mary protested, her blonde curls bouncing as she laughed. "Well, more than a little—but I have given you an excuse for a holiday." She put her cup down and leaned towards Ellie. "I know you miss Ben now he's in the army. And Aunt Harriet…" She grimaced.

"I didn't say anything about Aunt Harriet in my letters," Ellie pointed out.

"That's how I know you're not getting on with her. And I know what she's like. Sometimes, Ellie, you're too nice for your own good. You know I won't think any the worse of you if you say what you think. You cannot deny you'll enjoy being away from her demands, and Father's, can you?"

"No." Something inside her lightened at the idea of a few weeks of freedom. "But what am I to do if you don't need me to help with the children?"

"Whatever you like! We have already bought you a subscription to Hargrove's Circulating Library, so you may spend a month reading novels if you wish, and Father will never know!"

Ellie tried to keep a straight face. "Mary! Such deceit!" She smiled. "I may read one or two." Or a dozen.

"Henry recommends gentle exercise for me, so we will walk on the Stray together, and attend the theatre—"

"How sinful!"

"Indeed! There are assemblies, too, and we can drive to Knaresborough and see the petrifying well. You can do whatever you wish! It will be lovely to have you stay for a time. I have friends in Harrogate, but it's not the same as having you here, Ellie."

She tried to remember her first impression of Martin, Henry's childhood friend. He was of an age with Henry, so nearly eight years older than her, and a large man—tall and broad, not fat—with sandy hair and a friendly smile. He'd seemed shy at first, but they talked easily enough once they had got to know each other a little. He was kind and considerate of others' feelings, and Mary's children loved him, calling him Uncle Martin. Although he lived some thirty miles away, he came to Harrogate several times while Ellie was there, staying a few days each time. He'd eaten with the Cowpers rather than at his hotel, gone out for walks with Mary and Ellie, and driven them to local beauty spots when Henry was too busy with his patients to accompany them.

Had Mary and Henry thrown the two of them together on purpose? Given that their initial friendship had developed little further, she couldn't believe that Martin had been so attracted to her that he'd left his farms several times in a single month to court her. He *had* said he needed a woman about the house, and that had been true. The farm had been clean enough, but the rooms were gloomy, the furniture dark and heavy—it was bright and cheery now. And she'd helped Fanny to increase their income from the hens and the dairy.

When Martin had proposed at the end of the month, he'd said only that affection could develop but that he was confident they would deal well together. They had, except that she had hoped for more than friendship. And children—Martin would have made a good father, had she been able to conceive.

She turned over impatiently. If Mary and Henry had pushed them together, she should be pleased. There was no knowing what would have happened had she stayed in Quernby. By now, she could be turning into an embittered spinster like Aunt Harriet, or have become so desperate to escape that she accepted someone completely unsuitable. Running the farm was far different from attempting to cater to Aunt Harriet's decrees and Father's demands.

She should be content, but she was not—not without children, and passion in her marriage. She could be, perhaps, with just one of those things, but there seemed little prospect of either.

A couple of days later, Ellie brought out the book of recipes she'd bought in Thirsk. Agnes' lips pressed together as she eyed it and folded her arms. "If my cooking isn't good enough, Mrs Wilson, you only had to say so."

Ellie had expected this reaction, and knew that Agnes' belligerence was due to worry about her position.

"Not at all, Agnes. You manage the kitchen well—we wouldn't want to lose you. But I thought we might try some new dishes." She turned the pages to instructions for cinnamon pudding. "I bought some spices in Thirsk to make this. We will make it together."

Agnes unfolded her arms and squinted at the page. She could write lists of supplies, and read them, but Ellie wondered if perhaps she wasn't confident enough to read books.

"We'll teach Kate as well," Ellie added. "I'd have to read the recipe to her, of course, but she's good at the mixing."

Agnes' expression softened. Ellie reached out and put a hand on her arm. "Agnes, learning new skills will make you an even more valuable part of the farm."

The cook finally nodded. "We'd best make a start, if it's to have time to boil. I'll get Kate." She headed for the door into the yard.

Ellie tied an apron over her gown, then went to the door when Agnes did not return. She heard someone call Kate's name. Dan Cole?

"Is something wrong?" she asked, when Agnes came back.

"Dan saw her go down to the bottom field. Probably talking to the lambs. He's gone to get her."

"Let's get started." Ellie read out the list of ingredients, and Agnes fetched the items from the pantry. Kate returned as they had everything laid out ready and went to the scullery to wash her hands without being told.

"What's that in your hair?" Agnes' voice was sharp, and Ellie looked up from the instructions. Kate's hair was in its usual messy knot, but adorned with a length of bright red ribbon.

"A nice man gave it to me." She eyed the jars of flour and raisins. "What are we going to make?"

Nice man? Ellie and Agnes looked at each other without speaking. Kate would cry if she thought she'd done something wrong, so the questioning would have to be subtle.

"We're making a new kind of pudding, and you are going to help."
Kate nodded eagerly.

"And when you've mixed it, you can tell us about the nice man."

It was a simple enough story, when it came. She'd been watching the lambs playing when a man had walked up the lane beyond the hedge. He'd stopped at the gate and admired the lambs, and said that a pretty lass like Kate should have a pretty ribbon for her hair. Then he'd asked about the new man at the farm, and gone away again when all Kate could tell him was that he was digging the garden.

"Did you recognise him, Kate?" Agnes spoke softly, despite her anxious expression.

"Mmm." Kate was more interested in tasting the pudding mixture than answering the question, but she responded when Agnes repeated the question. "He came here before."

"What did he look like?" Agnes asked.

"A man." Kate's face creased up, and Ellie sighed. They'd get little more out of her.

"Here, Kate, help me spoon it into the cloth."

When the pudding was tied up and boiling on the range, Agnes sent Kate to the scullery to wash the mixing bowls.

"Mr Wilson's cousin," she said to Ellie, as soon as Kate had gone.

"It must have been, yes." Luke Palmer wasn't the only person to come to the farm, but everyone else came on business, or to see Martin. If they'd stopped to talk to Kate, they would have come on up to the farm afterwards, but they'd had no visitors today. And who else would be asking about new employees?

"What could he want?"

"Nothing good." And the thought that he knew they'd taken on a new hand sent a shiver down her spine. Was he spying on them? "I will mention it to Mr Wilson."

"She mustn't go down there again."

"We can't confine her to the yard; that wouldn't be fair," Ellie said. "I'll tell Fanny and Jake to keep a watch."

. . .

Martin didn't have anything further to suggest when Ellie discussed the matter with him that evening, although he did agree that it most likely had been his cousin. The incident slipped to the back of Ellie's mind when nothing happened over the next week. Dan Cole made a large vegetable patch and dug in manure, leaving it ready for sowing carrots, turnips, spring onions, and peas.

Dan's task at Knowle Farm complete, Martin took him to meet the horses. Ellie went with them, taking a tin of parkin and several meat pies that only needed reheating in the basic oven that was all the kitchen at Bank Side possessed.

"Dan's going to assist you all for a while," Martin announced, when the four men had assembled in the kitchen. They nodded a greeting, most with a sympathetic grimace at their first glimpse of Dan's scars, but they were more interested in the food Ellie had brought. Bill licked his lips, then turned to Dan with a sly grin.

"Newest one allus does the cooking," he announced.

Dan shrugged and smiled. "If you want. I learned to make a decent rat stew in Spain."

Ellie couldn't tell whether or not he was joking and, from their expressions, neither could the others.

"Serves you right, Bill," Martin said with a laugh. "Come on, Dan, I'll introduce you to the stallions."

Ellie went with them to make friends with the other mare that was to become a lady's mount. This was a pretty bay with black mane and tail and a white splash on her forehead. The men at Bank Side had already named her Star, and Ellie was content with that—it suited her.

"Can we stable her at the farm as well as Mist?" Ellie asked, when Martin returned.

"For a while." Martin cupped his hands to help her into the saddle. "I was thinking of taking one or both of those mares to York next month," he said, as their mounts walked up the lane towards the moor. "I might find buyers at the races. Want to come with me? We'd spend a few nights there."

It would be interesting, and a change of scene.

"You can buy a new gown or two," he added. "That habit is rather the worse for wear."

Ellie laughed. "I had some new novels in mind." But he was right about the habit—she'd had the drab grey one since before her marriage. Perhaps something in a deep red?

That reminded her of Kate's ribbon and its likely giver. "Agnes will worry in case your cousin calls when we are both away."

"I've been thinking about that. Now we've an extra body here, we can spare one of them to stay at Knowle if neither of us will be at home. One who can be trusted to use my shotgun effectively."

"Is that really necessary?"

"Probably not, but just in case. Dan will do. We don't need to decide for a few weeks—we'll see how well he settles in, and what Sam thinks of him."

"In that case, yes, please. I'd love to go to York." Then she remembered Mary—her baby was due in the middle of June. "I was hoping to visit my sister before she is confined. She will be getting too big to go about much."

"Go after the races. Agnes and Fanny can manage well enough for a week or so."

"I will, thank you."

They rode on in companionable silence.

Ellie's contentment lasted well into May—until the day one of the hens that had stopped laying was destined for the pot. As she passed through the kitchen on her way to the stables, Agnes brought the plucked and gutted bird out of the pantry.

She'd never liked the smell of raw meat, but never before had it made her dash for the scullery, hand pressed to her mouth. As she leaned against the sink, sucking in lungfuls of air that smelled of nothing more offensive than soap, the nausea gradually eased to a faint, lingering discomfort. What had come over her?

"You all right, missus?" Agnes' anxious face peered around the door—without the dead bird, to Ellie's relief.

"I felt a little strange, but it's passed now." She straightened her shoulders. "I was just on my way to see how Star is getting on after yesterday's ride." She and Martin had ridden for miles across the moors, a longer ride than Star had managed so far, and Ellie had been as tired as the horse when they returned.

Agnes nodded and returned to the kitchen, but her expression said she wasn't convinced. Ellie took a deep breath, holding it until she was safely in the yard. The smell in the stable was far stronger than that faint aroma of raw hen had been, but she felt only the comfort of familiarity. She stroked Star's nose, then she went out into the garden and stood gazing over the vegetable patch.

Rain overnight had given way to a glorious day, the sun warm on her face and shoulders, turning the hawthorn blossom in the distant hedges into a white glow. The cows grazed contentedly in the home meadow, now sprinkled with cowslips and buttercups. Green shoots were showing all over the vegetable beds, and the geraniums by the front door made splashes of colour against the sandstone. She was lucky to have all this.

Count your blessings and stop wishing for things you cannot have.

She still felt bone-tired, though. More than could be explained by the extra riding she'd been doing recently—she hoped she wasn't sickening for something.

That reminded her that she had last month's accounts to check, and reluctantly she returned indoors. Dismayed to find that Agnes had left the now-dismembered hen on the chopping board, she hurried through the kitchen and up to her bedroom. She rummaged through the drawers in the chest—somewhere, she had a vinaigrette that she'd never needed. When she found it and lifted the lid the smell was faint after long storage, but there was enough sharpness to dispel the last, lingering aroma of meat.

Retreating to the parlour and her account books, she remained there until the evening meal, by which time the kitchen was filled with the savoury smell of gravy and fried onions. Afterwards, when the men had gone outside and Martin to the parlour, Agnes drew Ellie to one side as Kate and Fanny carried the dishes to the scullery.

"You've been more tired than usual, lately, missus."

"I suppose so."

"I haven't washed rags for you in a while. When were your last courses?"

CHAPTER 10

*E*llie's mind stopped working for a moment. Last courses?

"I... I can't remember, Agnes."

"Think on, missus. Being tired, feeling ill at smells... could be all sorts of things. But if you're late as well..." She smiled. "I hope I'm right—it'll be good to have a little 'un around the place."

Tom?

No, it couldn't be. Not after one night, when she'd failed to have a child for years. *Wanted* a child for years.

"Don't take on now, missus." Agnes patted her arm. "You can ask your sister when you visit her in a couple of weeks. She's had more children than me. See what she says."

"Agnes... Please don't say anything to anyone else." What excuse to give? "It... it would be such a disappointment if I'm... I'm not with child."

"'Course I won't. Wait 'till you're sure, then master should be the one to get the good news first." She gave a brisk nod, and went to supervise the washing of dishes.

Good news? It would be if the child was Martin's, for he had wanted children, too. But he would know the child wasn't his. Martin, who was waiting for her to join him in the parlour as she always did.

As she walked into the hallway, she swallowed against a sick feeling that had nothing to do with smells. She could not sit and make polite conversation in the parlour, not with this possibility on her mind.

Opening the parlour door, she spoke without entering. "Martin, I'm going to retire. I'm feeling a little tired."

The concern on his face as he stood and approached almost undid her. "You don't look well, Ellie. Pale."

"I will be all right, Martin, really. I just need to rest."

He looked into her eyes, and it was all she could do not to drop them. He would have to know, but not yet. Agnes might be wrong, but Ellie had a horrible feeling that she wasn't.

"Sleep well, then," he said.

She didn't. The guilt that she'd tried to suppress over breaking her marriage vows resumed its full force. This time, she could not pretend that it might not matter because she would not do it again, and there was the added apprehension of what might happen to her and the babe.

If she was with child. A sensible woman would wait until she knew for certain, but she was feeling far from sensible. And, rack her brain as she might, she could not recall having her flow since before Aunt Harriet's funeral, and that had been nearly two months ago now. Never had she been so late that she'd missed two.

What would Martin do? He would be within his rights to ask for a separation, leaving her with no means of supporting herself. Although that would reflect on him, too, it would be far worse for her. She'd worried about this from time to time, but then it was only because Martin might find out. Now that he *would* know what she'd done, the possibilities were truly frightening.

Could Mary help her? But Martin was Henry's friend, and might not allow Mary to take Ellie in. Father? With his rigid ideas about right and wrong, he was perfectly capable of denying her.

Tom had given her a way of contacting him if she needed anything. She hadn't thought much of it at the time; what could a barren woman need after such an encounter? She had his mother's address in Kendal. But what use was that? He might be able to send her some money—eventually—if Martin disowned her. How long did it take a letter to reach Spain? Writing to Ben and receiving a reply had often taken months.

No, her only hope was Mary. Or that Martin would forgive her and accept the child as his—but that seemed more than she could hope for.

"Look what you led me to, Ben," she whispered. "*Carpe diem* indeed!"

But through all the worry and guilt, she still could not wholly regret what she had done.

Ellie awoke heavy-eyed the next morning. The sun shone, but a sheet of thin, high cloud was forming in the western sky. This weather might not hold.

That gave her an extra excuse to reinforce the decision she'd made between her few spells of fitful sleep. She would not be able to pretend to Martin that nothing was wrong today, not without compounding her lies.

"You don't look any better, Ellie," Martin said when they met on the stairs. "Go back to bed, and I'll send for the doctor."

"No, Martin." She put a hand on his arm to stop him. "I am just tired." True. "I will feel better for breakfasting in my room, in the quiet, if you don't mind."

"Of course. I'll get Agnes to bring up a tray."

"I do feel a little unwell. I was thinking I should go to Mary's today instead of after the races, so I can consult Henry. Can you spare Dan to drive me there?"

"I'll send Jake up to Bank Side with a message. Dan isn't doing anything that cannot be put off until he returns."

"Thank you." She turned and went back to her room to pack some clothes. An hour later they were on their way, trundling behind Lass in the gig with Ellie's trunk strapped to the step at the back and a basket of food at their feet. Agnes had assembled bread, cheese, and ham, and bottles of ale so they could eat on the way.

Dan seemed to sense her sombre mood for, after a few words of greeting, he said little, only checking that she was warm enough when the clouds thickened, and if she was agreeable to giving Lass a rest after a couple of hours on the road. Although the turnpike was not too busy, Lass had never been a fast mover and they didn't arrive until early afternoon.

"Ellie!" Mary waddled into the hall as the maid opened the door. "I saw you from the window—I thought you weren't coming for another week or so?"

"Mary. Are you well?" Ellie gave her sister a hug. "I'll tell you why in a moment. Can your man direct Dan to the livery?"

"Of course. Martha, can you see to that, please? Then make sure Cook gives him something to eat and finds him somewhere to sleep." The maid hurried off, and Mary led Ellie into the tiny parlour at the back of the house. Ellie had always liked this room. Although it was small and the window looked out only onto the yard behind the house, Mary had decorated it in a primrose yellow, picked out with white, and filled the walls with watercolour landscapes and flowers. Two comfortably padded chairs were set either side of a small table, and the fireplace was flanked by a bookcase on one side and an escritoire on the other. Mary eased herself into one of the chairs. Ellie removed her bonnet and pelisse and laid them over the chair drawn up to the escritoire before sitting down.

"How are you, Ellie? Are you well?"

Now Ellie was here, she didn't know how to start. Mary gave her a searching look; Ellie tried to keep the trouble from her face, but Mary was hard to fool.

"Well, we are bound to be interrupted as soon as the children realise you're here. Perhaps you will tell me in a little while. How did Aunt Harriet's funeral go? You didn't say much in your letter."

Ellie turned to the new subject with relief. "As any other funeral. I wouldn't have recognised her from Father's eulogy."

Mary rolled her eyes. "A woman of all the virtues, our Aunt Harriet."

"How are *you*, Mary?"

Her sister grimaced. "As well as can be expected when I'm this big. Henry suggested I take on another maid to help look after the children now I'm too ungainly to run around after them." Her expression lightened. "I'm glad you've come, Ellie. You can take them out for walks, if you will, and tell them all about your lambs and calves and horses."

"I'll be happy to. How is Henry's practice?" Any talk to put off the moment she had to confess to what she'd done. *If* Mary thought she was with child.

"Expanding. He's thinking of taking on an assistant. With that, and this little one," Mary patted her swollen belly, "we might need a larger house."

She was about to say more, but childish shrieks heralded the arrival of the three children. John managed a dignified entrance, but the girls burst into the room and ran over to Ellie.

"Auntie Ellie! Have you brought us presents?"

"Sorry, missus." The nursemaid entered behind them. "They saw you arrive and wouldn't settle."

"Hello John, Margaret, Ann." Ellie smiled at them. "I'm afraid not. Not this time."

Margaret stuck her lip out and Mary chuckled. "Aunt Ellie will come and see you later, Margy. *If* you're good."

Margaret smiled as Ellie winked at her.

"Come back to the nursery." The maid ushered them out.

"They're looking well," Ellie said.

"They seem to shooting up. It hardly feels like any time at all since I had John. Hand me that cushion, would you?" She leaned forward, and Ellie pushed the cushion behind her back. "Thank you, that's better. I can't wait to get rid of this one, and I've another month or so to go."

Silence fell while Ellie wondered how to broach her problem. But she needn't have worried.

"Now, Ellie, we've had our interruption, so you may tell me why you've come early. And don't pretend there's nothing wrong," she added, when Ellie didn't speak. "You look tired and worried."

"I am tired," Ellie admitted. "Very tired. And… and I missed my last two courses, and nearly disgraced myself when I smelled raw meat."

A wide smile spread across Mary's face. "That sounds promising, Ellie. Missing two courses… Oh, Ellie! I'm so pleased for you!"

Mary had to be told. Ellie closed her eyes, gathering her courage. "It's not Martin's." There, it was out.

"Not Martin's?" Mary whispered the words, with a glance towards the closed door.

Ellie shook her head, not able to meet her sister's eyes.

There was a long silence. "Whose?" Mary asked at last.

"Someone… someone at the coach accident—I told you about that in my letter."

"About the accident, yes. Ellie—were… were you forced?"

"No. Not at all."

Another long silence while Ellie held her breath, feeling a nausea that was nothing to do with her pregnancy. Then Mary struggled to her feet. "We cannot talk here—"

"You still want to talk to me?"

Mary reached a hand out and grasped Ellie's. "You're my sister—of course I want to talk to you!"

"Oh, Mary!" Her voice wobbled as she spoke, the relief at Mary's response bringing unexpected tears to her eyes. Mary was not like their father, or Aunt Harriet—Ellie should have known that her sister would not disown her.

Mary gripped her hand tighter. "Come to my bedroom—we will not be interrupted or overheard there. No tears, Ellie. Not yet."

Ellie managed to hold the tears back until they were safely in Mary's bedroom. Mary and Henry's room, for they shared a bed.

"Henry won't be back for an hour or so." Mary sat on the bed and patted the cover beside her. Ellie sat, and finally wept when Mary put an arm about her shoulders.

"I'm sorry, I shouldn't—"

"Cry all you like, Ellie. I'd give you a handkerchief, but that would mean getting up."

Ellie gulped, and took a deep breath. "I've got one." She took it from her pocket and blew her nose.

"Now, let us deal with the practicalities first. How are you so certain that the child—if there is one—is not Martin's?"

"We don't share a room like you and Henry do." It still felt rather shameful to admit to having a husband who was not interested in her in that way. "We never have. And he hasn't... I mean, he... not for more than six months."

"Ah." Mary's arm about her shoulders tightened. "He will definitely know, then."

"Yes. And he may... I mean, any man—"

"It takes two to make a marriage a success."

Ellie stared at Mary, surprised by her response.

Mary smiled. "If Martin hasn't been treating you well, he—"

"Martin hasn't been mistreating me, Mary. Just not... not trying any more to have children. I'm content, apart from not having a family. I mean, I *was* content. But Father..." The remembered hurt of his words came back to her. "He told me I was wrong to have married, that I should have stayed and worked in the parish, Mary. He said that a barren wife was no use to a husband."

Mary's mouth drew into a thin line. "Ignore him, Ellie. If you can."

"I try. Aunt Elizabeth gave me the same advice."

"Aunt Elizabeth is right, too."

Ellie gave a little gulp that was almost a chuckle, then sniffed and blew her nose again.

"Come, Ellie. It's done, and I will help you." Mary gave her shoulders a squeeze. "Do you want to tell me how it came about? You don't have to if you don't wish to."

Surprisingly, she found she did want to. Mary would stand by her regardless, but Ellie would feel comforted if her sister understood why she had done it. "It began with me thinking about Ben. You recall that he told us to remember the happy times, and that he'd never regretted joining the army?"

Mary nodded.

"I never really understood what satisfaction he could get in such a life. When the coach crashed…" She looked at Mary.

"I remember what you said in your letter."

"The man who stopped to help was an army captain. I asked him why *he* enjoyed the life. And we talked about other things, too." It wasn't what they'd said that had been important, though. "Mary, I felt as if he'd shared part of himself with me, that we were close. I mean, not close like us sitting—"

"I know what you mean."

Close like Mary and Henry seemed to be. "And he *wanted* me, Mary, in a way Martin never has. And I him—I've never felt like that before." It must be like the feelings that Mary and Henry had for each other, shown by the way they shared glances, little touches when they thought no-one could see.

Mary took Ellie's hand but didn't speak. Ellie saw a crease forming between her brows.

"Mary?"

"There's something I must ask Henry."

"About whether you can help me if Martin—?"

Mary shook her head. "No. Ellie, whatever Martin says, or Henry, I *will* help you."

Of course Henry had to be told. It was not a secret that Mary could keep from her husband. And Martin was Henry's friend. Ellie wasn't sure what Mary could do if Henry would not help, but the fact that Mary wanted to cheered her.

"Ellie, I think it would be better if we asked Martin to come here, where you have me—us—to support you. We need to talk to Henry when he comes home, then we can send a message back to Martin with your man when he returns in the morning."

That was sensible. If Martin did disown her, she would not have the shame of having Agnes, Fanny, and the others overhearing everything. Although they would all find out eventually, once she'd gone.

Ellie and Mary remained in the bedroom and caught up on all the normal news while Mary took the opportunity for a lie down. They talked about how Mary's children were progressing, how Aunt Elizabeth was keeping, and wondered how Father would manage and if he would pay for a proper housekeeper.

"My marriage is certainly better than staying with Father would have been," Ellie said. Or it had been until now. "Martin is a good man, and we deal well together. It was lucky he had the time to visit you so often when I first came here."

"It was—they usually meet in Thirsk, or somewhere else between here and your farm." She frowned. "I wonder if it *was* by chance."

"It doesn't matter now. Truly, Mary, if Martin will forgive me, I am content." It had been Ellie's decision to accept Martin—Mary should not feel guilty or to blame in any way for how the marriage had turned out. And now she would have a child to love and cherish.

"Ellie, let me explain to Henry, will you?"

"If you wish." She had no desire to see the possible disgust in Henry's face when he learned of her lapse. She did need his help, as well as Mary's, and Mary was the best person to ensure that.

There was a knock on the door, and Henry came into the room. "Hello, Ellie, I wasn't expecting you yet! I see we've got one of Martin's Misfits in the kitchen."

"Henry, you should stop calling them that!" Mary swung her feet to the floor. Despite the scolding words, Ellie could hear the affection in her tone.

"Sorry, my love." He looked at Ellie. "Are you well, Ellie? And Martin?"

"I want to talk to you about that," Mary said.

"I'll go and read to the children." Ellie made her escape, and managed to hide her anxiety until it was time for the nursery tea. Mary came to join them, whispering that Henry would help before giving her attention to the children.

At dinner, all Henry said was that Mary had explained, and Dan would set off early in the morning with a note asking Martin to come. He seemed... worried? Annoyed? Ellie wasn't sure, but she did sense that whatever he was feeling wasn't directed at her.

That was more than she had hoped for, but it wasn't Henry she'd betrayed.

CHAPTER 11

*E*llie spent most of the next day fretting about Martin's arrival, and what she could say. Although she didn't worry aloud, her inability to settle finally led Mary to send her out for a walk.

"Take the children to give you something else to think about. Help John look for birds, or the girls for flowers."

It was a good idea, and the nursemaid was grateful for some unexpected quiet time. The afternoon was warm and sunny, and the children enjoyed running around on the open grass parkland of the Stray. John and Margaret had mud on their shoes and stockings, so they returned to the house through the back entrance. Ellie removed her own bonnet and pelisse, and left the nursemaid cleaning up the children.

In the hallway, Mary was standing outside the door of Henry's consulting room. She turned her head as Ellie approached, putting a finger to her lips. "Martin," Mary mouthed, and beckoned Ellie closer as she bent to return her ear to the door.

No. She was not going to add to her sins by being caught listening at doors. When she didn't move, Mary shrugged and stood upright, one hand pressing into her back, and they went into the parlour. Ellie asked her why she'd been eavesdropping.

"Martin arrived a quarter of an hour ago, and Henry insisted on talking to him in private first. I said he should have let *you* explain."

He should have, but the coward in her wasn't sorry that he hadn't.

"Ellie, I thought it was just chance that Martin came here when you first visited. I couldn't hear very well through the door, but it sounded as if Henry arranged it."

Did that matter now? No-one had forced her to marry him. "Martin said he wanted a wife to help him with the farm," Ellie said. "*You* thought I needed a husband to escape from Father—rightly so. We've both got what we wanted. If Henry thought we might suit each other, I don't see anything wrong with that."

"But he sounded displeased when he took Martin into his office. I can't understand why."

"You can ask him," Ellie said, as she heard their voices in the hall. Her heart raced uncomfortably now the time had finally come to confess to Martin.

There was a knock on the door, and Henry put his head in. "Martin's here, Ellie. Will you come and talk to him?" If he had been annoyed before, he didn't seem to be now.

The door opened further. Martin stood behind Henry, his expression… She couldn't make it out. But not disgusted or angry, to her great relief. "Shall we walk outside?" he asked.

"My pelisse is probably still in the back hall." Ellie led the way, and Martin held the pelisse for her. That was a promising start. Once they were on the street, he offered his arm. She didn't know what to say, how to begin. They slowed to avoid a group of women walking the other way—this was no place to talk. "Shall we walk on the grass?"

Martin veered off, and soon they were beyond earshot of other people enjoying the sunshine. "You are with child," he said at last. A statement, not a question.

"Yes." It was easier to admit to it, walking beside him like this rather than facing him.

The muscles in his arm tensed. "Who is the father?"

"No-one you know. No-one I will see again."

"You do not wish to go away with him?"

That was not a response she had expected. Ellie stopped and turned to face him—he looked worried. Anxious, even. "No. I will not see him again." A small part of her still regretted that this was the case.

His expression did not change. "You seem very certain. Does that mean he does not live around here?"

"I told you about the coach accident. He was the man who stopped to help. We talked, and I felt I knew him. It did not... He did not feel like a stranger, not then."

Why wasn't he angry?

"Why, Ellie? It doesn't seem like you."

At least he did not think her some kind of loose woman—and she did owe him some kind of explanation. "He wanted me; he was attracted to me. In... in a way you are not."

He looked away, his jaw clenching.

"And I to him," she added, almost as a whisper. "I'm sorry, Martin." He held out his arm so they could walk on, and she took it, feeling the tense muscles beneath his coat. But he did not speak. Finally, the waiting was too much. "Martin, what will you do?"

He stopped again. "Do? What...?" He closed his eyes and rubbed a hand on his forehead. "Ellie, you do not think I would put you on the streets, do you?"

"I... I have thought so many things since I found I was with child." She should have known the man who had taken in Fanny and Kate would not turn her out. That would have saved her some worry over the last few days. "No, you would not. But you could send me away."

"No."

The tension within her uncoiled a little. But what was he thinking? She could not understand why he was not angry, or even reproachful.

"Martin, I broke my marriage vows. Do you not mind?"

"I do mind, very much. But not in the way you're thinking." He took both her hands in his. "I mind that I could not give you a child, and that you were unhappy enough to... to do what you did." He smiled, but his eyes were sad. "Ellie, when we wed, I hoped for children as you did. And now we will have one. If you will stay with me."

"Of course I will." How could she do anything else? "I'm sorry I—"

"Do not be. You have given us a gift." He squeezed her hands, then released them and took out his watch. "There is more to be said, but not here, I think. It is too late to set off for home now, and the horse needs to rest in any case. Do you wish to stay with your sister as you had planned, or will you return with me in the morning?"

"I will come with you." She needed some time alone for her mind to make sense of what had been said, and she could manage that more easily at home.

They turned back, and Ellie remembered what Mary had said. "Martin, Mary thought that Henry was displeased with you. Was she right?"

"Yes, but I cannot discuss it now, and I ask that you persuade Mary that it is a matter between you and me. If not, this evening will be… difficult."

Something significant then. "Will you tell me when we get home?"

"I will, I promise."

Conversation at dinner that evening was stilted, with everyone determinedly sticking to talk of everyday things. Ellie and Martin rose early the next morning, while Mary was still resting in bed. Henry joined them for breakfast, and then Ellie crept into Mary's room to say her farewells.

"I'm so pleased you didn't need my help in the end," Mary said, sleep still in her voice. "Will you be happy, Ellie?"

"I think so." Content, at least. It might depend on what else Martin had to say, but her current situation was so much better than the misery she had anticipated on the way here that she put that to the back of her mind. "I'll do my best to be. I'll come for a proper visit when… when things have settled down."

"And we'll keep you away from the kitchen!"

The memory of the chicken smell almost made Ellie gag, and Mary laughed. "You'll feel sick and tired, and your feet will probably swell and you will look like a beached whale—but it's worth it in the end."

Ellie grimaced. "I'll take your word for it. Look after yourself, Mary."

"Henry makes sure I do." Mary's eyes were closing again by the time Ellie shut the door.

Martin had driven himself, and guided the gig through Knaresborough and north onto the busy turnpike. He was concentrating on driving, and had a crease between his brows as if he was thinking, so Ellie didn't try to talk. With most of her worries assuaged, she had more inclination to look about her at the slowly changing scenery; the hawthorn in the hedgerows was in full bloom, and the crop fields were green. Halfway back they stopped for refreshments and to give the horse a rest. Martin stopped again a couple of miles beyond Thirsk.

"We're nearly home, Martin. Why are we stopping?"

He had a determined look about him, mixed with apprehension. "I think we should talk before we go back to the farm."

"Here?"

"No, not here." One side of his mouth lifted a little. "I thought we could walk up onto the moors. Talk where we cannot be interrupted or overheard. If you're not too tired."

"No, I'll enjoy the exercise."

He drove on past the turning for the farm and found a place to leave the gig where the horse could crop the grass while it waited. Ellie leaned on Martin's arm as they walked up a path in the woods, through glades with celandines, wood anemones, and bluebells and out onto the moor. But once there, he still seemed reluctant to talk.

"Martin, you said you would explain why Henry was displeased with you. Is that what this is about?" Then, when he still didn't speak, she laid a hand on his arm. "Martin, if we are to go on together, as a family, you must tell me."

"I am afraid it will give you a disgust of me. That you will want to take the babe and go."

Had he committed some crime? "It cannot be any worse than what

I have done, can it? Even though we are not attracted to each other in… in that way, we like each other, do we not?"

"Yes. I *do* like you, Ellie. But my lack of interest in you… in coming to your bed…" He stopped and drew a deep breath. "That is not a fault in you, but in me."

"Or just that the combination of the two of—"

"No, it's not that. I do not feel that way about any woman. I… I feel that way about other men. *Some* other men."

Ellie's mind seemed to freeze. Other *men*?

Martin—the man she had married, had lived with these last five years? Attracted to men, not women?

She had heard of that, of course, in unpleasant terms: sodomy, unnatural crimes. A sin against God and man, and a hanging offence. It wasn't something she had ever given much thought to—why would she?

"I didn't choose to be this way," he added, a note of desperation in his voice. "I would change if I could, but I cannot help it."

Surely no-one would choose to be that way, with all the trouble it could cause? She shivered, a chill not caused by the breeze. "If you cannot help it, there is nothing to be done. We are married, and now we have a child on the way."

His anxious expression faded, and he almost smiled. "You are cold —come, let us walk."

She didn't contradict him, but took his arm and they picked their way slowly across the rough turf. "Why did you marry me? Was it just to have children?"

"I do want children, but that was not why Henry suggested I meet you."

What other reason could there be? Then it struck her—Martin's cousin, Luke Palmer, who would do harm to Martin if he could. And sodomy was punishable by death. "Does your cousin know?"

"He suspects. If he had any evidence, I would have been hanged by now. He… insinuates. When he talks about justice being done, he doesn't only mean his idea that he's entitled to the farm."

"And you—and Henry—thought that if you were married, people would be less likely to believe him?"

"Yes. It hasn't really worked, though. Luke is still sniffing around trying to cause trouble." He laid his free hand over hers where it rested on his arm. "Ellie, I value your friendship and I don't want to lose it. I do not regret being married to you, except for the disservice I have done you. That is why Henry was displeased. When he helped us to meet, I thought I could... satisfy you in a way a wife should be, and I told him so. He would not otherwise have encouraged the match. But I was wrong. It wasn't a hardship to lie with you, but it was not something I desired, either. We had been trying for years, with no child, and it did not seem as if you enjoyed it. That is why I stopped coming to you."

"I don't want to lose your friendship, either, Martin." She shivered again—there was much to think about. "Let us go home. *Our* home."

"And soon, God willing, we will have our child to look after."

They turned their steps towards the woods and the path back to the gig.

Ellie's feelings fluctuated wildly in the next few weeks. Sometimes she was angry with Martin for cheating her out of a true marriage, then she would remind herself that she had cheated, too. She resented Henry conspiring with Martin, but recalled that Henry had been displeased with his friend for not making Ellie happy. Both of them had meant well—and marrying Martin *had* allowed her to escape from Father and Aunt Harriet. Then there was Martin's confession— she knew sodomy was a crime, but it was difficult to think of it that way when it was a kind man like Martin admitting to it.

Life at the farm went on much as it had before, and Ellie's thoughts and emotions gradually became less intrusive and turned more towards the new life growing within her. Agnes had not told anyone else about Ellie's likely pregnancy, but Ellie's bouts of nausea became more frequent and Martin talked about redecorating one of the empty bedrooms, and soon everyone knew. She didn't go to the races with

Martin, but went to Harrogate to see Mary instead, asking her more about what would happen as the baby developed, and what she would need when it was born.

A few days after Martin returned from York, they went up to Bank Side together. When she'd handed over Agnes' latest pies and cakes, Bill took a chair into the yard for her, and she sat with a cup of tea while stable life carried on around her.

She thought how difficult it must be for men who shared Martin's inclinations, if they cared for one another. They had to conceal their feelings unless they were alone, or risk death. The glances and little touches that Mary and Henry shared—they must not let themselves do any of that.

Martin came to join her, leaning on the sun-warmed wall behind, watching the gait of two of the three-year-olds as Bill and Dan led them around the yard. Dan—one of Martin's Misfits.

"Chestnut would make a good hunter," Martin said, and talked about the length of the gelding's back and neck, the slope of his shoulders. Ellie listened carefully—the horse business was the main part of their livelihood.

On the drive back to Knowle Farm, when there was no chance of being overheard, Ellie asked about the Misfits. "Martin, do you take on your 'misfits' because you feel like a misfit too? You cannot help being attracted to men, and they cannot help what happened to them."

He glanced at her, then back at the road. "My nature makes me aware of the unfairness of so many things in this life."

Real unfairness, not the fabricated resentment that his cousin held. "What will they do if you... if anything happens to you? I mean, I don't think your cousin would keep them on."

"I have a will leaving both farms to you, I told you that. When the child is born, I'll add him—"

"Her," Ellie said with a grin. Not that she minded which it turned out to be.

He chuckled. "Him or her. I'll add the babe to the will, with you as sole guardian. It will be in your hands, Ellie. But cheer up—I'm not planning on going anywhere."

"Might your cousin have a case for taking over the guardianship? As a male relative, I mean?"

"No sensible man would think so, although he could try. But it would cost him money that he hasn't got to take it to the Court of Chancery. What are you thinking?"

"Make Henry a joint guardian. You trust him. I don't know him well, but I trust my sister's judgement."

"I think you're worrying unnecessarily, but I will do that if you wish."

"Thank you."

Martin would make a good father, Ellie thought. They would both love and protect their child, and she was determined to be the best wife and mother she could.

CHAPTER 12

Two years later
Tarbes, France, March 1814

Tom stirred from his drowse at the raised voices beyond the door of his room. The woman of the house wasn't happy at having several of Wellington's wounded officers billeted with her and made that known at every opportunity. The smattering of French Tom had picked up as his battalion fought its way across the south of France wasn't sufficient to understand her complaints, and he normally let the diatribes wash over him. At least she wasn't berating *him* this time. The food she provided was edible and the room clean—that was enough.

Assistant Surgeon Levin entered, shutting the door behind him and rolling his eyes. Despite his pain, Tom managed a grin.

"You may well laugh, Allerby, but I have to listen to the same complaints twenty times a day. Now, let's have a look at this shoulder."

Tom winced as Levin peeled the bandage from his right shoulder. Twisting his neck, he could just make out the stitches over the bullet hole. The flesh around the wound was red, but the doctor nodded in approval.

"My arm's not going to fall off, then?"

"It's a bit early to be sure, but it's looking promising. You'll live to... well, perhaps not fight another day, but it's good that you've managed to get this far without signs of infection."

"Not fight?" Tom tried to sit up, then his breath hissed through his teeth as he collapsed backwards, liquid fire shooting down his arm.

Levin tutted. "Didn't I tell you to rest it as much as possible?"

Yes, he had.

"You're lucky, you know. Half an inch to the left would have hit a major artery. You'd have bled to death before anyone could help. You may never get full movement back in the joint, though. Shoulders are complicated things. But you'll have plenty of time to think about it. I'm arranging for transport home—it will be a few months, at the very least, before we know how well the joint will heal. You should be well enough to leave next week."

Resting his head back on the pillow after Levin left, Tom wondered how he would manage. He couldn't imagine his shoulder being mobile enough to pull a shirt on over his head or get his arms into a jacket. He'd probably even need someone to cut up his food for him to start with, like an infant.

And if it never healed properly—what would he do then? But the effort of thinking was too much, and he drifted off to sleep again.

The next day Tom called "come" to a tentative knock on his door, and a boy stepped cautiously inside.

"Captain Allerby?"

"Yes."

The lad could only have been ten years old, with a round face and dark hair currently sticking up in all directions. Too young to be a drummer boy. His clothing was far from new, but several rips had been mended and it was as clean as could be expected for someone who had, presumably, been following the army. "If you please, Captain, Mr Levin sent me. He said you might need some help." He had an odd accent, traces of an Irish lilt overlaid on something northern. "He give me these to bring you." He held out a couple of letters.

Tom used his good arm to push himself into a sitting position. He could do that today without too much pain, if he was careful, but it had been as much as he could manage to use the chamber pot without swooning. "You'd better come in properly."

"Oh. Sorry, sir." The lad crossed the room and put the two letters into Tom's hand.

Tom glanced at the directions—both were in his mother's hand. One was quite thick, probably enclosing a letter from someone else. He remembered the flashes of anticipation on the previous occasions Mama had done that, but in the two years since he'd seen Ellie the enclosures had never been from her. He should not hope that this would be, either.

A shuffling reminded him that he had an audience. "What's your name?"

"Finn Robson, sir." The boy sniffed and looked at his feet. Looking more closely, Tom could see red around his eyes.

"Well, Finn, I don't bite."

The lad looked up and attempted a smile. "No, sir."

"Where are your parents?"

"Me da was Sergeant Robson, sir, in the 43rd. He..." Finn gulped. "He..."

Tom didn't recognise the name; Robson must have been in someone else's company. Killed in the recent action, Tom guessed. He patted the bed. "Come and sit down." He waited until Finn sat. "What about your mother?"

"She got a fever when we were still in Spain." Finn was staring at the floor once more.

What a position to be in—both parents gone and stuck in a foreign land. Tom rubbed his hand through his hair. "Have you got any relatives?"

"Me da said if anything happened, I was to go to his brother. My uncle. In Darlington. But I don't know where that is." Tears were threatening again, and Tom looked away while Finn sniffed and wiped his nose on his sleeve. "Mr Levin said Da's friends in the company collected some money for the journey. He's lookin' after it for me. But I don't... I don't..."

"You can travel with me," Tom said. Which was, no doubt, exactly what Levin had intended. Finn wouldn't have enough money to get himself to England, let alone all the way to the north country; the men hadn't been paid in months. And one so young was bound to be robbed at some point if he travelled alone. "As you can see, I won't be able to do much for myself."

Finn looked at Tom properly for the first time, a spark of interest in his eyes as he took in the bandaged shoulder. "Is Mr Levin goin' to cut your arm off?"

"Good grief, you horrible brat!" Tom was amused by the lad's curiosity and bluntness—and both were better than tears. "No, not if I can help it. What can you do? You must have helped your... your father."

"I helped me mam, mostly. Carryin' water and the like. Choppin' veggies."

"Brushing clothes?"

He shrugged.

"Well, you can try your hand with my uniform." Tom nodded to the corner of the room where his ruined jacket and filthy trousers were draped over a chair. He had spares in his trunk, but it would give Finn something to do. "See if you can get the landlady to give you some water and a brush."

"I don't understand what she says."

"Try. Before you go, see if there's a handkerchief in the pocket and bring it to me." Tom lay back—carefully—as Finn searched the pockets. He found the handkerchief and frowned as he inspected it. He looked at Tom, curiosity in his expression, but Tom only held his hand out for it. He wasn't about to explain why he had a woman's handkerchief. Finn handed it over, then took the jacket away.

Tom closed his eyes, holding the small cotton square. Memories of his time with Ellie—the talking as well as the intimacy—had seen him through many dark nights after friends had been killed. He felt that she'd seen into his soul—fanciful though that sounded. Seen an act he was ashamed of and not excused it or said it didn't matter, which he couldn't have made himself believe. Instead, she convinced him that he'd done the best he could, and that was good enough. That he had nothing to blame himself for. He'd never been able to talk to anyone else like that.

Would she be married again by now? Should he try to find her?

Dismissing those questions—for now—Tom turned to his letters, breaking the seals and unfolding them awkwardly with his left hand. He read the single sheet first. It was the usual hope that the letter found him well, and news of Mama's doings and those of the people in Kendal he knew. Nothing of note, but a welcome connection with home. It was only the last line that gave him pause—she hadn't heard from Frank in several months.

Frank's last letter to Tom had been even longer ago, but he'd assumed the missives had got lost in transit. Frank had never been a frequent correspondent, but he might have written more often to Mama.

The thicker one was dated more recently, and the enclosure was also in his mother's hand.

My dear Tom,
Mr Mortenson sent the enclosed to me. I know there is nothing you can do while you are still in France, but I thought you ought to be aware of the situation. I have not heard from Frank since my last letter to you.
I do hope you are safe and well and will be able to return home soon.
With much love
Mama

Mortenson was Frank's former business partner. Frank had written sometime last summer to say he'd set up his own business. At the time, Tom had assumed he had done so because things were going well; perhaps that was not the case.

The enclosed letter was addressed to their mother and began with an apology for bothering her.

I am very concerned about Allerby. The dissolution of our partnership was reasonably amicable, but relations later became acrimonious, although I don't know why. There was certainly no ill will on my part. I have no hard evidence for what I tell you here, only hearsay— but consistent hearsay from many people is often worth attention. There are rumours of unpaid bills, of tradesmen considering using debt collectors, and of briefs not handled with professional care. Allerby's problems appear to have begun around the time he separated from his wife.
The situation between us is not such that I can approach Allerby myself, but his brother, if he can obtain leave, may be able to address the problem. Forgive me for interfering in your family's affairs, but I assure you I have only done so with the best of intentions.

Tom dropped the letter. Of course he would help if he could—both for brotherly affection and because Mama was worried. Not without reason.

He recalled his brief visit to Frank's house. Or what had been his house at the time, as Frank had a new address now. His wife had seemed a little discontented, but for them to live apart meant there must be something much more serious wrong. Whatever the reason, Tom should see if he could help. The hole in his shoulder would spare him the need to explain the situation when asking for leave—he'd got his furlough, whether he wanted it or not. And just when Wellington had really got Boney's troops on the run.

Help Frank, take Finn to his uncle, give his shoulder time to heal— and perhaps while he was doing all that he might make some enquiries about Ellie, who had been heading for York.

York, a month later

Tom's shoulder merely ached when he descended from the stage coach in York. A powerful ache, to be sure, and he still needed the sling, but he didn't have the debilitating tiredness of the days following his injury. The four days it had taken to get to the French coast in a jolting carriage had been agony, and he hadn't been at all sorry that poor weather kept them waiting to sail for several days, giving him a chance to rest. He'd spent most of the time at sea lying on his bunk and that, together with the week he'd just spent in Kendal being fussed over by Mama, had done him good. Finn was looking healthier, too—Mama had found him some better clothes and fed him well.

He'd caught up on the news while he was in Kendal. Details of the final battle of the war had reached home at about the same time as the news of Napoleon's abdication and the peace with France. Sadly, word of the latter had not reached Toulouse until after the battle. How must the wounded from that engagement feel, or the kin of the dead, to know that they had fought after the war had ended? All those deaths and injuries for nothing.

"There's your trunk, sir." Finn pointed. The yard of the Green Dragon was teeming with people and horses—not a place where either of them would get a decent night's sleep. Tom caught the eye of a porter and arranged for his trunk to be kept until he'd found some-where to stay. The porter directed him to a quieter part of town, and Tom set off with Finn trotting behind him. It was good to stretch his legs after so many hours in the coach—and even better to think he didn't have to be cooped up in one of the infernal things again for some time.

The Prince Rupert was the second inn he tried. It had a room free, and the scent of frying onions and roasting meat hinted at tasty meals.

"It's not big, sir," the landlord said, opening the door to the room and standing back. "But the sheets be clean and aired. There's a truckle bed for your... your lad."

"Batman," Tom said. The landlord wasn't the first to be puzzled by Finn's status, and didn't look convinced by Tom's explanation. And rightly so, for Finn was far too young for that, but he liked the title.

"This will do nicely—I'll take it for three nights to start with. Send up some hot water, if you please."

Feeling refreshed after a quick wash, Tom debated what to do. It was only mid-afternoon, so Frank should be in his office. Turning to ask Finn to get his greatcoat, he caught a look of pure misery on the lad's face before Finn realised he was being observed and managed a more neutral expression.

Come to think of it, Finn had been growing less and less talkative all the way from Kendal. He'd chattered readily enough on the journey north from Portsmouth—tales of his life with the army and comments about the passing scenery. For all the hardships and danger, it seemed that Finn had had a happy childhood, with parents who had cared for him. Not to mention the rest of his father's company. The boy would find it strange, not being in the midst of so many people he knew.

"What's wrong, Finn?"

"Nothin'." Finn looked at his feet.

An obvious lie—he'd have to coax it out of the boy. Walking around the city would give them something neutral to talk about, and he had some exploring to do. "Get your coat; we'll go for a walk." That made Finn look worse, not better, but what could he do if the lad wouldn't talk?

Tom asked directions to the nearest bookshop and bought a plan of the city, then headed for the coaching inn to get his trunk delivered. Finn stopped when the inn sign came into view. Tom didn't notice for a few paces, then turned back to see him still standing at the corner, his lips clamped together as if he was about to cry.

"I'm going for my trunk, not to put you on a coach."

It seemed he'd guessed correctly—Finn looked less miserable, but not much. Tom sighed. "Wait there. I'll be back in a minute."

Arrangements made, Tom led Finn to the open patch of ground near the Minster and found a quiet spot to talk. "Don't you want to go to your uncle?"

Finn shook his head. "I've never seen him. What if he doesn't like me? Or if he already has children of his own?"

In which case, he might not be able to afford another mouth to feed. "What do you know about him?"

"Da called him my Uncle Joseph. Ma said he doesn't like the Irish."

That didn't bode well. Tom gazed up at the towering stonework above them, but there was no inspiration there. The obvious solution —for now—was the only one.

"I'm not going to send you on your own, anyway. I still need a servant." That wasn't quite true, but near enough. "You can work for me until I have time to take you to Darlington, and I won't leave you there if your uncle doesn't want you. Will that do?"

Finn nodded and rubbed his sleeve across his face.

"I do have rules, though." Tom pulled a handkerchief from his pocket.

Finn looked wary.

"The first one is to use this, not your sleeve."

Finn took the handkerchief with a wobbly smile and blew his nose.

"Good. Now, you can see this from most parts of York." Tom pointed up to the towers of the Minster looming above them. "If you get lost, or go exploring on your own, you can always find your way back to here. The Prince Rupert is down the road between the Minster and that church." He waited until Finn nodded before they set off for Frank's office.

The office was in a shared building; a small painted sign beside one of the doors in the downstairs hall announced *F. Allerby, Attorney*. There was no response when Tom knocked, even though it was not yet four o'clock. After a minute, Tom knocked again, harder.

A door opened behind him. "He's not there." A young man with ink-stained fingers stood in the doorway of the office opposite.

"Do you know when he is expected? Or his clerk?"

"I'm afraid not, sir. His clerk hasn't been in for nearly a month, though. If you'll excuse me?" The man didn't wait for an answer, stepping back into his own office and closing the door.

That didn't sound good. Not at all. He could try Frank's lodgings, but his shoulder was paining him now and he just wanted to rest.

"Come on, Finn. Let's go and find some food."

CHAPTER 13

*A*fter breakfast the following morning, Tom sent Finn off with enough coin to buy some food, along with instructions to learn his way about the centre of the city. Then he set out to find Frank, deciding to start at his home. From the way the address was written, Frank lived in a room in a lodging house.

The building was on a narrow street; the door had peeling paint, but the steps looked recently scrubbed and the windows were clean. The entrance hall was dim, but there was enough light to make out that the stairs had been swept, and Tom's hand on the banister came away clean. Perhaps Frank hadn't sunk as far as he'd feared.

He had to knock several times, but eventually there were sounds of movement within. A bleary-eyed Frank opened the door a fraction and stuck his head around it.

"Tom?" The door opened a few more inches, and Frank rubbed a hand across his face. "What are you doing here? I thought you were still... I mean it's only a few weeks since Boney..."

Tom took in the shadows beneath his brother's eyes with concern; Frank's cheeks were thinner than he recalled. Mama had been right to worry.

"Are you going to let me in?"

"Oh, yes. Sorry." Frank stood back and held the door open. The parlour wasn't large, but there was space enough for a small table with two upright chairs, and an armchair by the fireplace. The grate held only the dead remains of a fire, even though the air was chill. The room was dusty, but probably only a few days' worth. There were several unwashed dishes and a glass on the table, together with a couple of empty wine bottles. Frank's hair was unbrushed, his waistcoat unfastened, and he wasn't wearing a neckcloth. Had he just got out of bed? Anyone who had to work for a living would have been up and about hours ago.

"Sit down, Tom." Frank sat opposite and nodded at the sling. "Injured? Is that why you're back so soon?"

"Bullet through the shoulder. It's mending."

"Toulouse?"

"No. A small engagement a few weeks before. I've got leave for a month or two. Thought I'd come and see how you're doing."

"I'm well enough." But Frank's tone was unconvincing, and he seemed to realise it as soon as he'd spoken. "Sorry, bit of a sore head this morning."

As Tom had surmised from the empty wine bottles. And the single glass implied that Frank had been drinking alone. "Coffee'll help." He looked around, but couldn't see any means of making a hot drink. "Shall I fetch some? Or do you want to finish dressing and come for breakfast with me?" The used plates beside the empty glass were somewhat reassuring—it seemed Frank wasn't so far gone that he'd stopped eating.

"Just coffee. Thank you."

"Food?"

Frank shook his head and winced. "Not yet."

By the time Tom returned with a pot of coffee, Frank had combed his hair and washed his face—as evidenced by still-damp tendrils around his forehead. Tom sat at the table and poured for him; Frank downed it and held the cup out for more. He sipped the second more slowly, frowning at Tom over the edge of the cup.

"I suppose Mama sent you."

"She's worried about you," Tom said. "You haven't written to her for months. I looked for you at your office yesterday and learned that your clerk hasn't been seen for some time."

Frank just grunted.

"I thought, when you first wrote to let me know you'd set up on your own, that it was a sign of your business doing well."

"Clearly not," Frank snapped, then rubbed his face again. "Sorry." He drank more coffee and set the cup back in its saucer. "You're not going to leave me in peace, are you, little brother?"

"No. Do you really want me to?"

Frank sighed and shook his head. "No, not really. Unless you're going to order me about like one of your company."

"Ha—I'd send you to put your head under the pump, then have you marching around the barracks to teach you not to drink so much next time." He laughed as Frank winced again. "A bit of fresh air might do you good, though. Unless you feel like telling me now what's been going on?"

"I'd rather wait until my head's a bit clearer," Frank admitted. "Besides, the cleaning woman is due to come in this morning, so we're likely to be interrupted."

"How long—an hour? I'll come to your office."

Frank just grunted and emptied the rest of the coffee into his cup as Tom left.

An hour later, Tom loitered in the street outside Frank's office wondering if his brother was going to come. Things didn't seem to be quite as bad as Mama had feared; Frank had decent lodgings, still had his office, and could afford a cleaning woman. But that was very different from the house and prosperous business partnership he'd had two years ago.

Frank was only ten minutes late, with a muttered apology as he unlocked the door. The outer room of the office was furnished with a clerk's high desk and a couple of hard chairs, all covered in a film of dust. The desk in the inner office had piles of paper stacked around the edges, and there were more bundles on the cupboards lining the wall.

"You'd better sit down." Frank sneezed as he moved papers from a chair, raising a cloud of dust and not seeming to notice several sheets fluttering to the floor. He slumped into his own chair behind the desk.

"Couldn't you get your cleaning woman to come in here?" Tom asked.

"She's included with the lodgings, and I owe a month's rent," Frank said, staring gloomily at the papers. "The woman who did for me here stopped coming at the same time as my clerk."

When Frank failed to pay them, no doubt. Perhaps things *were* as bad as Mama had thought. "How dire is it?" Tom asked. "Am I going to have to fend off bailiffs?" He waited, but his brother only glowered at him. "Frank—things are not right with you. I'm not going to just ignore that if there's anything I can do to help." He waved a hand at the papers. "Is this the problem, or the result of something else?"

There was a long silence as Frank looked down at his hands, clasped on the desk before him. "I set up my own business because... because I couldn't work with Mortenson any longer. I didn't really have a name for myself, so I didn't get as much work. Even then it was mostly simple things like making wills, marriage settlements and the like."

"You worked well with Mortenson for several years, didn't you?" Tom asked. "That's why he took you into the partnership."

"Things change." Frank stood and opened a cupboard, bringing out a stoppered decanter and two glasses. He poured what looked like brandy into one and offered it to Tom.

"Not at this hour." Tom's worry deepened—drinking at this time of day did not bode well.

"I keep it for clients," Frank said, but the defensiveness in his voice suggested that it wasn't the only reason.

"You don't have to tell me what's wrong if you don't want to, but I wish you would."

Frank drained the glass, making himself cough, but then put the decanter back in the cupboard and shut the door. "It began with Susannah." He slumped back into his chair, not looking at Tom. "She was beautiful. Still is. You know that—you met her."

"Yes, I remember."

"Very young—Mama would probably have said too young. But she was a fascinating creature. I couldn't understand why she wanted me when she must have had so many other suitors. She was forever gadding about to parties and assemblies and so on. With me, when I had the time, but with others when I was too busy. And I often was. And the house—do you remember the house?"

Tom nodded.

"She had it all redecorated, new furniture, new curtains. Her dressmaker's bills... I asked her to not spend so much, and that led to arguments."

"What has this to do with Mortenson?"

"Would you work with a man who'd cuckolded you?"

Mortenson? A man who'd cuckolded his business partner wouldn't have bothered to write to Mama, would he? Or say that he didn't understand the acrimony between them. "Are you sure he did, Frank? Did he admit it?"

"No. He told me we'd have to part if I didn't mend my ways. Accused me of not taking enough care with things. Well—he might have had a point there. I was preoccupied with the money Susannah was spending, and made some mistakes. I did try to pay more attention, but when Susannah told me..."

Tom waited without speaking.

"No, she wasn't telling, she was taunting me. Said I didn't give her what she needed. That I wasn't a proper husband." Frank scowled. "Mortenson *was*, apparently."

"If she was taunting you, perhaps it wasn't true," Tom suggested. "Or you may have misunderstood what she meant."

Frank shrugged and refilled his glass. "Doesn't really matter now. She went to live with her sister. That allowed me to give up the lease on that house and sell some of the fancy furniture." He looked around the office. "Some days I just can't face coming in, or dealing with people's petty disputes. It just seems… pointless, really."

There was little Tom could do about Frank's relations with his wife, but she wasn't his only problem. "Your office appears to need sorting out. Does anyone owe *you* money?"

"Possibly. Probably… My clerk was in charge of making sure people paid."

That was something he could help with. Finn could earn his keep by cleaning the place.

Over the next couple of weeks, Tom was kept busy with Frank and his business affairs, aided by numerous pots of coffee. Finn fetched food and drink from a nearby inn in between practising his letters—under protest—and keeping the offices swept and dusted. They spent their evenings together; sometimes Tom would relate stories of his time in the Peninsula over a few pints of ale. At other times, though, Tom had to listen to brandy-fuelled accounts of Frank's courtship of his wife, how lovely he'd thought her, and then a litany of her actions since.

Tom had prodded Frank into sorting his papers into completed jobs and ones in progress—although there were distressingly few of the latter. Then between them they'd written to all the clients who had not yet settled their invoices. One afternoon when Frank was elsewhere, Tom had gone in search of Mortenson to thank him for his letter. Mortenson had been happy to see him, even saying he might be able to put a little work Frank's way if Frank's unexplained resentment would allow it. Tom was more convinced than ever that Frank was wrong about his former partner, but he couldn't think of a way of asking Mortenson about it without causing offence.

Mortenson had also given Tom the details of an attorney in Darlington who could help find an address for Finn's uncle. Tom had decided it would be better to write first. If the uncle was unwilling to take the lad in, it would save them both an abortive trip to Darlington.

His mind often wandered to Ellie during that time—should he try to find her? Could he? Might she be married again by now? But family came first, and any such attempt would have to wait until he'd done what he could to get Frank back on his feet.

By the end of a fortnight, some of the outstanding invoices had been settled and Frank was no longer in danger of being evicted from his rooms or being dunned. Others would need to be followed up in person. That was not a task Tom relished, but it would give him the opportunity to get out of Frank's office and away from the city. The May sunshine was warm; he would hire a horse and ride to the clients in the villages and towns within half a day from York. He could take Finn with him—the lad seemed to like animals and would enjoy seeing the countryside.

"It's the races next week—the Spring Meeting," Frank said, when Tom told him his plan. "You won't find a lot of them at home."

That was why the city was becoming more crowded than usual. Tom had been so deep in details of mortgages, wills, leases, and conveyancing that he hadn't thought about the reason for it.

"D'you fancy a day or two at the races?" Frank asked, a gleam of interest in his eyes.

"Yes, why not?" Even if he'd had no inclination for it, this was the first spark of enthusiasm Frank had shown for anything. It would make a change for all of them, and he'd be glad to spend a day *not* looking through legal documents and invoices. Finn would love it.

The racecourse was a mile or so outside the city—not far enough to warrant hiring a horse or carriage. Tom was happy to stretch his legs on the walk, with Finn trotting along behind him and Frank puffing to keep up. He ignored his brother's protest—the exercise would do him good. When they arrived, Tom gave Finn some coins to buy something from the food vendors and told him not to get into trouble.

Frank produced a list of races with odds pencilled beside some of the runners. "Fancy a bet?"

"Not today." Or any other day—he couldn't afford to lose what little cash he had left. Nor could Frank.

"Don't worry, little brother." Frank grinned. "I'm not so far gone I can't remember Mama's rules."

"She never gave me rules about gambling."

"Really? Don't you remember the row when Papa won on Daedalus in the Derby?"

Tom shook his head. But he'd been only fourteen at the time, and Frank seventeen.

"Perhaps Mama made sure you were out of the way. It was a real shouting argument—the only one I ever recall them having."

"I thought Daedalus winning was a good thing?"

"Oh, it was, considering the amount Papa had put on him. The odds were only six to one."

"Good heavens. He must have bet a hundred guineas or more." He didn't think it would have beggared the family to lose that much, but it might have been a close thing. Let alone the damage to his father's professional reputation.

"More than that, I think."

"But he still went to the races after that?"

Frank chuckled. "Mama made him promise that he would only bet a certain amount, and when he lost that he must stop. I'm not sure he always stuck to it, but close enough." He pulled a handful of crowns from his pocket. "My allowance for the day." He looked Tom in the eye. "I may drink too much at times, Tom, but I haven't pickled my brain yet; I'm not going to waste your efforts of the last two weeks by spending more than this. Now, I'm off to put some money on the first race."

Tom's pleasure in the day wasn't from the prospect of winning bets, but in the time away from the office in the sunshine. In enjoying the spectacle. Murmurs amongst the crowd grew, and Tom found a position to watch the first race. He didn't know anything about the runners or their owners, but he got caught up in the excitement of the crowd, the speed and grace of the animals racing past, and the cheers.

While waiting for the next race, Tom wandered away from the grandstand to where the crowds were thinner. His shoulder still hurt in the evenings, even when he'd used his sling and done little more than look through Frank's paperwork; he didn't want people bumping into him. Here, spectators sat in their open carriages, some with spyglasses to watch the finish over the heads of the crowd. There were glossy barouches with crests on the doors, curricles, and a collection of lowlier vehicles—gigs and farm carts.

Tom's stomach reminded him that it was a long time since breakfast, and he turned to go in search of food. Then something made him look back; a memory.

His gaze passed over the vehicles again, stopping on a woman sitting in a gig. She was talking to a man standing beside it while a younger man—little more than a boy—adjusted a nosebag on the horse.

They were some distance off, so he began to move closer, feeling a flutter in his belly—surprise and eager anticipation. And hope that he wasn't mistaken. The woman's hair was partly hidden by a bonnet, her face in the shade of its brim, yet he knew her. A turn of her head lit her face as she looked in his direction, and even though he was too far off to make out her features properly, he recalled the way her eyes shone when she smiled, the soft sound of her laugh.

Fate had found Ellie for him.

He'd taken several steps in her direction before his rational mind caught up. He wanted to go to her, but should he? She'd had a way of contacting him and had not—although he had given her his mother's address in case she needed help, not because he'd asked her to write to him. There was animation in her movements as she talked, and a broad smile for the man she was addressing. His initial joy at seeing her faded into dismay. Was he too late?

"There you are, Tom!" Frank had a huge grin on his face. "Firecracker won at four to one." He laughed. "I'm richer by a whole pound!"

Tom managed a smile. This was more like the brother he remembered, and it was good to see. And perhaps Frank could help him now. "You know a lot of people, Frank. Do you recognise that pair?" He pointed discreetly to where Ellie was still talking. "The woman in the green pelisse sitting in a gig, and the tall fellow in the brown greatcoat."

Frank squinted, then his brows rose. "Looks like Wilson—comes to most of the race meetings. I investigated him last year. The woman must be his wife."

CHAPTER 14

*E*llie was married.

Why wouldn't she be? She was attractive in personality as well as in her person. Their encounter was more than two years ago now, and although he'd thought about her many times since then, there was no reason to expect she'd done the same. Why shouldn't she have found herself a new husband? Lucky dog, whoever he was.

"Tom?" Frank said. "Is something wrong?"

Tom managed a smile. "Pangs of hunger." Disappointment, more like, turning his stomach into a leaden lump. He was too late, and he hadn't realised until now how much he'd been hanging onto that dream of seeing her again. Finding out if there could be something more than just a night spent together.

But he couldn't share his feelings with Frank. "Come on, let's get something to eat. Which runner d'you fancy in the next?"

It wasn't until Frank was cheering on his choice in the final race that Tom wondered about the surname. Wilson. Her name was Wilson two years ago, which meant she must have married a cousin of her late husband, or someone who had the same name by coincidence. Not particularly likely, but far from impossible.

Or she had been married when he met her. That would mean she hadn't been a widow, but a woman who'd cuckolded her husband with a man she'd met only hours before. And it also meant she'd deceived him about being a widow.

Could he have been so wrong about her? The Ellie he'd held in his thoughts all this time wasn't a deceiver, but he *had* only known her for a few hours. He tried to recall the earlier part of that evening in the inn. She'd been wearing black; he'd thought she was a widow, and the Ben she'd talked about had been her late husband. However, he couldn't recall her specifically saying so.

When had she married?

He waited until there weren't too many people within earshot before asking his burning question as off-handedly as he could. "Frank, what did you investigate Wilson for?"

"Eh?"

"Wilson. That fellow you pointed out."

"Odd case, that. Why d'you want to know?"

Tom managed a nonchalant tone. "Reminded me of someone I knew. Thought he might be a relative of his."

"He's a farmer, lives up near Thirsk. Breeds horses. Someone, a cousin, I think, wanted to find evidence that his marriage was invalid."

"Did you find any?"

"No." Frank stopped and looked into his face. "Does it matter?"

Tom shrugged, ignoring the pain the movement sent through his shoulder. Although that was nothing compared to the hurt at what felt like a betrayal. "Just wondering. Seems a strange request." Time to change the subject before Frank got *too* interested in his reasons. "How much did you lose today?"

Frank laughed. "Oh, ye of little faith. I won!"

"More money to lay on the horses tomorrow?"

"According to Mama's rule, yes." He reached into a pocket and pulled out a handful of coins. "But not this time. You take the winnings; I'll start again with my original stake." He dropped the coins into Tom's hand. "You coming tomorrow?"

"No. Perhaps on Wednesday."

. . .

Tom let himself into Frank's office the next morning, late enough to be sure that Frank would be at the racecourse. He'd given Finn a few coins again, telling him to entertain himself for the day, and the lad had set off happily, presumably to the same destination.

The office was now very different from his first sight of it—Finn had become a dab hand with broom and polishing cloth. Not all the paperwork in the inner office was sorted into drawers, but there wasn't much left to deal with.

Slumping into Frank's chair, he spun it round to look at the drawers. "Investigated him last year," Frank had said of Wilson. Tom didn't recall seeing the name Wilson on any of the papers he'd looked through, but the papers were filed by the name of the client. Wilson's cousin could easily have a different surname. He was reluctant to start, partly because he wasn't sure he was going to like what he found, but also because he shouldn't be looking through private legal papers. He'd seen a lot of Frank's cases while he'd been helping him to sort out his affairs, but then he'd effectively been acting as a clerk would have done. He was not acting as a clerk now.

All he wanted to do was to find out when Ellie had married. Just that.

If she'd married after their night together, he was unlucky that she'd now found someone else. If it was before... Well, he'd think about that if it *was* so.

He took a deep breath and opened the first cupboard.

The bundles were stored in order of clients' names and, as he had suspected, there was no Wilson. He began a methodical search at the top of the left-hand cupboard. He ignored anything more than two years old, but it still took him hours.

The bundle he eventually found was thinner than most. It contained an invoice addressed to Luke Palmer, which Tom put aside without taking in the details. Two letters in Frank's hand, then a sheet in crabbed handwriting from someone with an indecipherable signature, although the 'Parish Clerk, Quernby' below it was legible.

I enclose a copy of the entry in the register for Miss Dennison. The banns were read as required. The certificate of banns for Mr Wilson should be available for inspection at Kirby Sutton.

The copy was pinned to the letter.

Married 18th June 1807, Martin Wilson, farmer, of Kirby Sutton, Yorkshire, and Eleanor Dennison, spinster of this parish.

Nearly five years before Tom had met her.

He shouldn't feel so disappointed. She was married now, so he had to forget whatever dreams he'd had of meeting her again and seeing if something more could come of their liaison. But the knowledge that those dreams had *never* been possible made their night together seem more like a romp with a willing camp follower and turned his subsequent wishes into a foolish dream.

A knock at the door interrupted his thoughts, but he ignored it. Finn or Frank would have just walked in; anyone else would be in search of Frank, and would go away if he didn't let them in.

Then he heard footsteps crossing the outer office. Swearing, he quickly stacked the papers and shoved them into the top desk drawer. Another knock, then the latch clicked.

"Captain Allerby."

Tom stood. "Mrs Allerby." Her appearance was different from his memory of their first meeting, although it was difficult to pin down exactly how. A plainer hair style, perhaps, and less rosy lips? A crease between her brows—not exactly careworn, but far from the youthful smoothness he recalled.

"I'd heard you were visiting Frank, Captain. I am glad to find you here alone."

Had she been watching the office?

"It's Frank," she said when he did not reply. "I wondered if you might talk to him for me?"

"About what?" Tom had barked out the question, as if interrogating a recalcitrant private. He sat back down abruptly, and rubbed a hand over his face. He should not let his disappointment about Ellie affect his dealing with Frank's wife.

"He… he has…" She took a shuddering breath. "He will not believe what I say, Captain, but gives credence to malicious gossip. He made me homeless by selling the house in Micklegate—I am reduced to living in a single room, and that has caused even more gossip."

"I thought you went to live with your sister?" That was what Frank had said.

Her lips turned down. "My sister has a growing family."

"I don't see how an intervention by me would help."

She blinked a couple of times, then lowered her eyes. "So many misunderstandings, Captain. It is hardly my fault that men find me attractive, but to… to accuse me of…" She broke off and gave a little gulp, pressing a handkerchief to her mouth.

Frank's wife was either a *very* good actress, or she truly was distressed. And he hadn't entirely believed his brother's conviction that Mortenson had betrayed their friendship.

"You told Frank he wasn't a proper husband, did you not?" He tried to keep his tone more questioning than accusing. "And that Mortenson was? How else was he to interpret that?"

Her mouth dropped open. Genuine surprise, Tom thought—no-one could make their face pale like that. Had Frank misunderstood what she'd said?

"I… I became friends with Mrs Mortenson. She has a lovely home, and a husband who is not away for a week or more every month. Mr Mortenson goes with her to assemblies and concerts, and al fresco events in the summer…" She waved a hand. "The Mortensons were happy for me to attend with them, but it is not the same as having my husband accompany me. I was lonely, and occupied some of my time by making our home as comfortable as Mrs Mortenson's. Then Frank became angry with my spending."

"Frank was a junior partner, Mrs Allerby, some twenty years younger than Mr Mortenson. As such, he was the one more likely to be sent on business beyond York. If you are unhappy that he had little time for you, bear that in mind. And his income would not have been as great as Mr Mortenson's."

"It isn't my fault that he's gambled his funds away." The words were muffled by the handkerchief, but distinguishable for all that. "He's at the racecourse now, isn't he?"

Tom felt his anger rising at the accusation, but if Frank had never explained his situation to his wife, he could see how she might think that. "He is. But Frank has never bet more than a few guineas, and has not started to now." Two days ago, he might have given more credence to her claim, but there had been no hint of deceit in Frank's manner yesterday when he explained Mama's rules. Now Tom was as sure as he could be that most of Frank's money problems had begun after his dissolution of the business partnership.

She gazed at him for a moment, then nodded. "I will take your word for that. But will you tell him what I have said? Please, Captain."

Tom sighed. "Very well. Now, if you don't mind, I have business to deal with."

She rose. "Thank you."

There was dejection in her posture as she left; Tom thought again that there must have been some misunderstanding between the two of them. Frank deserved the chance to try and mend things, and he would tell him what Susannah had said.

Once she had left the outer office, Tom locked the door against further intrusion. Was Ellie another such woman, lacking something in her marriage that made her unhappy? Something that she'd thought Tom could give her?

He would never know. With a sigh, he drained the glass, retrieved the papers from the drawer, and started to sort them into a tidy pile to return them to their place in the cupboard. He'd found the information he was looking for.

But as he put the papers back in order a phrase caught his eye, and his hands froze.

Son?

He pulled the paper out and scanned it—it was Frank's file copy of a letter he had written to Palmer. The last paragraph had caught his attention.

I advise you not to waste money on further enquiries of this nature.
As I explained, a child is illegitimate only if the parents are not
married at the time of birth. There is no doubt that Wilson was legally
married when his son was born.

Palmer's enquiry hadn't been about Ellie's marriage, not really. He had been making enquiries about the Wilsons' son.

Ellie had said she could not have children—but evidently she had been mistaken.

His hand trembling slightly, Tom looked at the date on the letter. March 1813. Twelve months after he met Ellie. A woman who'd thought she was barren having a child less than a year after being intimate with someone else...

Was *he* the child's father?

He'd always thought that he would have children one day—sometime in the future, when he found a woman he wanted to share his life with. To discover that he might have one now shook him, gave him a feeling of unreality.

What else was in this file? He spread the papers out; the unpaid invoice had an address in Northallerton, and the only other letter was a copy of one that Frank had sent to the parish clerk at Quernby, requesting a copy of the register entry. Nothing to give him any better indication of whether or not he was the father of Ellie's child.

If the boy *was* his, Ellie must have passed him off as her husband's. But what else could she have done in the circumstances?

Tom rested his head in his hands. Ellie was beyond his reach, and he had to try to forget her. But he couldn't, not with this question in his mind. He had to know if the boy was his. And if he was, whether he was being well treated. Ellie would do her best, he was sure, but what if Wilson knew, or even suspected, that he might not be the boy's father?

The only way to find out was to ask Ellie. If all was well, that would be the end of it. The boy was Wilson's son by law, and Tom would not break up a family to claim a child born into wedlock, even if he had the means to look after him.

Ellie might be at the races tomorrow, but her husband would be with her; what excuse could he give for approaching her? He didn't know anything about her background, so he couldn't try to pass himself off as family friend or acquaintance.

Finding out exactly when the child had been born should be his first step, as if the dates didn't fit with his ride over the Pennines two years ago, then he wasn't the father and he should not even approach Ellie. He did not want to create gossip that would harm the boy and his parents. No child deserved that.

The Quernby parish clerk had mentioned Kirby Sutton in his letter—if that was where Wilson's banns had been called, it was likely the boy had also been baptised there. The parish records would have the date, but he could think of no excuse for enquiring about a baptism less than two years ago, especially when the family in question still lived in the same parish.

The sound of the outer office door opening interrupted his thoughts. He shuffled the papers into a neat pile, but before he could do more, the inner door opened and Frank came in.

"Tom? What are you doing here on such a fine day?"

Of course, locking the door didn't work against someone who had a key. Tom could say he was checking for further unpaid invoices, but Frank would know it for a lie when he saw the name on the file. Besides, there had been enough misunderstandings and he didn't want to lie to his brother.

"I was wondering how I could find out whether or not I have a son."

CHAPTER 15

"Ha ha, very funny." Frank turned his head sideways and peered at the letter Tom had just been reading. "Palmer? The Wilsons..." His smile vanished and he sank into the chair across the desk, staring into Tom's face. "Good heavens, you're not joking!"

"No, I'm not." He could hardly blame Frank for making that assumption. Many men of his acquaintance would have treated the situation as a joke, and Frank couldn't know how often he'd thought of Ellie in the last couple of years. And how foolish he now felt about it.

Frank picked up the papers and scanned them. "It was Mrs Wilson you recognised at the races, not Wilson, wasn't it? Your last furlough?"

"Yes—the dates could fit. The coach accident... Do you recall me telling you about it?"

"I remember you mentioning stopping to help, but not that you—" Frank shook his head. "Well, you wouldn't have told me about that kind of thing."

"She was wearing black, and I thought she was a widow. I looked out the records to find out when she married, and found more than I bargained for."

"Why would the date of their marriage matter?"

Tom didn't reply.

Frank's expression changed from puzzlement to sympathy but, to Tom's relief, he didn't repeat the question. Whatever he'd surmised was likely close enough to the truth. Tom wasn't used to sharing his innermost feelings with anyone—that night with Ellie had been exceptional in many ways.

Frank fetched the brandy and two glasses from the cupboard, and Tom accepted a drink. It was rare that he felt he needed one, but this was one of those times.

"You said you wanted to find out if their child is yours?" Frank asked.

Tom nodded.

"Why? You do understand that you have no legal rights over him? Wilson regards the child as his, so, in the eyes of the law, who fathered the boy is irrelevant."

"I do understand that. I just want to know, that's all. And to know that the child is well. Wouldn't you?"

"I suppose so."

"Do you *know* Wilson, Frank? To speak to, I mean."

"I know *of* him—he has a good reputation as a horse breeder. And he came here last year to ask why I was making enquiries about his marriage." Frank pushed the letter from the parish clerk at Quernby across the desk. "That fellow also wrote to Wilson to tell him someone was asking for proof of his marriage. He—Wilson—wasn't pleased about it."

Tom sighed. "I thought about finding the date of the baptism from the local church, but news of that would get back to Wilson even faster."

"How would that help? Even if the child was born exactly nine months after your encounter, it wouldn't prove anything."

"If the date was definitely wrong, I wouldn't need to ask Ell— Mrs Wilson about it. I'm trying to work out a way of seeing her alone; I don't want to upset things between her and her husband."

"Best just leave well alone, then."

"That's easy enough for you to say." Tom was ashamed at the petulance in his tone. Frank was right.

"True." Frank didn't seem to have taken offence. "I'll give your problem some thought, little brother. Women, eh?" He stood. "See you later for dinner?"

"Possibly." He didn't feel like eating at the moment. It wasn't until Frank had gone that Tom remembered he'd intended to tell him about Susannah's visit. Well, there was no urgency in that.

There was nothing more he could find out here, so he put the papers back into their place in the cupboard and set off for what was currently his home.

When Tom walked into their room at the inn Finn was there, his nose red, one eye swollen, and his chin showing traces of blood imperfectly cleaned up. He was slumped in a chair, his expression a cross between weary and contrite. A letter lay on the table beside him.

Tom inspected him with concern. "Are you badly hurt?"

Finn jumped up, wincing slightly but no more than that. "No. Well, only a bit."

"Fight?"

Finn nodded, and Tom sighed. To be fair, he had been involved in fights often enough when he was Finn's age and shouldn't expect Finn to be any different. "What happened?"

"They called me a stupid Irish bastard and then told me to go home." His voice wobbled and he sniffed. "Took my money, too."

"How did they know you were Irish?" Finn's speech had a trace of an Irish accent, but it wasn't obvious. "Here, sit down while you tell me." It took a little coaxing, but Tom finally extracted a tale of three larger boys befriending him—so he thought—and asking about his family. Looking for an excuse to bully a smaller child, no doubt.

"No-one minded Ma being Irish before!" Finn said.

"There's nothing wrong with being Irish, Finn. Only fools judge someone by the place they were born. Have you eaten yet?"

Finn shook his head. "No money."

Tom didn't ask how long he'd been sitting in this room; he felt guilty enough already. He'd needed Finn's help when he couldn't move his arm—he should have looked after the boy better than this. "Let's get you cleaned up properly, then we'll have dinner."

The letter had Tom's name on it, and he read it while Finn was washing. It was from the attorney in Darlington, to whom Tom had written to ask about Finn's uncle. The attorney reported that Joseph Robson was an established blacksmith on the outskirts of the town, address enclosed. He was married with children, well respected in the area for the quality of his work, and making a good living. The attorney had made no detailed enquires but, from hearsay, judged that Robson was well able to support another child.

Tom felt a sudden pang at the idea of giving Finn into someone else's care. He'd got used to having him around, and would miss him. There was no choice, though—he wouldn't be able to look after the lad when he rejoined his regiment. Mama and Finn had liked each other during the week he and Finn had spent in Kendal, but that visit was far different from asking her to take on complete responsibility for the lad.

Finn cheered up as they ate, talking about the horses he'd seen at the races. It helped to keep Tom's mind off his own muddled thoughts. Tom broached the topic of the letter when they finished their meal.

"The letter was about your uncle," he began, and Finn's mouth turned down at the corners. "He's a blacksmith, with a good business. He should have enough income to keep you as well."

Finn frowned. "Doesn't he *want* me to come?"

"I haven't asked him yet. But you need somewhere permanent to live, Finn. I can't take you with me when my leave finishes. I'd have to find a boarding school for you."

Finn looked thoughtful. "Will there be horses at a blacksmith?"

"Possibly—the ones people take in to have their shoes fitted."

"What if my uncle doesn't like me?"

"We'll go and see him. Then you can decide if you want to stay with him or go to school." Finding a school that treated its pupils well would be a different problem, but he could find one near York, or perhaps Kendal, so that Frank or Mama could check on Finn's progress from time to time. "Now, you'd better get an early night."

Finn nodded and trailed off—not looking miserable, but not looking particularly happy either. But what else could Tom do?

He went in search of Frank, tracking him down to a nearby alehouse without too much trouble. "Come for a walk by the river?" he suggested. "It's a fine evening."

Frank agreed, and they made their way through the streets to the banks of the Ouse near the castle. Tom began by telling him what had happened to Finn.

"Can you keep an eye on him at the races tomorrow? He enjoys watching the horses, and it'd be a shame for him to miss the last day."

"Aren't you going?"

"I thought I'd hire a horse and see how my shoulder holds up to riding."

"If you wish." They walked on in silence for some minutes before Frank spoke again. "Something else on your mind?"

There was no subtle way to introduce the subject. "Your wife called at your office today while I was there."

Frank scowled, but walked on without saying anything.

Tom gave him the gist of what Susannah had said. "She is young, Frank—are you sure she wasn't just taunting you about Mortenson's greater income, and the time he spent with his wife? And you got on well with Mortenson when you worked with him. Is he really the type to cuckold his own business partner?" Tom didn't think it wise to mention that he'd been to see Mortenson. Not at this point.

Frank walked on, his scowl still in place.

"Neither you nor she is happy at the moment, Frank. Talk to her. You don't have to forgive her, but at least find out her perspective on what went wrong between you."

"All right. I'll think about it." Frank's agreement was grudging. "Let's go for a drink."

The weather was still fine when Martin and Ellie drove home from the races. Ellie was looking forward to being back with Jamie—she had worried about their son a little, and had missed him most of the time. Jamie had gone with her to both race meetings last year, with Fanny to help. But now he was seventeen months old and could walk, after a fashion, he was no longer happy to be carried about and a city thronged with racegoers wasn't the place for him to test his new skills. So Agnes and Fanny—not to mention Dan and Jake and most of the stable lads left at Bank Side—had been tasked with looking after him.

The Spring Meeting had gone well. Martin's idea of selling the best-looking horses as hunters or lady's mounts—depending on their temperament—had borne fruit over the last year, and he'd sold two animals at the races. And Lord Longhirst, with an already successful string of racehorses, had talked to Martin about breeding from one of the Bank Side stallions. She should be happy, but the man she'd seen in the crowd still bothered her.

He had the look of Tom Allerby—the solid build, the dark hair— but then so did many men, and he had been too far away for her to make out his features clearly. He had been looking in her direction until another man came up and spoke to him, then he'd turned away and walked off before she could act on her impulse to get closer to see if it *was* Tom. That was for the best, as Martin and Jake had both been with her and she would have been too flustered to invent a plausible reason for her interest in a stranger.

She had never really been able to put Tom out of her mind over the last two years, particularly when Jamie had been born. The memory of their short time together was something she cherished, but she had tried to think of it as part of her past. He had given her a son, even if he did not know it, and that had changed her life for the better. Knowing that someone wanted her physically had given her more confidence in herself. She would be forever grateful to him for both those things, even if the memories still made her yearn for the possibility of something more in her marriage—some sharing of deeper thoughts and feelings beyond the practical conversations about the farms and their son that she had with Martin. When she imagined what that could be like, it was always Tom she thought of.

"Are you worried about Jamie? They'll have taken good care of him, you know." Martin was looking at her in concern.

Ellie managed a smile. "I've missed him."

"Do you wish you'd stayed at home?" Martin's expression was half amusement, half sympathy. "You were a great help selling the white mare—"

"Snowflake." Ellie corrected him without thinking. Martin's reluctance to give his horses anything but merely descriptive names had become a standing joke between them.

Martin gave a theatrical sigh. "Snowflake. Watching you putting her through her paces was what finally convinced Sir Frederick to buy. And if his wife looks as good on the animal as you did, his friends might come and see me when they want a new mount."

"I'm glad I went. I enjoyed the races. And the shopping." The trunk strapped behind the gig held more now than when they'd set out: a new pelisse, a bonnet, a dozen books, and some dress lengths for Agnes and Fanny. The stable hands from Bank Side were returning separately in the wagon.

They turned into the track leading to the house, and Fanny appeared around the side of the building with Dan close beside her and Jamie in her arms. As they drew closer, Ellie could see Jamie wriggling. Fanny put him down as Ellie jumped from the gig.

"Mama!"

Ellie picked him up, happiness bubbling up as he wrapped his arms around her neck. "Hello, Jamie. Have you been good for Fanny?"

Dan laughed and Fanny rolled her eyes as Jamie nodded energetically.

"Papa!" He wriggled, and toddled towards Martin when Ellie put him down.

"What's he been doing?" she asked, amid the shrieks as Martin tossed him in the air.

"Eating worms. Got into the henhouse and fell over. Had to scrape egg yolk out of his hair."

Ellie couldn't help laughing, and Fanny joined her. "I'm glad you're back, missus. He minds you better than he does me. Tea?"

Ellie nodded and followed her into the kitchen, unfastening her bonnet. "Has Palmer been around?"

"Not that anyone's noticed, missus. And I've been keeping a look-out. So has Agnes."

Dan would have been vigilant, too. Over the last two years, most of the incidents in Palmer's campaign of harassment had been minor. The most potentially damaging had been when a dog got into a field of new lambs the previous year, but Bates' dog had raised the alarm and Dan had shot the animal before it killed a second lamb. There was no proof it was Palmer's doing, but Martin thought it was just the kind of thing he *would* do, and no-one had come looking for the dog. Some time later, Kate had come in from one of her wanders about the fields saying she'd seen the ribbon man again, but Dan had come along and sent him away. That was many months ago now, though.

She hoped Palmer had given up—she still couldn't understand how he thought the petty harassment would persuade Martin to give him money.

Tom returned to her thoughts that evening after dinner, when she was sitting with Martin in the parlour. The war was over now, and there had been speculation in the papers about returning soldiers—the country could not keep paying for such a large army when there was no further need for it. Some regiments would be sent to the war in America, the papers said, but some could be disbanded. Officers in those regiments might sell out or be put on half pay. Was Tom one of them?

The address Tom had given her was in Kendal—his mother's home. Why, then, would he be in York? Had he found out that Jamie was his son? Sudden worry knotted her stomach—if Tom found out, what would he do? Would he want to see Jamie? Or want to take him away?

She took a deep breath, trying to dismiss those thoughts. Tom had seemed to be a kind man, and she could not believe that he would try to take Jamie away from her, or the man he loved as his father.

"Penny for your thoughts?" Martin's newspaper rested on his lap. "You were miles away."

"I was thinking about the end of the war." That was the truth, in a way. "It doesn't seem real, somehow." Peace had been declared six weeks ago, but the war had been a presence in everyone's minds for so long—most of Ellie's life—that it seemed strange to think it was finally over and there was no further threat of invasion.

"I don't suppose they'll disband many cavalry regiments—not right away, at least. I'm planning on concentrating more on good quality animals suited for normal riding, and the stage coach companies are always in need of horses. We will have some drop in income, no doubt, but the farm pays its own way, and we'll still be doing well enough even if Bank Side only makes half as much."

"That's all right, then." She'd known that, really. Martin often discussed his plans with her. And she shouldn't worry about Tom either. The man at the races might not have been him. Even if it had been, there was no reason for him to come in search of her.

CHAPTER 16

*D*uring the next week, Frank busied himself with new work that had come his way, without too much prodding from Tom. Tom spent several afternoons on a hired horse riding to nearby villages with some of Frank's remaining outstanding invoices. He kept his journeys short, not wanting to strain his shoulder too much. By the end of the week, he thought it was healed enough to stand a full day or two on horseback, although he still could not raise his hand above his head. He was restless, in part because of the uncertainty about his future in the army, but mainly because he couldn't help wondering whether Ellie's child was his son. And what he would think or feel if the child *was* his.

The latter thought had intruded into his mind too often for comfort. And his initial conclusion that the only way of resolving his questions was to speak to Ellie had not changed. She would be back at home now, with the races long over.

Tom told Frank he needed a couple of days away from the office and the city, hinting at a friend to see, and rode out of York the next afternoon on wet roads under a grey sky. He should have told his brother what he intended, of course, but he had only the vaguest of plans and didn't want Frank to talk him out of the trip. He would stay overnight in Thirsk and start the following day's enquiries by having a drink in the nearest tavern to the Wilsons' farm. He might be able to learn how Wilson was regarded in the area, and possibly the age of their son. A long shot, to be sure, but if the boy was too young to be his he wouldn't need to talk to Ellie. Frank had mentioned that the Wilsons bred horses, so he could pretend to be interested in buying a new mount.

The next morning he checked his map. The Wilsons' farm wasn't marked on it, but the village of Kirby Sutton was—the place where Wilson's banns had been read. He could ask for directions there. He just hoped the place had a tavern.

It did. The Farmers' Rest was next door to the church, the pair of buildings surrounded by half a dozen houses. It was a small tavern, the stable behind it only large enough to shelter a few horses. He loosened the girth and gave the boy loitering there a few pennies, then ventured into the taproom. He was the only customer, so he ordered a pint of ale and sat on a high stool at the bar.

"Quiet in here," he ventured to the landlord, and slid a coin across the bar. "Have one for yourself."

"I will, very kind o'yer, sir. Usually quiet at this time of day," he added as he poured a small mug for himself.

"I believe there's a place that sells horses hereabouts," Tom said. "Thought I might take a look as I was in the neighbourhood."

The landlord nodded. "Wilson; lives a few miles away. The horses are at Bank Side, though, a bit further on. He mainly breeds cavalry horses, but he does sell some for normal riding."

The door opened as the landlord was speaking. The man who entered wore work rough clothes, with a handkerchief loosely knotted around his throat and traces of dirt beneath his fingernails.

"Sexton," the landlord said, jerking his head towards the newcomer. "Who yer digging a hole for today, Isaac?"

"Old Mrs Philips. Burial's tomorrow."

The landlord shook his head. "Bad business, that. Philips'll miss her."

"Join us?" Tom said to the sexton. Two informants would be better than one.

"Don't mind if I do." He accepted the pint the landlord handed him and eyed Tom assessingly. "Don't see many strangers in these parts."

"I was asking about Wilson's horses," Tom said. "Seems his business might not be so good now the war is over. Pity—a good business in horses would be a tidy inheritance for his sons."

"'E'll be reet," the sexton said. "Likely makes a tidy amount from the other farm, and only one bairn to provide for." He had finished his pint, and pushed the empty mug towards the landlord. "I'll have another half. Thirsty work, digging in this weather."

The landlord glanced at Tom, who shook his head but slid another coin across the bar. "Have it on me. What kind of horses does Wilson breed?"

"Ones with four legs." The sexton cackled at his own joke. "No use asking us—all I know is that one end bites and t'other end kicks." His eyes narrowed. "Dunno why you didn't just go straight there."

Tom lifted his mug. "Came here for some ale, of course. But I'll be off there now if you'll direct me." He'd learned all he was going to here —any more questioning was likely to arouse suspicion.

He hadn't found out much at the Farmers' Rest, Tom reflected as he rode away, but he had learned something. Wilson seemed to be well respected in the area, and they had only one child. The only child in seven years of marriage, if he recalled the date on the certificate correctly. Ellie could well have believed she was barren—although remembering the sorrow in her eyes when she had said it, he hadn't seriously thought she'd lied to him about that.

He could easily be the child's father.

The landlord's directions were easy to follow, with only a few turnings in the winding lanes to negotiate. He came to a gate with a track leading towards a rambling set of stone buildings beside a field full of sheep with lambs. 'Knowle Farm' on the gate confirmed that this was the Wilsons' main farm.

Not wanting to loiter in the lane while he decided what to do, Tom rode on a little way to where the ground began to rise at the edge of the moor. Coming to a patch of woodland, he dismounted and leaned on a tree as he regarded the farm. He was close enough to see people in what looked like a vegetable patch beyond the rectangle of buildings, but too far away to make out much detail. A man was digging and, as he watched, a woman joined him, carrying a child on one hip. She paused by the digger, then went on into the field. From her gestures, she was talking to the boy about the animals, her affection for the child showing in every movement. She wore no bonnet, and the light hair he remembered gleamed in the sunshine. A bird flew overhead—a buzzard—and the two of them followed its flight, pointing upwards and turning as it headed for the moors behind Tom. He stepped back into the trees, not wanting to be caught watching.

He sat with his back against a tree, the image of the farm and its people still clear in his mind. That was the woman he had dreamed about for two years, with a child that could be his. He felt weighed down with loss—of the chance to get to know her better, a possible life together, and the son he couldn't acknowledge.

Should he still try to talk to her? He did want to know whether the boy was really his, although that was a selfish wish and should not decide his actions. But he also wanted to know that she was well and happy, and that her husband was not mistreating her in any way—as some men might do if they found out their wife was with child by another man.

Calling at the farm unannounced could arouse the suspicions he was keen to avoid. He could write a letter—or might there be some other way of contacting Ellie so that her husband did not find out? She'd had an address to write to him, though, and surely she would have done so if she needed help?

No, talking to her would be purely to satisfy his own curiosity, and he should leave well alone—as Frank had advised. He didn't want to just go back, but it was the right thing to do.

Decision made, he mounted the horse and set out to retrace his route; he could be back in York by mid-afternoon.

He didn't get very far. As he rode around a corner in the lane, he found a horseman blocking his way—a stable hand, by the looks of his clothing. He had burn scars across half his face, and he held a rifle.

Tom stopped his horse, keeping his hands on the reins. There was a pistol in one of his coat pockets, but although the man's rifle wasn't cocked or pointing at him, it would take only a second to lift it and fire. Besides, this was an unlikely place for a robbery, and a thief would already be aiming the weapon at him.

"I told Palmer I'd gut him if he showed his face near the farm again," the man said, in tones the more menacing for being quiet. "The same goes for you, or anyone else he sends."

Palmer?

If Wilson was concerned enough to have someone at the farm keeping watch for intruders, Palmer must have done more than just enquire about the legality of the Wilsons' marriage. And this man had come armed. Palmer wasn't merely a nuisance—he could be a threat. To Ellie, and to her son.

That changed things.

Tom had no right to protect them, but he couldn't leave without asking Ellie whether he could help in some way.

"I'm not working for anyone," he protested, trying to think. Could he take advantage of this situation? He'd ruled out calling at the farm pretending to be a family friend as he couldn't make that plausible; her husband would know more about Ellie's family than Tom did. But this man would not have that knowledge, nor was Ellie here to be surprised into an incautious comment.

"Why were you watching the farm?" the man asked.

"I was wondering what to do." A request from a friend, perhaps?

The click as the horseman cocked the rifle was loud in Tom's ears.

Keep it vague. "I'm just returned from France," he began. "A dying friend asked me to give a message to Mrs Wilson, but all he told me was that she lives on a farm near Thirsk. I wasn't sure if this was the right place."

The man's brows rose. "Why not just go and ask at the farm?"

Tom shrugged. "I didn't know if Mrs Wilson would want to see me." His hand moved towards the pocket where he kept his notebook, but he thought better of it as the rifle moved. "If I write a note, will you give it to her?"

"Your name?"

"Allerby. Captain."

The man stared at Tom, then finally nodded. Tom tore out a page and scribbled a line, asking only to speak to Ellie. Then he twisted it into a screw and held it out. "If you don't want me near the farm, I'll wait here."

Tom dismounted as the man headed off, watching as he rode out of sight behind the farm buildings. Then he retreated into the cool shade of the trees to wait.

"Did you talk to him?" Ellie asked, as Dan led his mount back towards the stables. "Is it Palmer?"

Dan was staying at the farm for a few days while Martin was away on business, and had spotted a man on horseback watching the farm. Now Dan was back and the man was still there.

"No, missus. He said he wanted to talk to you. Gave me a note." Dan had a twist of paper in his hand, but did not hold it out to her. "Said his name was Allerby. He weren't sure if you'd want to see him."

Ellie felt as if her heart had stopped for a moment, then she reached out and took the note. Her hand shook, but Dan did not seem to notice.

There were only a few words. *Please can we talk? Tom*

The man she'd seen at the races *had* been Tom. But why was he here? She felt a little glow of pleasure that he had come to find her, quickly swamped by worry. How had he discovered where she lived? Did he know about Jamie?

If Tom thought he might be Jamie's father, what would he do? He had no legal right to have anything to do with her son, she knew that. But not having a right didn't stop some men trying to do what they wanted to—just look at Palmer.

She'd dismissed those fears a week ago when they returned from the races. But knowing it *was* Tom, and that he was only a couple of fields away, made her less sure. Even though she had known him for such a short time, she could not really believe that the man she'd shared that evening with could be anything like Martin's cousin, but she must find out what he wanted in case she was mistaken.

"I'll go and see him now."

But Dan didn't move out of the way when she went to walk past him to fetch her bonnet.

"Are you sure, missus? He could be lying. Could be working for Palmer."

Ellie shook her head. "I cannot see how Palmer would know to use that name. He was a friend of my brother, I think."

Only after she said it did she wonder if she might be contradicting something that Tom had said to Dan, but Dan showed no surprise. Instead, he followed her around to the front of the house, still leading the horse.

"I'll keep my eye on him while you talk."

"I'm sure there'll be no trouble, Dan."

Ellie.

Tom took in her face as she approached. She looked lovely, with a healthy glow to her skin that he recalled well. But there was wariness in her eyes, not the friendship or humour that had endeared her to him at that inn and in his memories since then.

He suddenly felt nervous, uneasy. Had his dreams changed his memories of that night? Made of her something unreal? Even if they hadn't, the events of two years could change a person.

He wanted to smile a greeting, to step forward and take her hand. But she was married, with a son, and might well have come here only to send him on his way.

She came to a halt in front of him, beneath the trees. "Captain Allerby. I am happy to see you survived. Are you well?"

Tom swallowed disappointment; her expression was stiff, the

greeting one she might say to any acquaintance who'd been in the war.

"Thank you. A damaged shoulder, merely, which is mending."

She nodded, and her face relaxed a little.

"Are *you* well, Ellie?"

"Yes. That is… How did you find me? Why are you here?"

The first part was easier to answer. "I saw you at the races, and asked someone who you were." He hesitated, then said it anyway. "I intended to try to find you when I returned from France, until… That is, I thought you were a widow. When we met before."

Her brow creased in puzzlement. "Why would you think I was…? Oh, I was wearing black because I'd been to my aunt's funeral."

"That interfering woman said something about you being a widow, and you didn't correct her. Although it was none of her business, of course. I assumed the Ben you talked about was your dead husband."

"He was my brother—did I not say that?"

Her gaze became unfocused. Were her memories of that night together as vivid as his?

"Perhaps I didn't." She met his eyes. "We became very close after our mother died. I still miss him, but what you told me helped me to focus on his enjoyment of life." She put out a hand as if to touch him, but dropped it. "I can never thank you enough for that, Tom. Ben was so keen to join the army, but he knew the risks and accepted them."

"I'm pleased I could help."

Ellie rubbed her arms as he spoke, and Tom looked at her pelisse—it was much thinner than his coat, and the sun's warmth had not penetrated beneath the trees. "Shall we walk while we talk?"

She hesitated, then nodded. "Up onto the moor, perhaps?"

CHAPTER 17

*T*om had to hurry to keep up as Ellie set off at a brisk pace. He smiled to himself as he followed—this was the woman who had ridden off into the storm without a qualm. He hadn't thought her the kind of woman to betray her husband, but how well did he really know her? Perhaps she had a reason?

And what of his actions? Would he have even gone into her room if he'd known at the time that she was married? He ought not to have done, that was certain, but after the way she had been in his thoughts since that night, he couldn't now say what his previous self might have done.

Their pace slowed as the track through the woods became steeper, but she still had breath enough to speak. "*Carpe diem* was one of Ben's sayings."

"Seize the day?"

She turned her head to look at him, then away again. "Exactly. And he also told me, several times, that I... anyone... would regret things *not* done." She shrugged. "I am not... not an adulteress by habit, Captain, if that is what you are thinking."

. . .

"I'm not." Tom said the words without thinking. When he'd first discovered that she wasn't a widow after all, he had briefly wondered if she made a habit of sleeping with chance-met men, but her response to their intimacy had not been those of a wanton.

They came out of the woods into the sunshine of the moor. For a few moments there was only the faint whisper of the breeze in the heather and the liquid warbling of a skylark overhead. Ellie lifted her face to the sky, then gazed around and went to sit on a small outcrop of rock beside a stunted hawthorn tree. Tom sat beside her.

She turned her face to his, her smile tentative. "I last saw Ben here, on a day very much like this. There were curlews calling then, and ever since I've associated them with him. I avoided this place in the two years between his death and our meeting, but after we talked... Well, I could enjoy it again, and remember mostly the good times. And now the curlew's call sounds joyful to me, not mournful."

The sharing of their thoughts and concerns had meant as much to her as it had to him—that knowledge made Tom wish once more that she had not been married. He almost told her so, but that was pointless and not why he was here. Asking about her son wasn't the main reason, either, not after what her man had said about Palmer. But this was likely to be his only chance to find out.

He took a deep breath. "You have a son."

Her smile faded, but she answered readily enough. "Yes. James Benjamin, after Martin's... my husband's... grandfather and my brother. We call him Jamie."

"I knew you wanted children."

"I thought I was barren. I was not lying when I told you that, but it appears I was mistaken, and the problem was not with me." Colour rose to her cheeks. "That is one reason... that is why I cannot regret what we did together, even though I should not have done it. You gave me a son."

He almost asked how she could be sure, but the only answer would be that her husband had not been going to her bed at the time the boy —Jamie—was conceived. That could also explain why she'd asked him

145

to stay that night. But it was none of his business, and he was not going to embarrass her by asking.

Jamie *was* his. She would not have said so if there was any doubt about it.

He had a son, but not one he could ever acknowledge. How could he feel so sad at losing a child he'd never met? Whose existence he hadn't even suspected a week ago?

"My husband knows," Ellie went on, talking faster now. "He forgave my... my action, and is happy that we have a child. He is a good father, Tom, and I wouldn't want anyone to try to take—"

"Ellie, stop!" The idea that he might break up her family by trying to claim Jamie as his son brought back the hurt. What she thought of him should not matter, but it did. "Ellie," he went on more gently, suppressing the urge to reach out to her. "I wanted to know, that is all. And to be reassured that all is well with you and the child. With Jamie. I would love to know him, and to be a father to him, but I cannot subject you or Jamie to the scandal that would ensue. Nor would I ever try to take him from you."

Ellie felt limp with relief; there was sincerity in his face and voice. Was there hurt, too? She felt ashamed of her fear that he might cause trouble for them if he knew.

"You helped me, too, Ellie. The memory of that night got me though some difficult times. I hoped that when I returned..." His words tailed off and he looked away, his jaw set. "No matter; that is past."

It did matter. She had deceived him, although not intentionally, but what was done could not be changed.

"I'm glad I could help you." What more could she say? The knowledge that Tom had been thinking of her as she had him gave her a warm glow inside, but wasn't going to help her to forget him. A vision of life with the three of them together crossed her mind. She dismissed it. There was no future for her with Tom, even if he still wanted more than this meeting. She could not bear to leave Jamie behind to be with Tom, nor could she take Jamie away from Martin—for Martin's sake as well as Jamie's. And either action would cause scandal that could dog Jamie's life and harm Martin's business, and possibly give Martin's cousin more reason to suspect his inclinations.

"Is Jamie happy?" Tom asked.

"He is." She swallowed a lump in her throat. "Martin loves him as if he was his own son, and everyone else dotes on him, too. The others don't know that Martin did not father him."

Tom took off his hat and ran a hand through his hair. "Ellie, I was watching the farm to see if there was a way to speak to you without others knowing. But I realised that getting an answer to my question wasn't worth risking your happiness, and I was on my way back to York when your man stopped me. And now—even though your husband already knows of me, I can't think he will be pleased that we've talked. Will your man tell him?"

"Don't worry about that. I told Dan you were a friend of my brother. But I will tell Martin myself—I owe him that much. If he *is* unhappy, he will not harm me or Jamie. He could never do so."

If he'd been leaving, why had he changed his mind? "Why did you send a note instead of going on your way?"

Tom didn't answer immediately, his gaze fixed on something behind her. Ellie turned to see Dan sitting on his horse at the point where the trees on the slope gave way to rough moorland grass. In sight, but well out of earshot. She waved, and after a moment Dan turned his horse and rode away down the slope. "It was only Dan Cole —come to check all is well, I suppose."

"You have a good protector," Tom said.

"I do, yes."

"Ellie—why do you *need* protecting?"

Ellie frowned, and Tom wondered if she would answer. It was her husband's business to look after Ellie and Jamie, not his, but he wanted to. He couldn't bear the idea of something happening to her that he might have prevented.

"Your man assumed I was working for Palmer, and threatened me with a rifle. Is Palmer a danger to you?"

"He is my husband's cousin." Her frown deepened, and her next words came out sharply. "You said Palmer, not 'someone called Palmer'. As if you know him."

"I know *of* him. The person I asked about you at the races was my brother. He is an attorney in York, and he knows where you live because Palmer asked him to investigate your marriage a couple of years ago."

Her frown gave way to surprise. "Investigate? What is there to investigate?"

"I'm afraid I looked through my brother's files. That's where I found out you had a son. Palmer was trying to prove Jamie was illegitimate. I don't understand how he thought Jamie might not be your husband's child, for how could he know about our meeting?"

"He couldn't. He probably thought it because... because he wished it. If he *knew* anything, he would have spread gossip and scandal long ago."

That hesitation—there was something she hadn't told him. "Ellie, that does not explain why your man came brandishing a rifle to see me off. *Is* Palmer a threat to you?"

"A nuisance rather than a threat." She dropped her gaze to where her fingers twisted together. "But it's possible he might become a threat."

"Tell me?"

She let out a breath and shrugged. "He has the idea that he should have one of the farms, and keeps asking Martin for money. Martin did give him some in the past, but the requests became demands, and kept coming, so Martin refused. Now he... harasses us. It began with little things, like making snide comments about our lack of children. Then a couple of years ago he started causing actual harm—damaging the henhouse so a fox could get in, and letting a dog into the field with the lambs. Things like that. It sounds silly to worry about such little incidents. But I didn't know about him trying to prove Jamie illegitimate." Her shoulders slumped. "I keep hoping he will stop, and I worry that he will do something worse."

"If I can help in any way, Ellie, let me know. I'll be in York for some time—you can write to my brother's office in Davygate. He might be able to assist if I have returned to my regiment—Palmer is no longer his client, as that job is finished."

"Thank you. It's the not knowing what he will do that worries me at times—probably much more than it ought to."

Could he help there? Alleviate her worry, at least. "I could try to find out, if you permit. He hasn't paid Frank yet—I could talk to him under that pretext. He will not know it has anything to do with you."

Her face brightened, but then she shook her head. "It is best we do not see each other again, Tom, much though I wish it could be otherwise."

"I wish it, too." They weren't the same people they had been two years ago, but he still felt the connection between them, the physical attraction as well as the emotional one. Something they could have built on, if only they were free to do so. "My offer isn't an excuse to see you again, but to do what I can to prevent any harm coming to you or Jamie. You will only hear from me if I find out anything you need to know."

"In that case, yes. Thank you."

Good. "May I tell my brother what you have told me about Palmer? It will go no further, and it is possible that his legal knowledge may be of use."

She considered a moment, her gaze distant, then nodded. "I don't see why not. Much of it is already known—by our farm workers and some of Martin's friends." She stood and shook out her skirts. "This must be goodbye." Her smile was sad. "I expect Dan will be waiting for me in the woods, so I will go first. Be well, Tom."

She held out her hand and he grasped it. Not shaking it, as friends would, but just holding it. Holding her in the only way he could. Then she was walking away.

"Be happy, Ellie, and make Jamie happy, too." He spoke the words out loud, even though she was too far away to hear them.

He'd found out what he'd come to discover. Ellie's son was his, but also not his. And Ellie—she wasn't really the woman he'd been dreaming about these last years, but the reality still attracted him. She was still someone he thought he could have shared himself and his life with, if only circumstances had been different.

He stood there for ten minutes or so, gazing across the rolling expanse of the heather. Ellie found peace here, but Tom had never felt so lonely.

Martin had not yet returned when Ellie got back to the farm. Dan had been waiting for her, but after she assured him that all was well, he rode on ahead. She needed the time alone while she walked to settle her mind. Having indulged in a few brief moments of what might have been, happy at the idea that Tom had been intending to find her, she resolutely turned her mind to practical matters. She was pleased that Tom was back safe from the war, but thinking about him could only upset the contentment she'd tried so hard to achieve.

Dinner was on the table by the time Martin arrived, and there was no chance to speak to him privately. When the pigeon pie and vegetables had been served, Fanny asked Dan about the man they'd seen spying. Ellie suddenly had difficulty swallowing the food in her mouth.

"Weren't nothing to do with Palmer," Dan said.

"He was a friend of my brother's." Ellie got that in before Dan could say any more. Although that was what she'd told Dan, she hadn't been sure he believed her. She would tell Martin the truth when they were alone. She felt Martin looking at her, but kept her eyes on her plate as Fanny and Bates discussed one of the cows that was looking sickly.

When they retired to the parlour, Martin handed her the customary glass of port and settled into his chair. Normally, he'd have told her about his trip—even if there was little more to describe than the state of the roads or the weather. But he was frowning, and the silence began to feel awkward, nerve-racking.

"Why would a friend of your brother not just come to the farm, Ellie? It was him, wasn't it? That's why you talked to him on the moor instead of here."

They both knew who he meant. Ellie tried to read Martin's expression. Was he worried or angry? She wasn't sure.

"Yes. I was going to tell you, but this has been the first time we've been private since you got home."

Martin nodded, his frown not changing. "What did he want?"

"He saw us at the races, and he found out we had a son. He just wanted to know whether... whether he—"

"Whether he was Jamie's father? What does he want with Jamie?"

Of course—if *she* had worried that Tom might want to take Jamie away, why wouldn't Martin think that, too?

"Nothing, Martin. He only wanted to know, nothing else."

Her answer didn't reassure him. "How can you be sure of that? How can you trust him—a man who... who slept with another man's wife!"

Ellie bit back a retort. Because she had asked him to stay, that aspect of Tom's behaviour hadn't really struck her until he'd told her of his assumption a few hours ago. But she could see how Martin would think that made Tom untrustworthy. "I was wearing black after Aunt Harriet's funeral. He thought I was a widow."

Martin's expression relaxed a little. "And now that he knows?"

"Nothing. He wanted to know that I was well, and Jamie. He won't come here again. I will not see him again."

He still wasn't happy. She tried again. "Martin, I could not leave Jamie, and I will not take Jamie away from you, for both your sakes. My seeing him will not change that."

He stared into this glass for some time, then finally lifted his head and nodded. "I'll have to take your word for all of that. But how did he know where to find you?"

"His brother told him who you were. Your cousin had employed him—his brother, I mean—to check on our marriage. A coincidence, to be sure, but he could have found out by other means eventually."

"Allerby?"

Ellie was as surprised as Martin looked. "You know him?" Then she was suspicious. "*How* do you know? Are you still hiding things from me?"

"I didn't want to worry you."

She could see he meant it. Suspicion turned to exasperation. "I will worry *more* about what you may be concealing from me. What has this attorney to do with us? And how did you come to know about it?"

"The parish clerk at Quernby wrote to me, telling me someone had requested a copy of our marriage entry in the register. He gave me Allerby's name and address. I went to see what it was all about. Luke was apparently trying to demonstrate that Jamie is illegitimate. A pointless exercise—I can leave the farms to whomever I wish."

Ellie was curious about Tom's brother, but it was best not to ask. "Very well. But Martin, will you promise not to hide these things from me in future? Otherwise I will worry that something *has* happened that I don't know about."

"I promise. And will you promise me that... that seeing your... the other Allerby will not change things between us?"

"I will."

Their meeting would change her thoughts and feelings—for a while, at least—but she could not let that affect her dealings with Martin or anyone else. She'd achieved a degree of contentment before Tom reappeared; she had to hope she could do so again. It was only when she was preparing for bed that she recalled Tom's offer to look into Palmer's activities, and that she had not told Martin about it.

No matter—what could Tom find that would be serious enough for him to contact her?

CHAPTER 18

*T*om reached York late that evening, too tired to do anything more than return the hired horse and fall into his bed. When he awoke the sun was already high and Finn's truckle bed empty. His shoulder still hurt, even after a night's rest. Any travelling in the near future would have to be by coach.

He had a quick breakfast in the taproom, then settled his arm in the sling and set off for Frank's office. Now he'd found Ellie and spoken to her, he didn't know what to do with himself. He could chase up a few more invoices, but that task would soon be finished. Could he be of any further help to Frank? He needed to do something to keep his mind off Ellie.

Finn was sitting on the high stool at the clerk's desk in Frank's outer office, his feet dangling in mid-air and a slate and copybook before him. "You're up, then!"

"So I am," Tom said, cheered by Finn's grin. The signs of his fight at the races were fading, too. "Are your letters improving?"

The smile vanished as Tom inspected the wobbly writing. It was legible, but couldn't be described as neat.

"Not bad. Keep practising. Is he in?"

Finn nodded, returning to his task with a grimace. In the office,

Frank got up to take another mug from the cupboard and poured Tom some coffee from a pot on his desk. "Still hot enough, just about. Did you enjoy your trip?"

"Well enough." He took the cup and sat down.

"Did you manage to talk to her?"

"Yes, I…" Tom blinked. He hadn't told Frank where he'd been going. "How did you know?"

Frank chuckled. "I guessed."

Tom sighed. "I fell into your trap, didn't I?" He shouldn't mind—he'd used the same technique when questioning soldiers about their misdeeds. He was pleased to see Frank looking well rested and clear-eyed—his brother hadn't hit the brandy bottle too hard while he'd been away.

"Did you find what you wanted to?" Frank asked

Tom didn't want to reply—he hadn't really come to terms yet with the knowledge that he'd fathered a child. He had asked about Frank's private life to help him, not just out of curiosity. But Frank deserved an answer.

"Yes, Jamie Wilson is my son. No, I'm not going to try to meet him or see him."

Frank's head tilted to one side. "Are you pleased? Or the opposite?"

"I don't really know." Ellie was happy she had a child, and he was pleased for her—but he wasn't going to discuss Ellie with Frank. "I also found out more about Palmer." He repeated what Ellie had told him about Palmer's harassment. "The invoice I saw was unpaid; I thought I might use that as a reason to see him."

"To what end?"

Tom shrugged. "Just general reconnaissance, really. He sounds vindictive, causing worry and harm even though his actions are of no benefit to himself. If there's any chance he might try anything more serious, it would be useful to know beforehand. I did ask Mrs Wilson if I might do so," he added, seeing Frank's frown. "It's not an excuse to see her again."

"Fair enough."

"Frank, why did you take Palmer's job? You knew it was futile before you wrote to that parish clerk."

Frank shrugged. "Palmer called not long after I left Mortenson and I wasn't busy. I explained that there was no point, but he persisted. I gather he'd been shown the door by several other attorneys. In the end it was easier just to do as he asked. Does this mean you're about to head off to wherever the fellow lives?"

"Northallerton," Tom said. "He came a long way to find an attorney."

Frank shrugged. "Perhaps the local one knew he was unlikely to be paid."

"I'll not go for a few days, though—that'll give time for my shoulder to feel better. And if Finn's uncle replies in that time, I'll take him to Darlington and stop at Northallerton on the way back."

"All right." Frank picked up a pen and fiddled with it before looking back at Tom. "I've been thinking…"

"Go on."

"It's been good having you around, Tom. I needed a kick up the backside to help me get back to all this." He waved a hand around the office. "How long are you staying in York?"

"Until my shoulder is fit for purpose. A few more weeks, perhaps longer. I might need to go to London at some point to see an army surgeon about it."

"Do you… I mean, I could find a bigger place, with two bedrooms. Would you stay with me? It'd be cheaper between us than you continuing to pay for a room at the Prince Rupert. It's too easy to drink too much when I'm alone in my room."

"There's Finn, too—for the moment, at least."

"We'll make space."

"Very well." Tom resigned himself to more evenings listening to Frank's woes, but it would be worth it if it helped him. Now might be the time to mention another source of help. "Frank—one reason Mama was worried about you was that Mortenson wrote to her. He was concerned about you."

Frank's lips became a thin line. "He should mind his own damned business."

Tom ignored that. "Go and see him, Frank. He was your friend once. He didn't strike me as the kind of man who would betray a friend and business partner in the way you assumed. He could put more work your way."

"I'll think about it."

It wasn't quite an agreement, but it would do for now. Although Tom was wondering if Frank had spoken to Susannah yet, he decided that this wasn't the best time to ask. He stood and picked up his hat. "I'll start looking for new lodgings then."

He left Frank staring into space. Finn was happy for an excuse to get out of the office, and they set off together to enquire about rooms to rent.

Several days later, while he was concluding arrangements for a new set of rooms, Tom received a letter from Finn's uncle, saying that of course he would give the lad a home.

"Do I have to go?" Finn asked, when Tom told him what the letter said. "I like it here."

"I like having you here," Tom said. "But I'll be going back to the army soon. You can't come with me, you know that."

Finn nodded reluctantly.

"We'll see what your uncle's like, as I promised."

Finn made no further protest, and they boarded a north-bound stage coach the next morning. Tom's shoulder was feeling much better, but not so much so that he was about to try riding fifty miles. The stage would be quicker, too.

They reached the smithy in the early evening. It looked prosperous —a solid building in good repair, with an adjoining house. Joseph Robson was a large, brawny man, as might be expected of a black-smith, and his wife thin and tending to the sour-faced. But they welcomed Finn warmly enough, and made no objection when Tom asked to see where the lad would sleep. Mrs Robson led the way up to a tiny room under the eaves.

"Do you like it?" Tom asked Finn, when Mrs Robson left them there.

The bed was yet to be made up, but Finn sat on it and prodded the mattress. "Bed's soft enough."

"You won't feel lonely on your own here?"

Finn shrugged. "I don't know their children. It might be better here."

"Very well. Let's go and talk to Mrs Robson."

"It looks a very comfortable little room," Tom said, not exaggerating by much. "We'll fetch Finn's bag from the coaching inn. Has he missed dinner?"

"I'll find him something when you get back," Mrs Robson promised.

"Well, what do you think?" Tom asked, when they were well out of earshot.

"Seems all right." It was said without enthusiasm.

"Your uncle said in his letter that you could make yourself useful with the horses—you'll enjoy that. And if you really don't like it, you can write to me and I'll see what I can do. You can write well enough for that." He tore a page out of his pocketbook and wrote down the address of Frank's office. "Here, keep this safe. I'll come round in the morning before I get the coach back. All right?"

"All right."

The next morning, Finn cheerfully reported a fine supper and comfortable bed. The other Robson children had seemed friendly as well, so Tom bade him farewell and set off to look for Palmer. With no Finn to distract him, his thoughts turned not to Ellie, this time, but to Jamie. Jamie, whom he'd only seen from a distance and would probably never see again. Would he turn out as resilient as Finn? As talkative and trusting?

He hoped so. And without the trials Finn had had to endure in his short life. That was why he was getting off this coach at Northallerton instead of going straight back to York.

· · ·

Tom had a quick pint and a bite to eat at the Golden Lion in Northallerton, and arranged for a room for the night. The waiter gave him directions to Palmer's address, and Tom found the place in a back street. The house was recently painted and spotlessly clean, and the woman who answered the door was well dressed in sober brown with lace on her cap and around her neckline.

"I'm looking for a Mr Luke Palmer, ma'am." Tom doffed his hat. "Does he still live here?"

She raised her brows. "Another one after him? No—he moved out of here six months ago when he couldn't pay."

A nuisance, but Tom wasn't surprised. "Sorry to bother you, but do you know where I might find him?"

She sighed. "Try the Plough." She pointed down the street. "Turn left at the end, then the second or third street on the right."

"Thank you."

She shut the door almost before Tom finished speaking. He found the Plough easily enough. It looked like a drinking establishment—too small to have rooms for guests, and no signs of anyone eating. It smelled like it, too—of spilled ale not cleaned up, and stale tobacco smoke. He ordered a pint of ale and asked if the barman knew someone called Palmer.

"Comes in most afternoons. Plays cards in the back room." The barman jerked his head towards a door at one end of the room, and finished pouring the ale. "See his coin before you play, though."

"Is he there now?"

"Didn't see him come in."

"Take a look, will you?" Tom slid the price of his ale across the bar, and added another coin. "But don't tell him I'm here."

The barman rolled his eyes, but the coins disappeared. He shook his head when he returned. "Not yet."

"Let me know if he arrives?" He placed another coin on the bar and took a seat near the open window, where the breeze helped to dilute the fusty air. He hoped he didn't have to grease the fist of too many more people—he was low enough on funds already.

It was nearly two hours before the barman caught his eye. Tom had downed another couple of pints of ale by then, and learned far more than he ever wanted to know about tanning and working leather from a loquacious customer. He muttered some excuse and crossed to the bar.

"Just went in," the barman said. "Blue jacket."

Tom nodded his thanks. The four men around the table looked up as he entered, the man who was dealing pausing for a moment with one card held in mid-air. Fortunately only one of them was wearing a blue jacket. He looked nothing out of the ordinary—of medium height, running a little to fat, with thinning sandy hair.

"Mr Palmer? A word with you, if you please."

"I'm busy," Palmer muttered, his attention on the cards in his hand.

"I have come some distance to find you, Mr Palmer. I'm sure you would prefer to discuss our business in private." When Palmer made no move, Tom took the folded invoice from his pocket and placed it on the table, then retreated and leaned on the wall by the door— giving the impression, he hoped, of someone prepared to wait as long as it took.

"See what he wants, Palmer, or read the damned note," one of the others said. "We're waiting."

Palmer slapped his cards down and unfolded the invoice, his brows drawing together. "What's this?"

"An invoice for work done. An invoice that is more than a year overdue for settlement."

"He didn't succeed. Why should I pay?"

"Attorneys do not do business on those terms, Mr Palmer." As the man well knew. "Do you also believe that you should not pay your gambling debts if you lose the game?"

"What's this, Palmer? Being dunned again?" The speaker chortled, but there was an edge to his voice. "Don't want you getting a clap on the shoulder before you've paid what you owe us, do we?"

Palmer stood. "I told you—I'll be coming into money soon. I'll pay."

"You've been saying that for the last year, and you never come up with enough to pay *all* you owe. See if there's anyone else wants to make a fourth on your way out, will you? Someone who *can* play and pay." The speaker gathered up the dealt cards and began to shuffle them, ignoring Palmer's scowl.

Tom picked up the invoice and followed him out onto the street. Palmer stopped at the entrance to an alley—this was no more private than the taproom would have been, but the passers-by would take less interest in an argument here than Palmer's acquaintances in the Plough.

"How dare you embarrass me in front of my friends?" Clearly furious, he nevertheless managed to keep his voice down.

"If you'd paid the money owed, I wouldn't have needed to talk to you at all."

"I'll come into some money soon." Palmer's manner reminded Tom of a sulky child, but this was no laughing matter. The actions of this man had led to Wilson having an armed man to protect his wife and household.

"Really? Wasn't that what you were trying to do when you employed my brother?" He waved the invoice at Palmer. "That didn't work. We need the money now, not in another year or two."

"Your *brother*?"

"Yes. What of it?"

"Nothing." He took the invoice and peered at the amount. "It's not a great deal of money; it cannot be urgent."

"If it's not a great deal of money, you won't have any difficulty paying it, will you? If you don't, you'll find yourself in a sponging house soon enough."

Palmer sneered. "You won't do that. It'll cost you more than this is worth to get a warrant."

"Wrong. An attorney can get a warrant cheaply." Tom had no idea whether that was true, but Palmer wouldn't know either. "And if I ask around, I'm sure there will be plenty of tradesmen here willing to share the cost to get you to pay what you owe. Or even the *friends* you were playing cards with."

That had been a guess, too, but a good one. Palmer swallowed hard, his Adam's apple visibly moving. "Like I said, I should be coming into some money soon."

"You said that to your friends, and they didn't believe you. How are you going to get this money?"

Palmer's eyes slid sideways and he shuffled his feet.

Not a legal scheme, then. "The money, Palmer. I just want the money—I don't care how you get it. If you can convince me you *will* get money, and soon, I'll wait. If not, expect a visit from a bailiff."

Palmer tugged at his neckcloth. "I... Let me think about it."

"You've got until this evening. Where's a good place to talk in this town?"

"The Dog and Duck. Back Lane." Palmer pointed. "That way."

"Be there at eight."

Palmer nodded and scurried off. Tom sighed and headed for the Golden Lion to while away the time. What should he do if Palmer had a plan that didn't involve the Wilsons? Perhaps warn the potential victims. And if Palmer didn't show up, all he would have achieved would be to confirm his impression that Palmer was a vindictive wastrel.

CHAPTER 19

"Success?" Frank asked, as Tom walked into the sitting room of their new lodging.

"That depends on what you count as success." He found the invoice in his satchel and put it on the table, then slumped into an armchair. "I didn't get the money, but Palmer has a plan to repair his finances. It may work, but even if it doesn't, it will be deeply unpleasant for Ell—the Wilsons."

"Go on."

Tom loosened his neckcloth. He felt grubby—from the journey, and from associating with a worm like Palmer. "He spent some considerable time on a self-pitying rant about how unfairly he's been treated—by Wilson, his grandfather, and apparently also everyone to whom he owes money. But basically, he is planning to get Wilson hanged for sodomy."

Frank sat up straighter in his chair. "Sodomy? Really? How is that supposed to help him? If Wilson has any sense, he'll have made a will leaving the farm to his wife and son."

"Palmer seems to think he could get that overturned—some nonsense about Wilson inheriting some of it from his mother, not through the male line. If not, he'll try to get guardianship of the boy."

Or he had some plan to get rid of Ellie and Jamie, too. Tom had manged to resist the impulse to throttle Palmer. He'd even entertained himself on the journey back by trying to think how he could dispose of Palmer without being found out, though he knew he could never bring himself to do so—premeditated murder was very different from killing men in the heat of battle. "He wasn't explicit, but I think he's found a local man who'll state under oath that Wilson forced him behind a tavern."

"And such things, once in the open, will be talked of widely even if proven to be false."

Tom hesitated before speaking again, but Frank was the brains here and needed all the facts. And suppositions. "The thing is, I think it's possible there may be some truth in it. He—Palmer, I mean—seems to have suspected that Wilson is that way inclined for some years. That might be why he initially tried to prove that Wilson is not the child's father." It could also explain Ellie's actions and responses that night at the Boar's Head.

"Or it could be a random accusation."

Tom shrugged. "We can't know. Wilson wouldn't admit it if we asked him. Does that make you disinclined to help me?"

"Innocent until proven guilty," Frank said, with a shrug. "Does it discourage you?"

"No. For the same reason as you, and to protect Mrs Wilson and her son. But also because I've known—still know—a few officers who I'm pretty sure have similar... tastes. It doesn't stop them being damned good soldiers, and good friends, too. As long as they're not forcing their attentions on unwilling men, what they do with their own bodies is up to them, as far as I'm concerned."

"It's a sin against God?" Frank made it a question.

"Then they can answer to God when they die. What do you think?"

"Each to his own. As you say, it's up to them."

"I persuaded Palmer that he couldn't be seen to be involved in the plot if he wanted to get Wilson's farms afterwards. So now I'm a co-conspirator, helping him for a cut of the proceeds." The nature of Palmer's plan had taken him by surprise, and that had been the only thing he could think of in the moment to enable him to keep track of what Palmer was doing, even though the idea disgusted him.

"What did you promise to do?"

"I offered to find out about Wilson's recent movements, to ensure that the so-called evidence his witness provides cannot be easily disproved. You are not included in this conspiracy, by the way."

"Good of you."

Tom wasn't sure whether his brother was being sarcastic, but Frank appeared to be thinking hard now and he didn't want to interrupt.

"Are you sure the evidence is fabricated?" Frank said, after a while.

"Pretty sure, yes. If it wasn't, why wouldn't the man just go to the constables? Why would Palmer be involved at all?"

Frank stared into space again, so Tom stood and glanced at two letters lying on the table with his name on. One was from Mama; the other had an army frank on it. He quickly broke the seal on that one and skimmed the text, letting out a silent breath of relief that he still had some time before having to report to his unit. He didn't want to be ordered elsewhere before the threat to Ellie and her family had been removed.

Mama's packet enclosed a letter from a friend in his battalion describing their current billet in a town not far from Toulouse and the way they were being wined and dined by the leading residents, who were apparently glad to finally be free of Bonaparte. But there were rumours they were soon to return to England.

"News?" Frank had come out of his abstraction.

"Not exactly. I'm to report to the second battalion at Hythe in four weeks." To be prodded by the regimental surgeon, no doubt, before they decided whether he could rejoin his company. Even though his shoulder still pained him when overused, he almost had full movement back. Apart, perhaps, from not being able to scratch all of his back with that arm, but that could hardly matter. The men would likely be given a few months rest before being shipped off to another campaign, so even if his shoulder muscles needed building up, there would be time.

"Not back to France?"

"No—the first battalion is about to be brought home."

"Oh well, at least you'll still be in this country."

For a few months, possibly. But the south coast was nearly three hundred miles away. "Did you come to any conclusion about the Palmer matter?"

"Only that this should be dealt with before it gets as far as a court, if possible, and before you have to leave. I'll have a word with Mortenson—I went to see him yesterday, as you suggested, and made a start on putting our friendship back as it was. He might know who the local magistrate is near Wilson's farm. And Wilson will have to be warned—and give his blessing for us to interfere."

"Do you have a plan?"

"I have some ideas. I'll let you know when they deserve to be called a plan."

Contentment didn't always come easily to Ellie during the days following her talk with Tom. Her usual activities about the farm and with the horses kept her busy enough, but too many things reminded her of things she could not have. Playing with Jamie, and yearning for more children. Sitting with Martin in the evenings, and wishing for someone who *wanted* to share her bed. And when Martin stayed overnight at Bank Side, as he did from time to time, she wondered if one of the men there was his lover, and resented that he could have what she could not. These were all things she had thought of from time to time before Tom came, but now the thoughts came more often and were harder to dismiss.

A couple of weeks after seeing Tom, they had a visitor who brought it all back to her again. They had been up to Bank Side, showing Jamie the horses while Martin talked business with Sam. Agnes met them at the kitchen door when they returned.

"There's a man come to see you, sir. I put him in the parlour and gave him some tea. He's been here near on an hour."

"Who is he?" Martin asked.

"Oh!" Agnes fumbled in her pocket and handed over a card.

Someone come about horses, Ellie guessed, pulling the ribbons of her bonnet. Harmless, almost certainly, as both Dan and Fanny were around and wouldn't have hesitated to see off anyone they even suspected of being from Palmer.

Martin handed the card to Ellie.

F. Allerby, Attorney, York.

Tom's brother. Her heart raced for a moment—but Agnes had referred to one man, not two. He had come alone. She didn't know whether to be glad or sorry.

"Thank you, Agnes. Put the kettle on again, will you?" Martin waited until she'd retreated into the kitchen before turning to Ellie. "Do you know anything about this?"

There was a hint of suspicion in his eyes, but it vanished when Ellie shook her head.

"In that case, it can only be something to do with my cousin. If you meant what you said about wanting to know everything, you'd better see him with me."

"I will, thank you. I'll just go and change out of my riding habit."

When she arrived in the parlour, Martin and Mr Allerby were talking about the weather—cool for June—and what would happen now the war with France had formally ended with the signing of the Treaty of Paris. She had a few moments to take in Mr Allerby's appearance before the men noticed she was there. There was familiarity in the colour of his eyes and hair, the shape of his face, but he was of a slighter build than Tom. And a little taller, she thought, as both men stood.

"Are you sure you both wish to be present?" Mr Allerby asked, once the standard greetings had been exchanged and they had all sat down. "The matter is somewhat delicate."

"I have no secrets from my wife," Martin said. "Pray proceed."

Mr Allerby gave a small shrug, and took several sheets of paper from his satchel. "It has come to my notice that Luke Palmer is likely to attempt to have you arrested, Mr Wilson. On a charge of committing unnatural acts."

It took a few moments for what Mr Allerby had said to sink in, then Ellie clenched her fists, her nails digging into her palms. What Martin had feared for years—the very reason he'd married her—had happened.

Mr Allerby looked towards her, one brow slightly raised, as if to check whether she still wanted to be present. She focused on Martin—his face was white, his jaw clenched. Fear, she guessed, in case his cousin really did have some evidence. An innocent man faced with such a charge would be angry. She hoped desperately that Mr Allerby assumed the latter.

"Go on," Martin said, forcing the words out. "I presume there is more." He gestured to the papers with a hand that shook slightly.

Mr Allerby consulted the paper. "All I know so far is that there is a witness who will testify that he was propositioned by you behind an inn in Northallerton." He glanced at Ellie before he continued. "It is not clear at present whether the accusation is that you propositioned him, or that you forced him."

"I haven't been to Northallerton this year," Martin said. "Nor last year either."

Mr Allerby went very still, then dropped the paper onto the others in his lap. "If I may give you some advice, Mr Wilson, it would be better to answer such an accusation with a more general denial." He paused, as if choosing his words carefully. "A denial only that you were not at the location in question leaves your reply open to the interpretation that you are not guilty of this *specific* incident."

Suggesting that he might have done something similar at some other time? A sick feeling settled in Ellie's stomach. Did Mr Allerby know about Martin's nature? How could he?

Martin blinked. "I... I hadn't thought... That is—"

"Pray do not say anything just yet, Mr Wilson. Not without thinking carefully first." He looked from Martin to Ellie and back again. "Let me reassure you that I have had no personal contact with Palmer since he instructed me to look into your marriage last year. I am not acting on his behalf, nor will I do so in the future. Anything you say to me will go no further without your explicit permission."

Martin stared at Mr Allerby, and the silence became uncomfortable. Although Ellie felt fear for her own future, and Jamie's, she was facing scandal and pity, not a possible public trial and hanging. There was nothing Ellie could do or say to reassure Martin at the moment, but she could give him time to think.

"How did this come to your notice, Mr Allerby, if you have not been in contact with Palmer?"

Mr Allerby seemed glad of the distraction. "I said no personal contact, Mrs Wilson. Palmer had not paid my invoice for the work I did for him and my... my representative went—"

"Captain Allerby?" The sick feeling receded a little. Tom had done what he had promised, and it seemed it was a very good thing that he had.

Mr Allerby hesitated before nodding. "He found out what Palmer is intending."

"Are you here at his request?"

"Yes, in part, but once I knew what Palmer intended, I could not stand by while a man was accused using a false witness."

"You worked for Palmer before." Martin had found his voice, although he sounded dazed.

"A mere letter of enquiry, on a matter that would not achieve the end he wanted. I explained that, but he insisted. That is far different from becoming a knowing accomplice in a fraudulent prosecution." He stood. "You need to think about how you wish to proceed from here. You could deal with this yourself now you have warning, and there are other attorneys you could use. However if you wish to retain my services, I may be able to work out something that will not only negate this threat but make Palmer less likely to be given credence in future. You have my card." He bowed his head.

"Mr Allerby," Ellie said. "Would you mind waiting while we discuss the matter?"

"If you wish. I will take a walk in the lane and return in... Will half an hour be sufficient?"

"Yes, thank you. I will show you out."

When she returned to the parlour, Martin was still sitting where she had left him. "It was likely to happen at some point." He sounded defeated already. He looked it, too, with hunched shoulders and gaze fixed on the floor. The risks of Martin's... association... with other men had occurred to Ellie from time to time since that day when he had confessed on the moor, but for him it must be an ever-present threat.

"Your cousin's accusation is baseless, Martin."

"Mud sticks, Ellie. Once the suspicion is out in the open—from someone other than Luke—there is no going back. You only have to read about the crowds who go to see condemned men hanged."

"Martin!" Ellie knelt on the floor in front of him so she could look up into his face. "They cannot find you guilty based only on a lie from one man."

He shook his head. "You don't understand. People will ask questions. Someone will talk to the men at Bank Side and—"

"They are all loyal, are they not? And even if they know the truth, surely they would not say anything?"

"The others... They must suspect something, Ellie. They're not stupid. They may even... I mean, it has been known for someone to be given a pardon in return for giving evidence... If it comes to a man risking his own neck or mine, then I don't—"

"Stop!" Ellie waited until he looked at her properly. "Let us hear what Mr Allerby suggests."

He frowned. "Do you trust him, Ellie? If I was not here, your... that is, Allerby's brother could take you and Jamie—"

"No, that is not why Mr Allerby is here. If Captain Allerby wanted to be rid of you, why would he warn us at all? I don't know Mr Allerby, but I do trust that his brother would never resort to false accusations. Nor would it gain him anything—do you think I would ever associate in any way with a man who had done that?"

"No, no. Of course not." He put out a hand, and Ellie laid hers in it. "I should not have thought it. As you say, we should talk to Mr Allerby again. He doesn't *know* the truth about me, but it is best not to have anyone else suspecting my… my guilt."

"It's not something you can help," Ellie said, getting to her feet. "I'll fetch him."

Ellie saw Agnes and Fanny peering through the open kitchen door as she passed through the hallway on the way to the front door. She kept her gaze on them, and the door closed. She and Martin would have to think what to tell all the servants and farm hands, but not yet.

Mr Allerby was not far away, and returned as soon as he noticed Ellie approaching. He didn't have much more to say, only that he hoped he could arrange for the matter to go no further than an informal hearing with a magistrate, and it was best if they did not know what he was planning. He sounded very positive, and Ellie was relieved to see that Martin no longer looked so despondent.

"We will tell the others it was a problem with your contract for cavalry horses," Ellie suggested, as Mr Allerby rode away down the lane. That was better than implying a problem with a horse they'd sold, which Dan or the others might take too much interest in.

"Good idea. Ellie—thank you." He squared his shoulders. "Let's go and see what Jamie has been up to in our absence."

CHAPTER 20

*T*hornton Court, the home of the nearest magistrate to the Wilsons' farm, was midway between Northallerton and Thirsk, which suited the plan very well. Frank had stayed in Thirsk last night, and should, by now, have received the message Tom had sent this morning and be on his way to Knowle Farm. Tom drove in silence, wanting to have as little as possible to do with the lying weasel beside him. Francis Cullton was a pretty young man with, to Tom's eyes, overlong fair hair, a smooth complexion and a weak chin. Just the kind of fellow that many people expected a man with Wilson's supposed inclinations to take a fancy to.

The preparations before Frank's plan could be put into operation had taken nearly three weeks, and involved Tom in several trips to Northallerton and the surrounding area. He'd taken the opportunity to go on to Darlington on one of those occasions, to find that Finn seemed to have settled well in his new home; the boy was enjoying helping with the horses needing shoeing and generally making himself useful around the forge.

Palmer's original plan had been only half-formed—he had found a witness to bribe, but hadn't thought through any details of the supposed encounter. Frank had suggested they change Palmer's original plan and set their lie in a place not too far from Wilson's home that neither Palmer nor Cullton was familiar with; they decided on Richmond. Tom presented the location to Palmer as being close enough to the farm for Wilson to get there without too much trouble, while being far enough away for him not to be recognised. Frank had also obtained a list of Wilson's business trips over the last few months and picked a date when he could prove he'd been in York. That way, if their plan failed and the magistrate did decide to take the matter further, Wilson had an alibi. They hoped to achieve more than that, though.

"Do you remember all you have been told to say?" Tom asked. "It won't do to hesitate in front of the magistrate." Tom tried to keep the distaste from his voice.

"Yes." Cullton nodded, with a sulky scowl. "Red Lion, Richmond. Constable wouldn't believe me."

"Good." They had been through it already this morning, before they left Palmer in his lodgings. Tom relapsed into silence again. He would be glad when this deception was over. If everything worked it would be worth it, but the whole business left him feeling tainted. Even Frank pointing out that none of it would have been necessary if Palmer hadn't embarked on a criminal conspiracy didn't help much.

The magistrate's home wasn't the grand manor house that Tom had expected. It was old, certainly, and must have had ten or more bedrooms, but there were no added wings, fancy architectural adornments or landscaped grounds. Tom left the gig on the gravel by a large stable block and went to knock on the front door, nudging Cullton with one elbow to remove his hat. "Remember, I've only given you a ride here. Nothing more."

The manservant who opened the door didn't look surprised at finding two total strangers on his doorstep. Once Tom had explained their business, they were shown into a small chamber close to the front door furnished with nothing more than a few hard chairs. They waited for nearly an hour; Cullton became more and more restive as time passed, and jumped to his feet when the door opened. Tom put a hand on his arm to calm him—all his efforts would be wasted if Cullton blurted out the wrong thing now.

The manservant showed them into another spartan room—this one had a table with a high-backed chair behind it in addition to a selection of the same hard chairs as in the anteroom. Roseworth looked like a typical country squire—of middle age with greying hair, and dressed in a coat of good cut but plain fabric.

"Well? I understand you have some information for me?" He looked from Tom to Cullton and back again.

Cullton twisted his hat in his hands and nodded. "Yes, sir."

"Your name?"

"Francis Cullton, sir. From Richmond."

Roseworth turned his gaze on Tom. "And what is your involvement in this matter?"

"A mere bystander, sir. I came across this young man needing transport, and it seemed that my assistance could be useful to see justice done."

"All the way from Richmond?"

"No, he found his own way to Northallerton."

Roseworth didn't look convinced, and with good reason, but shrugged and returned his attention to Cullton. "What is this all about, then?"

"In… Indecent acts, your honour."

Roseworth's brows rose. "Just 'sir' will be quite sufficient. I am not a judge. Who are you accusing?"

"Wilson, sir. He has a farm near here."

"I know him. I hope you have good evidence for what you say, young man. Slander against a respectable man like Wilson is a serious offence."

This was the point at which the whole thing could have ended if Cullton had succumbed to his nerves and admitted what Palmer was paying him to do. Tom hoped he would, but hadn't felt he could point out the possible consequences of being found out to Cullton without bringing his own role into question.

Cullton swallowed hard, but Palmer's promised reward must have been large enough to overcome his hesitations and he stammered out the rehearsed story. Of an encounter in a tavern in Richmond, of Cullton stupidly agreeing to accompany Wilson outside, then Wilson not taking no for an answer when Cullton had discovered what Wilson really wanted. The way he hung his head could have been taken for shame at having to admit what he'd been subjected to.

"The constable at Richmond said it was nothing to do with him, your hon— I mean, sir," Cullton said. "And even if it was, he wouldn't arrest a landowner without some higher authority. So I came to you to have him arrested."

To Tom's relief, Roseworth didn't need any prompting to take the action Frank had hoped for, now that this farce had to be played out fully.

"I'm not summoning the constable for such a matter, and for such a man, without hearing his side of the story first. I'll speak to him."

"Today, sir?" Cullton shuffled his feet. "It's just that I can't take another day away from my job or I might—"

Roseworth's lips compressed, and he regarded Cullton through narrowed eyes. "I suppose it will have to be today. A man deserves to have his accuser face him."

"If it would help, sir, I can take this young man to Wilson's farm," Tom offered. "There would be no difficulty then about returning him to his home afterwards. Besides, I've heard that Wilson has some fine horseflesh for sale." A feeble excuse, but it would have to serve.

Roseworth's scowl made plain what he thought of unconnected persons butting in on things that clearly weren't their business, but the look he gave Cullton also conveyed his reluctance to take the man up in his own carriage. "Very well. Let's get this over with."

The weeks since Mr Allerby had called were difficult for Ellie, and must have been harder still for Martin. This latest threat from Luke Palmer was far more serious than anything he'd tried before, and the need to pretend to the servants that nothing was wrong made things worse.

Not only that, but Ellie had once again been trying to forget the attraction she felt for Tom, the feeling that there was something stronger between them than the physical intimacy they'd shared. Knowing that he would soon be returning to his regiment had helped to dampen her growing yearning after they'd talked on the moor. But this time she knew he was still nearby, most likely in York with Mr Allerby. Within a day's journey.

They had received a letter from Mr Allerby a few days after he called, asking about Martin's recent absences on business. It was couched in vague terms—lest it fall into the wrong hands, she suspected. It was somewhat reassuring that Mr Allerby seemed to have some plan in hand, but she did not see how those details would help.

She went riding to try to take her mind off their troubles. Sometimes she went by herself, and being alone on the moors helped a little. But wherever she was, her mind kept coming back to Palmer's plot and Martin's likely fate if Palmer won—she could not bear to think of that happening to him.

There was also the worry about what would happen to her and Jamie if Martin was no longer there, but Mary's husband and, probably, Tom's brother would help if Palmer tried to wrest the farms from her.

It was easiest when Martin accompanied her, with Jamie up on the horse before him. Their son's presence meant they could not discuss the matter for, although he could only understand simple questions, he was beginning to repeat words he'd overheard. He seemed to relish the new sounds, even if he had little idea what they meant. Instead, they talked to him about horses, about the birds they saw, and made him laugh by attempting to imitate the calls. They were bitter-sweet excursions; times that should have been some of the happiest of her life, with a son she loved and a good friend who loved Jamie, too.

Then one sunny afternoon Agnes put her head around the parlour door where Ellie was going over the household accounts. "It's that man again, missus. Coming up the lane."

"Which man?" There was no worry in Agnes' expression, so she could not mean Palmer.

"Him that came about the horse contracts, a few weeks ago."

Mr Allerby—and Martin was at Bank Side. Her heart began to race as she wondered what he wanted, what had happened. "Can you find Jake and tell him to ride to Bank Side to fetch my husband? And you and Fanny make sure Jamie stays out of the way, please." She went to the front door as Agnes hurried towards the stables, and waited as Mr Allerby approached.

"Good day, Mrs Wilson." Mr Allerby removed his hat and made a little bow. "Is your husband at home?"

"He's at our other farm, I'm afraid, but I have sent for him." Mr Allerby didn't have the look of a man bringing bad news, and her anxiety abated a little. She led him into the parlour and asked Agnes to bring tea. "Has something more happened?" she asked, when the door was safely closed.

"Nothing to be concerned about, Mrs Wilson. In fact, I hope the matter may be resolved permanently today. I am expecting... hoping, rather... that Roseworth will call on your husband with the witness Palmer has—"

"Mr Roseworth? The magistrate?" Was Martin about to be arrested?

"Yes, but do not worry. We have a plan, but it's best that you do not know of it. There are two things I need you to do though. The first is, should Roseworth ask, to tell him I am here about some matter connected with... purchasing land, or enquiring about what would be involved in enclosing part of the moorland. Something like that."

Ellie nodded, Mr Allerby's composed manner calming her. "We told the servants that your last visit concerned a problem with my husband's contract to supply cavalry horses."

"That will do very nicely. The other is... Well, it is possible—likely, even—that my brother will be with the magistrate and the witness. It will be best if you do not recognise him—I don't want the magistrate to know that there is any link between Tom and this household. Or me, come to that."

Ellie nodded, although she thought the magistrate might see the family resemblance in the two brothers.

"Now, should the magistrate arrive before your husband, will Mr Wilson need to be warned not to recognise Tom?"

"No—they have never met."

"That is good. Now, while we wait, tell me more about the business of breeding horses for the cavalry."

It was half an hour before Martin arrived, looking as worried as Ellie had been—as she still was. Mr Allerby explained again, and then spread out several papers on the parlour table, a few with impressive seals. "If our plan works it will become evident that I am here in connection with Palmer's false accusation. However, it would be better if the magistrate does not realise that at the start."

So much deception. But forced on them by the actions of others.

"It is possible that nothing will happen," Mr Allerby went on. "In which case we will all have waited several hours in vain. There is no need for us to sit here the whole time—the scene will be set just as well if we appear to be having a break from legal matters."

They passed the time by showing Mr Allerby around the farm until they saw two gigs turn through the farm gate and come to a stop not far from the farmhouse. A middle-aged man got out of the first, a much younger man out of the second, but the two drivers remained with the vehicles. With a catch in her breath, Ellie recognised Tom at the reins of the second gig, but he made no move to approach the house. Martin walked over, Ellie and Mr Allerby behind him, and met the two men by the front door.

"Roseworth?" Martin said, giving a good impression of being surprised. "What can I do for you?"

Mr Roseworth looked uncomfortable. "A... A somewhat delicate matter, Wilson. If I could have a word in private?"

"A legal matter?"

Mr Roseworth nodded. "I'm afraid so. Well, a criminal matter, in fact. This… this person," he indicated the young man, "has made a very serious accusation against you."

Martin glanced towards Mr Allerby, who nodded. "Mr Allerby is an attorney acting for me on a contractual matter. As he is here, would you have any objection to him being present while you explain?"

"No, no objection." Mr Roseworth seemed relieved by the suggestion.

"If you will come this way?" Martin led the way into the parlour, where Mr Allerby gathered the scattered papers together and sat down at one end of the table, Martin beside him and Ellie behind. Mr Roseworth took the remaining chair, leaving the young man shuffling from one foot to the other and twisting his hat in his hands.

The reassurance Mr Allerby had given her was fading now the magistrate was here, and a knot of worry settled in Ellie's stomach.

Mr Roseworth looked in her direction. "If you will excuse us, Mrs Wilson…"

"I have no secrets from my wife, Roseworth," Martin said. "What's this all about? I've never set eyes on this person before."

Mr Roseworth scowled, but turned his attention to the young man. "Introduce yourself."

"Cullton, sir."

"Go on," Mr Roseworth barked, when Cullton seemed at a loss for words. "Repeat what you told me earlier."

"I… I live in… in Richmond, and…" He swallowed hard.

"May I?" Mr Allerby said to Mr Roseworth. "Witnesses often respond better to specific questions. We haven't got all day, after all."

"By all means." The magistrate leaned back in his chair.

"Your occupation?" Mr Allerby asked.

"Um. Draper's assistant, sir."

"And you encountered Mr Wilson." He waited for Cullton's nod. "Where did you meet him?"

Cullton's gaze jerked from the magistrate to Martin, and then back to Mr Allerby. "Er, I… I met him in a tavern. He asked me to go

178

outside with him, and offered me money to... to... And then he... he made me... That is, he pushed me over a barrel and..."

"Forced himself upon you?" Mr Allerby asked, and Cullton nodded, his face a picture of misery. As he might look if relating a real experience, Ellie supposed, but she didn't think Mr Roseworth was convinced by his performance. Martin was scowling—as any man might at hearing such an accusation, but she could see that his fists were clenched below the table.

"Let us spare Mrs Wilson the details of the alleged act," Mr Allerby said. "And before my client has to submit to the indignity of having to deny such a scurrilous accusation..."

Thus avoiding the risk of saying something that might lead the magistrate to wonder if there was some truth behind it after all. Ellie's confidence in Mr Allerby increased.

"... let us have some more details of where the alleged incident happened." The pen and ink were still on the table, and Mr Allerby drew a blank sheet of paper from his satchel. "When was this meeting?"

"In April. The sixteenth."

Ellie relaxed a little. Martin had gone to York in April.

"Over two months ago," Mr Allerby stated as he wrote it down. "This tavern in Richmond—what is it called?"

"The Red Lion, sir." Cullton sounded more confident now.

"Now, if your story is true, you should be able to describe the room in the tavern where you say Mr Wilson talked to you. Please do so." Mr Allerby's tone made it clear it was not a request but an order.

"Had fox heads on the wall, sir," Cullton said, as if he'd been expecting the question. "There's a stuffed pheasant in a glass case over the fireplace. Pictures of hunting on the walls." He screwed up his face, as if trying to remember. "Yard of ale glass hanging over the bar."

"I know that place well," the magistrate said, an odd note in his voice. "The usual barmaid is called Rosie, I think? Thin woman, black hair."

"Yes, sir. That's it." Cullton nodded, a smile of relief spreading across his face.

Mr Roseworth's brows drew together, his voice sharp. "There's just one problem. You have described the Fox and Pheasant, where I frequently enjoy an ale after the hunt. I am not familiar with the Red Lion in Richmond, if it even exists, but I doubt it would have exactly the same things on the walls, and certainly not the same barmaid. It's you who should be arrested for slander."

Cullton stood still for a moment, then sprang for the door. His footsteps sounded in the stone-flagged hallway, then she heard the rattle of the front door opening.

Ellie felt limp with relief. The threat was over. This one, at least.

CHAPTER 21

*A*lthough Tom was on tenterhooks to know whether Frank's plan was working, he was also glad to be excluded. Sitting in the same room as Ellie without betraying his feelings would have been difficult. Very difficult. As it was, the faint scent of lavender drifting from the bushes lining the front path reminded him of their night together.

He loitered by the gig for a while until, restless, he left the other driver with both horses and walked down the lane a little way. That was better than wandering around the farm trying to get a glimpse of his son. When he returned, the man with the burnt face was several yards from the gigs—without a rifle, this time. Dan Cole, Ellie had called him.

"You again," Cole said, when Tom was close enough to hear. His expression was wary, but not as hostile as the first time Tom had seen him.

"I'm here to help." Although not with Wilson's explicit permission.

"Is this something to do with Palmer?" Cole indicated the other gig. "I don't reckon the magistrate's come about a horse."

"That's Wilson's business to tell, not mine."

Cole didn't seem offended at Tom's refusal to answer. He pointed to his damaged face. "I lost a few positions because of this—some womenfolk couldn't look at me without having a fainting fit. But the missus gave me a job and Mr Wilson agreed. There's a lad at the farm with a limp, things like that. Martin's Misfits, some folks call us. Not meant nastily, usually, I reckon."

Tom nodded, trusting that this conversation was going somewhere.

"The point is," Cole went on, "I like it here. And I want it to stay that way." There was a firmness to his voice that was almost a threat.

"I'm not trying to change that."

Cole stared into Tom's face, his eyes narrowed, then he nodded. "You said you were Captain Allerby. What regiment?"

"43rd Foot." Had Cole been in the army himself? Tom wasn't accustomed to being questioned by anyone other than his superior officers, but Cole was one of Ellie's allies here.

To Tom's surprise, Cole grinned. "Light Bobs? You were late!"

It took Tom a moment to work out what he meant. "Talavera?" The Light Brigade had marched fifty miles or so in the summer heat, in little more than twenty-four hours, arriving only to find the battle over. He looked at Cole's face. "Is that where you got that?" Dry grass on a hillside had caught alight, burning many of the men too badly wounded to escape.

"Tried dragging my mate away from the fire. He didn't make it."

"I'm sorry. Did they give you a pension?"

Cole shook his head, and held up his left hand. "This don't work well enough to load a musket fast, but it don't stop me working. I'm not complaining. As I said, I like it here."

"The Wilsons have a good protector."

"I do what I can." Cole smiled—a small smile, but enough, Tom hoped, to indicate that Cole no longer regarded him as a threat. Then he turned and walked away.

Tom paced up the lane again, but hadn't got far when the sound of running feet on the gravelled path made him turn around. Cullton swerved around the two gigs and into the lane, skidding to a halt as he spotted Tom. His head turned from side to side, but the hedges here were thick and unbroken, and before he had chance to run back the way he'd come, Tom had reached him and grabbed his jacket.

"We've got to get away!" Cullton wriggled, but Tom had a firm grip. "I did my best, but what you told me to say didn't work. Please—if that magistrate gets me, Palmer'll see *me* hanged instead."

Suddenly the man's apparent willingness to do Palmer's bidding became clear. Cullton was as much a victim here as Wilson—or nearly so.

"Shut up," Tom hissed. "You don't want the magistrate's driver to hear you." He shook Cullton's shoulder, and the man finally stopped pleading.

"It's your fault. You told me what lies to tell, and now the magistrate will—"

"It's not you I'm after," Tom said, keeping his voice low. "It's Palmer —I want him totally discredited. Understand?"

Cullton's mouth fell open, then he collected himself enough to croak an answer. "Yes."

"Palmer caught you with another man, I imagine, and threatened to report you unless you did as he told you?"

Cullton nodded, his face ashen. Beyond him, Frank and Wilson were approaching, with Roseworth and Ellie not far behind them. Tom kept his focus on Cullton.

"We've not much time. You're going back in there, and you're going to let me do the talking. Palmer was *paying* you—have you got that?"

"They'll still lock me up, and Palmer will say I've failed to—"

"No." Cullton might well be guilty of sodomy, might even have taken money for it—but blackmail was a crime, too, and Cullton's crimes had not harmed anyone. So far.

"Ah, you caught him…" Roseworth frowned at Tom. "What did you say your name was?"

"I didn't. Captain Allerby, sir. 43rd Foot."

"Allerby?" Roseworth looked from Tom to Frank, his brows drawing together. "What is going on here? You're making a May game of me!"

"There has been some deception involved, sir, for which I apologise." Tom kept his gaze from straying to where Ellie stood. "But it was to prevent a greater harm."

"If we might explain?" Frank asked. "Mr Wilson should know, too, in case he wishes to press charges for defamation against..." He glanced at Cullton. "Well, let us hear what Cullton has to say first."

"I will get some refreshments sent into the dining room." Ellie met Tom's eyes for a brief moment before turning back to the house. Had she smiled?

"Very well." Roseworth stalked off, indignation in his stiff gait. Frank followed him, one hand grasping Cullton's arm. Wilson lingered, looking Tom up and down. Assessing. Not actually hostile, but not far from it.

Tom met his gaze, trying not to resent this man who had Ellie as a wife. Was Wilson about to berate him for being intimate with her? "I'm not here to interfere with your family. I'm only here because my brother's plan required it."

Wilson pressed his lips together, then nodded. "Thank you."

Tom followed him into the parlour and stood beside Cullton. Frank and the magistrate were already seated at the table. There was no sign of Ellie.

"Why did you lie?" Frank asked, before the magistrate could speak.

Cullton glanced in Tom's direction, and hung his head. "Palmer was to pay me. And *him*..." He pointed at Tom. "*He* told me what to say. All that stuff about the Red Lion."

"Palmer is my cousin, Roseworth," Wilson said. "He has been conducting a campaign of harassment against me and my family for some years. This attempt, however, is far more serious than anything he has done so far."

The magistrate nodded, and turned to Tom. "And your role, Captain?"

"I beg your pardon for lying to you, sir," Tom said. "I discovered Palmer's plan by chance. We—my brother and I, that is—thought that merely informing Wilson of Palmer's plan would not prevent another such false accusation in the future. I volunteered to help Palmer. He was glad of my assistance in getting Cullton to see you without involving himself in the matter. He thought that might raise suspicion, given that he has a long history of harassing Wilson in various ways. My intention in describing your local inn to Cullton, pretending it was the tavern in Richmond where Palmer had set their fiction, was to unequivocally demonstrate the falsity of his statement."

"You went to a lot of bother for strangers." Roseworth still looked suspicious.

"No-one deserves to be subject to such accusations, sir, particularly when the nature of them could lead to a capital charge."

Frank took over. "Our intention was to discredit Cullton as a witness and, ideally, to have his evidence that Palmer was behind it. Cullton has never seen my client before today, and has no motive to act against him."

"Do you wish me to have Cullton arrested for making this false charge?" Roseworth said to Wilson, sounding more weary than angry now. "Or Palmer?"

Cullton looked towards the door, but Tom's hand on his arm prevented another attempt at escape.

"If I may make a suggestion?" Tom said. "With your permission, Wilson?"

Ellie sent Agnes into the parlour with glasses, a jug of ale, and Martin's brandy decanter. Then she went out to the vegetable patch where Fanny was sitting on an upturned crate while Jamie looked for worms and beetles.

"Is everything all right, missus?"

"Yes, thank you." Or it would be shortly, but she was happy to leave the men to it now she knew Martin was no longer in danger.

"Will you watch him now?" Fanny added. "Don't want to leave the butter making too long in this weather."

Ellie nodded and took Fanny's seat on the crate as she hurried off.

Tom had avoided her gaze, and it hurt, even though she knew it was the sensible thing to have done. Just the sight of him had made her feel slightly breathless—she wouldn't have been able to stop herself returning a smile and giving away her feelings.

She inspected Jamie as he tottered over to the next vegetable bed. He still had the largely unformed face of a young child, but she could see hints of Tom in his features. Not enough for others to notice, she thought; not yet. But it would not do for too many people to see Jamie and Tom together. Or to suspect that she had a partiality for Tom.

"Beel!" Jamie squealed, picking up a large black specimen.

"Beetle," Ellie corrected automatically, jumping to her feet in time to prevent him tasting it. "Put it down. Come and say hello to the lambs."

It must have been half an hour or more before one of the gigs set off down the lane. She could make out two people in it; neither of them looked like Tom. "Time to go back," she said to Jamie, and picked him up, in spite of his protests that he could walk. She should not, but she wanted to see Tom before he left. Now the danger was over, this might be the last time she ever set eyes on him. And he should be given a chance to see Jamie, at least, after all he had just done for them.

By the time she reached the farmhouse, Cullton was in the remaining gig. Martin stood by the front door with his back to her, talking to the Allerby brothers. Tom looked in her direction, then moved towards the gig, away from her.

Before she could feel the hurt again, he stopped and turned, and she realised he was now out of Martin's sight. He looked at Jamie, still in her arms, and then into her eyes. His smile was tentative, wistful, even, but it warmed her and she couldn't help returning it. Then he abruptly turned to gaze up towards the moors and she saw that Jake was bringing Mr Allerby's horse and Martin had turned to look in her direction. She put Jamie down and forced another smile as she walked up to the group of men by the door—she should be happy this danger had been averted.

"I'll stay the night in Thirsk," Mr Allerby was saying, "and take the letters to Roseworth tomorrow. I'll let you know how much the other matter costs." He turned to Ellie and bowed. "Good day, Mrs Wilson.

Please feel free to consult me if Palmer causes any more trouble; I will do what I can to help."

"Thank you, Allerby," Martin said. "Both of you."

Mr Allerby nodded, thanking Jake as he mounted the horse and rode off. "Wilson, Mrs Wilson," Tom said. "I was happy to be of service." Then he, too, nodded and strode towards the gig.

"What happened?" Ellie asked, taking Martin's arm and leading him into the house before she was tempted to watch Tom leave. "Did you pacify Mr Roseworth?"

"Allerby did. Or rather, the Allerbys did, between them. Allerby is to write a set of letters for Roseworth to sign and send to all the magistrates in the area, informing them of Palmer's slanderous accusations and warning them not to give credence to any such claims in the future."

"That's good. What about his witness? Isn't he as much to blame?"

"Allerby—that is, *Captain* Allerby—didn't seem to think so, but didn't say why. It wasn't difficult to persuade Roseworth that it would do more harm than good to prosecute him for it—the less the thing is talked about the better. The 'other matter' Allerby referred to... The captain said it would be best to ensure Cullton left the area completely. He suggested giving him the coach fare to somewhere distant, and enough money to tide him over for a while."

"Did Cullton agree?"

"Readily."

"So we are safe." She took in Martin's frown. "Aren't we?"

"Oh. Yes. Thanks in part to your... to Captain Allerby."

Martin looked as if he had to force the words out. Ellie couldn't blame him—it must be hard for him to feel indebted to a man who had wronged him, even if unwittingly.

"But we can't let down our guard, Ellie, in case he tries something like it again."

～

"We won," Frank said, as they watched Cullton climb into the London coach outside the Three Tuns the following day. Tom had left Cullton with Frank while he went to Northallerton. He'd avoided the ale houses where he'd talked to Palmer, having agreed with Frank that it was best to leave Palmer to wonder what had happened.

He retrieved Cullton's possessions from his lodgings and spoke to the draper for whom Cullton had worked. To his surprise, the shop-keeper considered Cullton a diligent and helpful assistant. He didn't enquire why his employee had decided to leave the area so abruptly, and Tom wondered if he, too, suspected that Cullton indulged in forbidden activities. But he did take a few minutes to write a char-acter for him.

"Cullton has won, in a way," Tom said, as the coach set off. "He's away from Palmer's blackmail, with a character and some money in his pocket. I imagine he'll take better care not to get caught in future."

"The Wilsons have won, too," Frank said.

"I'm not so sure about that. Palmer has been promising all and sundry that he was about to come into some money. He has gambling debts, and probably owes tradesmen, too, to the degree that the bailiffs are likely to be called in soon."

"He's shown his hand now," Frank said. "He can't try the same thing again, and Roseworth would be suspicious of anything that happened to Wilson."

"Palmer didn't strike me as the type for violence, but who knows what he might do now he's getting desperate? If Wilson ends up dead —which is what Palmer really wants—it's of no use to him that Palmer may swing for it later."

"With you to protect them, they needn't worry."

It was said light-heartedly, but Tom couldn't return his brother's smile. "This is serious, Frank. I could hardly discuss it in front of Roseworth, but I don't think Wilson has fully grasped the fact that Palmer's aims have changed. Before, it was petty harassment, as far as I can gather. I think this is the first action he's attempted that could have resulted in Wilson's death."

"Sorry, Tom. I *am* taking it seriously."

"Besides, I won't be here, remember? I have to be in Kent two weeks from now." Another coach pulled into the yard. "This is ours, I think. I don't know what else can be done, and we can't discuss it on the coach, but we could both give it some thought."

By the time they reached York, all Tom had managed to think of was to encourage Frank to offer Wilson his legal assistance if it was needed, but that was unlikely to be enough.

CHAPTER 22

"Letters, missus," Agnes said as she knocked on the parlour door and entered the room. "Jake just got back from Thirsk." She laid them on the table. Jamie looked up from his place on the rug, but seeing no sign of food, returned his attention to the wooden animals spread out around him.

"Thank you." Ellie examined the letters as Agnes left. Two were addressed to Martin—the one from York had Allerby on it as the sender. *Not* in Tom's hand.

Had Palmer found another way to attack them? They hadn't heard anything from him, or about him, in the month since his attempt to have Martin arrested. Ellie found that worrying rather than reassuring. She was tempted to open the letter, but resolutely put it to one side. Martin would tell her about it when he read it.

The third was for her, from Mary. The letter was mostly Mary's usual relation of everyday events, confirming that she and the children were well, and Henry was as busy as usual. But she finished by announcing that she thought she was increasing again.

A brother or sister for Mary's other four children. Something that Jamie would never have.

Ellie put the letter down and closed her eyes. She should not envy

Mary for her happy marriage and growing family, but she couldn't help it. In the weeks since Tom had come with Palmer's lying witness, the discontent she'd begun to feel after they'd talked on the moor had intensified. Whenever Martin went to Bank Side, her suspicion that he had a lover there would return, together with her resentment at the unfairness. She could not do the same without risking breaking up their family.

Martin had offered to try again to conceive a child, if that was what she wanted, but she had declined. She had not done so in the years when Martin came to her bed regularly, before they had given up hope, so she was unlikely to do so now. And lying there while Martin... Well—it would make her feel like the cows or mares being serviced. Particularly as she now knew that Martin did not want her in that way. As unsatisfactory as those early episodes had been for her, she had thought Martin had enjoyed them.

Although the sky was still covered in cloud, the earlier rain had stopped and she needed something more than the novel she was reading to distract her. "Jamie, shall we go and see what's growing in the garden?"

The rain was inconvenient—it had come on suddenly the day after everyone who could wield a scythe had cut the hay fields. But there was lighter sky in the west, so the crop might yet be salvaged. She might even go out with a rake herself to help turn the wet grass. Exercise didn't clear her mind of thoughts of Tom, but it helped.

Jamie soon lost interest in the garden, and demanded to "find Papa". She looked at his shoes and dress, already liberally coated with mud, and sighed. It was just as well that Kate didn't mind washing muddy garments.

"Come along, then. We'll walk down the lane." Martin had said he would be back before it was Jamie's bedtime.

They didn't get far, having stopped to pick a handful of meadowsweet from a damp ditch, "to say thank-you to Kate when she cleans your clothes." Jamie gave her the rather crushed stems at the sound of approaching hooves, and tottered along faster until Martin came in sight. Jamie shrieked in delight as Martin leaned down and pulled him up to sit in front of him, holding him safely with one arm.

Seeing them together made Ellie ashamed of her envy—Martin would do anything for their son, and he did all he was capable of for her, too. She really should be grateful for what she had.

That evening, when they retired to the parlour, Martin handed Ellie a letter—the one from Mr Allerby. It didn't contain good news, from his expression. Ellie unfolded it and ran her eyes quickly over the usual greetings.

As you requested, I have made further enquiries about Luke Palmer in Northallerton and the surrounding towns. The situation appears to be much the same as when you came to my office.

Ellie looked up. "When did you go to his office?"

"About a week after they brought Roseworth here. I was in York to discuss Fleet's stud fees with Lord Longhirst's man of business, and I called to ask Allerby if he knew what Palmer had done after his plot failed. Allerby had already asked around in Northallerton and discovered that he hadn't been seen in the previous few days, but there were a lot of people wanting to find him."

Martin could have told her at the time, but there was little point in making a fuss over it—he was telling her now. She returned to the letter.

No-one admitted to having seen him, and the creditors I spoke to at the time are still owed money and beginning to talk about bailiffs. The landlords of several alehouses he was known to frequent informed me that he has not been back, and if he did return he would not be welcome until he had paid off his gambling debts.
There is little else I can do on this matter unless Palmer makes another move, but I am happy to provide any further assistance you require.

"This is good, is it not? If he's not in the area, he'll find it difficult to cause more trouble."

"In a way." Martin didn't appear to be convinced. "But it does show he's still in need of money." He held out his hand and Ellie passed the letter back. "I was just letting you know, Ellie. What I really wanted to talk to you about is the August meet."

"Are we to make a holiday of it, as we did in the spring?"

"If you wish, of course we may. I will go, because I've entered Fleet in the Sixty Guinea Sweepstakes race."

"Sixty guineas?" Ellie was surprised at the amount. It was as much as they would get from selling two horses. Perhaps it always cost so much? This was the first time Martin had entered a horse in an official race meeting.

"I know it's a lot, Ellie, but it's the best way to get Fleet seen. If he wins, we'll get five or six times the amount back. If not, as long as he makes a decent showing, he'll get noticed, and I can charge more for stud fees. People might come to me for hunters, too."

"An investment, then." She should have known Martin would have a good reason for spending that amount of money. "Is Sam to ride him?"

"He's the best one for it. We had Fleet up on the moors for a gallop this afternoon, and he's going well. He's the best prospect we've had since I started breeding for speed, Ellie." Enthusiasm lit his face as he talked on, listing the gentlemen who might be interested in having Fleet cover their mares, and how the extra money should compensate for the likely reduction in their income from cavalry horses.

Well, a week in York was something to look forward to—aside from the excitement of the races, York had more and bigger shops than Thirsk.

Tom winced as the army surgeon prodded the scar beside his shoulder-blade.

"Still hurts, does it?"

"Only when you poke it like that," he muttered.

"Hmm. Well, you can put your shirt back on. What did the surgeon who patched you up say about it?"

"He wasn't sure I'd get full movement back." Tom didn't like this man's frown. The results of this examination could decide whether he went back on active duty or was relegated to some kind of administrative task that might see him left in England when orders came for the first battalion to be sent abroad. The really unsettling thing was that he wasn't sure which outcome he wanted.

"Have you? Show me."

Tom tucked his shirt into his trousers and raised his arm above his head, then swung it around—forwards, down, and then as far behind him as he could, ignoring the twinge in his shoulder.

"Both together." The surgeon watched carefully. "Hmm. Not quite the range of movement as your good arm, but enough."

"I'm fit for duty then?"

"Not so fast, young man. I want to see that you can wield a sword properly before I make my final decision, but I'll give you a couple of weeks to exercise first." He made a note in a ledger while Tom picked up his neckcloth and shrugged himself into his jacket.

What next? It was late afternoon—too early to settle himself in the mess, and half the officers from his battalion were on leave in any case. The sky was clear, the August sun still warm on his face, but a cool breeze brought the tang of salt from the Channel. He'd call at the adjutant's office to see if there was any mail for him, and walk on the beach.

There was a letter from Frank; he tucked it into a pocket and set off. He was reasonably familiar with this area, his battalion having trained nearby to become part of the Light Brigade, then being posted further up the coast in Kent when the threat of a French invasion was high.

On the beach, Tom stood looking at the sun glittering on the sea. The coast of France was across this stretch of water, hidden by the curve of the Earth. The threat from Napoleon was over now, and the idea that they were at peace still felt very strange to him. At peace with France, at least; there were other conflicts, but they didn't feel as immediate as an enemy less than thirty miles away across the water.

Looking about him, he found a piece of driftwood to sit on and took Frank's letter from his pocket. In the two months he'd been in York, he'd got used to having Frank to talk to in the evenings, particularly in the later weeks when Frank had mostly weaned himself off the brandy, and had been less maudlin about his marriage. There was plenty to talk about with his fellow officers, to be sure, but he missed Frank's company.

Breaking the wafer, he unfolded the letter and began to read.

Dear Tom,

I hope this finds you well. I am beginning to prosper, at last.
Mortenson is sending some business my way, and I suspect he may be
open to resuming our partnership at some point, but I am not going to
suggest that yet. There's enough business to keep a clerk occupied, and
I've articled a young man from Leeds.

That was good—the lad's parents would have paid Frank to train their son. But the next paragraphs gave him pause.

I am continuing to meet Susannah, and we have decided to try living
together again. In rooms, though. I do not feel ready yet to go to the
expense of leasing a house. I was on the point of moving to smaller
lodgings, but I am glad I did not. She can have your room.

Tom shook his head, then smiled as he read Frank's next words.

I can guess what you are thinking, but I am being careful. I will not
end up in the same situation as before. I explained my finances to her,
and compared my income to the bills she ran up while we were in the
Micklegate house. I'm not sure she understood it all, but she did
appear to realise that I wasn't merely being tight-fisted. And that I
have yet to repay all of it.

At least he was aware of the potential for disaster.

I continued to enquire as to Palmer's whereabouts, with no results, and wrote to Wilson to that effect. And your boy Finn turned up at my office last week, having (he said) walked from Darlington. He wanted you, but I told him you were in Hythe. I offered to put him up for a few days, but he never arrived at our lodgings, so I assume he returned to Darlington.

The last part of the letter was only wishing him well. Tom folded it and put it back in his pocket. Then he stood and walked along the beach, feet crunching on the pebbles.

Finn had been content enough only a few weeks ago when Tom visited him—what had happened in the meantime to make him run away? If he'd wanted to escape badly enough to walk all the way to York, Tom didn't believe he would have returned to Darlington. So where was he now?

Damn. All he could do was to get Frank to check whether Finn *had* gone back to his uncle and perhaps find a suitable school for him. If Finn wasn't in Darlington, there was nothing he or Frank could do.

Ellie and Jamie weren't his responsibility, either. Less so than Finn, really. But he couldn't forget Palmer's animosity towards his cousin, and his own belief that Palmer would make another attempt to harm the Wilsons. It was bad enough here in Hythe, where he was within two or three days' travel of York. When the 43rd were sent abroad—and, as light troops, they were likely to be—he would be an ocean away. Did he want that?

The sweepstake Martin had entered was on the second day of the August race meeting, and Jake had driven Ellie and Jamie to the racecourse early enough to get a good viewing position close to the finishing post. Martin would join them later, after the race, but now he was off somewhere with Sam, making sure Fleet was ready for his first event. Fanny had the day off, to watch the races or tour the shops in York, as she pleased.

Watching the 'horsies' would only entertain Jamie for so long, so Ellie had come armed with a selection of candied fruits and other sweets in case she needed to bribe him into sitting still for a while. For now, he sat beside her in the gig babbling unintelligibly to his new toy horse. Telling it to look at all the other horses around, she thought, but she couldn't be sure. She'd let Jake go off to get a better view, and he'd elbowed his way to the front of the crowd; Ellie didn't expect to see him again until the racing was over.

"Papa horse?" Jamie asked as rising noise from the crowd indicated that the first race was about to start.

"Not yet, Jamie. Papa's horse is in the next one." She helped him to stand on the seat, steadying him with a hand twisted in his clothing as he jumped up and down with excitement. The horses rushed towards them, then passed in a thunder of hooves, almost drowned by the shouts of the onlookers. Ellie didn't enjoy it as much as she usually did, her mind focused on Fleet's upcoming performance and worry about Martin's disappointment if Fleet didn't do well.

The time before the Sixty Guineas seemed endless, as a hollow feeling settled in Ellie's stomach, but it was replaced by a surge of excitement as the race started. She put her arm around Jamie this time so she could give her whole attention to the runners, squinting at the distant line of horses to find Sam's blue coat and cap. She clenched her fists, digging her nails into her palms as she finally identified Sam, urging his mount on from third position. Only third! But he wasn't far behind the leader—could they win? Then the roar of the crowd became even louder as the horses dashed past. They were so close to each other that it was impossible to make out who was in the lead, and a cheer rose louder still as they passed the finish post.

"Papa?" Jamie asked, looking around.

"He'll be back soon," Ellie promised, crossing her fingers against the untruth. Whether or not Fleet had won, Martin would be busy making sure he was cooled down properly. And if they *had* won, he might be talking to possible customers.

She finally found out from Jake—she could see from his beaming smile as he limped towards the gig that the news was good, and she grinned in response, happy for Martin and all the men who had worked with Fleet.

"He won?"

"Yes, missus. Just by a nose, I think, but Sam pulled ahead just at the last." He was almost bouncing with excitement. "Do you...? I mean, can I—?"

"Go and see them, Jake."

He grinned again, and left as fast as he could. Ellie settled down to wait, relaxed enough now to enjoy the sunshine and the bustle. Perhaps tomorrow she would spend the day in York with Jamie. They could walk by the river and feed the ducks. With some of Martin's winnings, she could buy enough fabric for new gowns for Kate, Fanny, and Agnes. Martin would have something in mind to help the menfolk celebrate, although it was likely to involve ale rather than new clothing.

She didn't see much of Martin until the next morning. She'd heard him stumble into the adjoining room in the early hours, so she wasn't surprised when his breakfast consisted solely of copious quantities of coffee.

"Too much celebration?" Ellie tried to keep the amusement out of her voice. She could hardly blame him, after achieving an ambition he'd had for years.

"A little," he admitted, giving a wry smile in response. Ellie didn't bother him for details of the race, but told him her plans for the day and received a ready agreement to her intention of buying something for their female servants. She would learn all about it later.

CHAPTER 23

*E*llie enjoyed a walk along the river with Jamie after breakfast, and he sat quietly enough in the draper's shop playing with a length of ribbon while Ellie and Fanny chose materials for new dresses. Ellie bought two lengths for each of them in the end—a light printed muslin for the rest of the summer, and heavier wool for winter wear. And she elicited a blush from the normally imperturbable Fanny when she mentioned that she thought Dan would approve of the dark blue wool that set off her eyes. Then she sent Fanny back to the hotel with the parcels while she took Jamie to a haberdasher to buy trimmings and fastenings.

Her enjoyment of the day was diminished when Fanny rejoined them. "Saw that Palmer, missus," she said as soon as the shopkeeper was out of earshot. "Lurking by the hotel."

"Did he try to speak to you?"

Fanny shook her head. "He saw me, but he didn't follow me here."

What need to do so, when all he had to do was to wait for them to return to the hotel? Ellie had been planning on doing just that, to give Jamie time for an afternoon nap, but now she wasn't sure. Palmer had never yet offered violence, but that didn't mean he wouldn't. She could return, and say she was not to be disturbed. But the hotel's private parlours had been reserved by other people, so she would have to go to her room. She'd feel trapped, having to stay there until Martin returned.

She felt like swearing—why did Palmer have to appear now, when things were going so well?

"Missus? If it's that Palmer you're worried about, he can't do nowt here—not with so many people about."

"I don't want to even speak to him, Fanny. Or let him get too close to Jamie."

"Hmm, can't blame you for that. But the lad's tired."

Tired, and likely to become fractious. "We'll go to a different hotel and have some food," Ellie decided. "Or... No, I've a message to deliver first." If Martin had retained Mr Allerby to check on what Palmer was doing, he should be told that Palmer was in York. She asked the shopkeeper for directions as she paid for her purchases, and Fanny picked up Jamie and followed her out onto the street.

Mr Allerby's office was only a street away, and she found it without too much trouble. Inside, Mr Allerby's door was answered promptly when she knocked.

"Can I help you, ma'am?" The clerk was young—hardly old enough to shave. "I'm afraid Mr Allerby is at the races today."

She had expected that. "Is Captain Allerby with him?"

"No, ma'am. The captain rejoined his regiment last month, I understand. Can I take a message?"

Oh. Tom was no longer in York, possibly not even in the country. That should make no difference—it was Mr Allerby who had offered further help, not his brother. She should be pleased that Tom's shoulder had healed well enough for him to return to duty.

"Ma'am?"

"I'll write a note, if I may?"

The clerk provided her with paper and pen. She wrote only that she had seen Luke Palmer in York, and gave him the address of their hotel. Folding it, she gave it to the clerk and returned to Fanny. "Now we will find something to eat."

. . .

Ellie's attempts to avoid Palmer came to nothing when they returned to their hotel after eating elsewhere. Fanny took Jamie straight up to their room while Ellie went to order tea for herself and Fanny.

While she was waiting for the serving girl to attend her, she heard someone stop behind her. This was a busy hotel, and Martin would still be at the racecourse, so she didn't look. Not until he spoke.

"Good evening, Mrs Wilson."

She turned, keeping her expression blank. "Mr Palmer."

"I hope I find you well?"

Ellie inclined her head, not bothering to reply.

"I would like a word with my cousin. Do you know when he will return?"

"I'm afraid not. Excuse me." She didn't wait for a reply, but stepped around him and went upstairs. She would send Fanny down to order tea.

Something struck her as odd about the encounter. That it had happened at all, for a start, but also Palmer's manner. Not threatening, or angry, as she might have expected following his unsuccessful attempt to get Martin arrested. Did he know what had happened? She cast her mind back to what Martin had told her. Mr Allerby hadn't found Palmer after that incident. If Tom had seen him, wouldn't Mr Allerby have mentioned it?

Perhaps Palmer only knew that his plan hadn't worked, and not *why* it hadn't? He might even think that Martin didn't know about it at all.

Did it matter? Perhaps not—but it might be worth warning Martin. There was paper and ink somewhere in Martin's room; she could send Fanny with a note to walk towards the racecourse in the hope that she would see Martin before Palmer did.

Fanny came back an hour later, saying she had given the note to Mr Wilson. It was another half hour before Martin arrived. Ellie left Jamie dozing in his bed and closed the door of Martin's room behind her.

"Did Palmer find you?"

He dropped his satchel on the floor and his hat on top of it, and ran a hand through his hair. "He did. Thank you for the warning, by the way. He *didn't* know what happened that day." He smiled, but without humour. "He still doesn't know the details, just that I am aware of his failed plot against me."

"What did he say?"

"Oh, he congratulated me on Fleet's win, and said that as it had been a family farm, he was sure I'd wish to share some of the winnings."

"What? The effrontery!"

"Indeed. I pointed out that it was my hard work—and the lads at Bank Side—that had earned the reward. Then I told him *he'd* find himself in gaol if he ever approached a magistrate again with lies about me."

"Good."

"Not really." He turned towards the mirror and started to remove his neckcloth. "He was shocked that I knew about it, then furious. He'll find some other way to set the law on me, Ellie." He turned his head at a knock. "That'll be the hot water I ordered. Dinner in half an hour?"

Ellie nodded, and went back to her room. What would Palmer do next? What *could* he do?

If only Tom was still in York. She would feel safer knowing he could be called upon if necessary.

The back room in the King's Arms smelled of brandy and cigars. Tom looked up from the cards he was dealing as a waiter stopped beside him.

"Captain Allerby?"

"Yes?"

The waiter bowed. "I'm sorry to disturb you, sir, but there's a corporal outside asking to see you. He wouldn't say what he wanted, but insisted he would wait." The waiter's face conveyed his disapproval. Officers playing cards and buying drinks were welcome in this hotel—lower ranks cluttering up the entrance clearly were not.

"Come on, Allerby, are we playing or not?" Stanton sounded impatient.

Tom hesitated—this place was a mile from the barracks, so the corporal had not only made enquiries as to where he was, but had walked some distance to find him. He tided the cards back into a stack and set them on the table.

"You're not leaving, Allerby?"

"I am, I'm afraid." He turned to the hovering waiter. "My bill, if you please."

"Damme, Allerby, no need to run off. It's only eight!"

"Nevertheless." Tom nodded, settled up, then stepped outside to see who—or what—awaited him. Although the sun had set over an hour ago, there was still some light in the sky. As he hesitated on the pavement, a shadowy shape stepped up and saluted smartly.

"Captain Allerby?"

"Yes?"

"Corporal Bonner, sir. Captain Ffyles' company. I was on gate duty this afternoon." He turned his head. "Come on, you said you 'ad to see 'im."

Another, much smaller figure shuffled out of the shadow towards the pool of light in front of the hotel door. Even before he could see, Tom guessed who it must be.

"Finn?"

Someone pushed past behind Tom, and he took Finn's shoulder. "Come, let's get out of the way."

"Did I do right, sir?"

"You did indeed, thank you, Corporal. You can leave him with me now." Tom felt in his pocket and handed over a few shillings. The corporal could have just sent Finn away, but hadn't.

"Thank you, sir." Bonner's smile turned into a wide grin as he saw the value of the coins. He saluted again and marched off.

Tom contemplated the drooping figure in silence. It was several weeks since he'd received the letter from Frank telling him that Finn had been in York. Had he been on the road all that time? What had he done for money?

"When did you last eat?"

A sniff and a shrug were the only answers.

"Come along, then." He strode off down the street, looking for an alehouse that wasn't too rowdy, nor full of soldiers—the presence of an officer would only cause embarrassment. He found one a couple of streets away from the sea—it was bustling, but not full, and Tom made his way to a table at one side of the room. The place was a dim fog of tobacco smoke, but there was enough light for Tom to make out Finn's gaunt appearance and filthy clothes.

He ordered soup and bread, and ale for himself. If Finn hadn't eaten for days, a large meal would likely make him sick. Finn cast a wary glance at Tom's face as he picked up his spoon, then began to eat.

"You don't have to go back," Tom said. Although what he *was* going to do with him would take some thought. While Finn was eating, Tom had a word with the waiter, who returned with a meat pie wrapped in a napkin. Finn eyed it, hunger clear in his face. "You can have it in a little while," Tom said. "You'll be ill if you eat too much at once." Although it might be wise to let the lad have more food before walking back to the barracks. "Why did you run away?"

"My uncle turned nasty after Da's pay come. Made me sleep in the workshop, and didn't give me the same food the others had. He took the money Da's mates collected, too. Said he was owed it for feedin' me."

Ah. Had Robson known that money would be forthcoming? It was possible the army had contacted him as the sergeant's next of kin, and he'd welcomed… *appeared* to welcome Finn to get his hands on the back pay.

"How did you get here?"

"Walked. Got a ride on a wagon now and then."

Tom nodded, and pushed part of the pie across the table. "Eat it slowly, now." That Finn could walk three hundred miles wasn't all that surprising—he must have walked across Spain behind the army, after all. But he'd been with his family in Spain. This time he'd done it alone; that showed a great deal of initiative.

Initiative or not, what to do with the lad was going to be a problem. One he could think about later, though. The first thing to do was to get him cleaned up. He wasn't going to attempt that in his room in the mess, but there'd be a family at the barracks who'd happily do it for him in exchange for some coin.

Mrs Tattersall was a sergeant's wife, known throughout the battalion for her kind heart and practical common sense. She'd inspected Finn, tutted, and sent Tom away, saying she'd sort the lad out.

"I'll see you later," Tom said to Finn, when the lad seemed reluctant to leave him. "I promise."

Finn nodded, and trudged off after Mrs Tattersall while Tom went in search of his own dinner. A couple of hours later the mess steward came to tell him he was wanted outside.

Mrs Tattersall was alone; Tom took her into an empty anteroom. "Is he all right?"

"He will be now," she said, taking the seat he indicated. "I've washed him and his clothes, and put him to bed with my lads. He can borrow some of Fred's things until his own are dry. But you should know that someone's been beating him."

Tom had suspected as much. "Recently?"

"No. There's bits of old bruises showing; some weeks old, I'd guess."

Robson, then, not as a result of some unfortunate encounter on his journey. And although Tom hadn't insisted that Finn go to his uncle, he hadn't really given the lad much of a choice.

"He didn't want to talk about it," Mrs Tattersall added.

Tom rubbed his face. "His father was killed at Tarbes, mother died before that, while they were still in Spain. The surgeon sent him back with me, and I took him to his uncle."

"His kin did that?" She frowned. "Does he have to go back there?"

"Not if I can help it. But I don't know what to do with him. Unless you can...?" His voice tailed off at her grimace.

"Not unless you can pay, sir. It's hard enough making ends meet."

"Sorry." He should have worked that out for himself—there would have been other difficulties, too. "I'll think of something. Can you look after him for a few days? Best feed him up before we do anything else."

"I can do that, yes."

Tom tried to work out how much she would need, but then just gave her all the coins he had in his pocket. "Let me know if you need more. And get him a change of clothes, if you can."

"I will, thank you, Captain."

Tom watched her go, then returned to his ale. The book he'd been reading lay ignored on the table while he considered his latest problem.

It had been an impulsive suggestion that the sergeant's wife would take the lad. One that only a little thought would have ruled out. Finn seemed to have latched onto Tom as his protector, and was determined enough to have walked for weeks to find him. Passing him off to a sergeant's wife would work while they were in barracks, but Mrs Tattersall might not win the ballot next time the regiment was posted abroad. The odds were always poor, with only a limited number of families officially allowed to accompany their menfolk. And that would mean leaving Finn in England with a family who were no relation. Not to mention the fact that Sergeant Tattersall might object to some of his wife's attention being given to a stranger.

No—if he was posted abroad, the only solution was to send Finn to Frank to find a school for him.

CHAPTER 24

*E*llie closed the door to Jamie's room quietly. It had taken nearly half an hour to get him to go to sleep, and she didn't want to disturb him now. Downstairs, instead of heading for the kitchen she stepped out of the front door. Dusk had fallen while she'd been busy with her son, and now the western sky was streaked with red. Ellie breathed the cool air with its faint scent of phlox, enjoying the peace after Jamie's fractious crying. Out here, there was only the faint cackle of jackdaws settling into a distant tree and leaves rustling in the breeze.

Agnes came out of the door to stand beside her. "Is Jamie all right, missus?"

"He is now. The oil of cloves helped." She would be glad when he had all his teeth.

"Bill came from Bank Side to say one of the mares is sick, missus, and the master might not be back tonight."

"Which one?"

"Ginger, he said. Funny, thing—Kate was reet bothered about it. I said you might take her when you go to Bank Side tomorrow."

Ellie took in Agnes' worried frown. "Of course I will."

· · ·

Martin had not reappeared by the time they finished breakfast the next morning, so Agnes packed the results of the previous day's baking into two baskets while Jake harnessed Lass to the gig. Jamie co-operated with donning his coat and shoes when he learned they were going to see the 'horsies', and Ellie handed him up to Kate before taking the reins. She would have enjoyed the walk, as the breeze was warm for September and the sun shone between gaps in the clouds. But Agnes and Fanny were to do laundry today, and could not supervise Jamie at the same time.

Mick opened the gate as the gig approached, eyeing the baskets with a grin.

"How's the mare?" Ellie asked, jumping down and reaching for her son.

"Master reckons she's on the mend, missus." He jerked his head. "In the end stall."

"Can I see her?" Kate asked, and trotted off at his nod.

"I'd best see Kate don't disturb her," Mick said, and followed. Dan and Martin appeared in the kitchen as Ellie was unpacking mutton pies and fruit cake.

"Excellent. That cake'll go nicely with some coffee." Martin slumped into a chair as Dan hung the kettle above the fire.

"Mick said the mare will recover—is that right?" Ellie asked, sitting down opposite him.

"I think so. Could take some time though. Good thing we'd already started weaning her foal." He seemed tired, and the limp way he sat in the chair made Ellie wonder if he'd been up with the animal all night. He looked up at Dan. "Go and fetch Kate in, will you? The mare needs to rest. Probably needs to be put in a clean stall, as well."

Dan went off, and Ellie deposited Jamie on Martin's knee while she found the coffee and made a large pot. Then she took plates off the shelf and cut the fruit cake into large slabs. Martin wouldn't have been the only one up all night.

Kate came back alone. Dan came in later, when most of the cake and coffee had gone.

"You'd best come and see this, sir," Dan said to Martin. With a sigh,

Martin stood and followed him out, Jamie on one hip. Curious, Ellie went with them. They didn't go into the stalls, but to a pile of muck in one corner of the yard.

"Mick were cleaning out the mare's stall," Dan explained. "Take a look."

They appeared to be normal droppings to Ellie, but Martin handed Jamie to her and crouched down to examine them more closely. He poked at something on the surface. "Acorn husks?"

"Quite a lot of them." Dan stirred the pile with a shovel. "She ate enough acorns to give her colic."

"Damn." Martin straightened. "Has she been out of the field?"

"A gate were left open last week," Dan admitted. "But we got them all back within an hour."

"She must have eaten them more recently than that."

Dan nodded. "Dunno where she got them, though. Didn't think there were many oak trees around."

"Best send someone to check the hedgerows," Martin said. "It would only take one tree, if she ate everything on the ground. Make sure there aren't any left lying around."

"Right, sir."

"Now go in and get your cake before the others eat it all."

"It's time you came home," Ellie said to Martin when Dan had gone.

"Very well. I'll just have a quick word with Dan."

Jamie wriggled in her arms. "No, Jamie, you can't play here. Wait until we get home. Come, you can hold the reins." She put him up on the seat of the gig and gave him the reins, going to Lass' head while Jamie pretended to drive.

Martin drove them back, Ellie and Jamie beside him and Kate sitting on the narrow backwards-facing seat behind them with her legs dangling.

"Acorns?" Ellie asked.

"Poisonous to horses," Martin said, glancing at her. "You didn't know?"

"No. I had no occasion to. My father bought hay for his horse, and it's never been mentioned here."

"It doesn't happen often."

"Could someone have given them to her?"

"Palmer, you mean?" Martin frowned. "No-one's told me about strangers around. And why harm one of the horses at all?"

"Revenge?" Ellie suggested. "When you wouldn't give him any of your winnings."

"Why Ginger, in that case? Why not Fleet? Poisoning him would be revenge indeed."

A sob came from behind as Martin turned into their lane. Ellie twisted round in the seat. "Don't worry, Kate. Ginger will be fine. And her foal."

~

"Hit it harder."

Tom tightened his grip on the surgeon's old sword. Its blade was already full of nicks and dents, and he was about to add to them. He swung again, putting more effort into it. This time he couldn't hide the wince as the impact with the wooden post sent a stabbing pain through the muscles around his shoulder.

"Now from the other direction."

He made the first stroke a gentle one, then repeated the action with more force. Swinging across his body and outwards exercised different muscles, but it didn't take many strokes before his shoulder began to protest.

"Hmm. I think we will omit downward attempts for now."

Tom followed the surgeon back into his office and propped the old sword in a corner before sitting down and rubbing his shoulder. "What's the verdict?"

"Have you tested it that way before?"

"Several weeks ago, yes." Not long after the surgeon had first inspected his wound. "It's improving, but slowly."

"You'll be fit for active duty in a few weeks." The surgeon leaned back in his chair. "There are rumours we're being sent off to America soon—six to eight weeks, probably. The men will have had a few months' rest by then. I'll suggest you be given duties with headquarters if you're still not fully fit—although by the time we've crossed the Atlantic you'll probably be ready for action." He nodded as Tom left.

The surgeon's verdict left Tom with mixed feelings. He was pleased to be told he should eventually regain full use of his shoulder—who wouldn't be? But he'd been having doubts about his future, and he realised that he'd half hoped that the surgeon's verdict would make the decision for him. Which was stupid, he knew, for that meant he'd been hoping his shoulder would *not* pass muster.

Back in the mess, he ordered an ale and sat down to think. The years in the Peninsula had made him forget just how tedious peace-time army life could be. Normally he'd be busier drilling his company, but many of the men were on leave and the battalion was officially resting. If the surgeon was right, they'd be off again soon—but a month or more on a ship across the Atlantic would be even more tedious than living in barracks.

Then, as ever, there was his worry about Ellie and their son. Someone who had attempted to get a man hanged to gain money wasn't likely to stop. And now he had Finn to look after, too. Keeping Finn with him while he was with headquarters would be possible—Finn could make a passable servant if he tried. But in all conscience, he could not take the boy with him into action.

"Bad news?" It was Lieutenant Junor. He sat down with his own pint of ale.

"No." No-one else would doubt that it was good news. "Passed fit to stay on active duty." A quick grimace crossed Junor's face. "You wish I'd been told to sell out?"

Junor shrugged, then sighed. "Not really. But dead men's shoes and all that. There's not much chance of a vacancy now we're home."

"Rumour has it we're off to the Americas soon, so you might get your wish. Whose demise did you have in mind?"

Junor grinned, taking the words as Tom had meant them. "Very funny. It's just that I've come into some funds and I've got enough to purchase a captaincy now, but I don't want to leave the regiment."

Lucky Junor. Tom's rise to lieutenant, and then to captain, had been field promotions—the dead men's shoes Junor had referred to—without the need to purchase. He'd never have got so far otherwise.

"You're the senior lieutenant?" The one who would be given first opportunity to purchase a vacant rank.

"No. But I asked around, and I'm the most senior of the ones who have the money for purchase."

"You've plenty of time." Junor was not yet in his mid-twenties—and that made Tom feel old. He didn't have enough to buy a major's commission, so there was a good chance he'd remain a captain until he retired. Something else to take into account, but not at this moment. "D'you fancy a game of piquet?"

They played for penny points, and Tom ended up several shillings down. He blamed lack of concentration, although Junor was also a very good player. He thanked the lieutenant for the game, and went to find out how Finn was getting on.

The lad had slept most of the previous day, being woken by Mrs Tattersall for meals and then retreating to his mattress again afterwards. But today when Tom asked for him at the men's quarters, Finn came out looking not only clean but rested, the shadows around his eyes gone although his expression was wary.

"Come with me; we'll go to the beach." Tom set off towards the gate—there was little privacy in barracks, and it was often easier to talk over difficult matters while walking.

"Tell me about it," Tom said, once they were away from the barracks. The tale came out in fits and starts, with much prompting from Tom. It seemed Finn had been treated as well as the Robsons' own children to start with. Finn had handed over the money collected by his father's company, told by his uncle that it was needed to buy him new clothes. Then a man had come asking for Finn, who had confirmed that his uncle clothed and fed him. When the man left, Finn's new clothes were given to his cousins, he was banished to a pallet in the smithy for his bed, and spent all his time tending to the horses brought for shoeing, working the bellows at the furnace or sweeping up. It also sounded as if he'd been half starved, which Tom might not have believed had Mrs Tattersall not mentioned the remains of bruises.

"And he hit you when you complained?"

Finn nodded. "Said he'd got Da's money now so I was just another useless mouth to feed, and no son of an Irish whore would ever be any good." His bottom lip stuck out. "Ma wasn't a whore! It wasn't right of him to say that."

"D'you know what I think?" Tom said, keeping his voice calm. Finn shook his head. "A man who says someone is good or bad because of where they are born is not a good person. And someone who pretends to like you only to make money is a very bad person." He briefly considered whether Frank could get Finn's money back, but it was probably more bother than it was worth.

"What's goin' to happen to me now?" Finn's voice wobbled.

"I don't know yet. But I'll sort something out—*not* your uncle. Now, do you know how to play ducks and drakes?" A suitable diversion, Tom hoped, to take the lad's mind off his future.

"No. What's that?"

So Tom showed him how to choose flat stones and throw them so they bounced across the surface of the sea. It wasn't the best of days for learning, with not much smooth water between the waves, but Finn got the hang of it quickly and became quite competitive. They finally stopped when Tom's shoulder protested at the effort; Tom was surprised how much time had passed. He'd enjoyed himself. Was that what it would be like playing with a son?

Not feeling like talking, he sent Finn back to the barracks alone, and walked along the beach. Would he ever have a son of his own? It would not happen while he was in the army—following the drum was no life for a woman, even if he could find someone who connected with him in the way Ellie had. As she still did. Nor was leaving a wife in England for years at a time something that he would do. If he was to wed, it would be to a woman he wanted to be with all the time.

He'd been sixteen years in the army—nearly half his life. It had suited him until now, but he wasn't sure he wanted to spend the rest of his days being ordered from one place to another. He could ask to go on half-pay, but he couldn't live comfortably on that income, even if his colonel would agree to it.

No, it was stay in or sell out. The more he thought about it, the more it seemed right to remain in England. Junor was a good officer; Tom would have no qualms about leaving his men if Junor was to take over.

There was still the matter of earning a living, though. He kicked at a stone—so many things in life came down to money. Either the lack of it, or the desire for more. There were limited opportunities in civilian life for a man whose main skills were killing enemy soldiers and preventing his men looting. He could try for a position in the militia, but the idea of being used to control his own countrymen did not appeal to him.

But looking at it in a different way, the skills he did have involved managing men, and it wasn't only soldiers who needed managing. He'd have to do it without the threat of flogging that too many officers resorted to, but he'd never found that particularly effective in any case. Digging the navigations? There were plenty of teams of men involved there. Even in a factory, perhaps, although he'd rather not spend his days indoors. Farming? How much did it cost to buy a farm and settle down?

He would get the price of a captain's commission when he left, even though he hadn't originally paid for it. That was the equivalent of several years' pay. The interest would not be enough to live on if he invested it, but it would give him time to find some other way of earning a living. He wasn't making this decision so he could remain close enough to help if Ellie needed him, but that was an advantage of selling out.

He'd sleep on it, but if this feeling of rightness was still with him tomorrow, he'd make an appointment to talk to the colonel.

CHAPTER 25

*E*llie went up to Bank Side again several days later, to ride a gelding that Martin was thinking of selling as a lady's mount. She didn't take food this time, as Agnes and Kate had walked up the day before; Kate had returned much happier than she had been, saying that Ginger was getting better now.

Dan accompanied her onto the moors, as Martin wanted to go through the racing calendar with Sam. It wasn't the first time she had ridden the gelding, so when they came out of the trees they headed for the smooth areas where they could gallop. There was a stiff breeze, and Ellie felt wind-blown and exhilarated by the time the horses had been put through their paces.

"Time to go back?" Ellie asked. Dan nodded, but didn't follow as Ellie turned her horse to the west. "Is there something amiss?"

"I think so." He spoke hesitantly. "I'm not sure... I might be wrong."

"Talking about something can help you to get things straight in your mind." It sometimes worked for her. "Shall we walk?"

"Kate came to Bank Side yesterday," Dan began as they led the horses towards the track down through the woods. "She went to see Ginger."

"Yes, she told me," Ellie prompted, when he hesitated again.

"Thing is, missus, I heard her talking to her. Kate talking to Ginger, I mean."

"She talks to most of the animals."

"She were apologising."

That was odd. "Are you sure? Not just saying she was sorry Ginger had been unwell?"

"No, missus. 'I didn't mean to make you sick', she said, and 'I didn't know they were bad for you'."

Ellie met Dan's eyes. "You think that Kate gave the acorns to Ginger?"

Dan nodded. "It's not just that. We went round the hedgerows, like the master said. There's one big oak on Bank Side land, and some small ones. There weren't no acorns under the big one."

"That could just mean that Ginger ate them, could it not?"

"The horses haven't been in that field. Only way there could be none lying around is if someone picked them up."

"One of the men?"

"They say not, missus. No need, see, if the horses weren't there."

"But why would Kate do that? Unless someone... Dan, have there been any strangers around?"

"Haven't seen any."

Which was not the same as there not having been anyone. Ellie stopped and closed her eyes for a moment. Would this harassment never end?

"I don't reckon Kate would take it into her head to feed acorns to the horses, missus. Nor why anyone would want to harm Ginger. But most horses don't like acorns anyway. If someone suggested she feed acorns to Fleet, and he didn't like them, she might have tried some of the other horses."

"And poor Ginger does like them," Ellie finished. "*Does* Fleet like acorns?"

"We could find out, missus, but I didn't want to give him any without the master's permission. If he does like them, one or two wouldn't be enough to hurt."

"We'll ask," Ellie promised.

Back at Bank Side, Ellie waited until Martin had finished his business, and took him to one side so Dan could explain.

"I think it's far-fetched," Martin said, "but you can try Fleet with a few acorns if you wish."

Ellie watched with him as Dan offered a few acorns to Fleet. The stallion put his head down, sniffing at the offering, then he tossed his head, his top lip curling up to show all his teeth.

Dan offered the acorns again, and Fleet took a step back, turning his head away. "I think he don't like them, missus."

Ellie couldn't help smiling at the understatement as they went back out into the yard.

"That proves nothing," Martin objected.

"It doesn't *disprove* Dan's idea," Ellie said. "The only way is to ask Kate."

"I'll have a word with her." Martin scowled. "She's been told often enough not to talk to strangers."

"Let me talk to her." Ellie put a hand on his arm. "If you speak to her like that you'll frighten her and we'll never find out anything." She turned to Dan. "I'll let you know what she says. If what you suspect is what happened."

It took most of the afternoon. As any suggestion that Kate was being reprimanded usually resulted in floods of tears, Ellie tried an indirect approach. She started by telling Agnes and Fanny what Dan had surmised, and then said that they would spend the rest of the afternoon baking cakes and pies, summoning Kate to help. She slipped questions into the conversation, and eventually confirmed—to her own satisfaction, at least—that Kate had collected the acorns and fed them to Ginger. She hadn't talked to strangers; she knew she wasn't supposed to do that. But the man who'd suggested that a nice reward for Fleet winning in York would be to have lots of acorns to eat said he worked at Bank Side. In Kate's mind, that meant he couldn't be a stranger—which was logical in an odd kind of way. But no new workers had been taken on at Bank Side since Dan arrived.

"Was it the man who gave you the ribbon last year?" Ellie asked, trying to keep her voice light.

"No!" Kate sounded offended. "I remember I'm not to talk to him."

"That's all right, then." Ellie smiled. "Can you chop those apples, Kate?" And a little later, when the pies were in the oven, Ellie casually asked if Ginger was the only horse who liked acorns.

"Fleet didn't," Kate replied, her brow creased with the effort to remember. "Nor did Socks or Chestnut or Primrose." Her voice turned into a wail. "Ginger liked them, so I gave them all to her. I didn't know!"

Agnes hurried around the table and hugged her, and Ellie patted her shoulder. "You know now, Kate, don't you?" Kate nodded vigorously. "And you won't feed any of the animals without asking one of the men first?" Kate shook her head, and Ellie left it at that for the moment. Later, when Kate had calmed down, she would impress upon her that the acorn man was a stranger and she mustn't talk to him again.

"Kate mentioned Fleet first," Ellie said that evening, when she and Martin were having their after-dinner port together. "She was past the stage of being questioned further, but it was clear that Fleet was the target."

"It would seem so." Martin sighed. He must be even more weary of his cousin's activities than she was.

"What are you going to do to protect the horses?"

"There's not much I can do," he admitted. "The stallions will have to be kept in the stable, and watched when they're put into the paddock. The rest will have to take their chances."

"What about this stranger? I'm going to stop Kate going up to the farm alone for a while, but he might try something else. I suppose your cousin paid him to do it."

"More likely to be a promise of payment," Martin said, "if what Allerby said was correct."

It took Ellie a second to realise he was referring to the letter the attorney had sent, describing Palmer's debts. Her mind had gone straight to Tom—but Tom had hardly spoken to Martin when he was here.

"But I'd lay odds he won't have paid whoever it is," Martin went on, "because nothing happened to Fleet. Ellie—don't worry. When we were children, he got up to enough mischief, but he rarely did the deed himself. It was almost always someone else who got the blame."

"He damaged the henhouse," Ellie pointed out.

"A minor thing that could never be proven. Allerby said Palmer paid that Cullton lad to lay information against me. And if Fleet had been poisoned, Kate would have got the blame. I can't put the law on him for that—we'd need to find the man who talked to Kate, and then prove that Palmer promised to pay him to do it. Besides, can you imagine having Kate tell her story before a magistrate?"

She could imagine only too well. They could never subject Kate to that.

"Ellie, he won't put himself at risk of arrest, or attack me himself."

She was not convinced. "He's already employed someone, for the acorns. Now Kate has seen that man, he could employ someone else."

"He could try. But word will get around that he cannot pay, and who would risk breaking the law themselves if they are unlikely to be rewarded?"

"Should you take on more men? Or do the ones you've got have enough time to keep a look out for someone lurking around in the area?"

"I'll have a word with Dan and Sam," Martin promised. "And I'll tell them to take extra care when I'm in Manchester the week after next."

She had to be content with that.

Ellie managed to put her worries about Palmer to the back of her mind for nearly a week. Until the day that Agnes told her she'd seen a stranger in the fields between the two farms. He'd been too far away for Agnes to describe his appearance, but she didn't think it was one of the stable hands from Bank Side.

Martin wasn't particularly worried by it. "It could have been anyone, Ellie. And what harm can someone do, just walking in the fields? I'll have someone ride around to check the hedges and gates, if that will make you happier?"

Ellie nodded, but couldn't rid herself of the feeling that Martin wasn't taking his cousin's actions seriously enough. He was basing his confidence on what he'd known of Palmer when they were young—but people could change. Was there anything that could be done to keep Palmer away from the farm? Some sort of order from a court, perhaps? Although that would not work if Palmer hired men to do his bidding, it might still be worth trying.

The next day, when Martin was at Bank Side, she wrote a letter to Mr Allerby describing the acorn incident and asking if there was any way of preventing Palmer from bothering them again. She gave it to Jake to post when he went into Thirsk the following day.

Nothing more happened, and Martin set off for Manchester at the end of the following week as he'd planned. Dan continued with his work at Bank Side during the day, but slept at Knowle Farm overnight —Ellie found it reassuring to have him close by in case something did happen. Then, four days after Martin left for Manchester, she received a letter from him. He'd had word of someone living in Shrewsbury who might be a useful partner in breeding racehorses, so he would be away at least an extra week.

Ten more days of worrying about the man that Agnes had seen, not just three.

"Tom! I didn't expect to see you so soon." Frank stood and walked around his desk as the clerk retreated to the front office, closing the door behind him. "I only got your letter last week." He clapped Tom on the shoulder.

"Things were well in hand by the time I wrote." Although it had taken over a fortnight to extricate himself from the army. "I don't want to interrupt your work; just called to let you know I've arrived." Before retreating to his bed at the inn, even though it was only mid-morning. He never had been able to sleep on an overnight coach.

Frank looked at the papers on his desk, then shuffled them into one pile and locked them in a drawer. "This can wait. Come out for a drink? Ale," he added. "I haven't gone back to my old habits."

"Coffee would be better."

"Coffee it is, then."

"Good journey?" Frank asked, when they were settled at a corner table in a nearby coffee house.

"As good as it ever is, being cooped up inside a coach. And that after hanging around London for days waiting to see various clerks at Horse Guards."

Frank laughed at his grimace. "Where are you staying?"

"The Prince Rupert, same as last time. I left Finn there."

"Finn? Where did you find him?"

"He walked to Hythe."

"Good heavens! I'm sorry—if I'd known he was that desperate I'd have made more of an effort to look for him."

"You couldn't have known, and he's not your responsibility."

"He's not yours, either." Frank frowned. "That isn't why you sold out, is it?"

Tom shrugged. "Partly, but only a part. There were a number of reasons. I don't know what I'm going to do with myself yet, but I've enough money to tide me over while I find something."

"Nothing to do with that letter from Mrs Wilson, then?"

"Letter?" Tom's attention sharpened. "What letter? The last I heard from you was when you told me Finn had come here."

"I wrote to you..." He paused, his gaze becoming unfocused. "Two weeks ago, or a bit longer. The second letter only arrived a couple of days ago."

"The other one? For heaven's sake, Frank, why didn't you tell me straight away? What did they say?"

"I'll show them to you." Frank stood and summoned the waiter to pay.

In his office, Frank extracted two sheets of paper from a drawer and handed one to Tom. It described a poisoned horse and the Wilsons' suspicion that Palmer was behind it.

"*Is* there some kind of injunction you could take out to keep Palmer away?" Tom asked, when he finished reading.

"It's possible, but Wilson would have to request it. From what his wife says, it doesn't seem as though he's sufficiently worried to try. This one might concern you more." He handed over another letter.

It did. Tom scanned it quickly, then read the key parts a second time.

> *...away on business longer than expected... stranger seen in the nearby fields several times... don't like to employ extra men from the area in case Palmer has already paid them to act for him... will ask Mr Roseworth... wondered if you had any other advice for me in my husband's absence.*

"Did you have any other advice?"

Frank shook his head. "Roseworth seemed a capable man, sensible to ask him. I wrote to that effect."

Sensible, yes. But if Wilson hadn't been concerned enough about the situation to stay at home, would Roseworth take Ellie's worries seriously? "I'll go."

"I thought you weren't going to see Mrs Wilson again."

"I won't. I'll try to talk to their man Cole. Ex-soldier. If he thinks there's nothing to worry about I'll come straight back."

Tom headed for the livery stable and arranged for a horse to be ready in an hour. He needed to eat or he'd be no use to anyone when he arrived, so he took Finn to a nearby tavern. "I'm going away for a few days," he explained as they ate. "I've paid for the room, so you can stay there until I'm back."

Finn didn't speak, but the hand holding his laden fork fell back to the table and he stared at his plate. Tom castigated himself—Finn had kept close to him ever since they left the barracks at Hythe, even waiting in the street near Horse Guards while Tom was dealing with the sale of his commission. He wouldn't want to be left alone here, and who could blame him after all he'd gone through?

Could Frank help? No—Susannah was living with him now.

"Or you can come with me."

Finn looked up with a watery smile.

"You'll have to do *exactly* as I say, though," Tom added. Finn usually did, but if there was to be any danger he had to keep the lad out of it.

"I will." With renewed appetite, Finn ate the rest of his meal.

Half an hour later they rode out of York with Finn sitting behind Tom on the hired horse.

"Not too far now," Tom said as they came to a village. "We'll stop to ask directions." He hadn't approached Bank Side from the south before.

The Whitestonecliffe Inn had only a few customers, one hunched behind a newspaper in a window seat, and another pair absorbed in a game of dominoes. Tom bought some slices of mutton pie to eat on their way, and the landlord gave them the required directions. The place had even fewer customers as they left; the man reading the newspaper had gone, leaving it behind him.

The late afternoon sky was grey; not even the yellowing leaves on the trees could brighten the dull day, although the sky to the west was clear. The directions were easy to follow, and it wasn't long before Tom dismounted by the gate at Bank Side. From here the main yard was visible between the house and another stone building, but there was no sign of activity. He waited for a minute, hoping someone might have seen him arrive, but no-one came.

"Hello!" he called, not wanting to just go in. He called again, and eventually someone appeared. "Is Cole about?"

"Aye, somewhere. You're just in time, I reckon. I'll fetch him." He ambled off, seemingly in no hurry.

When Dan Cole appeared he greeted Tom with a nod, casting a curious glance at Finn. "Captain. What can I do for you?"

"Mrs Wilson is worried about Palmer—she wrote to my brother about it. He's an attorney in York. I came to see if I could be of assistance."

"Why didn't you go straight to Knowle Farm to ask her?" Cole asked, leaning on the gate.

"This place was on the way." That would have to do as an excuse. Cole narrowed his eyes for a moment, then shrugged.

"What did that other man mean when he said I was just in time?" Tom asked.

"I stay at Knowle Farm at night while the master's away. I were just about to set off."

"Mrs Wilson *is* worried, then?"

"She is." Cole eyed the tired horse. "You'd better come in. That fellow looks like he could do with a rest while we talk."

CHAPTER 26

Cole showed Finn where to take the horse, and led Tom into a dim kitchen that smelled faintly of tobacco smoke. They sat at the table.

"You said Mrs Wilson wrote," Cole began. "Did she mention Palmer trying to poison Fleet?"

"Yes. And that there's been a stranger about."

Cole nodded. "Not seen him myself, but Agnes, at the other farm, saw him a couple of times, and one of the lads here did, too. Don't think it were Palmer, though."

"He's paid others to act for him before. When I was here a few months ago it was because Palmer had tried to get Wilson in trouble with the law. If he'd succeeded, Wilson could have been in real danger." Cole opened his mouth, but Tom hurried on, wanting to avoid any explanation of exactly what Palmer had attempted. "Palmer thinks he'll get his hands on the two farms if Wilson is out of the way. He won't, but that doesn't seem to have stopped him trying. He's deep in debt and needs to pay off his creditors. He's very likely to be planning something else."

"I dunno what's to be done." Cole looked dispirited. "Master's keeping the stallions in the stables instead of the fields, but there's not a lot else we can do."

"Keep watch at night?" Tom suggested.

"Pickets and patrols? Chance'd be a fine thing. Trouble is, the others here all think it were spite on Palmer's part, because the master got Fleet's winnings and his cousin got nothing. And why should he? None of us knew he'd tried to harm the master directly."

"Poisoning Fleet could well have been mere spite, but that doesn't mean he won't try real harm to Wilson. Mrs Wilson said she would ask Roseworth, the magistrate, for extra men—do you know whether she did so?"

"I drove her there a couple of days ago. Seems he said something about discussing it with the master when he gets back."

What use was that now?

"I'll take a look around before I go down to the other farm," Cole went on, "but unless the master gives the order, I can't make the others take watch about at night."

"I could stay. Tonight, at least, if you have room for us both."

"My bed'll be empty, but that's not fit—"

"I was thinking more of some straw in the stables. And that'll be luxury compared to some places I've slept."

"The lad, too?"

"He's not mine, although he seems to have adopted me." Tom explained Finn's situation. "I'll not ask him to keep watch, but he'll be happy anywhere dry and warm."

"All right—I'd be easier in my mind." Cole stood. "Let me show you around." Out in the yard, he pointed to a long building to one side, with a stone stair to a door on the upper floor and small windows. "Most of the men sleep up there. Mainly stalls underneath —only two mares in there at the moment. Hay in there…" He pointed to a barn across the yard as he walked over to a building that made the fourth side of the square. Inside, Finn was standing by Tom's hired horse in one of the stalls lining one wall. He came to join them as Cole stopped by a handsome bay animal in a spacious loose box at one end of the building. "This is Fleet—won at York this year." Pride shone in Cole's face as he said it. "Blackie, down the other end, is our other stallion."

Cole moved on, and stroked the nose of the fourth horse in the building. "This poor lady is Ginger, the one that got poisoned. She's still not right. All the other animals are out in the fields." They heaped a pile of clean straw in one of the empty stalls for Finn to sleep on, then Cole introduced Tom to the other men before leaving for Knowle Farm.

The men happily shared their evening meal with Tom and Finn, taking it in turns to keep a watch outside. It was not done without some grumbling, but Cole had insisted before he left. The evening passed quickly, the men talking amongst themselves about Fleet and the other horses. Finn listened with avid attention until his yawns became too large.

"I'll take watch now," Tom said, and left the others to their talk and ale. He took one of the kitchen chairs with him and placed it by the doorway at Fleet's end of the stable. Finn bedded on his straw, wrapped in a borrowed blanket. Checking that the pistols in his pockets were primed, Tom settled down for a long night.

Keeping watch when there might be enemy soldiers about was sensible, Tom thought an hour later. Trying to stay awake all night because a stranger had been seen in the fields a few days ago seemed more like being over-cautions. And doing it for a woman who was married to someone else made even less sense.

Too much time to think, that was the problem. He wasn't doing it just for Ellie, but for Jamie. And all the men here who didn't deserve to have their livelihood put at risk if Palmer did more damage.

All was quiet—there was only an occasional snort or movement from the horses, or a rustle of straw as Finn turned over. And this chair was damned uncomfortable.

The afternoon's clouds had cleared, and the yard was half in shadow, half in moonlight. Enough light to walk around and revive himself a little. He stepped into the other stable building—the mares slept, and faint sounds of snoring came from the men in the room above. He went on past the hay barn and round to the front of the house. There was no movement, no unexpected noises, but he felt a growing sense of unease.

Completing the circuit of the buildings, he returned to his chair, but the feeling persisted. He'd learned to heed such feelings in Spain. There had been nothing wrong, more often than not, but on a couple of occasions his company had avoided an ambush by changing their plans.

He stood and moved the chair inside, keeping himself in the shadow of the doorway as he watched. Was that a moving shadow, or a trick of his eyes? There was nothing for the breeze to move, nothing to hear, and only the smells of manure and horses, and a lingering scent of smoke from the banked fire in the kitchen.

The kitchen that was downwind of his position—and a banked fire should not make much smoke at all. Cursing, Tom ran across the yard to the building where the men slept, but there was nothing amiss.

The hay barn?

Back in the yard, the smell of smoke was stronger. "Fire!" He shouted as loudly as he could as he ran towards the barn. The wicket door was ajar, and he stepped through it. Although he was breathing smoke, it was not yet choking—if he could see where the fire was, might the hay barn still be saved?

"Sir?" Finn's voice.

Tom went back through the wicket. "There's a fire. Wake the men. Get a lantern. Hurry."

Finn dashed off, shouting, and Tom lifted the bar holding the main doors shut. He could do nothing without light.

Moonlight showed only empty floor, and rakes and pitchforks stacked against a wall. There was a loft above, but the smoke was coming from the bundles of straw stacked at ground level. Where was the fire?

There, a faint glow off to one side.

"Damn." The stallions were worth more than the hay crop. Sprinting across the yard again, he met the men coming the other way. "You two with the lanterns—see if you can deal with the fire. You, check the horses in your building." The third man set off at a run, and Tom made for the stallions, arriving at the same time as Sam Barnaby.

"Check the straw," Tom said, starting at Fleet's end as Sam began at the other. No fire here, thank God, although the animals were snorting and tossing their heads.

"What happened?" Sam asked.

"Fire in the hay barn, but it's not been going long. I didn't see anyone running off so they could still be here. Best to get Fleet out of harm's way?" He made it a question.

"I can take him to Knowle," Sam said.

"The other stallion?"

"Can't lead him—the two of them will fight. Someone else'll have to ride him there."

"I'll send someone on when we've dealt with the fire."

"Saddle's across the yard," Sam said, and hurried off.

Tom considered the other animals—they would be better off in the adjacent field, away from the smoke. And out of danger, should the fire spread to the other buildings. He was leading them out as Sam returned with saddle and bridle.

"Sam—don't ride along the lane. Go through the fields. Someone might be waiting."

Sam's hands stilled for a moment, then he nodded in understanding and continued saddling the stallion.

"Tell Cole to stay at Knowle, *not* to come back with you. And take this." Tom handed over one of his pistols. "It's primed—you know how to use it?"

"More used to a shotgun, but yes." He checked the girth, mounted Fleet and rode off.

The smoke was thicker in the yard as Tom headed for the barn.

Ellie listened, wondering what had woken her. She'd been more attuned to noises in the night since Jamie was born, but she could hear nothing out of the ordinary now. She wouldn't sleep again unless she checked, so she threw the covers back and pulled on a robe. It took a few moments to light a candle, then she padded across the landing to Jamie's room. He was sound asleep, a mere lump under the covers. Then, through the window that faced the yard, came the clop of hooves.

Martin? No—he was not expected back for several days yet. It must be someone from Bank Side.

In the kitchen she exchanged her candle for a lantern and ventured out into the yard. The air was chill, and she hurried across to the stable, stopping at the entrance as she recognised Sam talking to Dan.

Had something happened to Fleet?

"Fire in the hay barn, missus," Sam said. "The new man said to get Fleet safe away from Bank Side in case it were that Palmer."

And there was Fleet, placidly munching hay in one of the stalls as if nothing had happened. But the hay barn... To lose this season's hay harvest, and possibly the barn as well, would not be as bad as losing Fleet, but it would still be a major loss even if the fire didn't spread to any of the other buildings.

Ellie took a deep breath, then another. Worry about the facts, not imaginings. "Is the fire out, Sam? Was there much damage? Should you and Dan go back—?"

"No, missus. He said Dan were to stay here, to make sure you were all safe. I can go back, though, if I can have a different horse."

"Yes. Yes, of course. Is anyone hurt? Should I come with...?" What? Bandages? Laudanum? She had treated nothing more than fingers or hands burnt by touching hot cooking pots.

"There weren't no-one in the barn when it took light," Sam said.

"You should stay here, missus," Dan interjected, lifting the saddle off Fleet and putting it onto the horse in the next stall. Sam fitted the bridle, and Dan went with him to the gate, closing it again as Sam trotted off down the lane.

"Dan, who is the 'new man' giving orders?" Ellie asked, when he returned. Orders that Dan was obeying.

"Captain Allerby, missus. The one that were a friend of your brother."

Ellie was glad of the darkness to hide her expression. Being pleased they had an ally was fine. Being so happy that it was Tom was not. Mr Allerby must have shown him her letter, and he'd come. But now Tom was fighting the fire, along with the other men at Bank Side.

"How bad is the fire, Dan? Did Sam say?"

"They'd only just found it when Sam left, so it can't have been going long. There's nothing we can do but wait, missus. And best not wait out here in the cold."

"You're right." Ellie headed for the kitchen, but stopped and turned back when she realised that Dan was not following.

"I'll stay out here, missus."

On guard. She wouldn't sleep now, not until she knew the worst. "Coffee?"

"That'd be grand."

It took a while to blow the banked fire into life, then boil water, but the coffee was finally brewing. Ellie poured two large mugs, wondering at how soundly everyone else in the house seemed to be sleeping. Perhaps she wasn't making as much noise as she thought.

Dan was standing in the entrance to the long barn when she took his coffee out to him, looking very much like the soldier he used to be. She wasn't surprised to see Martin's hunting rifle leaning on the wall beside him.

She had just handed the mug to him when he turned his head at a faint, sharp sound.

"Best get back indoors, missus. That was a gunshot."

Praying that no-one had been hurt, Ellie crossed the yard. Another shot sounded as she reached the kitchen door.

The situation in the barn wasn't good, but Tom thought it could have been a lot worse. The three remaining men were busy with rakes, pulling lumps of smouldering straw into the empty space in the middle of the barn, wet cloths tied across their faces to protect them from breathing the smoke. Finn was carrying buckets from the pump in the yard, the men emptying them onto the fire as quickly as he could bring them. Tom held his lantern aloft, giving them more light and inspecting the still-stacked straw and peering up at the hayloft above.

"Reckon we've saved it, sir," one of men said. "If he really wanted to burn the place down, he'd have set fire to it in more places."

"And he'd have lit the hay, not just the straw," another said. "That'd cost a lot more to replace."

Why hadn't he? From Palmer's behaviour so far, even if the fire had been a distraction or bait, as Tom suspected, he would have taken pleasure in the extra destruction that burning the hay would have caused.

"I need to tell Mrs Wilson what's happened," Tom said. "I'll take Blackie, if one of you can catch him and direct me across the fields."

One of them propped his rake beside the door and went off—Tom had learned their names, but couldn't make out faces in the dim light.

"Can you manage now?" he asked the remaining men. "Don't leave this."

"We'll put it out, sir. Don't you worry."

Tom sent Finn to collect their things, and filled a few more buckets from the pump while he was waiting for the stallion to be saddled.

One of the men lifted Finn up behind Tom, and they were away across the fields. Not fast; by moonlight it was difficult to tell shadows from holes that might injure the horse. They must have been halfway to Knowle Farm when Tom heard a shot—the sound was distant, but unmistakable. Ahead, and to his right—where the lane ran. That could have been aimed at Sam coming back. Blackie pricked his ears, but didn't seem worried by it.

"Did you hear that, sir?" Finn asked, from his perch behind the saddle.

"Yes. Can you see a gate onto the lane?"

Damn it—he'd told Sam to ride to Knowle across the fields, but he hadn't explained why. And the stable master would naturally come back to help.

Another shot.

"Gate's over there, sir."

Tom peered in the direction Finn was pointing, and urged the stallion into a canter. Without being prompted, Finn slid off to open the gate, then Tom hauled him up again. They could not go fast in the lane, for the hedges cast deep shadows onto the surface.

"If there's trouble, you get off and hide in the hedge."

"Can't I help?"

"No. If something happens to me, go and find Dan Cole at the farm further along this lane." Silence. "That's an order, Finn."

"Yes, sir."

Tom took his pistol from his pocket, and they rode on down the lane. He'd always hated engagements in the dark—there was too much risk of tripping on obstacles, or making a noise and alerting the enemy. Or shooting one of your own by mistake. The moonlight wasn't helping—an opponent could hide in the shadows, made darker by the patches of relative brightness.

All they could do was listen. And Finn's ears were sharper than his.

"Horse ahead, sir."

Tom reined in—now he could hear it, too. "Getting closer?" He kept his voice as quiet as Finn's had been.

"Think so."

It must be in the lane—the grass in the fields was soft and they wouldn't hear the hoofbeats.

"Off," Tom ordered, pleased that Finn obeyed without question. Then he dismounted himself—army horses were used to gunshots, but this stallion was an unknown quantity. "Hold him, but if he panics just let him go. Don't let him drag you."

Finn's hand came out to take the reins, and Tom walked on down the lane, keeping to the shadows, and paused as he came to a bend. But the horse, when it came into sight, had no rider. It slowed as it came near, and stopped readily enough when Tom grabbed its reins. It was sweating, and its eyes showed rather more white than they should, but it let Tom stoke its nose. Frightened by the shot, Tom guessed. And somewhere along the lane was a man without a mount.

"Finn, bring Blackie up." They would walk from here—he'd be less of a target than on horseback. "Follow me, but a bit behind."

"Yes, sir."

"Good lad."

The horse hadn't run far—Sam called out to him from the shadow of a hedge and stepped into the lane.

"Are you hurt?" Tom asked.

"No, sir. Someone shot at me. Missed, but I fell off when the horse bolted. He came into the lane, but I shot back and he ran off. I heard a horse."

"Long gone, then."

"The fire, sir?"

"Under control. You'd best come to Knowle with me."

Palmer had now directly attempted to murder a man, or hired someone to do so. Probably not the man he'd intended, but that shot had raised the stakes.

CHAPTER 27

*E*llie went back to her room, lit the lamps and donned her day dress, then stuffed her hair into a cap. All the time she was trying not to think of burning barns and injured men. She was worried about *all* the men at Bank Side, not just Tom. If only she could *do* something, not just wait for news. She checked Jamie on the way back downstairs, but he was still fast asleep.

Dan would spot anyone trying to enter the farmyard directly, but Ellie could help by keeping watch at the front of the house. She did her best to concentrate on looking and trying not to imagine the worst.

Having prepared herself for a long, anxious wait, Ellie was surprised to see riders in the lane only a few minutes later. Just two silhouettes against a moonlit background. They could be friends or enemies.

Dan had already heard them—he passed the parlour window on the way to the gate, rifle ready on one arm. She heard him call a challenge, then he opened the gate.

Friends then. Tom?

Ben's friend, remember. That is all.

Coffee. Even if they didn't want it, making it was something to do. She refilled the kettle and set it on the hob, then opened the back door.

Voices, indistinct. Bates or Jake? Dan must have roused someone to look after the animals. Then Dan saying something about the kitchen, and Tom answering.

"Is something wrong, missus?" Fanny had a shawl over her night-rail.

"We're about to find out." Ellie was glad it was only Fanny. "Try not to wake Agnes yet, she'll only worry."

"Sleeps like the dead," Fanny said as Sam came in, followed by Dan.

"Fire's out, missus," Dan announced, before Ellie could ask him. "No-one hurt."

And there was Tom behind him, streaks of dirt on his face and the carefully controlled expression she should have expected.

Ben's friend.

"Can we use the kitchen to talk, Mrs Wilson?" Tom asked. "There are things you should know, and plans to make." He glanced at Fanny, but said nothing.

"Of course. Please, sit." She took her usual place at one end of the table. Fanny went to the kettle, now boiling, and busied herself with the coffee pot, cups, and plates while the men sat down.

Ellie looked at Tom. "Dan said no-one was hurt. Was there much damage at the farm?"

"Some straw lost, but not too much, I think. The fire wasn't out when I left, but it was under control."

"What happened?"

"I smelled smoke," Tom began. "Woke everyone, got the horses out, and sent Sam here with Fleet." He looked at Sam. "I told you to go by the fields, not the lane."

"I did, sir. But I thought you meant because someone wanted to harm Fleet, and it were quicker to go back along the lane. You never said someone might take a shot at me."

"Yes, I'm sorry for not making it clear."

"Who was it?" Ellie asked.

"Sam scared him off by returning the shot," Tom said. "So we don't know. But given his past actions, it can only have been Palmer, or someone paid by him. Although it does seem an odd coincidence that he should do it on the same day that I arrive." He rubbed a hand through his hair. "I went for a walk around the outside of the buildings an hour or so after everyone else went to bed—that might have given him the chance to set the fire and make his escape."

"And if he knew you were coming right back, he didn't have time to burn the hay properly, nor yet do anything to Fleet," Dan added.

"I'm not sure that Fleet was the target this time. A random poacher shooting at Sam less than an hour after someone set a fire is too much to believe. The fire-starter, or someone working with him, fired that shot."

Ellie put her hands over her face. "If Palmer didn't know Martin was still away, it would have been *Martin* riding along that lane, not Sam. He'd have gone up to Bank Side as soon as he heard about the fire."

Tom was pleased that Ellie had worked it out for herself. He had wondered if he was making too much of what had happened, and hadn't wanted to distress her by suggesting it. There was worse, though.

"What can we do?" she asked, lifting her face.

Tom allowed himself a smile—this was the practical woman he'd met beside a crashed coach two and a half years ago. "Warn your husband, if possible."

"I can write, but the letter may not reach him before he returns."

"When is he expected back?"

"Towards the end of the week, but it may be sooner if his business goes well."

"He usually leaves his horse at the Golden Fleece in Thirsk," Dan Cole put in. "You could leave word there."

"Good idea. But that isn't the only problem." Tom looked beyond Dan. The woman who had provided the coffee was still there—in the background, but listening.

"Everyone will need to know eventually, Captain," Ellie said. "Fanny, come and sit at the table. You may as well hear it now." She met Tom's eye. "Fanny has a good head on her shoulders."

Tom nodded. "Two things. The first concerns your two stallions." Get the easy part out of the way first. "Palmer has failed again, and may still wish to harm them to damage your business."

There were murmurs of agreement around the table.

"They would be safer away from Bank Side. Not here," he added.

"Where, then?" Ellie asked.

"The magistrate who came here—Roseworth. I got the impression he respected Wilson?"

"I think so, yes."

"We could take the animals there and ask him to stable them for a while. Perhaps allow them to..." Was his suggestion too delicate for a woman's ears?

"To cover some of his mares," Ellie finished for him. "Just say what you have to say, Captain. It will be quicker in the end."

"Yes, then. What do you think, Sam?"

Sam opened his mouth, then closed it again. Not liking it, but not wanting to protest, Tom guessed.

"Should Sam stay with them, perhaps?" Ellie suggested. "It would not be fair to expect Mr Roseworth's staff to look after two extra animals. And I understand Fleet can be difficult at times. What is the second thing?"

"In trying to shoot Wilson, Palmer has shown himself to be even more dangerous than we originally thought. He wants the farms, and in his mind you and your son are also obstacles."

Ellie's mind seemed to freeze for a moment. Jamie? Palmer would harm her son?

Of course he would. He wanted the farms. Why had she thought he would try to get them only by legal means if Martin died? If Martin was murdered, rather—she should admit that this was what Palmer intended now.

"This must be a great shock to you, Mrs Wilson."

She swallowed hard, collecting herself before looking at Tom. There was sympathy in his face, but determination, too. "I didn't think Palmer would be so bold as to shoot Martin. But if it was him, then yes, Jamie and I are also in danger."

"You should leave as well."

"There's your sister in Harrogate, missus," Dan suggested. "Does Palmer know about her?"

Ellie tried to think. There was no reason why he would know.

"The papers my brother has mentioned only your original home in Lancashire," Tom said.

"The farm... I can't—"

"Don't you worry none about that, missus," Fanny said. "We can manage well enough on our own for a while."

"Very well, Captain. Dan can drive me to Harrogate tomorrow."

"No." Tom rubbed one temple. "I mean, I have a different suggestion, if I may?"

"Please."

"You... that is, the two farms will be one man short if Sam stays with the stallions. Wilson is away. You cannot spare Dan as well."

Tom could take his place here—but she had no right to ask that of him.

"I'm willing to stay," Tom went on, "but Dan knows the farms and the men. Would it be better if I take you?"

He didn't look happy at the prospect. "You have given up a lot of time for us, Captain. For which I thank you," she added hurriedly, realising that her words could be taken as the beginnings of a refusal.

"I have time on my hands." He pulled a watch out of his pocket. "Three o'clock. Can you be ready to set off at seven? It will be full daylight by then. And the warning to your husband would be better written by you."

She could not fit much luggage on the gig, but it would be enough. Mary would have spare clothing that Jamie could use.

"Mrs Wilson?"

"Sorry. Yes. I can be ready then." She stood.

"One more thing. I have a boy with me—"

"We'll find him a place here, sir," Dan interrupted. "And I'll keep watch until dawn—you get some sleep."

"Fanny can make up a bed for you, Captain." Ellie doubted she would get any sleep herself, but she had too much to do to return to bed anyway. There was the letter to Martin to write, and things to pack.

"Thank you, but I'm sure there'll be space over the stables. If you can show me, Dan?"

That was just as well. She'd be spending too much time close to him tomorrow as it was.

Dan brought Tom a bowl of hot water at six the next morning, and he shaved and managed to brush the worst of the sooty flecks from his greatcoat. He'd lain awake for a while, his body reminding him that Ellie was sleeping in the next building. So close, yet still forbidden. But weariness won in the end and he felt more rested when he awoke.

The sky was lightening as he walked across the yard. Inside, the kitchen seemed full of people. Fanny was at the range stirring something in a large pot, while the sizzling pan beside her filled the air with the aroma of frying bacon. An older woman Tom hadn't seen before sat at the table next to a much younger woman, little more than a girl.

Ellie was beside them with Jamie on her lap, listening to the older woman with a creased brow. Jamie was eating a bowl of porridge, a spoon in one fist and only a few traces of it on his face and on the napkin tucked under his chin. Tom could see a slight resemblance to Ellie in Jamie's face—something about the shape of the eyes, perhaps.

Then Ellie looked up, and his breath caught at the welcome in her smile.

A smile quickly suppressed, reminding Tom that he was supposedly here as a friend of her brother, nothing more. He pulled out one of the empty chairs and sat down.

"Porridge, Captain?" Fanny asked.

"Whatever's on offer, thank you."

She nodded briskly and set a full bowl before him, with a jug of cream and a pot of jam. He ate, aware of Ellie's movements but doing his best not to look in her direction. Dan appeared with Finn, and Tom took the opportunity to explain to the lad that he was to stay here for a couple of days, and to do what Dan said.

"Or Fanny," Dan added, from his other side.

"Or Fanny. Or anyone else here." Tom looked Finn in the eye. "I *will* come back for you." Finn nodded reluctantly, his mouth too full to answer. "Good. Eat up."

When they'd finished breakfast, Dan muttered something about the gig and took Finn off with him. In short order the kitchen emptied, and it wasn't long before Tom was summoned outside. Ellie stood by the gig with Jamie in her arms while Dan strapped a bag onto the rear-facing ledge behind the seat. The girl from the kitchen was there, too, in pelisse and bonnet.

"A chaperone, Ellie?" Tom asked, his voice quiet enough so only she could hear. "Do you think you need one?"

A brief quirk of her lips lightened the worry in her face. "No. Kate is the acorn-feeder. Easily led."

Simple, Dan had said. Persuadable.

"She'd be a liability in a crisis," Ellie went on. "But she's good at following orders, and Jamie knows her. He won't mind..." She glanced up at him, then away. "She can help Mary's nursery maid with Jamie."

What had she been about to say? But there was no time to ask. Sam came out of the yard, leading Fleet, followed by a man with Blackie. Seen in daylight, it was clear that Fleet was a magnificent animal.

Sam must have seen him looking. "You want to ride him, sir? I can drive the gig as far as the magistrates. We can tie Blackie to the gig, but not Fleet—he don't like that."

"Thank you, I would," Tom said. He rarely got the chance to ride such a superb horse. Tom talked to Fleet while Dan assisted Ellie and Jamie into the gig and lifted Kate onto the ledge at the back, next to the luggage. Then Dan held out a rifle and a small leather pouch.

"Take this, sir. There's others here I can use if needs be. It's loaded. Some spare cartridges as well." He looked from Fleet to the gig. "You could stow it on the footrest."

Tom had his own pistols, but he took the rifle with a word of thanks. There was no way of knowing how many men Palmer might have paid. Ellie's eyes widened as he pushed the rifle onto the foot-board behind her legs, but she made no protest. Sam climbed up and set off, and Tom followed the gig onto the lane.

It was seven or eight miles to Thornton Court. The horse harnessed to the gig wasn't the fastest of animals, and it took them well over an hour. Even so, the butler who answered Tom's knock at the front door informed him that Mr Roseworth was still at breakfast, and they would have to wait. The delay didn't worry Tom too much— he felt they were all safer already, away from the farm.

When they finally saw Roseworth—in the same bare room where he had received Tom and Cullton—Tom merely said that he was here to escort Mrs Wilson in her husband's absence and let Ellie explain. She did so clearly and succinctly, relating the bare details of the fire, the shot aimed at Sam, and their suspicion that an attempt had been made to poison Fleet. The magistrate's scowl deepened as she talked, although Tom thought that it was the threat to the stallion that produced the most ire. Roseworth readily agreed to stable the two animals, even before Ellie's vague suggestion that he 'make use of them'.

"That is most kind of you, Mrs Wilson. May I offer you some refreshment before you return?"

"Thank you, sir, but I must decline. I am taking our son to stay with my sister in... That is, I think he will be safer there."

Tom hadn't quite caught up on his sleep and a coffee would have been welcome, but he could understand why Ellie wanted to be on her way.

"Very wise." Roseworth nodded. "I wish you a safe journey."

Ellie dipped her head. "I'm sure my husband will come to discuss the matter further when he returns."

Her husband. It would take them some hours to get to Harrogate, and Tom would be sitting beside her in the gig all the way.

Keep reminding yourself she's got a husband.

CHAPTER 28

*E*llie settled herself in the gig again, with Jamie on her lap. Kate had played with him in a separate parlour while she and Tom talked to the magistrate, but rather than tiring him, it seemed to have made him more restless. Tom took up more space than Sam had, and the seat on the gig was not wide enough to put more distance between them. In spite of the distraction of Jamie's fidgets, Ellie was very aware of Tom's legs less than a foot from hers, his hands on the reins. Hands that had run through her hair, touched her skin, her—

As Tom turned the gig onto the lane, she wrenched her thoughts back to the present, trying to ignore the warmth low in her belly.

"I had a look at the map," Tom said. "Once we've left the letter for your husband in Thirsk, we go to Topcliffe where we join the turnpike to Boroughbridge. Is that right?"

"That's the way we usually go," Ellie confirmed. "Then Knaresborough and Harrogate. We generally take most of the day over it, and give Lass one or two rests. But we could hire a new horse at Boroughbridge if you want to arrive earlier than that."

"We'll see how she goes. I wasn't planning on returning until tomorrow, so there is no hurry." He looked up and grimaced at the thick clouds. "Not that the weather inclines me to loitering."

"We're wrapped up warmly enough." Good heavens, talking about the weather! But she had Jamie on her lap, who might repeat words, and Kate was sitting behind them. Kate probably wouldn't hear what they were talking about, but she might, so Ellie could not discuss anything too personal with Tom. She occupied herself with Jamie for a time, pointing out houses, trees, birds—anything to keep him from becoming bored and fractious. Eventually he snuggled into her for warmth and began to doze. And she had ignored Tom long enough. "Who is that lad you had with you?"

"Finn Robson. Son of an army sergeant, killed in the same engagement that I was wounded in. He didn't have anyone else, only an uncle in Darlington. The surgeon foisted him on me in France, when I was laid up. His way of getting the lad sent home." He gave a wry smile. "It was weeks before I could dress myself—Finn came in useful on the journey."

"Why isn't he with his uncle?" Not that it was her business, really, but it felt awkward to remain silent while sitting beside him.

"The uncle only took him because he had his eye on the pay Sergeant Robson was owed. Made the lad's life exceedingly unpleasant once he had that. Finn made his own way to Hythe to find me, with no money."

Hythe? "Isn't that on the south coast? Kent?"

He nodded. "Three hundred and fifty miles, give or take a bit. With no money. He was a sorry sight when he arrived."

"That shows a lot of determination. Or desperation."

"Both, I think. I couldn't send him back to such a place." He grinned. "He might regret it though. I'm going to insist he improves his reading and writing."

She shook her head, but couldn't help smiling. Was that another example of the helpfulness that had made him stop to assist a crashed coach? And had brought him here now to help?

Her white knight. The idea made her feel light inside, protected. Then she looked away, pressing her lips together against another smile. Tom would probably be revolted by the notion, much as Ben would have been.

"Finn will make himself useful while I'm away," Tom went on. "With Dan having been in the army, they'll have something to talk about. Dan will understand the kind of life he's had so far."

"And Fanny will feed him up." She paused while Jamie pointed out cows in a field, then asked a question that had been at the back of her mind since she first learned that Tom was at Bank Side. "How did you come to be here? I thought you had returned to your regiment?"

"I sold my commission. When I arrived in York yesterday, Frank showed me your letters. I came to see if you needed my help. As we agreed not to—" He broke off, turning his head to glance at Kate on the back of the gig, then went on more quietly. "That is, I went directly to Bank Side to talk to Dan. I thought he'd know the situation."

Avoiding her, Ellie thought. As they had agreed he should. "I'm very glad you came, Tom. Without you, we'd have lost the hay barn, perhaps more." They'd nearly lost Sam as it was.

"You need more men, Ellie. As long as Palmer is continuing this… persecution, someone needs to keep watch properly, at both farms. Ideally two to keep watch at each place."

"There is less farm work to do at this time of year. We may not need more." She shivered, and hugged Jamie a little tighter. "It feels as if we are besieged. Waiting for something to happen." Threatened.

"All you can do is prepare as well as you can. It's not reasonable to expect men who have been working to stay up all night. If you take on more men specifically to stand watch, they'll be better rested and more effective."

It did make sense.

"Palmer is being pursued by creditors," Tom went on. "Possibly bailiffs, debt collectors. If not now, he soon will be. He may not have the time to wait. If you wish… That is, if your husband wishes, I can find some suitable men and send them to you. If he doesn't want to accept my help, persuade him to let Dan approve whoever he finds."

Tom's calm discussion had begun to soothe Ellie's fears, but this was a reminder that Tom was not in charge. A chill settled inside her that was not all to do with the breeze. Martin *must* take it more seriously now. He must do more than just having a word with Dan and Sam.

Tom tried to read Ellie's expression as she looked down at her son. They'd talked easily enough to start with and she'd almost looked happy. And that made him happy, too. Which was not wise, not at all. Even his discussion of Palmer's possible actions hadn't seemed to cause her too much concern until he'd mentioned that it was up to her husband. He wanted nothing more than to stay and protect her; all of them. And to hold her close until she felt safe.

"Do you drive?" His question came out more abruptly than he'd intended.

"Yes. Why?"

Because I shouldn't be sitting this close to you all the way to Harrogate.

But he didn't want to say that to her with Kate possibly listening. "I was thinking it must be very uncomfortable for Kate on that little seat at the back. I could hire a horse in Thirsk and ride. It'll be easier on Lass, as well, without my weight in the gig, if you don't mind driving all that way."

"I... Yes, that's a good idea."

They said little else after that. He wanted to talk to her, to ask about Jamie and her life, to share his own thoughts and experiences. But she had a husband.

When they reached Thirsk, Tom pulled up outside the Golden Fleece and left Ellie with the gig while he went into the stables to hire a horse and to check that Wilson *had* left his mount there. A coin ensured that Wilson would be told to collect a letter from the landlord before he departed, then he took Ellie's letter and left it behind the bar with another coin.

They went on to Topcliffe before stopping for some food at the Angel. After that the going was faster on the turnpike. Tom rode ahead to pay the tolls for both his horse and the gig, and they arrived in Harrogate in the middle of the afternoon. And none too soon, for the air was feeling increasingly damp.

Once in the town, Tom followed behind the gig until Ellie pulled up in front of a tall narrow house in a terrace. He dismounted and went to Lass' head while Ellie knocked on the door. He couldn't see who answered, but Ellie turned and beckoned, and Tom left the animals long enough to take Jamie while Kate climbed down. An all too brief moment with the weight of his son in his arms, their faces close.

Then Kate took Jamie inside, and a manservant came out to collect the luggage.

Tom was beginning to feel he'd been abandoned when Ellie came out again. "Mary's man will direct you to the livery shortly, and Cook will have some refreshments ready when you return." She looked at his saddle bag. "Shall I have that taken in now? I'm sure Mary can fit you in some—"

"I'll find an inn for the night. I don't think it's wise for me to stay with your family. Do you?"

She hesitated, and colour rose to her cheeks. "No. I suppose not."

There was a gratifying tone of regret in her words, and he reproached himself for noticing. When this sorry business was over, he should go away and not come near her again. There would be— there *must* be—other women who could rouse similar feelings in him. Somewhere.

A spatter of rain brought him back to the present. "I assume your sister is happy for you to stay?" There didn't appear to be a problem, but it was as well to be sure.

"I haven't explained yet, but with Kate to help she should be able to manage Jamie for a few weeks. What time do you want to leave in the morning?"

Why would her sister need to look after Jamie? "Er… early. It's best if I get back as soon as possible. Do you want me to call before I leave in case you have a message?"

"I'm coming with you. Will eight o'clock be all right? I can be ready by then, but do say if you would prefer to leave earlier."

He should have guessed that a woman with her determination would not passively wait while others dealt with a problem. "You're safer here, Ellie." Keeping her safe was the whole point of today's journey.

"I cannot leave Agnes and Fanny to manage alone. Particularly now."

"They're not alone. They have Dan, and the other men at Knowle." And *they* were not Palmer's targets. "I'm sure your husband will send someone for you once it is safe for you to return."

Her chin went up. "If you will not take me, I will drive myself."

He couldn't stop her, of course. Even though he was exasperated at her disregard for her own safety, he couldn't help but admire her determination. "The plan was for me to drive the gig back to Knowle."

"With me in it. And if you take the gig without me, I'm sure I can hire one here."

And drive all that way alone? An image came into his head of her riding off into the rain on the day they first met. Astride, with her skirts up near her knees and the weeping woman and her child in front. Certainly she would drive home on her own.

"What about Jamie? What will happen to him if you come to harm?"

"I will be careful."

A voice called from the house. "Ellie? Are you coming in?" A woman stood in the doorway—not a servant, from her clothing. Ellie's sister, most likely.

"Eight o'clock, then." Better she return with him than alone.

"What was that about?" Mary asked, as she closed the door behind Ellie.

"Just arranging what time he will collect me tomorrow." Ellie pulled at her bonnet ribbon. "Where are Kate and Jamie?"

"Kate took him upstairs. Martha will look after them for now." Mary tilted her head a little, eyes narrowed. "Take your pelisse and bonnet off and come into the parlour. I will order tea, and then you may tell me why you have come with no notice, and why you are only planning on staying one night."

Mary headed for the kitchen, and Ellie wondered how much to tell her. She should have thought about it on the way here, but she had been distracted by Jamie's chatter, and Kate's. And regretting Tom's distance after he'd hired the horse, even while trying to convince herself that it was right, and for the best.

She must tell Mary the truth, of course, for Mary would hear most of it eventually. But there was no need to tell her *every* detail.

When the tea had been poured and the door closed, Ellie started with the attempt to have Martin arrested for sodomy. Henry already knew about Martin's nature, and she was sure Mary did, too, although they had never discussed it. But the tale she told mentioned only an associate of the attorney in York that Martin sometimes used. That was not the whole truth, but not a falsehood, either. The business of the acorns needed no prevarication, and nor did last night's fire, really. Tom had been acting as if he was one of Martin's men.

"Your new man seems very well dressed," Mary said, curiosity clear in her face. "Much better than the one who usually comes when Martin cannot accompany you."

"He's the attorney's associate that I mentioned," Ellie said, not meeting her sister's eyes and hoping her expression gave nothing away. "He happened to be in the area."

"That was—" Mary broke off at the sound of the front door opening, and a moment later Henry came into the room with a smile for his wife, then raised brows at seeing Ellie.

"Hello, I wasn't expecting to see you, Ellie. Is all well?" He cast a rueful glance at Mary. "Or have I merely forgotten something you told me, my dear?"

"I didn't give you any warning," Ellie admitted. "I hope you do not mind?"

"It's Martin's cousin," Mary said. "He's gone too far now, Henry. Something must be done."

"What has happened?" Henry sat down, looking at his wife then at Ellie, unsure who would explain.

Mary started before Ellie had time to marshal her thoughts. "Martin's away, and there's been a fire and a man shot at, so Ellie brought Jamie here to keep him safe."

"Very wise."

As Henry looked at Ellie, she sat up straighter, trying not to show her weariness, but Henry wasn't fooled.

"You can tell me the details later; you look as if you need to rest."

"Your bed should be made up by now, Ellie," Mary said. "Why don't you lie down before dinner?"

"Thank you, I will." But she would check on Jamie first.

Upstairs, Ellie found Jamie in the bedroom that she usually used when she was here. Kate was putting him into a clean nightshirt, and had turned down the bedcovers on the truckle bed.

"Martha said he should have a nap, missus," Kate explained. "There, Master Jamie, you're ready for a rest."

"Thank you, Kate. I'll look after him for a little while. Go down to the kitchen and ask them to give you some tea and cake."

Kate beamed a smile and hurried off.

"Play," Jamie objected, standing beside the bed.

"You can play later," Ellie promised, holding up the covers. "But you need a nap now. I'll sing you the song about the sheep."

He stuck his lip out for a moment, then climbed into the bed. And he was fast asleep by the time Ellie had reached the end of 'Baa Baa Black Sheep'.

Watching her sleeping son, Ellie wondered whether she *should* stay here. Was she really a target, as Tom suggested? She would take no chances with Jamie, but how could Palmer gain by her death or injury? That would merely serve to convince Martin of the seriousness of the situation.

Jamie would miss her. Although he knew his 'Auntie Mary' and his cousins, and he was used to being looked after at home by Kate some of the time, he had never been away from Ellie for more than a few days. That had been back in May, when she and Martin had gone to the races. And then he had been in familiar surroundings at Knowle Farm, not in a strange house.

Perhaps she would return here once Martin was back at the farm.

If only she knew when that would be—it could be very soon, or nearly a week. But Dan could not look after both farms properly. Although she could not fight, she could organise people and make sure a watch was kept at Knowle Farm, as Tom had suggested.

She smoothed Jamie's hair then lay down on her bed. Perhaps Tom would be satisfied with a promise to return to Harrogate. It could be an awkward journey tomorrow, if not.

It would be an awkward journey in any case.

CHAPTER 29

*T*om tied his hired horse to the back of the gig the next morning. Having Ellie take the reins yesterday while he rode had made sense, giving Kate a proper seat. But it would look strange if he turned the driving of the gig over to her this morning in front of her sister's house. He didn't know how Ellie had explained his presence, but a woman's sole escort would not normally make her drive. He said as much to Ellie when they were on their way.

"I said you were an associate of my husband's attorney," she explained. "I don't like telling untruths, but…" She lifted a shoulder.

"It is the truth, just not all of it." How deceit multiplied when there were things best hidden. "Are you sure you won't change your mind about returning?"

Her posture stiffened. "I did think about it, but there is no gain for Palmer in killing me."

There might be if her husband was dead, but Tom decided not to mention it—there was a set to her chin that showed her determination and he didn't want a dispute.

"No further argument?" Ellie sounded surprised, and he couldn't help smiling.

"You won't have left Jamie behind without careful thought, and I don't know all your circumstances. You are in a better position to decide your actions than I am."

Some of the tension left her body, although she still sat with her hands clenched in front of her. Without Jamie on her lap, there was enough room on the seat for them not to touch, but Ellie's proximity was still distracting. She seemed preoccupied and disinclined to talk, so there was little to divert his mind from wishing this kind of closeness could be a normal part of his life. Should he ask her to drive the gig again while he rode? Even as the thought occurred to him, she stretched out her hands, flexing her wrists and then rubbing her forearms.

"Too much driving yesterday?"

"I think so. I drive to Thirsk and back sometimes, but I am not used to driving so far. If I come to Harrogate without Martin, Dan usually brings me."

"I'm sorry."

"Don't be. I can drive for a little while if you wish to ride."

"No, I don't wish to." It would be wiser, from his point of view. He'd felt that the attraction between them was still mutual, but that might be wishful thinking. That he still wanted her was not in doubt, but he didn't know, and couldn't with honour ask, whether she felt the same.

Their short exchange seemed to have brought her out of her abstraction. "You said yesterday that you had sold your commission."

"Yes. It was time for a change," he added, before she could ask. "I've spent nearly half my life in the army, being sent hither and yon at His Majesty's whim."

"Where did you go besides the Peninsula?"

And, in spite of his resolution to try not to get into the kind of personal conversation they'd shared in that inn, Tom found himself describing the heat and humidity of the West Indies, what had seemed like a holiday in Guernsey after that, then boredom on the Kent coast waiting for an invasion by Boney that never came.

"You sound as if you were disappointed?" she questioned, a laugh in her voice.

"I was younger then."

"So old and grey as you are now." She nodded seriously, then her smile broke through.

Oh, hell. He turned his gaze back to the road ahead—he really should have let Dan take Ellie and Jamie to Harrogate. How was he to forget this woman?

"Tom, is something wrong?"

Only that you are married.

"No, I'm only wondering how someone as ancient as myself can earn a living now." And he threw caution to the winds and asked her to describe her life—what she enjoyed about living on the farm and what she didn't, how she took part in the running of it. And then about how much a man could depend on the expertise of the workers if he knew nothing himself. This conversation lasted until they stopped for refreshment and to give Lass a rest, then they moved on to other things he might do for a living. The ideas became ever more fanciful, and the way their eyes met in shared amusement served only to deepen his feelings for her. His love?

It must be love, this desire to be with her, to protect her, but also to share his life with her. He was in real trouble now, but there was no going back—he should make the most of her company while he had it.

The miles passed easily as they talked and laughed together. She told him of her childhood, and of Ben, without the sadness there had been before, and Tom thought her brother would have become a friend if they'd met.

Then, when they were only a few miles from Thirsk, Ellie stiffened beside him, her gaze fixed on a rider approaching around a bend in the road.

"Martin has returned sooner than I expected."

Ellie's surprise at seeing Martin changed to relief. He must have read the letter she left in Thirsk, or he would be heading for the farm. Tom could explain the details of what had happened and what needed doing, and she could go back to Jamie.

But relief changed to puzzlement as Martin drew nearer and she made out his expression. Not worry, or pleasure at seeing her, but something else entirely. Anger? Yes, but anxiety as well. Had Palmer attacked someone else while they'd been away?

Martin came to a halt next to them as the gig slowed to a stop. "Where is Jamie? And what the devil are you doing with my wife, Allerby?"

"I'm driving her back to the farm." Tom's voice sounded remarkably calm. He handed Ellie the reins, then got down and went to untie his hired horse.

Whatever had got into her husband? "Jamie is safe in Harrogate with Mary. I explained in my note, Martin."

"You said that you were taking Jamie to the Cowpers. There was nothing about who was taking you—why not, if you had nothing to hide?" Martin jabbed a finger in Tom's direction. "*He* gave his name at the Fleece and the stable boy told me. The pair of you took our son away, and now I find you touring the countryside alone with him."

Was he accusing her of running off with Tom?

Tom led his horse forward, and looked at her. "I can leave you in safe hands now, Mrs Wilson." But he hesitated, as if waiting for her agreement, so she gave the tiniest of nods. He mounted and rode off down the road without a further word.

Ellie felt abandoned, but another glance at Martin's face made her realise it was for the best. Any attempt at an explanation from Tom would only have inflamed the situation further.

By this time Martin had tied his own horse to the back of the gig. He climbed into the seat. "Give me the reins." He almost grabbed them from her hands, and flicked them to set Lass moving.

"Martin, what is wrong?" He should be angry with his cousin, not her and Tom. "I left the note in case you returned early. We took Jamie to stay with Mary to keep him safe. Did you even *read* my letter?"

He drove in silence, his lips pressed together, then his expression relaxed a little. "Were you really going back to the farm?"

"Of course we were. Martin, *did* you read my letter? All of it?"

He took a couple of deep breaths, then shook his head, shame-faced. "The stable boy told me you'd gone off with Allerby, then the first part of your letter said you'd taken Jamie to Harrogate. I..." He swallowed. "Ellie, I thought you'd taken Jamie away from me."

"You know I would not do that!" Now she was beginning to feel angry. "Or you *should* know. You are Jamie's father, and—"

"That's the problem, though, isn't it? You took Jamie away with his *real* father. That was all I could think about once I found you were with Allerby."

"Jamie thinks of *you* as his father, and I would never separate him from you, or you from him. You should know me better than that." It hurt that he could think she would do so.

He was silent for several minutes before he spoke again. "Why did you take Jamie away, Ellie? I... I jumped to a conclusion—an incorrect conclusion—when I found that Allerby was with you, and just set out to find if you really had gone to Harrogate."

Ellie sighed. "Someone set a fire in the barn at Bank Side, which was put out before too much damage occurred. They thought that the stallions might be in danger, so Sam rode Fleet to Knowle, and someone took a shot at—"

"Someone shot at Sam? Was he injured?"

"No. He fell off the horse, but he was unharmed."

"Thank God."

The words were quiet, but heartfelt. Martin cared about all his employees, but he seemed to be particularly affected by the news of Sam's close escape. She'd suspected he had a lover—could it be Sam?

But at the moment it was more important that Martin understood the danger he was in from Palmer, so Ellie explained what had happened after the shot, and why she had decided to take Jamie to Harrogate.

Martin listened without further interruption, but his next words made Ellie wonder if he believed her. "It seems a happy coincidence that Allerby was there just when this fire started."

"It does seem that way," Ellie said, wearying of his suspicion. "I wrote to Mr Allerby for advice when your letter said you were to be away longer than you had planned. Captain Allerby was in York, and learned that I was worried. He came to see if he could help, which is why he was at Bank Side when the fire started. He *discovered* the fire. If he had not been there, we could have lost the whole barn."

Tom may well have had motives beyond keeping them all safe. Nothing specific had been said between them, but she could no longer doubt that he felt far more than mere friendship for her. As she did for him. But however much she wanted to be with Tom, her first duty was to Jamie and Martin.

"Martin, if you do not believe me, just say so and I will save my breath."

He sighed. "I do believe you, Ellie, but you must admit I had reason to be suspicious when I found you travelling the countryside alone with Allerby. You said, when Allerby turned up earlier this year, that he would not come again. And you promised that seeing him would not change things between us."

"It seems to have changed you, not me." That wasn't quite true, but she hoped it had not affected her actions as well as her feelings. "Why all this suspicion? Tom drove me to Harrogate because Dan was needed to look after the farms while I was away."

"'Tom', is it?"

"Oh, for heaven's sake, Martin. Yes, I call him Tom—what of it?"

He didn't answer.

"You have a paramour, don't you? At Bank Side." Ellie made an effort to keep her voice low. They were on a public road, and although passers by would not hear enough of what they said to make any sense of it, she did not want to attract attention. "It's acceptable for you to… to…" She waved a hand, frustrated at her lack of knowledge. "Whatever you do when you are together. But I cannot even call another man by his Christian name?" She folded her arms. "If you intend to continue with this… this distrust all the way home, I would prefer you to ride. Or turn the gig around now and take me back to Harrogate. Jamie needs me, even if you do not."

Perhaps she had done wrong in thought, in still wanting a man who was not her husband, but she had not acted on it other than enjoying his company on the first part of today's journey.

His hands dropped, and Lass came to a halt. "I'm sorry, Ellie. I… *We* wanted a child for so long, and then you had Jamie and we were happy. Then Allerby appeared. I know he helped us, but things haven't felt the same since then."

"I've been worried about what else your cousin may do."

"I don't mean that. You have not seemed as happy since Allerby returned."

She had tried to hide her discontent, but Martin was more perceptive than she had realised.

"Ellie, I should not have married you, given my nature, but I cannot regret Jamie."

Ellie sighed. "Nor can I. You have to trust me, though, Martin. We have enough trouble now without you suspecting me of wanting to take Jamie away. I never would."

He set Lass moving. "I'm sorry. I should have known you would not."

The tension between them dissipated, although little more was said as they drove on through Thirsk and into the lanes beyond. Martin was abstracted, driving without taking notice of anything other than the road a few feet in front of them. So much so that Ellie had to draw his attention to a horseman approaching. The lane here was narrow, and they would have to slow to allow him to pass. He was a stranger to her, and Martin showed no sign of recognition.

The stranger didn't pass, but stopped in the road, effectively blocking it, and removed his hat to her. "Excuse me, but could you direct me to Kirby Sutton? I think I must have taken a wrong turning."

Tom rode ahead to Thirsk, wondering what had caused Wilson's hostility. Most men would object to finding their wife with a man who had cuckolded him, but Ellie had left a letter explaining their actions. It was unfortunate—he would have to leave it to Ellie to persuade her husband of the seriousness of the situation.

He didn't stop in the town, but rode on along the road that led towards Knowle Farm. He didn't want to leave Ellie—or her husband —unprotected and he was worried about Palmer.

The first time Tom had shot at another human being hadn't been easy, even though the man was about to shoot him. But Palmer, if that *was* who had shot at Sam two nights ago, had now taken the step of attempting to kill someone directly. It would be easier for him the next time. And if Palmer was desperate, as Tom suspected, he would try again soon.

There were too many people in Thirsk for Palmer to risk a murder attempt there, but he could easily have enquired at the Fleece and might know that Wilson had returned today. This road was the shortest route from Thirsk to the farm, and there were plenty of bends in the lane and dense hedgerows that could conceal an assailant even in broad daylight. Just the kind of place for an ambush.

Once out of Thirsk, he found a farm track and turned into it, then dismounted. It was nearly half an hour before the gig came in sight. Looking at Ellie and her husband as the gig passed the end of the track, he thought he'd made the right decision to stay within reach. Their posture didn't indicate that their disagreement had continued, but Wilson had the air of a man with his mind elsewhere. Not alert to his surroundings. There might not be much Tom could do, but even a warning shout might help if necessary. Or his presence as a witness could deter Palmer if he was still in the area and planning another attack.

Neither Ellie nor Wilson seemed to see him, even though he was only ten yards away and not attempting to conceal himself. He mounted and followed, keeping far enough behind so Wilson didn't notice him, but close enough—he hoped—to be of use.

There was nothing untoward that he could see, although the hedgerows limited his view of the lane beyond the gig. Some fields were bare after the harvest; some had sheep or cows grazing. The still-green leaves concealed twittering birds, and somewhere in the distance a shepherd whistled to his dog. The only other sounds were the creak of his saddle leather and the clopping of hooves on the stony road.

A rider came into view, his hat showing above the hedges, and Tom pulled one pistol from his pocket, giving a gentle kick to get his mount to move a little faster.

It wasn't Palmer. Tom saw Ellie touch Wilson's arm and point, and the gig pulled to the side of the lane to make enough room for the rider to pass. The rider stopped, too, and Tom urged his mount into a canter.

The man lifted his hat with one hand; the other was still on the reins. No threat there. But beyond him there was movement behind a hedge, a gleam of metal. A shot rang out as Tom kicked his horse into a gallop, passing the Wilsons' gig with only inches to spare.

The stranger hadn't fired the shot—his mouth had dropped open and his hands were both visible. Tom fired through the hedge, hearing a muffled cry as his horse attempted to rear.

He kicked his feet out of the stirrups and slid to the ground. He couldn't control the frightened animal as well as dealing with the stranger—who now had a hand in one pocket.

A pistol?

CHAPTER 30

The shot set Ellie's heart racing as Lass lurched forwards and Martin grunted. A horseman galloped past, hardly clearing the gig in the narrow gap between it and the hedge.

Tom? Thank heavens.

Another shot—had Tom fired this time? Then he swung down from his horse and ran to the stranger, pulling at one arm so both men tumbled to the ground.

"Ellie." Martin's voice was more of a groan, his face white. He'd dropped the reins and bent forwards, hands clutching his side. Hands wet with blood.

"Martin!"

Where was Tom? Why wasn't he helping her? With trembling hands, Ellie pulled out the fichu she was wearing beneath her pelisse and wadded it up, then eased Martin's hands away from his body. There was a ragged hole in his coat, the fabric around it dark with blood. She unfastened the buttons on his coat and waistcoat, sucking in a breath at the stain spreading across his shirt, even round to his back. "Here, hold this against it." He nodded without speaking, and pressed the wadded fabric to his side.

Ellie tensed as a further shot sounded, waiting for sudden agony, or for a sign that Martin had been hit again, but nothing happened.

No, not nothing.

The stranger was on the ground on his front, one side of his face pushed into the mud and one of Tom's knees on his back. Tom pressed a hand to his thigh, and it came away red.

"Tom!"

Tom swore, keeping the pressure on the man's back even as he prodded his thigh again. It was only a flesh wound, as far as he could tell. From his quick glance while tackling the stranger, Wilson appeared to be more seriously wounded, but Ellie's voice calling to him was strong.

Palmer—if that was who it was behind the hedge—had two weapons with him. Or he'd managed to reload a single gun. Unless he had three, Tom was safe for half a minute or so. He finished unwinding his neckcloth and tied the stranger's hands behind his back, then felt in the man's pockets. The pistol he found was loaded and primed.

Pain shot down his leg as he stood, but he *could* stand on it. "Are you hurt, Ellie?"

"No. But Martin is—"

"Lay him along the seat, if you can. And keep down yourself. I'll be with you in a minute."

With the stranger's pistol, he still had two shots. The hedge was dense, too thick to push through. The gig—he clambered onto the ledge at the back, wincing as he put weight on his injured leg and grateful that Lass was doing no more than toss her head at all the noise. Wilson's horse, still tied to the back, was showing the whites of his eyes, but was not panicking. Yet.

Now he could see over the hedge—there, a man running towards a horse tethered to a tree near the far edge of the field. Tom took aim as best he could from the unstable platform and fired. The distant figure stumbled, but Tom couldn't be sure whether it was due to his shot or if he had merely tripped. Or even if it was Palmer at all. But who else would it be? He was still running—more slowly now, but he was already too far away for a pistol shot.

The rifle—he'd checked the priming this morning before they set out. "Ellie—pass me the rifle."

Wilson lay on one side along the seat, his legs awkwardly curled forwards. Ellie was kneeling in the remaining space, one hand against her husband's side. She felt by her knees with the other.

In the field, their assailant was getting further away every second.

"Here, Tom."

He raised the rifle, hoping it fired true. It felt wrong to shoot a fleeing man, but he could still be a threat. Releasing his breath slowly, Tom pulled the trigger.

The man stumbled again, falling to the ground this time. By the time Tom had found Dan's little pouch in his pocket and reloaded the rifle, he was sitting up.

Sitting, not standing. Not attempting to rise. Out of action for now.

Ellie winced as the rifle fired above her head, then the gig lurched as Tom climbed down, the breath hissing between his teeth as his injured leg hit the ground. She lifted the edges of Martin's coat; the bloodstain was still spreading around his back, although her wadded up fichu seemed no wetter than before. There was a second wound in his back; the bullet had gone right through him. With trembling hands, she removed his neckcloth and held it against his back. His face was still pale, but no worse than before.

Don't die. Please don't die.

In front of the gig, Tom had rolled the bound stranger beneath the hedge, out of the way. His hired horse was nowhere in sight, nor was the stranger's.

"Ellie, can you hold him in the seat if I lead Lass?"

She nodded. But instead of going to Lass' head, he untied Martin's horse and mounted it, then reached for Lass' reins close to the bit. It wasn't until she noticed his head turning from side to side as he rode that she realised that being on horseback helped him to see over the hedgerows. They could still be in danger.

Tom glanced over his shoulder at her. "Is your farm the closest house?"

"I think so. Yes. Yes, it is."

"Tell me if I turn the wrong way. And keep your eyes open—he might have had more than one accomplice."

Did that mean Tom had killed him? She found that she didn't care; all her attention was on getting Martin home in safety. They could not have been more than fifteen minutes away but the time seemed to stretch endlessly as she worried about the blood still seeping through the pad on Martin's wound, and the empty countryside beyond the hedges that was not empty at all.

They still had half a mile to go when Tom dropped Lass' reins and cantered forward, a pistol in one hand. Ellie's heart began to race. *Not more of Palmer's men, please!*

The fear of another attack left her as she recognised Jake and Dan approaching, with Bates running along behind them. They stopped to confer, then Jake came galloping towards her on Tom's hired horse. Jake's eyes widened as he took in Martin's reddened coat, and she caught only the word 'doctor' as he went past. Then Tom was beside her, still on Martin's horse.

"Bates will lead you home, Ellie. I'll take Dan and check on the man I shot—we need to make sure he can't do any more harm. Can you manage?"

Ellie nodded. "I'll manage."

Bates led Lass on. One more shot sounded as they were approaching home—distant, not close by.

If anyone was shot, please let it not be Tom or Dan.

Especially not Tom.

Tom was torn between accompanying Ellie and checking what had happened to their assailant. But Ellie had people at the farm whom she trusted, and he had no medical expertise. He should concentrate on ensuring that Palmer—if it was him—could do no more harm. There was also the accomplice to take care of; Tom hadn't tied the stranger's legs, but it wasn't easy moving fast with tied hands and they wouldn't have any difficulty catching him if he'd tried to escape.

"Found this horse just up the lane," Dan said, patting his mount's neck as they headed back to where Tom had left the accomplice.

It must belong to the stranger—the lad he'd sent for the doctor had ridden off on Tom's horse.

When they reached the scene of the shooting, the accomplice in the lane was sitting up, but had not moved from his position by the hedge. Dealing with him could wait.

"He was in that field." Tom pointed over the hedge. Dan nodded and they rode on, turning into the field through a half-open gate. The horse Tom had seen over the hedge was still tied to the tree. Their assailant was a huddle on the grass.

"He's moved since I left him," Tom said as they trotted over and dismounted. He hadn't gone far, though. A blood-soaked cloth tied around one thigh showed where he'd been hit. It *was* Palmer.

His eyes flickered open as Tom approached. "You bastard," he whispered. "If you hadn't turned up, I'd have had time to do a proper job with the fire." He took a shuddering breath and his voice became fainter. "Bloody Wilson, not coming back when he should. And Symonds—bastard wouldn't help me any more until I paid him."

Was Symonds the stranger seen around the farms recently?

"But I'd have got him today," Palmer went on. "No-one would have known who…" His eyes closed.

About to see if he was still breathing, Tom leapt back as Palmer rolled onto his back and lifted a pistol. Dan kicked at Palmer's hand, and the shot went wide. Tom swore at his own carelessness.

"No harm done," Dan said, one foot pressing Palmer's wrist into the ground as he bent and searched his pockets. He retrieved a second pistol.

"We'd better get him back to the farm. Although he'll hang for attempted murder anyway." He wasn't going to give Palmer the satisfaction of knowing that he'd seriously wounded Wilson.

"I'll fetch the wagon," Dan said. "Or d'you want me to keep watch over him?"

"No, you go. You know the way, and Palmer's not going anywhere. But we'll check on the fellow I left tied up first."

He had a lingering doubt about his actions—what if the stranger had only been a chance passer by? If that was the case, Tom had assaulted him. But even if he'd paused to think about it first, he would have done the same. The stranger had stopped the gig right by the place where Palmer was lying in wait.

The man looked as pale as if he'd been shot, but Tom had done little more than knock him over. Come to think of it, he'd put up very little resistance when Tom pulled him off his horse.

"Is he dead?" the stranger asked as Tom stopped in front of him. His voice had a distinct wobble.

"Not yet. Get up." Tom put a hand under one arm and helped him stand. "Walk. Dan, you ride and fetch a wagon back. Palmer may well die if we leave him there too long."

"I didn't mean him," the man said as Dan cantered off. "I mean the one he shot. Was it Wilson?"

"No, he's not dead either. You didn't succeed."

"Thank God!"

What?

"You deliberately stopped Wilson so Palmer could take a shot at him," Tom said.

"I didn't know what he was going to do! Please, you must believe me!"

An innocent man? No—he knew Wilson had been the target. "Explain. And start walking."

The man obeyed, stumbling now and then on the muddy surface, balance difficult with his hands still tied behind his back. "He owed me money. Palmer, I mean, not Wilson. And Palmer said that Wilson owed *him* money, but wouldn't hand it over or even talk to him."

"Go on." Talking helped Tom to ignore the pain in his thigh. He felt his breeches—the buckskin was stiff, but not wet. If it wasn't still bleeding, it could wait.

"He thought he could talk if they met on the road, but he said Wilson wouldn't even stop if he saw it was him. If Wilson saw Palmer, I mean."

Tom inspected the man's clothing. Beneath the mud, it was of good quality—not what he'd expect of a hired footpad. And he was young—little more than twenty, Tom guessed. "How did Palmer come to owe money to you? And what's your name?"

"Hersey. Cards."

"When?"

"Yesterday. In Thirsk." He stopped, waiting until Tom turned to face him. "You *must* believe me! I only agreed to help Palmer talk to Wilson. I didn't know he wanted to shoot him."

"You were reaching for your pistol when I pulled you off your horse."

"I didn't know who was shooting! It could have been at me."

That was plausible. Tom had seen plenty of prevarication in men trying to avoid punishment; Hersey didn't look as if he was lying. Tom decided to give him the benefit of the doubt for the moment. "Whether or not you're guilty, you're also a witness. Give me your word you won't attempt to escape, and I'll untie your hands."

"I promise." There was an almost pathetic earnestness in Hersey's expression. Tom thought he meant it—but if not, he had two loaded pistols.

Ellie saw Fanny and Agnes waiting by the gate when the gig finally approached the farm, Finn behind them. Fanny's eyes went from Ellie to Martin and back, then she spun around and ran into the house, taking the boy with her.

"We heard shots, missus, but…" Agnes wrung her hands. "Oh, dear, I never thought—"

"Not now, Agnes," Ellie pleaded as Bates led the gig through the gate. It was hard enough keeping her own anxiety under control, without having to cope with Agnes' lamentations.

Fanny reappeared with a blanket as they reached the front door. "Put this around him, missus. Bates, you help him down."

Martin was still conscious, and between them they managed to get him out of the gig. He swayed alarmingly—Ellie and Bates grabbed his arms to steady him. He staggered into the house, leaning heavily on Bates with Ellie supporting him on his injured side as well as she could. He sank onto the sofa, still making no protest. He hadn't complained during the jolting ride back in the gig, either, but the effort it took showed in his compressed lips and screwed up eyes.

"Leave missus to it," Fanny ordered, as the others lingered in the doorway. "Agnes, we'll need hot water." She inspected Martin. "Shall I bring more blankets down? I doubt we'll get him up the stairs, and it won't do him no good to be moved, neither."

"Yes, please. And pillows."

Thank goodness for a sensible woman who did not ask questions. Ellie took Martin's hand—it was cold and clammy, and the pulse in his wrist was racing. Tentatively, she moved the wadded cotton away from his wounds. They were still slowly oozing blood.

When Fanny returned, Ellie tried to make Martin as comfortable as possible with a pillow beneath his head, and others supporting him half on his side so he didn't lie on the wound in his back. She spread a blanket over him and settled into a chair beside the sofa. Fanny brought in a cup of tea, over-sweetened, which she forced herself to drink. What else could she do? She couldn't think.

"Ellie?" Martin's voice was faint.

"Hush now. We've sent for the doctor."

Was it her fault Martin had been shot? If she'd stayed in Harrogate as Tom wanted, Martin would have come to her there and she could have convinced him to take better care.

"Was it Luke?"

"I think so. Don't worry about that now. He won't hurt us again." She hoped that was true—Tom would do his best to keep them safe, she knew, but she wasn't going to mention him to Martin. Martin had apologised for his suspicions, but it was best to avoid anything that might lead to him becoming agitated.

She sprang up at the sound of hoofbeats in the lane, but it was only Dan. A few minutes later Fanny came into the parlour. Ellie went to the door, so as not to disturb Martin.

"Dan come for the wagon, missus, to collect that Palmer."

"Why do they need...?" Ellie rubbed her forehead. The reason should have been obvious. "Is he dead?"

Fanny shrugged. "That, or bad enough not to bother us. Good riddance."

Indeed. It was unchristian to think so, but she couldn't help it.

"Fanny, if... if Captain Allerby comes back, don't mention it in my husband's hearing." She kept her voice low, even though she thought Martin was asleep. Fanny's brows rose. "They... had a disagreement."

Fanny rolled her eyes, but nodded. "Don't you worry none, missus."

Now all she could do was wait for the doctor.

CHAPTER 31

Tom and Hersey passed Dan going the other way in the wagon, Bates sitting beside him. There was a pile of straw in the back and some blankets. Palmer would be more comfortable on his journey to the farm than Wilson had been, Tom thought savagely. The alertness of action had worn off now, and all he could think of was that he'd failed to stop Palmer shooting Ellie's husband. He'd have to explain himself to the magistrate if Palmer died. Or Wilson—God forbid. Life had been simpler in the army in many ways.

Finn came running out to meet them. "Dan said you were all right, sir. Is that true?"

"More or less."

"Fanny said to go round the back. This way, come on." Finn set off around the building at a run.

Fanny was waiting in the yard. "Doctor's not here yet. Missus doesn't want the master disturbed." She eyed Hersey, then looked questioningly at Tom.

"Is there somewhere to lock up this fellow?" Tom asked.

"Tack room. There's a bolt on the outside." Her gaze turned to Tom's torn and stained breeches. "Get yourself into the kitchen and I'll see to that."

"Er, thank you, but all I need is some water and a cloth."

"Ale? Food?"

"Yes, ma'am." Tom almost felt like saluting as she walked off. "Is she like that all the time?" he whispered to Finn.

"Pretty much." Finn grinned. "They have good cake here, though."

Ale sounded good. It would be sensible to wait for the doctor's verdict before taking Hersey to the magistrate. "Where's the tack room, Finn?"

They found a chair for Hersey and locked him in, then Tom headed for the kitchen to investigate the damage to his thigh. Palmer's bullet had only grazed the skin—a deep graze, but it was soon cleaned and bandaged. Fanny put ale, bread, and ham in front of him, and by the time he'd eaten and drunk, the doctor had arrived and gone to see Wilson.

Dan returned with the wagon not long afterwards. Palmer lay in the back, a blanket drawn up over his face. Tom glanced at Dan in quick suspicion—he and Bates had been away a long time.

"He were nearly at his last gasp when I got back," Dan said. "He tried to get to his horse, I reckon, and started bleeding again. I didn't do anything to hurry him off, if that's what you're thinking."

He had been. "I'm not sure I'd blame you if you did. Probably better for the Wilsons than having him stand trial."

"Where should we put him?"

Tom's main dealings with corpses had been supervising the digging of mass graves after a battle. Here, there would have to be a coroner's inquest. "Leave him in the wagon for now. I'll get the doctor to have a look at him when he's finished with Wilson. Then I'd best go to the magistrate. They'll want the body at the inquest, but I don't see why Roseworth shouldn't find room for it in the meantime. I'll take Hersey, too." While they waited for the doctor, he told Dan what Hersey had said.

"Right bastard, that Palmer," Dan said, when Tom had finished. "I reckon Hersey would have been dead as well by now, if you hadn't been there."

Ellie, too, most likely. They were both witnesses to Palmer's crime. His presence had saved them, at least.

Finn came out to see what was going on and, before Tom could stop him, pulled the blanket away from Palmer's face. Then he frowned. "He was at the inn where we stopped on the way here. Where we bought the pies."

Tom didn't recall seeing him there. "Are you sure?"

Finn nodded. "Readin' the paper, he was."

"He must have recognised you then," Dan suggested to Tom. "And maybe that hurried his plans along? That's what he meant about making a proper job of the fire."

"It's possible."

He hadn't come in the nick of time—his arrival had made Palmer set his trap earlier than he'd intended. And if he hadn't kept watch, Palmer would have had time to set a larger fire that would have destroyed the barn. That was little consolation to the Wilsons at the moment, though.

The doctor, when he came, gave Palmer's body a quick inspection and wrote down some observations in a notebook. Then he looked at Tom over his spectacles. "You will need to inform Roseworth."

"The magistrate. Yes, I'll go there now."

"Good. He has my direction. For the coroner's inquest." He nodded and rode off.

"Want me to come with you?" Dan asked.

"I think so, yes. You can bring the wagon back here when we're finished at Thornton Court. I'll ride into Thirsk and get a room. I'll just see how Wilson is before we set off."

The kitchen was empty, although sounds of activity came from an adjoining room. Tom looked through the door to find Fanny and the older woman—Agnes—talking quietly, their faces sombre.

"Captain." Fanny came over.

"How is he?"

Her mouth turned down at the corners. "Not good. Doctor didn't tell me no details, but we're bringing a bed downstairs for him. He's got some laudanum in him now, I reckon."

Too badly injured to be moved upstairs—that didn't sound good at all. "And Mrs Wilson?"

"Sitting with him. Do you want to see her?"

"I…" He ran a hand through his hair. "I thought she ought to know that Palmer is dead and—"

"Good."

Tom, taken aback at her frankness, just stared at her.

"I call a spade a spade, Captain." She folded her arms. "That man has caused nowt but trouble, though I never thought he'd go so far as to shoot Mr Wilson. He'd have finished at the end of a rope in any case, and it saves the master and missus having to have their family affairs made public in a trial, don't it?"

"It does. I need to tell the magistrate what's happened, and take Palmer and his accomplice. Can Finn stay here a little longer?"

"Don't see why not. He's a nice lad. Helpful."

"Thank you. However, I don't need to go immediately if I can be of any help here."

"I'll ask missus," Fanny said. "Step into the dining room, Captain, while I ask."

Fanny did not immediately reappear. Tom went to look out of the window, glancing at the clock on the mantelpiece. Five o'clock—the sun would be setting in something over an hour. But he doubted the people here wanted a dead body on the premises overnight—he'd go today, even if he had to ride on to Thirsk by moonlight.

Sounds of movement came from the stairs, then the hall—a bed being brought down, possibly. Remembering Wilson's hostility when they met on the road, he thought it would be better if he just stayed out of the way. Fanny would ask if they needed his help. It was another quarter of an hour before the door opened. Ellie's face was drawn, her hair in disarray, her gown streaked with blood. And she stopped by the doorway, not coming properly into the room.

"Ellie, I'm sorry." For her, for failing to keep Palmer away. For not being able to comfort her now.

"You did what you could. I don't know how you could have done more."

Been more alert? Insisted on accompanying them more closely?

"What did the doctor say?"

"All we can do is wait, and hope infection does not set in. Fanny said that Martin's cousin is dead. Is that right?"

"Yes."

She nodded. "I suppose Mr Roseworth will need to be informed."

"I can deal with all that. Roseworth will want to speak to you, I imagine, but not just yet."

"Thank you. I... I must get back to Martin." She met his eyes briefly, gave the smallest of smiles, and left.

Fanny came to the door as Ellie approached the parlour, blocking her way. "I'll watch him. Time you had a bath and something to eat. I've told Agnes to heat water."

"No, I must—"

"There's nowt you can do, missus. He went to sleep as soon as we got him into the bed. I'll send for you if he wakes, or if anything changes." Fanny had her don't-argue-with-me expression. "And you won't be no use to him if you're too tired."

She was right—Ellie had to admit it. But although ten minutes in hot water followed by bread and soup made her feel better physically, she couldn't stop her thoughts.

The doctor had said it was lucky the bullet had gone right through; it saved him having to try to get it out and subject Martin to even more pain. But the doctor had shaken his head when she asked whether Martin would recover. "I'm afraid it's too early to say. There is always a great risk of infection with an abdominal wound. Give him laudanum against the pain if he needs it, and persuade him to drink barley water or similar when he regains consciousness. I will call again tomorrow."

She returned to the parlour, and pulled a high-backed chair close to the bed as Fanny left the room. Martin's face was still pale and his breathing, although regular, was shallow. Fanny had stoked the fire, and the room was warm. Over-warm for her, but when she put a hand on Martin's forehead, his skin felt cold and clammy. The pulse at his wrist was fast.

Fanny came back with a tray carrying a jug of barley water and two glasses, which she set on a table next to the bottle of laudanum the doctor had left. Then she went back to the kitchen, closing the parlour door behind her, and Ellie settled down to watch.

Martin awoke late that evening with a hiss of pain as he attempted to move.

"Lie still," Ellie said, leaning over to put a hand on his shoulder.

"Thirsty."

She half-filled a glass with barley water and supported his head while he drank, then he sank back into the pillows. "I was shot?" He frowned, as if trying to recall.

"Yes."

"Was it Luke?"

"I'm afraid so." He'd asked her that before; did he not recall?

Martin closed his eyes. "We were friends when we were children," he whispered. "How could he...?"

She had no answer to that. Father would have quoted the Bible, no doubt, about the love of money being the root of all evil.

"Jamie?"

"Safe with Mary in Harrogate." He knew that—perhaps he just wanted to be reassured that nothing further had happened.

"What about Sam?"

"He's still with the stallions at Mr Roseworth's stables." Did he not remember what she'd told him as they were driving home? But if Sam was his lover, as she had suspected, perhaps he just wanted reassurance that he was safe?

"That's good. And you, Ellie. He didn't hurt you, did he?"

"No." She took a breath. "No, Martin, he didn't."

As he closed his eyes, she told herself that Martin could have seen for himself that she was not injured. She rested her head on the back of the chair, her eyes on the man with whom she'd shared her life for the last seven years. If Tom had been shot as well, which of the two of them would *she* have asked about first?

Fanny came and sent Ellie to bed for a few hours; Ellie obeyed, being too tired to protest. She only dozed, but did feel somewhat refreshed when Agnes came to wake her at dawn. "There's a bite of breakfast ready for you in the kitchen, missus."

"He took a bit more barley water," Fanny reported, when Ellie returned to Martin's side after drinking a cup of tea and forcing down a little porridge. "And I give him another bit of laudanum, like you said."

"Thank you."

Ellie felt his forehead again. He was hot now, his pulse as fast as before, but fainter. She closed her eyes for a moment—that did not bode well.

"Fanny, will you watch a little longer, please, while I have a word with Dan?"

Fanny nodded and settled back into the chair.

The early sun was just slanting into the yard, beneath a milky sky that would clear later into a lovely day. The fine weather seemed wrong in the circumstances, an offence to her feelings.

Ellie put that silly thought from her mind and followed the sound of voices to where Dan was helping Finn feed the horses. He said a word to the boy and came out into the yard. Now she was here, Ellie wasn't sure how she could explain the decision she had come to overnight. Not without betraying Martin. But if her supposition was correct, she was asking *for* Martin.

"Missus?" Dan prompted, his face solemn. "Is it Mr Wilson?"

"No. Well, not... I mean, he's asleep at the moment. He... he wanted to talk to Sam about the horses." She wished he really was well enough to do so. "Could you send someone to fetch him from Mr Roseworth's place?"

Dan went very still. "He's at Bank Side, missus. He came home with me last night."

Dan knew. After two years living at Bank Side, he could well have observed enough to work out that Sam was more to Martin than just a stable master and jockey.

"Is it urgent?" Dan asked.

"I don't know. But today. This morning."

"I'll ride up there now."

"Thank you."

As Dan went back into the stable, Ellie wrapped her arms around her middle. She was lucky to have people like Dan and Fanny to help her, but she felt very alone. And if Martin died…

Would Mary be able to come? And bring Jamie with her, perhaps? Martin would want to see him too, if… if the worst was going to happen. And Henry was Martin's friend.

She should write and let them know what had happened.

Tom rode from Thirsk to Thornton Court early the following morning. Roseworth had been entertaining guests when they arrived the previous evening, and had talked to Tom only long enough to hear the basic details and to agree that Palmer's body could be left there overnight. And, to Tom's surprise, he had recognised Hersey. The young man was the son of an acquaintance, and was provided with a room for the night.

Tom had ridden to Thirsk and written to Frank before going to bed, describing everything that had happened; he might need his brother's help at the inquest. Palmer was far from the first man he'd killed, but it was the first time he would have to explain his actions to a stranger. To a jury of strangers, who might not understand why he'd shot Palmer when the man was running away.

He found Roseworth breakfasting with Hersey, and accepted an invitation to join them. After that, their business was concluded surprisingly quickly. Roseworth had his secretary take down Tom's description of what had happened. His brows rose as Tom described his final shot at Palmer, but he accepted the explanation readily enough. Tom's fears eased a little—it would be for the jury to decide in the end, but Roseworth's lack of censure was encouraging.

Hersey corroborated the parts he'd witnessed, and Roseworth dismissed his secretary to make copies. "There will have to be a coroner's inquest," Roseworth said. "Tomorrow, if I can arrange it. If Wilson is not well enough to attend, I will need a statement from him."

"Wilson looked to be in a bad way, sir," Tom protested. "Wounds to the abdomen rarely turn out well."

Roseworth's lips turned down. "I'm very sorry to hear it—he is a good man. Please give my best wishes to Wilson and his wife, and I will wait as long as I can before calling there."

"Thank you, sir." Tom told Roseworth which inn he was staying at in Thirsk, then took his leave and headed for Knowle Farm.

Rather than going to the front door when he arrived, Tom rode around to the yard. Finn came out to take his horse with a cheery greeting, but Dan's face was sombre.

"How's Wilson?"

Dan shrugged. "Still alive, but the missus weren't too happy about him this morning. Doctor's due back soon, I think."

"She won't want me bothering her now, then. Roseworth will notify the coroner, and may need to talk to her. I'll stay in Thirsk for a few days, in case I can help with anything. Can Finn stay here a bit longer, d'you think? If you want to, that is, Finn?"

Finn nodded enthusiastically. "I like the horses."

Dan smiled. "I'll check with Fanny, but I think she'll agree."

"Thank you. Will you let Mrs Wilson know what arrangements have been made?"

"No need." Dan nodded towards the kitchen door. "You can tell her yourself."

Ellie stood in the doorway. Even from across the yard she looked tired, but she did smile. "Give me a minute, Captain." Then she stepped inside, reappearing a few minutes later clad in pelisse and bonnet. "I need some exercise. Will you walk in the lane with me?"

Tom offered his arm, but she shook her head, folding her arms in front of her as if she was cold. That was just as well—he wanted to take her into his arms to comfort her, but he must not.

"How is he?"

"Not well. He is feverish and weak, although still lucid. Tom, I must thank you for what you did yesterday."

"I did it for you, Ellie. And Jamie."

She glanced up at him, then back to her feet. "What happened at Thornton Court?"

Tom related what Roseworth had said, and they walked on in silence until Ellie said it was time to turn back. A frustrating silence for Tom. He wanted to help if he could, but he didn't know how. Practical matters he could deal with, but he had no position here.

"Ellie, you should not be alone to cope with all this. The farms as well as your husband."

"We have good people here, Tom. You have seen that. I sent Jake to Harrogate this morning, to ask if Mary can come, and bring Jamie back with her. There is no further danger, is there?"

"I don't think so. The stranger near the farms was an accomplice, but I gathered from what Palmer said that they had parted company. If he had other accomplices, he wouldn't have needed to trick Hersey into collaborating with him."

"Martin will want to see Jamie before… before…" Her voice broke on a sob.

He couldn't help it. He pulled her to him and put his arms around her, the way he'd held his mother after Papa's funeral. Ellie's hands rested on his chest, trapped between their bodies. She made no move to pull away, just rested her head on his shoulder while sobs shook her body. Gradually the shudders eased, and he released her as soon as she stopped leaning on him. He held out a handkerchief.

"I have one, but thank you." She blew her nose and mopped her eyes.

"Are you ready to return?"

She took his arm this time as they walked back to the house.

"Ellie, if you need help, just ask. I, or Frank, will help with anything you need."

"I will. Thank you."

And that was all they said. All they could say, although Ellie did give his arm a little squeeze before she released it and went into the house. There was nothing more he could do.

CHAPTER 32

One of Ellie's worries was eased; Tom didn't seem concerned that he might be in trouble with the law for killing Palmer. And she no longer felt quite so alone. Tom might not be here in body, but knowing there was someone not too far away who cared gave her some comfort.

Which was silly, for Mary cared, too. And so did the misfits, in their own way.

In the parlour, Martin lay with a cloth over his forehead, Fanny beside him with a bowl of water.

"Still feverish, missus." Fanny dipped the cloth in the bowl, wrung it out and replaced it. Ellie felt for his pulse—still faint, still racing. That could not be good.

The doctor, when he examined Martin several hours later, agreed. "I'm afraid you must prepare for the worst, Mrs Wilson. I have left some powders to be taken in water when he wakes—no more than every six hours, mind. And laudanum to minimise the pain—give him what he needs, and let him drink if he is thirsty."

"Is there nothing we can do?"

"Only hope and pray. I will call again tomorrow."

Martin awoke later that afternoon. The powders or the laudanum had allowed him to sleep without becoming restless, but he was still hot and cold by turns. She helped him drink some barley water, then mixed another powder and added a few drops of laudanum, but Martin turned his face away when she held the glass to his lips.

"Not yet. Want to talk."

She set the glass back on the table and drew her chair closer. He fumbled under the sheet covering him, and she drew it back so he could free his arm. His grasp, when he took her hand, was surprisingly firm.

"Thank you for sending Sam. Said goodbye." His voice was weak, with too-frequent pauses for breath, but the words were clear enough.

"Martin, please don't tire yourself."

"Don't pretend, Ellie. I'm dying, aren't I?"

She could not just agree, but his eyes were on her. "The... the doctor was not hopeful."

"Sorry what I said. 'Bout Allerby and you."

"You've already apologised, Martin. What you said doesn't matter now. Your cousin would have shot you again if he hadn't been there." Her as well, probably. Tom had risked his own life for both of them.

"Good man." There was a long pause before his next words. "Keep Jamie safe. Love him."

Ellie wanted to be able to tell Martin that he would see his son again, but she could not speak, nor hold back her tears.

"Don't cry, Ellie. Had a good life. You. Jamie. Sam."

"Yes, Jamie was a gift. You are a good man, Martin, to everyone. We've had some happy times together." She swallowed against a lump in her throat. "And you had a winner at York."

He smiled at that, although pain creased his brow. "People more important. Look after the misfits."

"I will." They would look after her, too.

"Laudanum now," he whispered.

She lifted his head so he could drink, then held his hand until he fell asleep.

· · ·

A carriage came up the lane that evening as most of the household were preparing for bed. Ellie heard the sounds of arrival, then Fanny let herself into the parlour.

"It's Mrs Cowper, missus. And Doctor Cowper."

So soon! Ellie hurried into the hall. "Mary! I didn't expect you to arrive so quickly."

"Oh, Ellie." Mary hugged her tight, then stepped back. "Your man made good time, and we came as soon as we could."

"I'm so glad you're here."

"How is he?" Henry asked, his expression becoming grave as Ellie repeated what the doctor had said. "May I see him?"

"Of course. He's in the parlour."

"Did you bring Jamie?" Ellie asked, as Henry took his medical bag into the parlour.

"He's asleep in the carriage, with Kate. I thought it best if he didn't wake. Shall I ask her to bring him in?"

"I'll go, missus," Fanny said. "Kettle's heating."

"Come into the kitchen, Mary. It's still warm in there." They sat at the table while Agnes made tea and coffee. Then Fanny carried Jamie in and Ellie hugged him on her lap while she drank her tea and wondered how much to say. Her letter had said that Martin had been shot by his cousin, and she didn't want to explain Tom's involvement. Not now.

"I haven't had a room made up for you," Ellie said. "I wasn't expecting you until tomorrow."

"Henry said he would sit with Martin," Mary said. "Shall I share your bed, as we did at home?"

"I'll keep you awake."

Mary gave a wry smile. "Don't worry about me. You look worn to a thread."

"Thank you." It would be a comfort to have Mary close by.

. . .

Henry crept into her bedroom in the early hours of the morning, putting a hand on her shoulder to wake her without disturbing Mary. She pulled a robe over her night-rail and followed him downstairs.

"I thought you would want to sit with him," was all that Henry said as he draped a blanket over her lap and another around her shoulders. So she sat beside Martin, holding his hand as his breathing became slower, with longer and longer gaps between breaths. He wasn't conscious, but she liked to think that he knew she was there.

Finally, Henry reached over and rested his fingers against Martin's neck, then disengaged her hand and pulled the sheet up to cover Martin's face. Ellie leaned forward, resting her head on her hands, and wept. Wept for the harm done by the selfish actions of his cousin; for a life cut short. For the fact that they had argued with each other during their last proper time together, returning home in the gig two days ago.

"He did love you in his way, Ellie," Henry said gently. "He told me. And having Jamie made him very happy."

"I know." She sniffed, wiping her eyes on the sleeve of her robe, then fishing a handkerchief out of the pocket. "I'm glad you are here, Henry."

"We will all miss him, Ellie. I will sit with him."

"No, but thank you. I will not sleep if I return to bed. You may stay, too, if you wish. He was your friend."

Henry stayed, and they sat in silence on either side of the bed. Ellie remembered the good times—Jamie's birth and Martin's delight in it. Their son's first words, and his first steps. Riding on the moors, the excitement of Fleet winning at York. And his goodness to others. The misfits, and his ready acceptance of Jamie as his son. And she was thankful that he had lived long enough after the shooting for her to say some of that to him.

Her tears flowed, and when dawn came she was puffy eyed and drained, but calm. She would mourn him for a long time, but acknowledging that he had enjoyed much of life, despite the difficulties caused by his nature, would help her to let him go.

She went back to her room to bathe her face and tell Mary. "I have to tell Jamie somehow," she said. "And everyone else here."

Mary, still rubbing sleep from her eyes, came over and gave her a hug. "Let me deal with Jamie until you have told the others. Send his breakfast up."

"I'll just look in on him before—"

"No, Ellie. You look dreadful—you might distress him. Tell him later, when you have collected yourself. Come, put a clean chemise on, and have some breakfast."

In the kitchen, Henry and Dan were sitting at the table with a cup of coffee while Fanny fried bacon and eggs. As Ellie entered, Fanny looked around, tears running down her face. Henry had already given them the news.

"I'm so sorry, missus."

Ellie just nodded, unable to speak for the moment.

"I sent Agnes and Kate out," Fanny said. "Such wailing and lamenting, as if it would bring him back."

"Thank you, Fanny." She didn't want the condolences of the menfolk, either. Not yet. "I'll have my breakfast in the dining room. Can you take something up for Mary and Jamie?"

Fanny nodded. Henry stood and accompanied her into the dining room. "Keeping busy helps," he said gently. "I will assist with whatever you need, although I cannot stay away from my practice for long. Mary will remain here for as long as you need her."

"Oh, Henry, I'm so glad you two could come."

"It's no trouble Ellie." He paused as Fanny arrived with a tray, and helped her to set out plates and cups, then served Ellie bacon and eggs from the platter. "Do eat something."

Ellie sighed, stabbing a piece of bacon with her fork, trying to think. The magistrate would have to be told, a funeral arranged. Would there have to be an inquest first? She must write to Papa. To Aunt Elizabeth, too.

"Henry, what must happen now?"

"I will help you to make you a list. But only when you have eaten your breakfast."

Ellie felt a little better with a full stomach. In the nursery, Mary had dressed Jamie and he was sitting at his little table with a bowl of porridge. He threw the spoon down and toddled over to her. Ellie picked him up for a hug, managing not to cry again.

"Papa back?" he asked, when she set him down.

Ellie glanced at Mary, who grimaced.

"Just tell him," Mary mouthed.

"Papa won't be coming back."

He scowled, then his face cleared. "Go see hens?"

Surprise robbed Ellie of words for a moment. "If you want to." She managed to get the words out in a normal voice. "Finish your porridge first."

"He doesn't understand," Mary said quietly. "He must be used to Martin being away on business for several days at a time."

"Yes. Perhaps he thinks I meant that Martin isn't coming back today." There could be no other explanation.

"Don't worry about it now, Ellie. You can tell him again later. He will understand eventually."

A gradual realisation might be best for him. A talk about what dying meant would have to wait until he was older, and would be easier for her to manage when her initial grief had abated. There were many other things she had to do.

The letter arrived the day after Tom had seen Ellie, handed to him by the landlord as he went for an afternoon drink in the taproom. The direction was in an unfamiliar hand, and he broke the wafer with some trepidation. It was from Roseworth, dated that morning, telling him that the inquest was to be held the following day and he was to attend at four o'clock in the back room of the Black Bull. The final paragraph brought bad news.

This is a day later than I hoped, but as Wilson succumbed to his injury this morning, I thought it best that both deaths be dealt with together.

Poor Wilson. And Ellie, and everyone else at the farms. He tried to suppress a sense of failure—he'd done his best, but his best hadn't been good enough to keep Ellie's family safe.

He'd be on trial, in a sense—the jury might not believe he'd shot Palmer to prevent him making another attempt to murder Wilson. Worse, though, was that they would probably require evidence from Ellie.

The coach from York drew into the Market Place late that afternoon, and, as Tom had hoped, Frank was on it.

"Thank you for coming."

Frank clapped him on the shoulder. "No trouble, little brother. It's time I could do something for you."

"I've reserved a room for you at the Golden Fleece." Tom picked up the bag the guard passed down from the boot of the coach and led the way. "Come down for an ale when you're settled in?"

The taproom was busy, so they left the inn and found a quiet tavern in a back street where they could talk without being overheard.

"Tell me all," Frank said. Tom started with the fire, and gave a brief account of everything up to his meeting with the magistrate the previous day. Then Frank had him describe the events in the lane in detail, nodding now and then as he listened.

"You shouldn't worry about the inquest," Frank said. "If the magistrate thought you were to blame in any way, he'd have called the constable. And you have two witnesses—one of them independent."

"It's up to a jury, though, isn't it?"

"Don't worry, Tom. The jury aren't just taken off the street; they will be men of property, not likely to sympathise with a debtor like Palmer, especially after what he did."

They talked of other things then, and ate dinner there before going back to the Golden Fleece.

· · ·

The following day, to fill the time before the inquest, they hired horses and rode up to the moors. Then Tom changed into the clean coat and trousers Frank had brought from York for him and set off for the Black Bull.

The room in the inn was laid out with a table at one end, behind which sat a thin man with sharp eyes. A clerk sat beside him, with pen, ink, and paper at the ready.

Twelve men sat at one side, and on the other was Ellie with a woman he recognised from Harrogate—her sister. Beside them sat Roseworth, Dan, Hersey, and the doctor Tom had seen at Knowle Farm.

The coroner was efficient, and not given to verbosity. The jury were sworn in, then he stated that both bodies had been viewed and described the location where the incident happened.

The doctor was called as first witness. He attested that both men had unquestionably died from gunshot wounds, and then asked to be excused as he had calls to make.

Ellie was next, looking pale but composed. She gave her evidence in a clear voice that wavered only a little, but she clutched her sister's hand tightly when she resumed her seat. Hersey explained how he had been an unwitting accomplice, then Tom was called. As Frank had suggested, he introduced himself using his army rank, and repeated Ellie's statement that he was a friend of the family. The only awkward point was when the coroner asked why, if Palmer had fired his pistols, Tom shot at him instead of apprehending him.

"He had two pistols, sir, and I had no way of knowing whether or not he had reloaded them. I could not quickly get through the hedge to pursue him. If he had retrieved his horse and followed us, he could have made another attempt on Wilson's life. Or he could have targeted Mrs Wilson as well. Wilson needed to be taken to his home as quickly as possible."

There were murmurings from the jury, and nods. Tom hoped they were of approval. Dan's evidence about Palmer's death was short and to the point, and the jury took only minutes to decide on their verdict.

"Well?" Frank asked, when Tom emerged into the taproom.

"Palmer murdered Wilson, and my actions were in defence of myself and the Wilsons."

"Told you it would be fine! Drink?"

"Not yet. I want to give my condolences to Ellie."

"Oh. Yes—I will accompany you."

"I am sorry you had to be subjected to such an ordeal, Mrs Wilson," Mr Roseworth said, once the jurymen had left the room. "I could have arranged for your evidence to be written and presented to the coroner."

"You did offer, Mr Roseworth, and my thanks for that. But I wanted to see that Captain Allerby was not blamed for Palmer's death."

"Yes, well. You need not bother your head further over this matter. I will see to the burial of Palmer. And pay my respects at your husband's funeral, if you permit?"

"Indeed, sir. It is to be three days hence at eleven o'clock, at St Oswald's in Kirby Sutton." It was only after Mr Roseworth had bowed and left that Ellie remembered that she'd meant to ask him about collecting the stallions. In one way it felt wrong to be thinking of such things with Martin so recently gone, but they had been his main interest for as long as Ellie had known him. She owed it to his memory, and to Jamie, to continue with his breeding programme.

Mary nudged her. "Here's your family friend."

Ellie turned to see Tom waiting by the door, his brother behind him, and went to meet them.

"Ellie, I'm so sorry."

The concern in Tom's voice and face made her eyes prick with tears. She could only nod.

"Is your sister staying with you?"

"Yes, for a week or so. Let me introduce you. Mary, this is Captain Allerby, and Mr Allerby. My sister, Mary Cowper. Her husband is... was... Martin's friend."

"I am pleased to meet you, Captain. Mr Allerby." Mary held out her hand, and both men shook it. "Henry had to return to Harrogate, but he will be glad to meet you if you come to the funeral."

Ellie caught Tom's questioning glance, and gave a small nod. "In three days' time, at eleven in the church at Kirby Sutton. You are both welcome to come to the farmhouse afterwards for refreshments."

"Thank you. We will see you there." They bowed and left, Tom pausing to say something to Dan as they passed in the doorway.

"The gig's ready, missus."

"Thank you, Dan."

"Was Captain Allerby one of Ben's friends?" Mary asked as Ellie drove them out of Thirsk, Dan riding behind. "I don't recall seeing him before he drove you to Harrogate with Jamie."

Ellie had to tell her sister at some point, and now was as good a time as any with no-one close enough to hear. "No, although I think they would have been friends if they had known each other. He's Jamie's father."

From her lack of surprise, Mary must have suspected something of the sort.

"A useful man to have around," Mary said. Ellie glanced at her, suspecting a double meaning, but could see nothing in her sister's expression beyond approval.

"A good friend." Perhaps one day he might be more than that, but that was all he could be now.

CHAPTER 33

The church was crowded for Wilson's funeral. As Tom walked in he spotted Ellie and Mary in one of the front pews, with a man who he guessed was Mary's husband. Behind them, some of the men from Bank Side filled the pew. Tom and Frank joined Roseworth and the doctor across the aisle as the church filled up with people from labourers to prosperous tradesmen.

The vicar's words about the deceased painted him as a kind and honest man, fair to his workers and a friend of many. And there was an approving murmur when he said that Mrs Wilson hoped they would take a drink to his memory at the Farmers' Rest after the service.

When the coffin had been lowered into the ground and the final words said, many people stopped to pay their respects to Ellie and then wandered off towards the inn. Tom did not join them. He even hesitated about accepting Ellie's invitation to return to the farm for refreshments, wondering whether it would be better to stay away from Ellie for now. But Frank was already at the reins of their hired gig, waiting for him to climb up. So they followed Dan driving Ellie in the farm gig, and the Cowpers, with several more carriages behind.

· · ·

A generous spread of cold meats and pies had been laid out in the dining room, and many of the guests made a good meal of it before taking their leave of Ellie. Tom recognised only Roseworth, who joined him by the fireplace with a glass of claret.

"Bad business, this, Allerby. Poor woman, she'll struggle to manage without Wilson."

"Indeed, sir."

"Just when Wilson was doing so well with his breeding, too. The stallions I'm putting up are fine animals. Still, she'll have no shortage of suitors once she's out of mourning. Tidy little business, the horses, and this farm is a productive bit of land."

As if Ellie needed the farms to attract a husband. Tom gritted his teeth, then managed a smile he didn't feel. "I'm sure she will manage until then."

Roseworth nodded. "Good head on her shoulders. Still, a woman alone—there'll be some will try to take advantage." He pulled a watch from his pocket and flipped the case open. "Must be off, I'm afraid." He drained his glass and left, stopping by Ellie only long enough to say a few words.

Most of the other guests had gone by now, and Ellie was talking to Frank. Or, rather, Frank was talking to Ellie, and she was nodding now and then as if absorbing information.

Tom turned his attention to a framed print above the mantelpiece, showing the York races. Four horses galloped in front of a crowded grandstand, cheered on by a group of men and a small dog.

"I was thinking of buying an uncoloured copy of that and getting the winner painted to resemble Fleet." Doctor Cowper had come to stand beside him. "We have not been introduced, but my sister-in-law told me what you did. May I thank you on behalf of my friend?"

Tom shook the proffered hand. "I'm sorry it was not enough."

"Martin had the satisfaction of seeing his ambitions coming to fruition." Cowper's gaze returned to the print. "And the joy of having a son at last."

Tom stiffened, then forced himself to relax. Even if Cowper knew that he was Jamie's father, he would not raise the issue here. "I'm glad Ellie has family so close."

"Not *so* close." Cowper grimaced. "And I cannot spare time from my practice to be here as often as I would wish. Mary will stay for a week or so, though."

Tom was about to ask if Ellie had no other relatives who could help, then remembered the fiction that he was a family friend who would know such things. But it was almost as if Cowper had read his mind.

"Her father… Well, suffice it to say that he and I do not care for each other. And he didn't approve of Ellie's marriage either. He has a parish near Lancaster."

"Too far to come for the funeral, I suppose." Although there had been time for a letter to have reached him and for him to make the journey.

"His letter said he was too busy." Cowper's expression made clear what he thought of that excuse. "Small loss, in my opinion, but it distressed Ellie a little. She has an aunt in Carlisle, who I think will come and stay for a while if Ellie asks her."

"That's good."

"And you, Allerby—I gather you're living in York at the moment?"

"For the moment, yes." Where was this conversation going?

"I hope Ellie may call upon you should she require assistance? I will do my best, of course, but I have little knowledge of farming or the breeding of horses."

Neither do I. "Yes, of course. My brother, too." He indicated Frank, still talking to Ellie. "He's an attorney."

"I know. Martin told me how the pair of you assisted him with that unsavoury false accusation."

Tom wondered exactly how much Wilson had told his friend, but there seemed to be nothing in Cowper's manner beyond a concern for Ellie.

"Good to have met you, Allerby. Now I must find my wife to say farewell. I need to return to Harrogate."

Ellie broke off her conversation with Frank to take Cowper's hand, then Cowper left—the last guest to depart, apart from himself and Frank. Tom walked over to them.

"As I was saying, Mrs Wilson," Frank said, "you may call upon me if you need a second opinion on any legal matters, for your husband will have had an attorney he uses regularly. He will be the best person to deal with the initial legalities."

"Thank you, Mr Allerby. And for your explanation." She turned slightly, to include Tom in the conversation. "I have just been asking how I must go about transferring the ownership of the farms."

"Will your husband's attorney not do all that for you?" Tom asked.

"Yes, but I like to know what is involved."

"That's good. Roseworth was saying that he fears some men might try to take advantage of your inexperience."

"I'll leave you to it," Frank said. He closed the door behind him, and they were alone.

Ellie looked into Tom's face as the door closed behind his brother, then dropped her gaze. The tenderness in his expression made her want to be comforted by him, held by him, as he had a few days earlier. But it would not do, not here where someone might come in at any moment. And they should not spend too long alone in the parlour together with the door shut, but she did want to have a few words in private.

"Tom, Martin did realise that what he accused you of was not true. He was grateful for what you did."

"That's good. I didn't want to cause a rift between you."

"You did not. I intend to carry on Martin's breeding programme, if I can." She grimaced. "I foresee some time spent going over the farm books to learn costs and prices. Still, it will keep me busy."

"If I can be of any assistance, do ask. I hate to think of you struggling with... Well, with anything."

"I will, thank you. After all, now you have sold out, you have nothing better to do." Her words were an attempt to lighten the conversation; he took it as she had meant it, with an amused crinkle of his eyes.

"Indeed. And where else might I get to ride an animal like Fleet?"

"Do you return to York now?"

"I think I must. Frank will need to go back, and you will wish to be rid of Finn."

"He's no trouble. In fact, I've hardly seen him." Fanny seemed to have taken charge of the boy.

"Hmm. When a lad of that age is invisible, it often means trouble. I'd better go and find him. Be well, Ellie."

She thought he was going to hug her again, but he merely touched her shoulder and left. She went to the window at the sound of wheels on gravel, to see Henry's gig being made ready, and the Allerbys' vehicle behind it. She went outside to make her farewells.

Mr Allerby's explanation of wills and probate stood her in good stead two days later when Martin's attorney called at Ellie's request. Mr Blaine was a man of little more than Martin's age, his dress sober and his face pale. Not a man who spent much time out of doors.

Ellie introduced Mary, and they went into the dining room. Mr Blaine took a folded parchment from his satchel and spread it out, squaring it carefully with the table edge. Then he brought out a little case, opening it to reveal a pen and stoppered bottle of ink. Setting a pair of spectacles on his nose, he began to read.

"This is the Last Will and Testament of me, Martin Edward Wilson, of Knowle Farm in the county of Yorkshire." He looked up from the paper, as if to check that Ellie was paying attention. "I hereby revoke all former wills and testaments made by me." He looked up again, and Ellie nodded. But it would take all day at this pace.

"Mr Blaine, is there any reason that I cannot just read the will myself?"

He pursed his lips. Ellie put her hand out, and Mr Blaine slid the paper across the table with an offended sniff.

Ellie positioned it so that Mary could read it as well. Martin had left Bank Side and all the horses to Jamie, to be managed by his guardians until he was twenty-one. The remainder of his possessions, including Knowle Farm, were left to her. She and Henry were named as Jamie's guardians. All as she had expected.

"It all seems straightforward, Mr Blaine. I assume I can carry on my husband's business as usual while you complete the necessary procedures to transfer ownership?"

"I… Yes. You will, naturally, wish to appoint a farm manager, and a man of business to deal with any financial and legal matters."

"Mr Blaine, I have not yet decided exactly what—"

"I have drawn up an agreement that will allow me to handle all the legal and financial details for you, Mrs Wilson, so you need not worry about any of this." He took another paper out of his satchel and slid it across the table, together with pen and ink. "You need only sign where I have indicated. Mrs Cowper should sign below as witness."

Ellie glanced at the agreement, then folded it. "Thank you, Mr Blaine. I will read this later and bring the signed document to you if I decide to retain your services."

Mr Blaine's brows rose, then drew together. Surprised that she had a mind of her own, perhaps?

"A woman cannot manage alone, Mrs Wilson. There will be difficulties that you do not anticipate or comprehend. Many of Wilson's suppliers and customers will not wish to deal with a woman."

"I will have Doctor Cowper to advise me, Mr Blaine. I assume there is no obstacle to getting the titles to the farms transferred to myself and my son? That is your role, as executor of the will, is it not?"

"Indeed. But matters would be much easier if—"

"Mr Blaine." Mary's voice was sharp, and Blaine looked as surprised as if a wooden doll had spoken. "My sister lost her husband only a few days ago. She should be given time to consider her future actions, and not be hurried into making decisions."

Blaine stiffened. "I meant only to help, Mrs Cowper."

"And I thank you for it, sir." Ellie's tone was conciliating. She wasn't sorry that Mary had interrupted, but it wouldn't do to put the man's back up. "Please do proceed with the transfer of ownership of the farms. I will let you know of my decision about this other matter within a week or two."

He sniffed, and refolded Martin's will. "I will take my leave, then, Mrs Wilson. Good day to you."

Ellie escorted him to the front door, and stood watching with Mary as he climbed into his gig and drove away.

"He might have been correct about one thing," Mary said. "About men not wishing to deal with a woman."

"I'm afraid so. Don't worry, I'm not expecting Henry to spend time advising me on farming, even if he had the time to do so."

Mary followed her into the parlour—now with all signs of Martin's last days removed. "He will happily help, you know that."

"I do." Ellie squeezed her sister's hand. "But I could not take him away from his practice, and an adviser thirty miles away is not ideal."

"Even if he knew the first thing about farming," Mary added, with a chuckle. "Are you going to use Mr Blaine as your man of business?"

"I think not. I will write to Mr Allerby, and ask if he can recommend someone in Thirsk. Now I must go to Bank Side, to talk with the men there. To explain that nothing will change for the moment. Would you like to come? Jamie always enjoys seeing the horses."

A few days later she went with Dan and Sam to collect Fleet and Blackie from Mr Roseworth. Sam sat on the ledge behind the gig— these days he was even less talkative than usual, with shadows around his eyes, but he continued to carry out his duties with his usual diligence.

Mr Blaine's doubts about her ability to continue the business were still in her mind. As she waited at Thornton Court for Sam and Mr Roseworth's groom to bring the two stallions out, she told Dan part of what Mr Blaine had said.

"He might be right, missus. I don't know about the people Mr Wilson dealt with, but I've heard many men say women don't have a head for business." He gave her an apologetic glance. "Might be true, in some cases, but there's plenty of women run shops, or dressmakers and the like."

"There's a bit more money involved in selling horses." And discussing the finer details of breeding animals could well be seen as improper, particularly by some of the estate-owners and titled gentlemen with whom Martin had done business.

"I don't reckon you need worry too much about the horses just yet, missus. There won't be no more mares coming into season now. Next year..." He shrugged. "Sam's not one for making decisions, but he's forgotten more about horses than most men ever learn. It'll do him good to have something more to think about right now, to keep him busy now the master's gone."

Sam must be feeling as sad as she was—more so, perhaps. She had Jamie, after all.

"I reckon we'll rub along well enough between us," Dan added.

It would be good if they could manage better than rubbing along. Even, perhaps, another Wilson's Wonder finishing first at York.

CHAPTER 34

"There you are." Frank slid onto the bench across the table from Tom and looked around for a waiter. "Have you ordered yet?"

"No." Tom set his book aside. It was a week since Wilson's funeral, and Tom had hardly seen his brother since then. Frank had gone to Ripon for a couple of days on a matter of business for Mortenson, and had been busy in his office the rest of the time. They'd arranged to dine together today.

Frank picked up Tom's book to read the title. "*Principles of Canal Construction?* You're thinking of investing your commission money?"

Tom shrugged. "No. But the men who dig the canals need supervision."

"By a good ex-sergeant, not an officer." The waiter came and they ordered roast beef, then Frank turned his attention back to Tom. "Blue-devilled, little brother?"

"I've been trying to improve Finn's spelling." And attempting to deflect the lad's seemingly continuous chatter about the time he'd spent at Knowle Farm. In truth, he was beginning to wonder if he'd made a mistake in leaving the army. Ellie and Jamie were no longer threatened, Finn would be happy fostered to a farm somewhere, and

Frank was back on his feet. But if he hadn't sold out, Palmer might have killed or injured Ellie and Jamie.

"You need an occupation."

"That's why I'm reading things like that," Tom pointed out. Their food came, and nothing much was said for a while.

"Farming?" Frank suggested, pushing his empty plate away.

"I doubt I can buy enough land with what I've got, and I've no idea how to go about it."

"Being out of doors would suit you though." Frank didn't wait for an answer, but took a letter from his pocket and handed it over. "This came today."

It was addressed to Frank; two sheets in Ellie's hand. He suppressed a stab of irrational disappointment that she should write to Frank, not him, and read through it. "I don't hold out much hope for this Blaine becoming her man of business."

Frank chuckled. "Indeed not."

"Are her reservations justified?" Ellie had not enclosed the agreement Blaine had proposed, but had quoted some of the clauses in it and her interpretation of them. They seemed overly restrictive to Tom, and from Ellie's acerbic phrasing in places, he suspected that Blaine had underestimated her understanding and let it show.

"*If* Blaine was a man I knew and trusted, it is the kind of agreement I would recommend for some elderly lady becoming incapable of making her own decisions, or the type of female who thinks of nothing but fashion and gossip. I don't know Mrs Wilson well, but I suspect that is far from the case."

"I think so, yes. A very practical and capable woman." Those were just two of her many attractions.

"I could send a different agreement for her to show Blaine, or you and I could become her men of business—subject to her agreement, of course." There was a knowing gleam in Frank's eyes that Tom chose to ignore.

"I know nothing about business matters," he protested. "And she only asked for a recommendation."

"Naturally, as I am based in York at the moment and that is rather too far for easy communication."

"At the moment? Are you thinking of moving?"

"Thinking only, for now. Mortenson has been in discussion with an attorney in Ripon about taking over his practice. The man wants to retire. I would deal with the business in that area."

"What does Susannah think about that?"

"She likes the idea, somewhat to my surprise. We may be able to make a fresh start in a new town. It's not decided yet." Frank tapped the letter. "Mrs Wilson says her husband only used this Blaine to look over contracts and so on, not for day to day matters, so there will be little she cannot manage herself once she has got the hang of things. If I do move to Ripon, it is only half the distance from her as York, so I could still advise her when necessary. However, I suspect that what she really needs is a representative to deal with men who might try to take advantage—*financial* advantage—of a woman."

"Or who don't want to do business with a woman."

"Precisely. And it would give you a good reason to see her. You do want to, don't you?"

"For heaven's sake, Frank, it's only a week since her husband died!" Whatever the relationship between Ellie and Wilson had been, she *was* mourning him. He wanted to court her properly, but it was far too soon for that.

"Think about it, Tom. You are an old friend of her family, after all."

"You know that's a fiction."

Frank shrugged. "A fiction that has been useful, and one it's too late to deny. And as such, it would seem strange for you not to lend your assistance, given that you live within a day's ride and have no other occupation at present."

"Who would know?"

"The local magistrate and the staff at the farm. Possibly others by now. But think of it another way—it would seem unexceptional if you *did* help. Consider it, Tom. I will reply to this tomorrow, to make an appointment to see her. Let me know if you will be accompanying me."

It would be a means to keep in touch with Ellie until her mourning was over. *If* she agreed. Although it could be frustrating, being close but not being able to show or speak of his feelings.

What if she said no?

~

Ellie found herself unexpectedly restless on the morning the Allerbys were to arrive. Nervous, even. Dan had driven Mary back to Harrogate the day before, and although she missed her sister's company, she did not feel as lonely as she had expected. Martin had often been away on business, or at Bank Side, and sometimes she went for hours at a time without recalling what had happened. Except when she was in the room that Martin had used as his office—there, reminders were all about her.

She had attempted to go through Martin's accounts and record books in the days following Mr Blaine's visit, but had got hopelessly muddled. They were more complex than the domestic and dairy accounts that she had routinely dealt with. The only thing she was sure of, as a result of that exercise, was that Mr Blaine had been someone that Martin consulted only occasionally. He had not handled all Martin's affairs in the way he had proposed doing for her. The relief she felt when Mr Allerby had replied, offering to go through everything with her, had given her the courage to look into it all again. This time she didn't worry about things she was unsure of, but compiled a list of questions. Quite a long list. Now, the dining table was covered in piles of paper and ledgers. There was no room to serve refreshments, but she thought they would not mind sitting at the kitchen table for that.

Fanny tapped on the open door. "Gig coming up the lane, missus."

Ellie felt suddenly breathless. *It's a business meeting, remember.* "Thank you. Put the kettle on, will you?"

"Looks like they've got that lad with them."

There was something in Fanny's smile that gave Ellie pause. Affection? "You look pleased about it, Fanny?"

She lifted a shoulder. "Brightens the place up, he does. The…" She swallowed. "The babe I lost would be about his age now. A little boy, it was, but he come too soon. I'll get the cake out." And she hurried back to the kitchen. Ellie smiled—from what she had seen of Dan and Fanny together, there might be another chance soon for Fanny to have a child of her own.

Ellie went to the front door to watch for the Allerbys, shivering in the cold wind that held a spatter of rain. Mr Allerby was driving, Tom beside him with his head turned, saying something to Finn. Then Tom looked around and met her eyes, his smile going straight to her heart.

Business meeting. It was too soon for anything else.

"Welcome. Thank you both for coming, and in such weather." She held her hand out, and they both shook it, Tom's grip lingering just a little longer than his brother's.

"You are most welcome, Mrs Wilson," Mr Allerby said. "We took the stage to Thirsk, so we have not suffered the damp for too long. I hope you don't mind that we brought Finn along as well? He's gone to find someone to help him with the horse."

"Of course I don't mind. Please, do come in."

They exchanged the usual pleasantries about the weather and their journey over tea and cake, then settled around the dining table.

"Mr Allerby, I am very grateful for your offer to explain matters to me. Once I understand things better, I will be able to decide whether or not I can manage alone."

"As to that, Mrs Wilson, I have a suggestion, but let us start with all this." He regarded the papers and books with what appeared to be remarkably like satisfaction.

"You look as if you will be enjoying yourself," Ellie said.

"He probably will, inexplicable though that may seem to us lesser mortals." Tom met her eyes in shared amusement.

Mr Allerby chuckled. "There's room in this world for all sorts. Now, where do you wish to start, Mrs Wilson?"

"I have some questions." Ellie handed him the list, and he ran his eyes down it.

"Hmm. If all the papers are here, perhaps I should look through this first. That way, I can give you a considered opinion, rather than you two sitting there while I think. Tom, why don't you tell her the other part of my idea?" He looked up from Ellie's list. "In another room, preferably."

"Ejected from your own dining room, ma'am?" Tom's flippant words were belied by his serious expression.

Ellie rose, suddenly nervous about what he might say. "Let us go into the parlour, Captain."

In the parlour, she hesitated, regarding the two chairs beside the fire, but instead moved to the table by the window. She could not talk to Tom sitting where she and Martin had spent their evenings. The table here was where she did the household accounts and wrote her letters. And this *was* a business meeting. She should not hope it might be more than that.

Tom took the other chair, but seemed reluctant to speak.

"Your brother mentioned another idea," she prompted.

"A suggestion, merely. One that you must feel free to refuse if you do not think it will answer. For whatever reason."

"Go on."

"Frank thought… We both thought that if you decide you don't need a permanent man of business, you may still need someone to go about the country to deal with others. For arranging mares to be covered by Fleet and Blackie, or selling hunters. Whatever else your husband did when he went away."

Ellie tried to concentrate on what he was saying, and not on the fact that it was Tom saying it. "I think I would need someone like that even if I had a man of business. Do you have someone in mind?" Himself, she hoped.

"Ellie, I don't know much about breeding horses, or—"

"Sam does, and you can learn. I could, too, I suppose, but I will have enough to do managing the farm." And not everyone would deal with a woman. "I trust you, which is just as important as knowledge. More so, really."

"Then, if it will help, I can do that for you."

If it will help...? She tried to read his expression—there was no reluctance in his face or voice, but little enthusiasm either.

"Why are you offering? Is it only because I will need a male representative?" If that was the only reason, she would prefer to find someone else. Someone whose feelings she had not mistaken. It might be too soon to talk directly of such matters, but...

Ah, perhaps *he* thought it was too soon to say more. But if he would not speak plainly, she must. *Carpe diem.*

Tom had hoped for a yes, and tried to steel himself against a no. He hadn't expected her to frown and ask him why.

"Tom, with all I have had to do since Martin died, I have always had the comfort that you would come if I needed help. And..." She hesitated, then took a deep breath. "Once Jamie was born, Martin was like a brother to me, or a friend, not a husband or lover. He was a husband only in law, and in that we were bringing up Jamie together."

Tom nodded—he'd surmised as much. What was she trying to say?

"Martin was a *good* friend, and an excellent father. A kind man. But even though it is not yet a fortnight since his death, I cannot help thinking about the future. I cannot bear the idea of your help being only a matter of business, if that is all it will ever be."

Only a matter of business? Had she really thought that? He leaned forward. "Ellie, no. It is the opposite." He couldn't blame her for doubting, for he had been trying his best not to make his feelings for her obvious. "All the time I was in Spain and France I remembered our time together, and it helped me through some dark times. Seeing you again these past few months..."

He did not want the table between them, so he stood. Ellie took his hand, and he pulled her to her feet and wrapped his arms around her. She settled into his embrace with a sigh, resting her head on his shoulder. "You are the one I want to spend my life with, Ellie, if you will have me. One day I will ask you to marry me, but we cannot do more than this, not yet." No matter how much he wanted to.

"I know." Her words were muffled; she pushed against him, but only moved far enough to lift her head. "One day I will say yes."

It was a struggle not to hold her close again, not to kiss her. He had to content himself with that promise, for now. For many months to come.

"I wish… I wish we did not have to wait," she said. "But to have you anything more than a business associate at the moment will set tongues wagging. I don't want there to be any speculation about Jamie."

There probably would be speculation, at some point, if Jamie came to resemble him more as he grew. But it was likely to be less damaging then than it would be now, so soon after Wilson's death.

Ellie tilted her head to one side. "Do you mind that Martin will always be regarded as his father?"

He thought he did, a little. "Your husband *was* Jamie's father until now—in his eyes and in the eyes of the world. Nothing can change that. How is Jamie taking it?"

"He doesn't understand that Martin won't be coming back."

He hugged her tighter for a moment, then, at a sound from the hall, released her. "Can I meet him? Properly, I mean—I didn't talk to him when I escorted you to Harrogate."

"Of course, if you wish."

"Tom?" It was Frank, just outside the door.

"Very diplomatic," Tom murmured, crossing the room to open it. Behind him, Ellie chuckled.

Frank stepped into the room. "I just came to say that it may take me a few hours to go through all the papers. Fanny will keep me supplied with coffee." He looked from Tom to Ellie. "Have you decided?"

"We have," Ellie said.

More than Frank knew, although Tom would tell him later.

"Tom," Ellie went on, "I know you have been to Bank Side, but you will need to meet the men properly now. Sam, in particular. We could go there together, and take Jamie with us. Mr Allerby, will you stay for dinner? We eat at five."

307

"Thank you, I would like that. Now if you will excuse me, I will get back to work." Frank closed the door behind him, with nothing more than a knowing look at Tom.

"There's one other thing," Tom said. "Finn. He's under my feet in York—no fault of his, but there's little to do for a lad of that age, unless I make him attend school. I haven't yet been in one place long enough to deal with that. I wondered if he could stay here. I'll pay for his board—"

"There's no need, Tom. We'll find some use for him, and if Fanny likes him, he can't be bad. Fanny likes you, too," she added, with a grin.

"I am honoured."

"You should be." Her laugh brightened her face. "Come, let's get Lass harnessed."

Jamie was playing in the yard and showed more interest in going to see the 'horsies' at Bank Side than in Tom's presence, sitting quietly on Ellie's lap as Tom drove there. Jamie probably regarded him in the same way as Dan Cole or any of the other men he saw about the farms.

Sam showed Tom around the barns and fields—giving far more detail than Dan had when he first came here. After ten minutes or so, Ellie pleaded fatigue and retreated to the kitchen, leaving Jamie in Tom's charge. Jamie babbled about the horsies to Tom as readily as he had to Ellie, and willingly accepted Tom's offer to carry him when Sam took them to look over the mares in a nearby field. The feel of the small body in his arms, trusting, gave him a sensation of tenderness he'd never known before. How much was due to the knowledge that this child was of his body, he didn't know, but he revelled in it all the same.

And in a year's time he would be doing this as Jamie's stepfather.

CHAPTER 35

*M*arch 1815

"Dammit! Hounds have lost the scent!" Roseworth sounded annoyed, but Tom wasn't sorry. He'd enjoyed the chase, but it was a raw day and the thin mist was turning to drizzle. Men and horses were spattered with a liberal coating of mud from the sodden fields. Enough was enough.

"We've had a good run considering the weather," someone else said. "Time for something to warm us up, eh?"

There was a murmur of agreement and the hunt broke up. The farmers in the group headed for the Fox and Pheasant; Roseworth invited the gentry back to his house. One of Roseworth's friends rode alongside Tom and introduced himself. "Dyson. Good mount you've got there, Allerby."

"She is." Tom patted the mare's neck. Storm—named for the dark colour of her coat—wasn't the fastest of the current crop, but she was good over fences. Tom had helped school her during this past winter —but not until Sam had schooled *him*. He now had a much better seat and, with the right mount, could clear hedges that he would never have attempted before.

"Roseworth tells me you trade them?"

"Not me, personally. I can arrange it with Mrs Wilson, though." Success! Although Tom enjoyed riding to hounds, he was really here to show off Ellie's horses.

"How old is she?"

"Four. This is her first season." Tom described Storm's sire and dam, and how she'd been trained. When they reached Thornton Court, Dyson followed Tom into the stables. Leaving his own horse to one of Roseworth's grooms, Dyson leaned on the partition watching Tom unsaddle the mare and brush her down.

"I'd like to try her," Dyson said, as they entered the house.

"Certainly. Come to Bank Side one day—Roseworth can give you directions."

"I will." They shook hands, and Dyson took a mug of mulled ale from a footman's tray, joining a group by the fire.

Tom sipped his own ale, wondering who to talk to. He still felt a little out of place at these gatherings. His army rank gave him some status amongst the landowners and gentry, but he had little in common with these men. That would change in time, he supposed, but he sometimes missed the camaraderie of an officers' mess. The men there had a common purpose, even when they came from very different backgrounds.

Roseworth joined him, a large glass of brandy in one hand. "Bad business in France, eh? I hear Boney's gathered quite an army on his way to Paris."

"I believe so. I know no more than you, though—only what I read in the newspaper." It was a worrying development—and depressing, too. All the lives lost in the war to contain Napoleon had been wasted by allowing him to escape.

"Just have to hope Wellington can see him off." Roseworth inclined his head in Dyson's direction. "You're doing well with getting business for Mrs Wilson, by the looks of it." He nudged Tom with one elbow. "You're in a good position with her, lad. Don't know what you're waiting for."

Tom took deep breath. Roseworth wasn't the first to make such a comment, and wouldn't be the last. Getting angry about the mercenary motives they attributed to him wouldn't help. "It's only six months since her husband died." As Roseworth well knew.

"Don't see what difference that makes." Roseworth squinted at him. "Does that mean you *do* want to marry her? Don't blame you. She's come here a few times with the black stallion—fine figure of a woman."

Tom gritted his teeth, and Roseworth chuckled. "Now don't take affront, I mean no disrespect to you or her. She does need a man to help with the business, or you wouldn't be here. Advantages on both sides."

Tom nodded, taking a mouthful of ale to avoid answering.

"Just saying that if you—both of you—*were* interested, I wouldn't think worse of you for getting on with it now. Nor would anyone else."

"Thank you, sir." He supposed the magistrate meant well. "I should be on my way, before the rain gets too heavy." Beyond the window, the clouds had darkened further; it was as good an excuse as any to get out of this conversation.

"Good idea. Come along again next time, eh? We might have more luck." Roseworth clapped him on the shoulder and wandered off.

By now Roseworth's grooms had finished dealing with all the visiting horses, and one of them helped Tom saddle the mare again. He had nearly an hour's ride back to Bank Side—shorter if he pushed his mount, but she'd done well today over heavy ground and deserved to take it easy.

Should he call at Knowle Farm on the way to tell her about Dyson's interest in the mare? No, he decided with regret. The news could wait until tomorrow, and if he stopped at Knowle to tell Ellie, he wouldn't want to leave.

Even though he'd dismissed Roseworth's suggestion of not waiting any longer to marry Ellie, the idea had lodged in his brain and his heart. It should be up to Ellie to decide; she was the one mourning a husband. But he was finding it increasingly difficult meeting her to discuss business when he wanted more than that. Would Ellie tell him if she was feeling the same, or would she wait for him to speak?

He should say something, he decided. But the rain was soaking into his coat and breeches, and Ellie deserved better than a proposal from the bedraggled creature he was becoming. Now was not the time. He rode past the turning for the farm, and on to Bank Side.

The yard and house looked very different now compared to the first time he'd seen the place. At the end of the previous year, Tom had started spending a few nights here each week, getting to know the men and the horses. Fanny had also moved in, going back to Knowle Farm for only a couple of days each week to supervise Kate in the dairy. She'd not only made a huge improvement in the food, but brightened the place up, too, with new paint on some of the walls, brighter curtains, and tubs of daffodils blooming around the yard. And in November she and Dan had married. Although Fanny wasn't showing it yet, it was common knowledge around the farm that there would be a baby Cole in the autumn.

Finn lived with them; Dan made a better father for him than Tom would have done. Dan had gone to Darlington one day and suggested to Finn's uncle that he should think about what the men in the late Sergeant Robson's company would do when they found out what had happened to the money they collected for Finn. The money had been repaid within a week. Frank's efforts to retrieve Sergeant Robson's back pay had not met with success, and they had eventually given up. Finn was thriving, and that was enough.

Sam joined Tom as he was unsaddling the mare in her stall. "Good hunt, sir?"

"Fox got away, but we might have a buyer for this lady." He patted Storm's neck.

"That's good. You get indoors, Captain. I'll see to brushing her down. Fanny's made some coffee."

Tom didn't argue. He'd discuss the asking price with Sam later, then confirm it with Ellie when he called tomorrow for his weekly discussion of business matters. The following day he would be off to Ripon for the next week. Frank still made use of him now and then, sending him to see clients who lived more than a couple of hours' ride away; doing that helped Tom to put some physical distance between himself and Ellie.

Now all he had to do was to work out how to suggest not waiting until the anniversary of Wilson's death.

~

Ellie placed the letter she wanted to discuss with Tom on the table, then resolutely folded the *York Herald* and put it into a drawer. She had read the newspaper article too many times already, and she should not let it distract her from business. Tom would be here soon, and she could ask the question that she hadn't been able to get out of her mind since it first occurred to her. Napoleon was now in Paris, with a large army. There would be more battles—would Tom be part of them?

She had seen him only once since the first news of the former emperor's escape from Elba, and all he had said then was a pithy comment about the incompetence of the guards who had let him slip through their fingers. How would she feel if he did go? He'd almost been killed in France—would he survive more fighting?

Stop it!

Ellie took a deep breath. All she had to do was ask him, and not dwell on possibilities that might not happen. But if he was to rejoin the army, she would make sure they were married before he left. There was no rule that said she had to wait a year.

"Captain's here, missus, and Sam," Agnes said from the doorway, and stood aside to let the men enter. Both men were smiling, and Ellie did her best to put her preoccupations from her mind. Tom would not look so happy if he was soon to be off to war again.

"Good news?" she asked, taking her usual seat at the table. The business matters had to be got through before she could speak to Tom in private. She looked away—with Sam present, Tom didn't have his special smile for her, and she should not show how his presence warmed her.

"One of Roseworth's guests was interested in Storm," Tom said.

Concentrate on business, Ellie.

"That's excellent news." Over the winter they had fulfilled the final part of the existing contract for cavalry horses, but the contract had not been renewed. That might change, given the current news from France, but she could not rely on it. She—they—should concentrate on sales of horses to private individuals, and this was a good start.

"He's going to come to try her out in the next few days," Tom went on. "He's married, I think. Perhaps you could arrange to be riding Chestnut when he comes? He might be persuaded to buy his wife a new mount at the same time."

Sam nodded. "Worth a try, missus."

"I'll do that." Ellie pushed the letter towards Tom. "This is from Lord Longhirst; he used Fleet to cover two of his mares last summer. He is asking Martin to take Fleet to his estate for a private race meeting."

"Good chance to show him off," Sam suggested.

"I thought it would be a good idea for you to answer it, Tom. News of Martin's death must not have reached him. Introduce yourself as the new business manager. That's the best way, until we know if he will deal with me."

Tom nodded, but his brow creased and she thought he was about to speak, although he did not.

"Is something wrong? I can write if you wish."

"No, I'll do as you suggest." Tom glanced at Sam. "Is there anything else today?"

Sam shook his head and stood. "I'll get back."

He nodded at Ellie and took his leave, but Tom made no move to do the same. Did he have something to say, too? Now they were alone, she didn't know how to start. It didn't help that they might be interrupted at any time.

The view from the window looked unwelcoming, with grey skies and bare branches moving in the breeze. But it wasn't actually raining. "Tom, would you care to ride on the moor with me?"

. . .

Tom had been thinking how to raise the subject of perhaps not waiting another six months, and the suggestion took him by surprise. The weather was raw, with a damp chill in the air—not the weather for enjoying the moors. But Ellie was no hothouse flower that would wilt in the breeze. Here, in the dining room that she used for business, he could hear the murmur of voices in the kitchen; on the moor, there would be no-one who might overhear if she turned him down.

"If you wish. Wrap up well, though."

They rode up through the woods and stopped at the edge of the trees. Tom had been up here many times over the winter, and he led the way to a small hollow, sheltered by the trees from the northerly wind. "Did you really want to ride?" She had seemed distracted during their discussion—did she have something to ask, too?

"No." She slid off her horse as he was dismounting. "I have a question for you."

He looped the reins over his horse's neck—there was grass here, and the animals would not wander far. "What is it?"

"Are you going to rejoin the army?"

What? "No. Why... Oh, because Bonaparte has escaped? I wouldn't do something like that without discussing it with you first. And I've no wish to rejoin." The years he'd served in the army were enough, quite apart from wanting to spend the rest of his life with Ellie.

She let out a long sigh, and rubbed her forehead. "No, you would not. But once the thought had occurred to me, I could not get it out of my head."

"I don't want to leave you, Ellie—you know that." He put out a hand to touch her shoulder, wondering if she would retreat, but she did not. Encouraged, he stepped closer and drew her to him. This remote spot had the advantage of privacy, but little else. With the many layers of fabric between them, and the biting wind, there was little danger of a kiss going too far, no matter how much he might want it to. Perhaps that was an advantage, though. One coupling out of wedlock was enough. He didn't know how he was to wait another six months if Ellie wished to stick to that.

He'd held her like this after her husband's death, but this time it was not for comfort. And this time she lifted her face to his and wound her arms around his waist. An invitation?

He bent his head and their lips met. Vivid as his memories of their night together had seemed, they were a pale shadow of the feeling that spread through him. Not just physical attraction, but that having this woman here in his arms was right. Was the way things were meant to be.

This was what she had been waiting for. Not only for the last six months, but for the last three years. Since she had discovered with Tom how things could be between a man and a woman. But even kisses that set her insides on fire had to end, and she moved her head back so she could see his face. He hadn't released her, and she was glad of it. His gaze on her lips was making thinking difficult.

"Too many clothes," he said with a wry smile and regret in his voice.

"Six months is a long time."

"It has been."

It had, but that wasn't what she'd meant. "The next six months will be, as well. Too long."

His grip tightened for a moment, then he stepped back and looked into her eyes, his face a mixture of hope and doubt. "Do you mean that, Ellie?"

She nodded, surprised when he laughed.

"I was working myself up to saying the same thing as you. Rose-worth…" His expression sobered. "Well, not to put too fine a point on it, Roseworth and others have been telling me I'm missing a good opportunity by not marrying you. And asking what I'm waiting for." He muttered something under his breath.

Ellie put a hand on his arm. "Don't listen to them, Tom. I know you're not here for the farms. But now you've been managing the horses for some months, it is natural we could have got to know each other well enough to want to wed." She smiled. "In fact, some might think I married you to save me paying a manager."

"Touché." He kissed her again, briefly, then reached for her hands. "Ellie, will you make me the happiest of men and accept my hand and my heart?"

"Of course I will. That is, yes, please!"

His hands squeezed hers. "Thank you, my love."

It felt so good to be called that, and know that he meant it.

Ellie already had his love, but she would have more, Tom vowed to himself. He suspected she'd never been told how lovely she was, inside and out, never been given flowers, or gifts to make her feel special. Their love was the most important thing, but being able to make her happy would be his pleasure, too.

Somewhere behind them a curlew called, and she tilted her head as if listening. "A happy sound, Ellie? Shall we seize the day and ride on to Kirby Sutton? If the vicar is at home, we can see about calling the banns."

Her joyous smile answered him without the need for words. "Yes, but may we have one more kiss first?"

EPILOGUE

Ten years later

The August sun burned down, making a heat haze shimmer over the moor. Tom was glad to be sitting in the shade of the tree on what he thought of as 'their' rock—the place where he and Ellie had talked when he first returned from France. They had been here together many times since, with an increasing number of companions. The man he had been then would have been surprised at how much he enjoyed having a large family around him.

Jamie sat beside him, tongue between his teeth as he concentrated on making a detailed sketch of a sprig of heather. He wasn't over-fond of reading, but he had taken to drawing as if born to it, and that had led him to an interest in nature—insects, plants, and birds. As Jamie had lost the chubby looks of childhood, he'd come to resemble Ellie far more than Tom, which had largely avoided people asking awkward questions about his parentage. They would have to tell him soon. Tom didn't think Jamie remembered much of Martin, which seemed unjust to the man who had been the boy's father for the first two years of his life, but Jamie should know the situation, at least.

Beyond Jamie, Ann was attempting to sketch the tree and Ben, seven last birthday, looked for beetles and worms for Jamie to draw.

Emily, still too young to spend most of the day on the moor, was at home with Ellie and new baby Lizzie, all being fussed over by Tom's mama. Tom and the older children had been banished for the day, to give Ellie some peace.

"Damn!" The word sounded odd in Ben's childish treble, and Tom tried not to laugh.

"What did I tell you about that sort of language?" He managed a stern voice. Short of completely banning the boys from seeing the horses, there was no way of preventing them picking up bad language. But they had to learn when not to use it.

"Language of the stables stays in the stables," Ben recited. "Sorry. But the beetle flew away!"

"Would you like to be captured by someone hundreds of times bigger than you?"

Ben sighed, and shook his head. Tom stood. Jamie and Ann would happily sketch for another hour or more, but Ben was getting bored. "Come, we will walk a little way, and I'll give you a farthing for each bird you can hear *and* name correctly."

"Skylark, peewit, curlew, plover," Jamie said under his breath. Then, loud enough for Ben to hear, "Kittywake, fulmar, woodpecker, gannet."

Ben had become too wise to that trick by now. "There *was* a woodpecker in the woods when we walked up."

"I'll let you have that one," Tom said. "What's Mama's favourite bird?"

"Curlew!"

"Good. Now, be quiet and listen, then you might be able to tell Mama you've heard one."

Ben did try to listen, but had identified only a skylark when he spotted riders on the horizon to the south and instantly lost interest in birds. "Horses!"

As the riders approached, Tom recognised Dan and Finn on two of the young horses coming to the end of their training. Finn was twenty-one now, and soon to take up a position as groom at Thornton Court. He was a bright lad, and had thrived with Dan and

Fanny. Tom wouldn't be surprised if he was managing Roseworth's stables in another few years.

"Want a ride home?" Dan said to Ben, reining in by them. Ben was soon sitting up before him, and Ann demanded a seat in front of Finn.

"I'll walk back with Jamie when he's finished his sketch," Tom said, and the two horses cantered off. But Jamie put his sketchpad down.

"Papa, when I go back to school, can I have drawing lessons?" Jamie had started school in Thirsk last year, riding the five miles each way in the summer months, and boarding during the week in the winter.

"If you wish. It would be in addition to your other lessons, though. You don't escape mathematics so easily!"

Jamie grimaced, but shrugged. "It will cost extra."

"We can afford it." Both the dairy business and the horse sales were doing well, and what else was the money for if not to feed and educate their family? "Have you finished your sketch?"

Jamie stood and handed Tom his sketch book, brushing dust from the seat of his trousers. To Tom's eyes, it only needed a wash of colour to make it look like a professional illustration in a botany book. Drawing lessons would be money well spent.

"Excellent. Shall we go? I believe Kate was baking this afternoon."

Ellie sat on the bench by the front door in the shade of the house, with Lizzie dozing in her lap. A few yards away, in the brightness of the sun, bees buzzed around the fading lavender flowers beside the path.

Emily came tottering out of the door, with Tom's mother behind her. Still curious at this new being in her life, Emily came and leaned on Ellie's knee, peering into Lizzie's face. "She's sleeping," Ellie said, deflecting a curious finger about to prod the baby. "For now." She met Mrs Allerby's eyes with a wry smile.

Mrs Allerby had moved to Ripon a couple of years after Tom and Ellie married, to be close to Frank and Susannah and their children, and not too far from Knowle Farm. She was a sensible, practical woman, but with a warmth and dry sense of humour that had sparked immediate liking in Ellie. So much so that Ellie regarded her as a second mother, and this Mama treated Ellie like the daughter she'd never had.

"Elizabeth is arriving tomorrow, is she not?" Mama asked, sitting beside Ellie. "I'm looking forward to seeing her again."

"The day after tomorrow, I think. I'll look out her letter when I go back indoors." Aunt Elizabeth was as welcome a guest as Mama, and the two got on well together. The house was rather crowded when they were both here, even with part of the stables converted to extra rooms, but nobody minded.

Emily sat on a patch of grass and played with a ribbon on her dress. Ellie leaned her head on the wall behind and closed her eyes. So peaceful—only the quiet sound of Emily babbling to herself and the buzz of the bees.

"Our peace is about to be interrupted," Mama said, removing her spectacles to peer into the distance. Ellie sat up, moving slowly to avoid disturbing the sleeping baby. Finn and Dan were approaching, with two of the children; she would let Kate and Agnes give them cake and lemonade. It was warm here, even in the shade. No need to stir herself just yet.

Ellie awoke to the sound of Lizzie crying, and sat up with a start as the baby was lifted from her arms. Mama and Emily had gone and Tom stood before her, jiggling Lizzie and letting her suck his little finger.

"You were dead to the world, Ellie. Do you want to go inside? It will be cooler there."

How she loved that smile, the laugh in his face.

She rubbed her eyes. "I suppose I must." She put up a hand and allowed him to pull her to her feet. They stood close for a moment, Lizzie cradled between them, then he dropped a kiss on her forehead and released her.

"I can smell apple pie."

Ellie shook her head. "You men and your stomachs. I suppose that's why you came back?"

"Of course. What more could a man want than a beautiful wife, a happy and healthy family, and apple pie?"

She laughed, joy filling her. "In that order?"

He kissed her briefly on the lips. "Of course."

And they went into the house together to join the rest of their family.

THE END

HISTORICAL NOTES

PLACES IN THE STORY

Most of the towns named are real places, and many of the pubs and inns are, too, although I haven't attempted to describe the interiors of the pubs as they would have been then.

For anyone who knows the area around Thirsk, Kirby Sutton is a fictional village roughly where Kirby Knowle is in real life. Knowle Farm and Bank Side are fictional, and are at the foot of the slope up to the moors somewhere between Boltby and Thirlby. My description of Knowle Farm is loosely based on High Paradise Farm, although that is at the top of the slope not the bottom. It is now a guest house and tea shop (and yes, I have sampled their offerings).

In Yorkshire, a 'bank' is a steep bit of ground, often the edge of moorland. If you're a cyclist and choose to ride up something with 'bank' as part of its name, you're in for a steep climb!

RACES AND RACECOURSES

Racing in Yorkshire originally took place in York and at Hambleton Racecourse. The latter was on the moors in an area about six miles north-east of Thirsk (not far from where the Sutton Bank visitor centre is today). The racing at Hambleton declined through the 18th century, but the flat area of turf was still used for training at the time of this story, and is roughly where I imagined Martin training Fleet and his other horses.

Racing in York has been taking place on the site of the current course since 1731. The first grandstand there was built in 1754, and it has been modified and rebuilt since.

Thirsk has a racecourse today, but it dates from early Victorian times.

There are images of some of the places in the story on my pinterest page:

www.pinterest.co.uk/jaynedavis142/book-the-curlews-call/

NAPOLEONIC WARS

Other than Tom's experience in the Spanish village, the incidents and battles referred to in the story are real.

The siege of Ciudad Rodrigo that Tom refers to when talking to Ellie after the coach crash happened in January 1812, and the victorious troops ran amok afterwards. Such behaviour recurred, to a much greater extent, after taking Badajoz a few months later, and this latter atrocity is better known (it is the start of Georgette Heyer's *The Spanish Bride*, which is based on a true story).

The Light Brigade (which became the Light Division shortly afterwards) arriving too late for the battle of Talavera is true, as is the grass fire on a hillside that killed many of the British wounded who could not get away.

The Battle of Toulouse took place on 10th April 1814. The French army in Paris surrendered to Allied troops on 31st March. Napoleon was marching on Paris when he heard news of the surrender, and he abdicated on 4th April. The news did not reach Wellington in Toulouse until 12th April.

FOLLOWING THE DRUM

When Tom is in Hythe and working out what to do with Finn, he refers to the sergeant's wife not winning the ballot. Each regiment was allowed to take only a limited number of soldiers' families with them, and lots were drawn before each foreign posting to decide who could accompany the battalion.

AFTERWORD

Thank you for reading *The Curlew's Call*; I hope you enjoyed it. If you can spare a few minutes, I'd be very grateful if you could review this book on Amazon or Goodreads.

Find out more about my other books, on the following pages or on my website.

www.jaynedavisromance.co.uk

If you want news of special offers or new releases, join my mailing list via the contact page on my website. I won't bombard you with emails, I promise! Alternatively, follow me on Facebook - links are on my website.

ABOUT THE AUTHOR

I wanted to be a writer when I was in my teens, hooked on Jane Austen and Georgette Heyer (and lots of other authors). Real life intervened, and I had several careers, including as a non-fiction author under another name. That wasn't *quite* the writing career I had in mind!

Now I am lucky enough to be able to spend most of my time writing, when I'm not out walking, cycling, or enjoying my garden.

ALSO BY JAYNE DAVIS

THE MRS MACKINNONS

England, 1799

Major Matthew Southam returns from India, hoping to put the trauma of war behind him and forget his past. Instead, he finds a derelict estate and a family who wish he'd died abroad.

Charlotte MacKinnon married without love to avoid her father's unpleasant choice of husband. Now a widow with a young son, she lives in a small Cotswold village with only the money she earns by her writing.

Matthew is haunted by his past, and Charlotte is fearful of her father's renewed meddling in her future. After a disastrous first meeting, can they help each other find happiness?

Available on Kindle and in paperback. Read free in Kindle Unlimited. Listen via Audible or AudioBooks.com.

AN EMBROIDERED SPOON

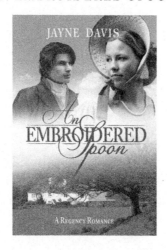

Can love bridge a class divide?

Wales 1817

After refusing every offer of marriage that comes her way, Isolde Farrington is packed off to a spinster aunt in Wales until she comes to her senses.

Rhys Williams, there on business, is turning over his uncle's choice of bride for him, and the last thing he needs is to fall for an impertinent miss like Izzy – who takes Rhys for a yokel. But while a man may choose his wife, he cannot choose who he falls in love with.

Izzy's new surroundings make her look at life, and Rhys, afresh. As she realises her early impressions were mistaken, her feelings about him begin to change.

But when her father, Lord Bedley, discovers the situation in Wales is not what he thought, and that Rhys is in trade, Izzy is hurriedly returned to London. Will a difference in class keep them apart?

Available on Kindle and in paperback. Read free in Kindle Unlimited. Listen via most retailers of audio books.

CAPTAIN KEMPTON'S CHRISTMAS

A sweet, second-chance novella.

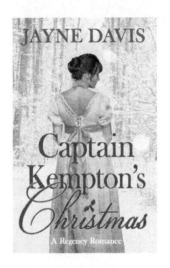

Can broken promises ever be forgiven?

England 1814

Lieutenant Philip Kempton and Anna Tremayne fall in love during one idyllic summer fortnight.

When he's summoned to rejoin his ship, Anna promises to wait for him. While he's at sea, she marries someone else.

Four years later, he is a captain and she is a widow. When the two are forced together at a Christmas party, they have a chance to reconcile.

Can they forgive each other the past and rekindle their love?

Available on Kindle and in paperback. Read free in Kindle Unlimited.

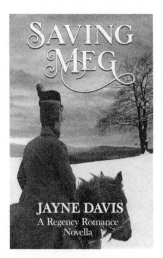

A soldier returns to keep a promise—but it will prove more difficult than he imagined.

Lieutenant Jonathan Lewis is devastated when his best friend, Fred, is fatally injured on the battlefield. He willingly promises to take care of Fred's sister and mother—after all, he has been quietly in love with Fred's sister, Meg, for years.

After a gruelling retreat across Spain, Jon finally returns to find England in the grip of a snowy winter. Thoughts of Meg have kept him going, but when he reaches her home, it is not Meg who meets him at the door but her cousin Rupert. Jon is devastated to learn that Rupert and Meg are to be wed in two days' time.

Despite Rupert's efforts to keep them apart, Jon manages to talk to Meg, who does *not* want to marry her cousin. Meg suggests that she would be safe from Rupert's threats if she married Jon instead.

Without hesitation, Jon sets off through the icy conditions and deep snow to get a marriage licence before Rupert can force Meg to marry him. But does Meg only want him for her safety, or could she love him, too? And can he make it back in time?

Available on Kindle and in paperback. Read free in Kindle Unlimited.

THE MARSTONE SERIES

A duelling viscount, a courageous poor relation and an overbearing lord–just a few of the memorable cast of characters you will meet in *The Marstone Series*. From windswept Devonshire, to Georgian London and revolutionary France, true love is always on the horizon and shady dealings often afoot.

The series is named after Will, who becomes the 9th Earl of Marstone. He appears in all the stories, although often in a minor role.

Each book can be read as a standalone story, but readers of the series will enjoy meeting characters from previous books. They are available as individual novels in ebook and paperback. The full-length novels are also available as a box set in ebook only.

A Question of Duty - Book 0 (Prequel Novella)

Sauce for the Gander - Book 1

A Winning Trick - Book 1.5 (Extended epilogue to Book 1)

A Suitable Match - Book 2

Playing with Fire - Book 3

The Fourth Marchioness - Book 4

A QUESTION OF DUTY

Prequel novella for the Marstone Series

Is a man's duty to his family or to the woman he loves?

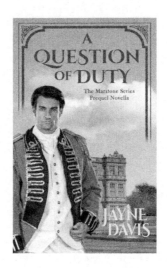

Albany, 1760

Returning home from his post in the Colonies, Captain Jack Stanlake finds himself a reluctant escort for Mrs Harper and her two daughters. Over the course of the Atlantic voyage, he finds himself taken with Miss Clara Harper.

Mrs Harper is set on finding husbands for her daughters—but that is not what Clara wants. Doing the bidding of a husband does not appeal in the least; not when there is a world out there she wants to discover. But after spending time with Jack, her feelings on the matter change.

There is, of course, a problem. Jack is the second son of the Earl of Marstone and Clara is a merchant's niece. For one of his background, marrying into trade just isn't done. Both must move on. Clara busies herself with her new life in London. Jack tries to push his feelings aside. But neither can forget the other.

To Jack's dismay, his brother has arranged a suitable marriage for him in his absence—one that will advance his family's status and prestige. His duty to the family demands he accept this union, but he cannot dismiss Clara from his heart and mind. Will he refuse his duty and marry for love?

SAUCE FOR THE GANDER

A duel. An ultimatum. An arranged marriage.

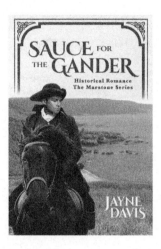

England, 1777

Will, Viscount Wingrave, whiles away his time gambling and bedding married women, thwarted in his wish to serve his country by his controlling father.

News that his errant son has fought a duel with a jealous husband is the last straw for the Earl of Marstone. He decrees that Will must marry. The earl's eye lights upon Connie Charters, whose position as unpaid housekeeper for a poor but socially ambitious father hides her true intelligence.

Connie wants a husband who will love and respect her, not a womaniser and a gambler. When her conniving father forces the match, she has no choice but to agree.

Will and Connie meet for the first time at the altar.

As they settle into their new home on the wild coast of Devonshire, the young couple find they have more in common than they thought. But there are dangerous secrets that threaten both them and the nation.

Can Will and Connie overcome the dark forces that conspire against them and find happiness together?

Printed in Great Britain
by Amazon

44422802R00188